FALL INTO TEMPTATION

BLUE MOON #2

LUCY SCORE

That's What She Said Publishing, Inc.

Fall Into Temptation

Cover by Kari March

ISBN: 978-1-945631-39-9 (ebook)

ISBN: 978-1-945631-40-5 (paperback)

lucyscore.com

111021

To Amber, the sister of my heart, if not my blood.

Wherever you stand
Be the soul of that place
— Rumi

1

_I_t was good to be home, Beckett Pierce decided. Even if home meant your across-the-street neighbor had put up his psychedelic Halloween homage to the sixties.

Beckett shook his head at the giant inflatable VW bus in the front yard and set an easy pace as he jogged down the sidewalk.

It was an early October evening, which in his opinion was the perfect opportunity for a run around town. Particularly since he'd been gone for ten days. A quick run after hours on a plane would let him stretch his legs and get reacquainted with his town. And since it was dark, he could do it without being stopped a dozen times by townspeople.

He loved his duties as mayor of Blue Moon Bend and the responsibilities of his law practice, but spending more than a week in the Caribbean sun at his law school friend's wedding had been a nice break.

Even if he was sure Edward was making a mistake by hitching himself for life to Tiffani the celebrity stylist.

Now, it was time to catch up on everything that had

happened while he was gone. And in Blue Moon, it was a lot. The town might be small, but it moved fast.

While Beckett was relaxing on the beach, his paralegal and right hand, Ellery, had found a tenant—a single mom of two—for his backyard guesthouse, the new owner of Half-Moon Yoga had set up shop and opened her doors, and his mother had announced she was moving in with her boyfriend Franklin Merrill.

Beckett had already decided to avoid the reality of that last change for as long as he could.

The evening was dark enough that he decided to chance his anonymity on Main Street. Most of the storefronts were closed, but he saw lights on at the yoga studio. Maris, the previous owner, had moved to Santa Fe to open her own crystal shop.

Beckett let his long legs carry him around the square to the large windows of the studio that occupied the first floor of a three-story brick building painted navy blue. It looked as though Maris's predecessor was significantly younger. And more limber.

Surrounded by a scatter of paint cans and brushes, a lone woman with miles of fiery red curls executed a perfect head-stand. The studio was a fresh shade of peacock blue and dotted with flickering candles, but Beckett only had eyes for the woman in the middle of it all.

Her legs, straight as lances, opened in an inverted split. She wobbled and then tumbled down into a graceful heap onto the mat beneath her. He could hear her laughter faintly through the glass. Fascinated, he watched as she tossed her hair over her shoulder and, undaunted, returned to her head-stand. This time, her split was rock steady.

She brought her legs down into a tight tuck and then jack-knifed them toward the ceiling, lifting up into a handstand.

Power and grace, he thought stepping closer to the glass. She tucked her chin and rolled forward and down into a cross-legged position. And then gave herself a high-five.

Beckett's phone rang in the pocket of his fleece. He pulled it out and winced at the screen. He wasn't ready for this conversation yet.

"Hi, Mom."

"I heard my favorite son was back in the country," Phoebe Pierce chirped in his ear.

"I heard my mother is getting a roommate."

"I will if we can find a decent place to buy," she groaned. "It's not exactly a hot real estate market in Blue Moon right now."

Beckett remained silent.

His mother sighed. "I had a feeling the news might not be warmly received."

Beckett scowled at the ground. "I don't want to argue with you, Mom."

"We're going to have to talk about this sooner or later, you know. Franklin is a wonderful man. I really need you to give him a chance."

"Mom."

"Beckett. You're important to me. You're the only middle son I've got. And Franklin's important to me, too. I need you to make room for him."

Make room for a man who wasn't his father?

John Pierce, in Beckett's estimation, had been the greatest man to ever live. He'd taught Beckett what love and loyalty and community looked like when you lived those principles day in and day out. The idea that some restaurant owner with his loud Hawaiian shirts and his baked ziti could just step into those shoes was laughable.

Beckett chose to ignore the fact that before he found out

that his mother was dating Franklin, he had actually liked the man. He was active in the Chamber of Commerce and always cheerfully giving back to the community. But none of that measured up to John Pierce's contributions to life and family in Blue Moon.

"Moving in together is serious, Mom. I'm just trying to look out for you," he argued.

Edward and Tiffani, his mother and Franklin. What was with people settling for incompatible partners? Successful relationships were founded upon shared similarities and goals. Not to be confused with indiscriminate physical attraction or fillers for loneliness.

He didn't want his mom getting hurt, especially not by someone who was so obviously not her type.

"We've given it a lot of thought and we both feel it's the right thing to do. I'm excited about it, and I hope you can be excited for me."

"Can we talk about something else?" Beckett begged.

Phoebe sighed again and let him have his way. "How was your trip?"

VICTORIOUSLY, Gia rolled back on the mat. Nailing the conversion from headstand to handstand was a pride-booster. But she was just as grateful for all of the stumbles and falls along the way. Earning her place with hard work and sweat was more satisfying than falling into something great, she decided. And with practice and focus, she'd learn to minimize the stumbles.

Gia stared up at the ceiling of her studio. Her very own yoga studio.

When life threw you curve ball after curve ball, eventually you had to hit one of them out of the park, she thought.

And this would be her home run. She had a gut feeling about the way everything had fallen into place. The newly available studio space. A charming rental that was walking distance to the studio. And being closer to her father was an added bonus. Growing up, she'd been so close to him as he took on the role of both father and mother—not to mention mediator when she and her sisters feuded. She'd missed him in the recent years when circumstances kept them apart.

But now, things would be different. She would be different. Life wouldn't revolve around the whims of someone so casually careless with hearts. The foundation she'd build here would provide the much-needed stability for those who depended on her.

Blue Moon—with its good vibes and quirky traditions— would be the fresh start that she needed.

Gia stood up and stretched her arms over her head. She tugged her paint-splattered tank top down and, hands on hips, studied the space.

The paint looked good. It was colorful but soothing. The rest of the space had received a tasteful facelift with new dimmable lighting, brightly colored cushions and soft throws, and Zen-inspired art on the walls. She had repainted the smaller studio in the back and changed out the vanities in both bathrooms.

A quick, surface clean, and she would be ready for the ribbon cutting tomorrow. She'd meet more of her neighbors and celebrate this new beginning.

The ceremony was representative of more than just a new business. It was a new start. A new home, a new way of life. A steadier one, with fewer mistakes and bigger rewards.

BECKETT TOSSED the handwritten messages in the recycling bin and reached for a glass. In ten days, he'd piled up fifteen messages from modeling agencies interested in representing him and his brothers.

He made a mental note to kill Summer when he saw her next.

Her article on his brother Carter and the family farm had garnered undue attention when it was published in a New York-based women's magazine. The article had been edited down to the equivalent of a *Playgirl* pictorial. The piece earned enough attention on its own, but when Summer published the original article on her blog, it had gone viral.

He and his brothers had since attracted ridiculous offers from both modeling agencies and women. Ellery took a great deal of joy in reading aloud some of the more creative offers that arrived via his business email.

He was filling a glass straight from the tap in his kitchen when the lights in the guesthouse caught his eye. Beckett checked his watch. Eight-thirty. It was early enough to stop by and introduce himself to his new tenant.

He walked out the back door, off the porch, and crossed the small patch of grass that separated his home from the guesthouse. It was a cozy two-story built to compliment his rambling Victorian. Two bedrooms upstairs, a doll-sized kitchen downstairs, and reasonable living and dining spaces, it was cozy and charming. And had rented faster than he anticipated.

He stepped onto the narrow porch and rapped his knuckles on the glossy black door. Through the glass, he saw a kid climb off of the couch and shuffle toward him. He had sandy-colored hair and suspicious eyes.

"Yeah?" The kid said.

"Hey. I'm your landlord slash neighbor," Beckett said jerking his thumb toward his house. "Is your mom around?"

"She's not my mom." The kid said it sullenly as if it were a constant point of contention.

"She kidnap you?" Beckett asked with an expression of mock concern. "If you're being held against your will, blink twice."

The kid's lips twitched into a smirk.

"I know the sheriff. I can have him over here in five minutes. It's pretty boring crime-wise here. He'd love to get his hands on a good, old-fashioned kidnapping case."

"She's my ex-stepmother," he said by way of an explanation. "And she's not here."

"Well, I'll stop by some other time and make sure she's not making you scrub floors or live in the closet under the stairs."

It was almost a smile this time.

"Later, kid."

"Later, landlord."

$\mathcal{C}$heerful from caffeine and a good night's sleep, Beckett breezed through the doorway into the section of his house that was dedicated to his law practice. Originally a parlor, the high-ceilinged room opened onto a glassed-in sun porch, making the entire space bright and comfortable.

Here he'd stripped the dark plaid wallpaper from the walls but left the waist-high wainscoting. Built-ins flanked the double doors that opened into the library that he used as a conference room. On the back wall was a large stone fireplace.

His office was through a set of ornately carved pocket doors toward the front of the house, overlooking the porch and driveway.

Ellery's desk faced the sun porch's entrance. From there, she did her best to control the never-ending stream of visitors. It was here that his worlds of politics and business intersected. Clients of his practice shared the sunny waiting space with town council members and residents with beefs or wildly inappropriate suggestions... sometimes both.

Beckett put Ellery's pink kitten mug down on her desk. His

paralegal swiveled in her chair, her desk phone cradled between ear and shoulder.

"Uh-huh. Sure Mrs. Parker. I'll let him know as soon as he's back in the office," she said into the phone. "You too. Bye now."

Her painted black lips stretched into a grin. Her ebony hair hung in lazy, loose curls pinned back from her face. Tiny skull earrings danced at her lobes.

"Mrs. Parker is *very* interested in talking to you about redoing her will, which is code for talking you into dating her daughter."

"Moon Beam?" Beckett winced. He had gone to school with Moon Beam Parker and had spent a very memorable portion of junior year with her, during which he lost his virginity in the backseat of his mother's SUV. The relationship had fizzled—as so many high school romances in Blue Moon —when Moon Beam left for a yearlong stay on a commune in Vermont after her parents' divorce.

"It seems Mrs. Parker became aware of the attention you're getting since that article and wants to lock you down for Moon Beam."

"Husband number three, am I?" Beckett said, dropping into one of the chairs in front of Ellery's desk. He sipped his coffee. "What else is on the agenda, besides marrying me off?"

"First things first," Ellery said. "Welcome back. You look tan and mostly happy."

"I am tan and mostly happy." He thought of his mother's news and suppressed a frown.

"Good." Ellery nodded briskly. "Here's a copy of your calendar for this week. I tried to keep the appointments a little light so you don't lose your post-island buzz." She ran through some of the highlights of the coming week, pointing with black tipped nails. "You also have a Chamber event at noon today. Ribbon-cutting at the yoga studio."

Beckett perked up. So he'd get to meet the beautiful and flexible yoga teacher today. That was a plus. The memory of her laughing in candlelight behind the glass of her studio tugged at him. All those red curls and that pale skin. There was something bewitching about her.

"Beckett?" Ellery was looking at him.

"What?"

"I asked if you met her yet?" Ellery asked, breaking through his thoughts.

He frowned. "No. I just got back last night," he reminded her.

"She's great. She's amazing actually," Ellery gushed. "She started teaching classes last week, and I signed up for a monthly package after my first class. I think you'll really like her. She's a good fit."

Before he could ask her what the limber, young yoga instructor would be a good fit for, they were interrupted by his nine o'clock who was thirty-five minutes early.

And so it began.

Beckett worked his way through appointments, research, and paperwork right up until he had to leave for the ribbon cutting. He grabbed the ceremonial gold shears that Ellery held up for him and headed out the door.

"Don't run with those," she called after him.

There was already a crowd gathered around the front door of the studio. They were all familiar faces. Elvira Eustace, with her more salt than pepper ringlets, was chatting animatedly with Anthony Berkowicz, the skinny editor of *The Monthly Moon*, who was holding a digital camera bigger than he was.

Anthony's mother, Rainbow, was impatiently staring at her

watch while Mrs. McCafferty of the catch-all general store McCaffertys talked her ear off.

The door to the yoga studio opened, and Rob from OJs by Julia stepped out carrying empty trays.

"Hey, Beckett," Rob greeted him.

Beckett nodded at the trays. "Does Julia have you doing deliveries now?"

Rob grinned. "She and the baby are directing everyone from home for another few days. It was all I could get her to commit to before she comes back to work."

"Three kids under five," Beckett shook his head. "You two are super heroes."

"Or insane." Rob shrugged happily. "What's new with you? How was your trip?"

Beckett's response was cut off by town councilwoman Dr. Donna Delveccio. Donna's entrepreneurial parents had raised three equally enterprising children. All told, the family owned and operated Blue Moon's dry cleaning business, medical supply store, and Delveccio Dental.

"Let's get this show on the road, Beckett," she said, rubbing her hands together. "There's a mini turkey club in there with my name on it, and I've got a cavity filling at one."

"Do we have a yoga studio owner somewhere around here?" Beckett asked, scanning the crowd.

Dr. Donna shrugged. "Maybe she's inside?"

"I'll see if I can find her and get you your turkey club," he told her. "Why don't you organize everyone, and I'll be right back?"

He made a move toward the studio's glass door and turned back. "What's her name?" he asked Donna.

"Gianna Decker."

Beckett entered the studio, noting that the painting supplies from last night had been cleaned up. A long buffet table, laden with sandwiches, snacks, and mini smoothies, was set up in front of the windows.

At the back of the room, the door to a second, smaller studio was open. It was empty. But down the narrow hallway, he noticed one of the restroom doors was closed. She must be in there. He decided to give her another minute or two when he heard the doorknob rattle.

"Is anyone out there?" called a muffled voice.

He hurried down the hall and arrived at the door in time to hear her groan.

"Seriously? Of all days," the voice said woefully. The handle jiggled again, harder this time. A swift thump replaced the jiggling. "I really don't like you right now, door!"

Beckett knocked and heard the yelp on the other side of the wood. "Are you stuck?" he asked.

"Oh my God! Yes, please help. The lock must be broken, and I have to get outside. Everyone's waiting."

Beckett tried the handle on his side. "Definitely stuck," he assessed.

"Gee, you think?" she asked dryly.

"Doors don't block sarcasm," he reminded her.

"Right. Sorry. I'm just flustered. Can you get me out of here?"

"No. I think you have to stay in there forever."

"Doors don't block sarcasm, you know."

Beckett laughed. "Sorry. Couldn't help it. I can get you out." He reached into his pocket and grabbed the ever-present multi-tool his father had given him. "I'm going to take the screws out of the handle on this side, okay?"

"Oh, good. I was afraid you were going to kick the door down."

"We'll save that as a last resort," he promised.

Beckett made quick work of the screws and popped the

handle off of his side. He heard the thunk of the interior handle hitting the floor. With his index finger, he pushed the striker release, and the door swung open.

She was sitting on the vanity, her bare feet dangling, peeking through the folds of her long skirt. The grin she gave him lit up the bathroom like fireworks in the night sky. Sliding off the countertop, she launched herself into his arms. He caught her purely on instinct, and his eyes widened as her full, soft lips landed on his.

There was nothing carnal about the kiss, he thought as she pulled back and slid to the floor. But it still affected him.

"Do you always kiss complete strangers?" he demanded gruffly.

Her wide green eyes sparkled. "I do when they rescue me from considerable amounts of embarrassment and life in restroom prison. I was just debating whether or not the hand soap in here was edible."

She looked like a fairy. Delicate and small, her ivory skin was dotted with a smattering of freckles. She wore her long red hair loose, cascading down her back. Her snug long sleeve shirt showed off a compact, curvy body.

"Now, if you'll excuse me, I need to go cut a ribbon," she announced, patting his arm as she stepped around him.

"You can't get started without me," he said, following her down the hall and into the studio.

She whirled around, her skirt billowing around her legs. "Don't tell me," she said, raising an eyebrow. "Beckett Pierce."

"At your service, it appears," he said with a mock bow.

"Well, isn't that interesting?" She smiled again, looking him over from head to toe. "Very interesting." Gianna turned her back on him again and slipped out the front door, leaving him frowning after her.

Back outside, Beckett found that Donna had organized

everyone into the appropriate positions, and the ceremonial tie-dye ribbon was stretched taut in front of the door.

Elvira handed the comically large scissors to him.

Beckett beckoned for Gianna to join him behind the ribbon. "Ready?"

"Let's do this." She grinned.

"On behalf of all of Blue Moon, I'd like to welcome Gianna Decker to our community," Beckett announced to the crowd. "I'm sure she will be an excellent addition to our town as both a business owner and neighbor."

The small crowd applauded enthusiastically, and Gianna waved.

Beckett held up the scissors to the ribbon and captured her hand with his free one. "Together?"

She looked up at him. Their gazes locked. He swore he saw a lifetime in those eyes before she winked. And together they snipped through the thick, colorful ribbon.

3

$\mathcal{G}$ia watched Beckett from across the studio as he chatted with a woman in a suit and two men who looked identical except for the color of their flannel shirts.

He was certainly easy to look at. The thick, dark hair waved a bit on top. His strong jawline and high cheekbones were a classical, appealing canvas for eyes so gray they were nearly silver.

He wore the navy suit with a careless comfort, keeping the look slightly more casual by forgoing a tie and leaving the top button of his unwrinkled button-down open. The cut of the suit hinted at spectacular shoulders, a personal favorite for her.

Beckett moved with confidence, made eye contact, and paid attention. It's too bad he was officially untouchable. Had his name been anything other than Beckett Pierce, she would have been tempted. Very tempted. But he was off limits, and even she could see disaster written all over this potential.

No, it was better to stick with her plan. Focus on her family and her business. Relationships were officially off the table for the foreseeable future until everything else was stabilized.

She couldn't help but wonder how Beckett would react when he realized who she was.

Picking up her green smoothie, she sipped. Rainbow Berkowicz wandered over to her side. "How's the new business checking account treating you?" she asked.

Gia grinned. All business from someone named Rainbow. Was it any wonder she already loved Blue Moon? "It's just fine, thanks. How's the banking industry these days?"

Rainbow launched into a dry analysis of current lending rates and what they meant for the local economy.

Willa, one of Gia's first students in the studio, floated over to them. Her wavy blonde hair flowed down her back, reaching her hips when it wasn't secured in a thick braid. "The new paint is just gorgeous. Very peaceful," she told Gia.

"Thanks, Willa. That's what I was going for." She felt a warm current rush up her spine as Beckett joined their little circle. "Are you coming to class tomorrow?" she asked Willa.

"I'll be here. I felt as loose as water after last class," Willa said with a dreamy smile. "Have you taken one of Gia's classes yet, Beckett?"

"Not yet, but I plan to," Beckett said with a politician's charm.

Gia raised an eyebrow. She knew an empty platitude when she heard one and tolerated them about as well as manicured nails on a chalkboard.

"Oh, you should." Willa nodded vigorously. "Gia is a wonderful teacher." A chirping noise sounded from the depths of Willa's tote bag. She dug out her cell phone. "And that's my cue to get back to the store. Those boots won't sell themselves! Thank you for lunch. I'll see you tomorrow."

"I'll walk out with you," Rainbow announced. They made their departure, leaving Gia with Beckett at her side.

"So you'd like to take a class, huh?" she asked. He may have saved her from a locked door, but little white lies were a personal pet peeve. A sin in her eyes, having lived with them for so long before. That was a major strike against him. She felt a little relief as his attractiveness dipped down to slightly more normal levels.

"Sure. Sometime." He nodded, frowning and looking mayoral.

She wasn't buying it and decided to call his bluff. "I don't know, Beckett," Gia said, baring her teeth in a fake smile. "The classes can be a little intense. I wouldn't want you to get hurt."

He looked insulted. "I run five miles a day. I think I can handle a little stretching."

He was cocky, but she'd take him down a notch in class. "I guess we'll see. I promise to take it easy on you," she said, her smile sharp as razors.

"When's your next class?" he demanded.

"Seven tonight."

"I'll see you then."

"Great," she said smugly.

4

$\mathcal{B}$eckett showed up at Half-Moon Yoga fifteen minutes early wearing gym shorts and a scowl. As soon as he'd left the ribbon cutting, he realized Gianna had manipulated him into agreeing to take a class.

It was sneaky and underhanded. Which rankled him as much as her initial suggestion that yoga would be too much for him. He didn't like that kind of manipulation from anyone, not even a beautiful woman.

He wasn't into the whole Om-ing, stretching deal but wouldn't dream of saying that to a woman who made her living that way.

He could have cancelled, had even considered it when he got back to his office. But that would give her the false sense of satisfaction that she had scared him off. A redheaded pixie and her downward-facing dogs weren't going to rattle him.

He had run track in high school. He hit the gym for early morning workouts five days a week and ran just as often. He had a protein shake for breakfast every day. He was in shape—great shape—and no bendy yoga guru was going to insinuate otherwise.

It was quite the eclectic crowd in the studio tonight. He recognized four of the starters from the high school football team taking up spots in the front row. Maizie from Peace of Pizza was brushing her white blonde bangs out of her eyes while her boyfriend, Benito, stretched.

In the corner by the window, Beckett spotted resident pothead and poker champion Bill Fitzsimmons sitting cross-legged with his eyes closed. His lips were moving, but no sound came out. He was wearing sweatpants that looked like they had lived through the seventies.

Beckett was just noticing how warm the studio was when Fitz stood up and took off his pants, revealing embarrassingly small spandex shorts. It took all his control not to start laughing... or crying.

Gianna, in cropped tights and a strappy tank top that showed off some spectacular curves, smiled from the front of the room. *That was going to be distracting*, he thought.

"Welcome," she called to him, with a hint of friendly cockiness in her eyes. "Let me get you a mat."

Beckett followed her to the shelving unit that held rolled up mats in purples and greens as well as a dozen foam blocks and soft blankets.

Gianna handed him a green mat. "You can set up anywhere. Just face the front of the room." She stood on tiptoe and grabbed one of the blocks off the shelf. "Here."

"What's this for?"

"It helps with modifications for some of the poses."

Beckett eyed her. "I doubt I'll need to modify anything."

"Suit yourself," she said with a wink and sauntered back to her mat.

Beckett took a spot in the back row and pulled off his sweatshirt.

The woman next to him smiled at him, and he recognized

her as the reigning women's champ of the Blue Moon Five-Miler for the past four years. She also managed to kick his ass every time they met up on the running trail.

"Hey, Taneisha. How's the training going?"

She greeted him with a toothpaste commercial-worthy grin. "I should be Boston-ready for next year. What brings you to yoga?" She flowed forward over her extended legs, reaching for her feet.

"Just supporting the small business community," Beckett answered evasively.

"What other mayor would willingly walk into a hot power flow class to show his support? Blue Moon is lucky to have you," Taneisha said, gliding back up and stretching her arms over her head.

"Hot power flow?"

Gianna cut off any response to his question from the front of the room. "Okay, everyone. We're going to get started. If you're new, don't worry." Her green eyes locked on to Beckett's face. "Just follow your neighbor, and I'll be around to help. So let's start in child's pose."

Four minutes into the class, and Beckett had a steady trickle of sweat working its way down his back and a growing concern that he wasn't going to survive the class. Gianna wandered around the room calling out instructions in a soothing voice that belied the fact that she was basically asking her students to work themselves up to and past death on their mats.

Beckett gritted his teeth and rolled forward, triceps shaking as they dipped into a low plank again. *Hadn't they already done like fifty of these?* This constant flowing—or vinyasa, whatever the fuck that was—wasn't awakening his body as she claimed it would. Instead it was drawing his attention to body parts that screamed in agony.

He was in great shape, wasn't he? Why did he feel like the Tin Man clunking around in shorts?

He shoved back to down dog again, a brief respite, before kicking one leg forward. He rose up, a second behind his neighbors, and reached for the ceiling, praying for a meteor to strike the studio.

Beckett was thinking about collapsing on the floor and taking a breather when he felt hands on him straightening his arms.

"Lift through your arms," Gianna said quietly. "That's right. Now extend through the spine like you're reaching for the ceiling through the top of your head." She ran her hands up his sweat-soaked spine in a sweeping motion that made his skin burn.

"Perfect," she said when he complied. He was acutely and uncomfortably aware of her hands leaving his body.

He had to admit, the pose felt better with her corrections. But it only lasted another second before she had them plunging through the sequence on the other side. Over and over he careened toward the floor praying his arms would hold him. The sweat was flowing so freely it was tickling his legs. A drop gathered on the tip of his nose and splashed to the mat as he swooped down.

Are my eyeballs sweating? he wondered.

He chanced a glance to his left. Taneisha's flawless skin was dotted with beads of sweat, and she was smiling her way through another sun salutation. Next to her, Fitz had stripped off his shirt and was now only wearing his ridiculous briefs.

There's a picture he wouldn't be unseeing anytime soon, he thought. But maybe the skinny hippie had the right idea in this situation. Beckett used the thigh-quivering chair pose to yank his t-shirt over his head. It landed with a wet thwack on the floor behind him.

Gianna had returned to her mat and flowed with the class on another round. She moved with ease and grace as if she'd been born flowing through yoga poses. He hated her gorgeous, graceful guts.

~

SOMETHING WAS NUDGING HIS FOOT.

Beckett opened an eye and swiped at the sweat that rolled into it.

Like a siren, she appeared in his line of vision. A shimmering mirage of evil beauty. Gianna grinned down at him.

"What was that?" he groaned, flopping his arms out to the sides.

"That was hot power flow yoga," she answered, sinking down next to him in a move as graceful as ballet.

"How do you move like that?" Beckett asked, studying her. She had a dimple in her chin and mischief in her eyes.

"Like what?"

"Like you're dancing. Everything you do is like dancing."

She was starting to look concerned. "How about we get some water into you?" she suggested.

Beckett rolled to his side and slowly worked his way into a seated position. The studio was empty except for the two of them. He vaguely remembered everyone bowing and saying "nama-something," but he didn't really recall the mass exodus.

Gianna handed him a bottle of water and a towel. "How do you feel?"

"Like I was steamrolled, wrung out, and hung up to dry."

She laughed then, a husky music. She patted his shoulder. "That's exactly how you're supposed to feel."

"You win," Beckett sighed and drank deeply.

"You hung in there for the entire class. I'd say this one ends in a tie," Gianna decided. She rose to her feet and reached a hand out to him.

Beckett debated not taking it but worried his legs would betray him. He let her pull him up to standing and glanced down at the mat.

"You're going to have to burn this one," he said, eyeing the body-sized sweat stain.

She grinned up at him. "Don't worry about it. I think I've got some industrial cleaner in the back somewhere." She headed over to the shelves, and Beckett picked up his still-sopping t-shirt.

Gianna returned with a spray bottle and another towel. "I don't think you're going to want to put that back on," she said, wrinkling her nose at his soggy shirt.

"Yeah," Beckett agreed, pulling on his sweatshirt instead. He picked up the block that he had ended up relying on like a lifeline and put it back on the shelf.

"Is this your last class tonight?"

She glanced up from his newly laundered mat, eyes trailing a little slower over his chest. "It is. You are free to go shower and drink several beers."

"Is that what you do after class?" he teased.

"Shower, yes. One beer and usually a giant dish of mac and cheese or something equally unhealthy."

Beckett's stomach growled in response. A shower, beer, and dinner were in his future, he decided.

"I'll walk you to your car," Beckett offered. Now that he was recovering some of his energy, he was reluctant to leave her. Especially since he'd be leaving her with the image of him barely conscious drowning in a pool of his own sweat. He could do better and perhaps recover a bit of his pride.

"Thanks, but I walked," Gianna told him, grabbing her bag from one of the cubbies along the back wall.

He felt a pang when she tugged a hoodie over her tank top. She had a beautiful body. One that demanded attention, even from the near dead. "I'll walk with you."

She eyed him for a moment. "Okay. That would be nice."

Beckett waited by the front door while she turned off the studio lights, and together they exited into the cool October evening.

"Which way are you?" he asked.

She slid her key into the lock and pointed to the left.

"Me too. We must be neighbors," Beckett commented as they started down the sidewalk.

"Imagine that," Gianna said with an amused look.

Beckett threw his sweaty t-shirt over his shoulder. "How do you like Blue Moon so far?"

"It's wonderful," she said. "Everyone's so warm. I love that my kids will grow up knowing their neighbors and walking to school."

"You have kids?" Beckett immediately looked down at her left hand. No ring.

She shot him an amused look. "Two kids and an ex-husband. You?"

"Zero kids and no ex-husbands."

Gianna laughed. "Any wives? Current or past?"

They walked past Karma Kustard, and Beckett waved to Pete, the owner, who was manning the counter.

"None. The Pierce brothers take our bachelorhood seriously. Well, we did until recently." He thought of Carter with his Summer.

"How many of you are there?" Gia asked.

"Three. I'm the good-looking one." He winked.

She rolled her eyes and tugged the hair band out of her

thick, auburn curls letting them tumble down her back. "You must be the middle child."

"How did you guess?"

"Like recognizes like."

"You're the middle, too?"

She nodded, tossing her hair over her shoulder and he caught a whiff of lavender. "I've got two sisters."

"Are you close?" he asked. He wondered if they looked like her. Gianna was a head turner. He couldn't imagine two more of her.

"Not geographically. I've got one bouncing around South Carolina and one in L.A., but we talk and email constantly. How about you and your brothers?"

He thought of Carter and Jax. Close was a good word for his relationship with them, especially now that they were all back home and starting a business together. "We're pretty close. So two kids, huh?"

Gianna nodded and stuffed her hands in the front pocket of her hoodie. "Yeah, they're pretty great. I'm hoping to be half the parent my dad was while I was growing up. If I can accomplish that, I can do anything," she sighed.

"How about your mother?" Beckett asked.

Gianna shrugged. "She left us years ago. My sisters and I were in our early teens, so you can imagine what gems we were then. But Dad hung in there and figured out how to fill both roles. He never once let us feel like it was our fault or that what we wanted wasn't important."

"He sounds like a good man."

"As close to sainthood as you can get." She nodded. "Your parents?"

Beckett caught a glimpse of his disheveled, sweat-soaked hair in the next storefront window and scrubbed a hand through it. Next time he saw Gianna, it was going to be in a suit after a shower, he promised himself.

"My dad was great. He put his heart into everything he did. He was never too busy for anyone who needed help." Beckett could still call up a hundred memories of his dad setting aside everything to have a conversation, to lend a hand, or just answer his incessant questions as a five-year-old.

"He sounds wonderful," Gianna said, guiding them off Main Street.

"He was. He died five years ago."

"Still miss him." It wasn't a question but an acknowledgement.

"Every day," Beckett nodded. It was true. There wasn't a day that went by without his thoughts turning to John Pierce.

"And your mother?" Gianna asked.

Beckett felt the familiar warring emotions of love and frustration that bubbled to the surface every time he thought of his mother the past few months.

"She's great," he said, keeping it at that.

They turned down another tree-lined street where the streetlights were spaced further apart. "Do you live on this street?" he asked her, frowning.

Gianna nodded and smiled. "I do. It's such a great neighborhood."

"I know. It's my neighborhood."

"Well, this is me." Gianna stopped on the sidewalk, her eyes sparkling.

"This isn't you. This is me. I live here," Beckett argued. The realization hit him as the words came out of his mouth.

"Hi, neighbor," Gianna said, cocking her head to the side.

"You're my new tenant." He was a dumbass. A complete and total dumbass, and Gianna had the pleasure of witnessing his idiocy over and over again.

She nodded. "I knew you'd figure it out eventually."

He had literally walked her to his own doorstep before realizing it. He was slipping. Yoga must have destroyed his brain.

"Ellery took care of the paperwork and your check while I was out of the country," he said, slowly piecing it all together.

"She did. She's a pretty amazing asset, by the way," Gianna said.

"She is." And his amazing asset had probably assumed he introduced himself to his new tenant when he came home. In fact, if he hadn't been daydreaming about the redhead before him, he probably would have heard Ellery telling him Gianna was his tenant. Her "good fit" comment suddenly made a lot more sense.

"How long have you known?" he winced.

Gianna looked like she was enjoying herself. "Since you introduced yourself at the ribbon-cutting. What kind of tenant would I be if I didn't know my own landlord's name?"

Shit.

"You're my tenant." He said it again as the implication settled. It didn't matter how attractive he found Gianna Decker. They had a professional relationship that must be maintained.

"This is—"

"Complicated," she finished for him. "You're lucky, Mr. Pierce, that I've sworn off complications and mistakes. Because, otherwise, I would have found you irresistible."

"Irresistible how?" Beckett asked before he thought better of it.

Gianna stood on her tiptoes and placed a soft kiss on his cheek. "Thanks for walking me home, Beckett."

She turned away from him and followed the walkway around the side of his house to the backyard.

Beckett touched his cheek and frowned after her. It was the second time she had kissed him, and he wasn't going to lie. It wasn't enough.

$\sim$

"WHAT'S WITH THE DOPEY GRIN?" Evan demanded when Gia let herself in the front door.

"I don't have a dopey grin. I have a self-satisfied grin. That's totally different," she corrected him.

"Whatever." He sighed and went back to his homework at the dining table.

"How's it going?" Gia asked, settling in next to him.

He shrugged his shoulders and frowned at the book in front of him.

"What do you think about school here so far?" Gia opened her water bottle and drank deeply.

Evan shrugged again. "It's okay, I guess."

"Is it a lot different?"

"There's a girl in my class named Oceana," Evan said, refreshing the screen of his tablet. He scrolled through some pictures and opened one. "This is her."

Gia peered at Oceana's school photo on the screen. In any other town in America, the perky little blonde would have been a cheerleader. In Blue Moon, she wore a hand-crocheted vest and lived on a sheep farm.

"This town is weird," Evan announced.

"I agree. Weird good or weird bad?"

"Mostly weird good. I guess. Like the teachers don't make us sit too long and stuff. They make us take stretching breaks, kind of like your classes. But the lunches are weird bad. At my old school we had pizza and nachos and stuff. Here they have this quinoa casserole crap."

Gia swallowed a laugh. "Maybe we should look at packing your lunch a couple days a week?"

Evan nodded. "I think that would be for the best."

"Your dad call tonight?" Gia asked, taking another drink of water.

"Nope."

She automatically squashed the annoyance and the desire to make an excuse for Evan's father. She and Paul had worked out a call schedule that promised the kids reliable, consistent communication with their father so he could stay up on what was happening with them.

And as was typical with her ex-husband, he continued to flake out on them, blissfully unaware of the damage that his inconsistency and lack-of-presence did to their little family.

Gia changed the subject. "How was Rora for you tonight?"

"She was good. She only made me watch two episodes of that dumb whiny cartoon."

Gia rolled her eyes heavenward. "She has to grow out of that show eventually, right? Every time it's on I want to put a frying pan through the TV."

"Yeah." Evan rewarded her with a small smile.

"So, listen. This was my last Friday night class. I have another teacher who is going to take over the time slot. So that means just Tuesday and Thursday night classes for me. How do you feel about being Aurora's official, compensated guardian on those nights?"

Evan leaned back and crossed his arms. His hazel eyes narrowed. "What kind of compensation are we talking?"

"For watching your sister from 5:30 to 7:30, I'm prepared to offer you five dollars." She purposely low-balled him.

"Fifteen," he countered.

"Ten."

"Deal," he said extending his hand.

She shook it solemnly. "And if you need a night off to do school work or hang out with friends or build creepy robots—whatever it is kids your age do—let me know, and I'll have Grampa watch Rora."

"Robots? Seriously, Gia?"

Gia held up her hands. "Hey, whatever floats your boat. No judgment."

"You fit right in with the rest of these weirdos," he told her.

She jumped out of her chair and put him in a headlock and covered the top of his head with noisy kisses. "I'm totally changing your name to Compost Heap Decker," she told him. He put up a struggle, but his laughter prevented him from wiggling free.

His sandy hair needed a trim, Gia noted. But they had worked out a deal back when he turned ten that he was in charge of haircut decisions.

"Hey, I was going to make an appointment to get my hair trimmed. I saw this crazy place called The Grateful Head. Let me know if you want an appointment. That's a play on a band, by the way."

Evan leveled the haughty gaze of a twelve-year-old at her. "I know who the Grateful Dead are."

Of course Paul Decker's son would know the Grateful Dead. Paul's finest gift to his children was a deep and abiding appreciation of music.

"Good, then I don't have to tell your dad that your brains are being consumed by pop artists and you want a life-sized One Direction poster for Christmas."

Evan had the good sense to shudder. "Dad would disown me."

"I'm going to grab a shower and warm up some mac and cheese," Gia said, rising. "You want any?"

"I guess I could go for some."

"Awesome." She started for the stairs. "Heavy carb date in ten minutes, and you can show me how to use the calendar app on my phone."

"Again?"

"It's not 'again' if it's a brand-new app. I didn't like the other one. This one has cool colors and alarms that sound like the ocean."

"I'm changing your name to Too Many Calendar Apps Decker," Evan called after her.

Once in the bathroom, Gia turned on the shower and reached for her phone. She dialed, took a deep, cleansing breath, and brought her phone to her ear.

"Hey, Cinnamon Girl." The sound of her ex-husband's voice simultaneously brought a smile to her lips and irked the hell out of her. It was the story of their relationship, being repeatedly charmed and disappointed by a man who refused to grow up.

"Hey, Paul. Did you forget something today?"

"Oh, man! Is it Friday again, already? I was so amped about this new gig I totally forgot."

"A new gig?" she asked, immediately regretting it.

"I'm filling in with this band at the casino for the next few weeks. Their drummer's having some legal troubles."

"Legal troubles?"

"House arrest for possession," Paul amended. "His loss, my gain. Can you put the kids on? I'll say hi now."

"Aurora's been in bed for half an hour," she reminded him.

"Right, right. How about Ev?"

"Listen Paul, I don't want to just hand him the phone and tell him it's you. He needs to know that you care enough to remember to keep your word when it comes to him."

"Uh-huh. Uh-huh."

She was losing him. She could feel it. He was getting

sucked into whatever video game or YouTube video he would obsess over until something shinier caught his attention.

"I need you to hang up with me and call Evan on his phone. And don't tell him I called you first." She said it slowly and carefully, as if instructing a toddler.

"Gotcha."

"And make it a video chat this time. It's been a while since he's seen you."

"Sure. No problemo."

She could envision him nodding into the phone.

"Okay. I'm hanging up now, and you're going to call Evan on his phone."

"I got it, G. Consider it done. Oh, listen. The support payment is going to be a little light this month, okay? Things are going down at work."

Gia closed her eyes and took another deep breath. If his child support payments dried up again, she was going to have to look for a second job. Again.

"I can hear you doing your 'don't freak out' breathing thing,'" he teased her.

"We'll talk about the support some other time, okay? Call your son."

"I'm on it. Good talking to you."

"Bye, Paul."

Gia waited until she heard Evan's phone ring downstairs before pulling off her clothes and stepping under the steaming water.

5

A long run early Saturday morning made Beckett reluctantly aware of how loose and energetic his body felt. He refused to attribute it to the yoga he'd endured the night before or the beautiful sadist who guided him through it. It was most likely the aftereffect of a nice, sunny vacation, he decided.

After a strong cup of coffee and his usual protein shake, Beckett decided to spend the rest of the morning catching up on work. But try as he did to focus on asset allocations for the Petrovic family and Pete McDougall's permit request for a custard truck, he found his thoughts returning to Gianna.

He was attracted to her. There was no doubt about that. He wasn't blind. Physically she was stunning. She was little, petite. But what she lacked in height, she made up for in sinful curves. And that face. A sprinkling of freckles on flawless ivory and green-gray eyes that always seemed to be laughing at some unspoken joke. Her wide smile warmed rooms while accentuating the sweet dimple in her chin.

He found her intriguing.

She was nothing like his usual type. The women he dated

were refined, restrained even. Focused on their careers, they had an appreciation of life's little luxuries. They wore tailored suits and spoke fondly of Italian vacations and the literary works of Marcel Proust and Joan Didion.

Gianna did not fit neatly into that category.

Not with her body-hugging spandex, wild curls, and the energy that sparked out of her. He bet she curled up at night with trashy novels and didn't even own a suit.

Yet the attraction for him had been instantaneous. There was power in that compact, curvy body. And that was as captivating as her physical beauty. She was strong and vibrant, making the memories of the women he'd always dated take on muted pastel shades.

She had kids. Kids meant complications, kids meant serious, neither of which Beckett was interested in. His best course of action was to avoid his new tenant as much as possible.

Beckett scrubbed his hands over his face. He needed to get out. Get a little distance from the wicked temptation in his backyard. While putting together his lunch, he'd actually stood at his kitchen window for ten minutes, hoping for a glimpse of her red hair.

He scrawled his signature across a document, hit send on an email, and dropped a stack of papers on Ellery's desk.

He'd pay his brothers a visit and check on the construction at the brewery. That would keep his thoughts from Gianna.

BECKETT FOUND his brother's girlfriend, Summer, putting groceries away in the sunny kitchen of the farmhouse. "Hey there, gorgeous," he said, greeting the stylish blonde with a kiss on the top of the head.

"Beckett!" Her wide blue eyes lit up, and she pulled him down for a hug. "How was the Dominican?"

"Beautiful, sunny. Paradise."

"Ugh," Summer groaned, shaking her ponytail. "I'm so jealous. Between the move, the magazine launch in January, and the brewery construction, we won't be able to leave the county let alone the country for years."

"You love it, and you know it," Beckett challenged her.

"I don't know what you're talking about," she sniffed, feigning innocence.

It was true; he only had to look at her to see the happiness radiating off her. Summer had come to Pierce Acres as a stressed out, overworked magazine editor to interview his brother Carter for a piece on organic farming. What had started off as a battle of the wills had turned into a flaming hot affair and, finally, a happy relationship.

Summer had quit her job, moved to Blue Moon, and was launching her own online magazine in the new year. She was the happiest person he knew, except for maybe Carter.

"So, tell me you'll stay for dinner tonight," she said, turning back to the open refrigerator.

"That depends. Are you cooking?" Summer wasn't known for her culinary skills.

She shot him a look around the door. "Don't be ridiculous. Franklin and your mom are cooking lasagna."

"Mom and Franklin?"

Summer nodded. "Jax, too, and I'm texting Joey to invite her."

"I'll pass. I've got things to catch up on," Beckett said, toying with the bowl of fruit perched on the granite island. "All those messages from modeling agencies wanting my body."

Summer winced. "Haven't they slowed down yet?"

The side door sprang open, and his older, bearded brother walked in. "Hello, pretty girl," Carter said, laying a sizzling kiss on Summer's upturned mouth.

"I'm surprised you can kiss her through all that fur on your face," Beckett quipped.

"Your brother was just telling me that he can't join us for dinner tonight because he has 'things to catch up on.'"

Carter plucked an apple out of the bowl and turned his attention to Beckett. "I call bullshit."

"It's a legitimate and reasonable excuse," Beckett argued.

Carter stroked a hand over his beard. "Nope. Bullshit."

"Beckett, I hate to do this, but I agree with Carter," Summer said, leaning her elbows on the counter. "I think you should talk to us about it."

"Talk to you about what? I have things to do. I was out of the country for ten days."

"You also have an intense dislike of Franklin," Summer pointed out.

"What is it about him that gets to you?" Carter asked, ranging himself behind Summer to rub her shoulders.

"I don't know what you're talking about," Beckett said crisply. "Being a responsible, productive member of society, I've got shit to do tonight."

"What shit do you have to do?" His younger brother Jax entered through the side door. Like Carter, he was wearing jeans and a t-shirt that had seen better days, and like all of the Pierce men, he had dark hair and steel gray eyes.

Carter's cavernous kitchen was starting to feel crowded to Beckett.

"I came over to check out the progress on the brewery. Can I at least do that without an interrogation?" he snapped.

He saw a long look pass between Carter and Summer.

"Forget it." He shoved through the door and stormed off the porch.

He heard the door open and close behind him. "Wait up," Jax called after him.

His brother jogged to his side. "Don't mind them. They're just disgustingly happy and feel compelled to make everyone else join their cult."

Beckett shrugged it off. "I shouldn't have snapped. I just have some things on my mind."

Jax clammed up as they caught a glimpse of Joey Greer's vintage pick-up as it drove past the lane. "Yeah. Me, too," he muttered.

The door to the kitchen opened and closed again. Carter caught up to them, hands shoved in his pockets and Summer's lipstick smeared on his mouth.

Beckett decided not to mention it. It's what brothers did.

"Calvin's crew is moving pretty fast," Carter said, ignoring the minor blow up in the kitchen as he led them around the little barn. The path served as a shortcut to the big, stone barn that would soon house John Pierce Brews.

It sat by itself on a rise surrounded by fields and pastures. A handful of pick-up trucks and construction vans were parked on one side.

Beckett stepped through the opening that would eventually be accordion glass doors to the stone terrace.

The massive main floor was looking significantly brighter thanks to the new windows that the builder added at strategic points. The thick walls, which would eventually be painted white, created deep windowsills. The wide-plank floors would be sanded down and refinished once the massive L-shaped bar was complete.

The rickety ladder to the top floor was in the process of

being replaced by a rustic staircase made from reclaimed barn wood. The railing they chose was a modern cable system.

Tucked under the loft near the end of the bar was a shaft for a small elevator. On the other end of the wall were the skeletons of two restrooms. Beckett waved to Calvin and his foreman, Joe.

"Looking real good, guys," he called out.

"Wait'll you see the brewery," Calvin said, pulling his Jets cap off his head to swipe at the sweat. "Really like that lipstick you're wearing there, Carter."

Carter dragged a hand over his mouth and swore. "You guys suck," he said to Beckett and Jax. And Beckett instantly felt a little lighter.

Carter led the way downstairs to the first floor. One third of the space would be used for the commercial kitchen, but the rest would be the heart and soul of the brewing operations.

Thick beams and stone walls reminded all who entered of the building's hundred-year-old past.

"I ordered the fermentation tanks last week," Jax told them, wandering around the space. "Carter and I were talking about the keg room placement. We thought having it over here would make sense. The lines could go straight up to the tap system above."

"Plus it's a straight shot to the doors for deliveries and supplies," Carter added.

Beckett shoved his hands in his pockets. He could finally start to envision it all.

"It's going to be a hell of an operation," he nodded. "We're going to need an onsite office, aren't we?"

Carter, arms crossed, leaned against a pallet of two by fours. "Jax had a thought on that."

Beckett turned his attention to his younger brother.

"The silo," Jax said.

The stone silo stood next to the barn, stretching toward the sky. Once a holding bin for grain, it had been empty for decades.

Beckett frowned thoughtfully. "How big is it?"

"Big. Twenty feet across."

He thought about it, rolling the idea around in his head. "We could have an office off of the upper floor, some storage, maybe even move the bottling stuff out there."

"Told you he'd be into it," Jax smirked at Carter.

"It's a good idea. Might as well make use of the space. What would it add to the timeline?" They were planning to open in the spring as it was now.

"The storage and bottling works wouldn't be a big deal. It might take a little more time to get the office space together, especially if we want any kind of plumbing over there," Jax told him.

Beckett nodded. "Let's do it. We can always finish off the office after we're open for business."

"Sounds good," Jax agreed.

"Now, the big question," Carter said. "How much longer before we can start brewing?"

"Once the tanks are in place, we can get everything else set up in a week or two tops," Jax said, scrolling through the calendar on his phone. "We can pretty much start fighting over who gets to do the first batch."

"Me."

"Me." Beckett and Carter frowned at each other.

"We're going to have to settle this like men," Beckett said.

"A duel at dawn?" Jax asked.

"We'll come up with something," Carter decided. "So while we're on the subject of change," Carter began. He pulled a black jeweler's box from his pocket. "There's hopefully going to be another one around here sometime."

He snapped open the lid, and Beckett pretended to shield his eyes from the sparkle inside. "Damn. Already? Didn't you just meet like four months ago?"

Carter grinned. "Don't even pretend like she's not the one. I just have to convince *her* that it's not too early."

"Summer's hell-bent on 'taking things slow' since everything happened so fast," Jax explained to Beckett. "Meeting Carter, quitting her job, and moving in is freaking out the control freak."

"Hey, that's my control freak you're talking about," Carter warned him.

"I meant it in the most adorable, complimentary way possible," Jax said, holding up his hands.

"Do you really think there's a possibility that she'll say no?" Beckett asked.

"I think she's more likely to say, 'ask me again in a year.'"

"So how are you going to do it?" Beckett asked, baffled.

"I'm going to make it seem like her idea and wait until the perfect time to strike," Carter said with a firm nod.

"I can't wait to see how this ninja engagement plays out," Jax said.

Carter couldn't wipe the grin off his face as he looked down at the ring again. "Do you think it's big enough?"

"No Pierce man has ever uttered those words before," Beckett told him, clapping a hand on his brother's shoulder. "It might be a little too big."

6

_B_eckett stayed behind at the barn to talk timelines and materials with the crew. At sixty-eight, Calvin Finestra considered himself to be in the prime of his life and had no intention of retiring. He climbed around on scaffolding like a man twenty years his junior and liked to take his wife of forty-four years line dancing every Friday night.

"It's good to see your brother so happy," Calvin told him.

"Carter? Yeah, Summer seems like she was just what he was missing."

"When are you getting yourself a woman?" Calvin asked, a twinkle in his brown eyes.

"When I find one that puts the stupid smile on my face like Summer does to Carter," Beckett told him.

Did he want to settle down someday? Of course. Eventually. He was a family man at heart. He'd bought a five-bedroom house for God's sake. But none of the women he'd ever dated had felt like Pierce family material. Well, of course, there was Joey.

One very brief make-out session eight years ago after Jax disappeared to the West Coast had left them both confused and guilty. They had vowed to pretend it never happened. Joey Greer, with her long chestnut hair and long, strong legs and wild stubborn streak was as close to a Pierce as you can get without the DNA. But she would always belong to Jax whether she wanted to or not.

Beckett was impressed with Jax's commitment. He had fully expected his younger brother to head back to L.A. long before now. Joey's frosty feelings hadn't thawed an inch toward him, but Jax was still sticking.

A glance at his watch told him he should get moving if he wanted to avoid seeing his mother and Franklin. He said his goodbyes to Calvin and the crew and headed back toward the house.

Standing between the construction on the barn behind him and the renovated farmhouse, Beckett was struck by the changes to the land he had known his entire life. Memories of growing up and running wild with his brothers lived side-by-side with the progress of today.

His brother would be married, and a new generation would grow up on Pierce Acres. A smile pulled at Beckett's lips. The change in Carter from when he first came home from Afghanistan wounded and scarred to now was nothing short of a miracle. The impossible healing came first from the land and the people of Blue Moon and then from the nosey blonde who loved the shadows right out of his brother.

But not all change was good.

He wouldn't think of a world without John Pierce as better than before. His father had showed him how to be a man. Everything Beckett learned in his life from farming to women to how to lead all came from his father. A legend in Blue Moon, his death had created a vacuum. One that Beckett had to step up and fill before he was ready.

Still mourning his loss, Beckett had worked side-by-side

with his mother to keep the farm going. And when their neighbors showed up day after day to lend a hand, drop off a casserole, or just sit quietly with his grieving mother, he had learned the meaning of community.

His love for Blue Moon was as wide and deep as his love for his family. And so, instead of moving away and joining a successful law firm like most of his classmates, he had come home and planted his roots. And had never once regretted it. He owed this town a debt of gratitude and hoped that one day his feet would fill his father's shoes.

A giggle and flash of red caught his attention. A little girl with bouncing red curls dashed around the side of the little barn, looking over her shoulder.

She turned her head just in time to avoid a collision with Beckett's legs.

"Hi!" she said cheerfully.

"Uh, hi. Who are you?" Beckett asked, scanning the yard for an adult.

"I'm Rora," she announced proudly.

"Rora?" There was something unsettlingly familiar about her.

"Uh-huh. What's your name?"

"I'm Beckett."

She brought a finger to her lips and shushed him. "Hi, Bucket! I'm hiding. Do you wanna play? You can hide, too."

Beckett crouched down next to her as she peered around the side of the barn.

"Here he comes," Rora whispered with excitement.

"Aurora, come on. I don't feel like chasing you." Beckett heard resignation in the voice of a young boy. "Let's go back to Grampa, okay?"

Beckett frowned. Had the farm been invaded by a family of strangers?

The little girl chose that moment to jump around the corner. "Boo!" she shouted.

Her roar turned to a squeal as her victim gave chase. She dashed back to Beckett, her tiny legs a blur. "Bucket," she shrieked. She raised her arms high and, without thinking, Beckett swung her up.

The boy half-heartedly jogged around the side of the barn and stopped short when he recognized Beckett.

"You again?" Beckett said. It was the boy from his guesthouse. Which meant...

"Van, this is Bucket," Aurora said, patting his shoulder. "He was hidin' with me."

"Your name is Bucket?" the kid asked.

"It's Beckett. And you can stop judging, *Van*."

"It's Evan," the boy told him.

Aurora rolled her eyes. "Dats what I said. Bucket 'n Van."

"So let me guess. Your mom," Beckett said, tickling Aurora's belly and making her giggle, "and your captor are the same person."

"Gia," Evan confirmed.

"And your grandfather—"

"He's not my real—"

"Yeah, kid. I got it. Who is he?" A feeling of dread was beginning to claw at his gut.

"Franklin Merrill," Evan answered.

"Shit."

The little girl in his arms gaped at Beckett. "You said 'shit,'" she said.

"I'm not taking the blame for that one," Evan said. He shoved his hands in his pockets and headed for the house.

"Bucket, 'shit' is a bad word. You shouldn't say it," Rora admonished him.

"Sorry, shortcake. I meant to say sugar. Hey, kid, wait up," Beckett called after Evan.

Evan paused and scuffed the toe of his sneaker in the dirt. "Hurry up, Bucket," he said with a deadpan face.

"Are you guys here for dinner?" Beckett asked, still carrying the little girl.

"Yeah. I guess Grampa wanted to introduce us to his new girlfriend or something. He was acting really weird."

The kid was smart and observant.

"Girls'll do that to a guy," Beckett warned him. "How do you think your... Gia will take the news?"

Evan shrugged. "She's always worried about him being lonely, and Phoebe doesn't seem like a crazy person or anything. She'll probably think it's great."

Beckett steered him to the side door, and they entered the kitchen that was already full of people.

His mother and Summer were layering noodles, cheese, and sauce in two casserole dishes. Carter and Jax were passing out beers and wine glasses while Franklin and Gia trayed up antipasto.

"Mama!" Rora chirped. "'Dis my friend Bucket!"

Gia's green eyes widened in surprise when she saw him holding her daughter. "Oh my God. Pierce Acres," she said, smacking a hand to her forehead. "I should have known."

She was wearing jeans today and an off-the-shoulder striped sweater that highlighted her curves without being showy. Her feet were bare, and her hair was pulled back from her face in a wild ponytail.

He couldn't stop staring at the line of her shoulder and neck.

"I take it you two know each other?" his mother, in a knit cardigan the color of blue bells, said coming around the island to give Beckett a kiss on the cheek.

Gia approached and plucked her daughter out of his arms. "Beckett is our landlord, and he did the ribbon-cutting at my studio yesterday," she told Phoebe.

Summer laughed from the other side of the island. "Small towns."

"Miss Phoebe, do you know Bucket?" the little girl asked his mother.

"I do, sweetie. He's my son."

"Mama, Bucket said 'shit.'"

The kitchen noise silenced except for Carter who choked on his beer.

"Did he?" Gia asked, looking at Beckett.

Rora nodded earnestly. "But it's okay, 'cause he meant to say sugar."

Phoebe burst out laughing.

"I have no idea what she's talking about," Beckett said innocently, snagging a beer. "Do you, Evan?"

He earned a smirk from the boy. "No idea," he agreed.

"Five seconds with my kids, and you've got them swearing and lying," Gianna said accusingly. "I'm putting you in time out."

Evan looked like he was going to argue the "my kids" statement but held his tongue.

"Mama, Bucket's too big for time out," Rora argued.

"You're never too big for time out," Gianna said, grabbing Beckett's arm and pulling him down the hall toward the farmhouse's front door.

She waited until they were out of earshot of everyone else. "I'm really sorry about this. I had no idea my dad was bringing us here or that you'd be here. He just said he had a surprise."

"Surprise, I'm moving in with someone." Beckett snorted.

"They're moving in together?" Gianna's eyebrows shot up.

"I guess he didn't get to that part of the surprise yet." He took a long pull on the bottle.

"That seems kind of fast." She frowned.

"They've been dating for six months," Beckett grumbled. "We've only known for three. And that's only because we caught him trying to sneak out of her bedroom one morning."

Gianna bit her lip. "I'm trying not to laugh because I can see you're upset by it. But..."

Beckett pictured Franklin's pajama-covered legs flailing off the porch roof. "It was a tiny bit funny," he conceded.

"If I'm getting my signals correctly, you're not happy about their relationship."

He wasn't happy with the way Gianna was looking up at him. She was standing too close to him. Those warm sea green eyes looked into him, her full lips parted just the slightest bit. A fiery tendril had escaped her hair tie to hang down her throat. He didn't realize until it was too late that his fingers were tucking the wayward curl behind her ear and then brushing down the graceful line of her neck.

He felt her pulse rate ratchet up under the pads of his fingers. Her skin was warm, smooth under his touch. Her lips, the color of the pinkest rose, parted even further. Under her spell, Beckett leaned down, leaned in until he could feel her breath on him. He brushed a thumb over her lower lip as he skimmed his hand over her jaw and neck. Soft, smooth, so alive.

Those stunning green eyes were heavy, her breath shallow.

An inch apart, swamped in her scent of soap and lavender, Beckett was lost.

A shout of laughter from the kitchen tore them apart.

Gianna sagged down on the bottom step. "I feel like I'm hyperventilating," she gasped.

Beckett bent at the waist and braced his hands on his knees. "There's not a milliliter of blood in my head right now."

"Forbidden fruit," Gianna said, fanning her flushed cheeks.

"Huh?"

"I want you because I can't have you, leading me to almost devour your face with our families fifteen feet away."

"Pretty sure I would have done the devouring," Beckett countered.

"Not helping." Gianna rose and straightened her clothing that didn't need straightening. "We can totally fight this, right?"

"Totally." Beckett shook his head.

"You're shaking your head."

"What?"

Gianna pointed at him. "You're not nodding 'yes.' You're shaking your head 'no.'"

Beckett frowned. "Sorry. I'm just..."

"Yeah, me too," she said, agreeing with his unspoken words.

Beckett leaned back against the front door, willing his erection to go away and his heart rate to return to normal. "Your kids are great," he said, changing the subject.

"Don't be sweet. I can't resist sweet," Gianna warned him.

"Your kids are monsters, and I hate your face."

Gianna laughed. "I hate your face, too. Your gorgeous, sexy face."

"Gianna," he warned her.

"I'm going to go make my monsters wash their hands. Are you staying for dinner?" She looked... hopeful.

"Yeah," he nodded.

"Good."

7

The Pierces assembled in the dining room, absorbing Gia and her family into their ranks. The dining table held all of them, including the late arrival of willowy Joey, who seemed to be the focus of the youngest Pierce's attention.

Gia devoured her helping of lasagna, admiring her father's vegetarian spin on one of her favorite family recipes. She had few childhood memories that weren't steeped in fresh basil and simmering tomato sauce.

While she and her sisters were growing up, Franklin Merrill was running two families: his daughters and his restaurants. Gia and her sisters had spent their formative years in restaurant kitchens. Gia had been waitressing herself through a bachelor's degree in plant sciences when she met Paul Decker, the sexy, charming, free-spirited musician.

It had been her twenty-first birthday. Paul was playing in the band at the bar where she and her girlfriends were ordering girlie drinks. She noticed him noticing her, and when the band took five, he took her number.

Six years, one unplanned pregnancy, and an unfinished

college degree later, Gia was older and wiser. Or at least wise enough to know that the handsome mayor seated across from her was off limits.

She had fallen for looks and lust before. She wouldn't do it again. She just wished Beckett would stop looking at her so she could stop her face from flushing.

Franklin paused his noodle cutting for Aurora to lean over and whisper something in Phoebe's ear. Phoebe giggled and nudged him in the ribs with her elbow. Franklin grinned back at her and brushed a kiss across her cheek as he reached past her for the salad.

Gia smiled.

It was good to see her father happy again. As far as she was concerned, he deserved all the happiness in the world. Raising three girls on his own had to have been a long, lonely period in his life. Seeing him smitten with Phoebe, a sharp, smart woman who raised three good men? Well, that was enough to send her heart soaring.

She was just starting to wonder if she could sneak a picture of the happy couple to text to her sisters when she spotted Beckett's frown. A frown directed at Franklin and Phoebe.

Disapproval pumped off him in waves so strong that Gia was surprised that no one else seemed to notice.

"So, Gia," Summer said from the other end of the table. "How's the studio going so far?"

Beckett's attention redirected to her.

"It's going well." Gia cleared her throat. "The student retention from Maris's classes to mine has been great, and I picked up a few new ones."

"I heard Fitz takes class there," Carter said, reaching for the salad.

An image of the skinny Bill Fitzsimmons in his yoga briefs

popped into Gia's head, and she bobbled her water glass. "Fitz is a regular," she said diplomatically.

"A regular naked weirdo," Beckett offered.

Gia laughed. "Beckett knows first-hand. He took a class last week."

"*You* took a yoga class?" Joey asked in disbelief, her brown eyes dancing.

"What's so unbelievable about that?" Beckett asked indignantly.

"Wait, wait, wait. Let me get a mental picture of Beckett Om-ing," Jax snickered.

"I'd like to see you take that class," Beckett said mildly. "You, too," he said to Carter who was chuckling.

"I wouldn't want to humiliate you in front of your constituents," Carter teased.

"I think you're both scared," Beckett announced.

"Pfft, it's yoga. You lay on the floor and stretch. No offense, Gia," Jax said, shooting an apologetic glance her way.

"None taken," she said sweetly. "Yoga's definitely not for everyone. There are a lot of people who can't handle it."

Beckett kicked back, clearly enjoying not being the intended target of her manipulation this time. "Yeah, Jax, you and Carter don't have the upper body strength that Fitz does. You'd just embarrass yourselves."

"It can be pretty difficult," Gia agreed in feigned earnest-ness. "I'd really hate to see one of you get hurt."

Carter and Jax exchanged a look.

"You know, you guys have been trying to figure out how to decide who gets to brew the first beer in the brewery," Summer began.

Joey caught on quickly. "Yeah. Why don't you have a yoga-off, and Gia here will decide the winner?"

"A yoga-off?" Carter sounded skeptical.

"Sure!" Joey said, grinning now. "Winner brews first."

"When's a good night for them to come in?" Summer asked.

Gia pretended to ponder. "How about Tuesday at seven?" The seven o'clock class was hot power flow.

Beckett winked at her. "I'm in."

"Me, too, Mama!" Aurora piped up. "I wanna yoga with Bucket."

Beckett reached over and ruffled her red hair.

"What do we do about Bucket's unfair advantage?" Jax asked.

"Yeah, Bucket already took the class," Carter argued.

"Gia can come up with a new routine for the class," Franklin offered. "That way no one has an advantage."

"That sounds fair to me," Summer chimed in.

"How do we decide the winner?" Carter questioned.

"Gia can judge," Joey decided. "She's the unbiased expert."

"I guess it's settled then," Gia said, pretending not to feel the weight of three Pierce brothers' gazes on her.

AFTER DINNER PHOEBE and Franklin volunteered to take the kids for a walk over to see the horses, and the Pierce brothers disappeared together to check out the construction progress on the second floor of the little barn.

The exodus left Gia, Joey, and Summer to handle the cleanup.

"I still say they did it on purpose," Joey grumbled, towel drying the pot that Gia handed her.

"All three of them have to go check out *my* new office as soon as the dish soap comes out? Suspicious," Summer agreed, tucking the salad bowl away in a cabinet.

"I wouldn't mind seeing your office," Gia said, dunking one of the lasagna dishes in the sink.

Summer wrinkled her nose at the remaining dirty dishes cluttering the counter. "We did fifty percent of the dishes. I think we can leave the rest for the boys," she decided. "We'll just go over there and kick them out."

"Let's refill and head over," Joey said, pulling the stopper out of the wine bottle.

Gia and Joey topped off their glasses while Summer debated on a second glass of wine or another chocolate chip cookie. The cookie won.

"These are sinful," she told Joey as they trooped out the door. "Do not leave them in my house. I swear I'm the only person in the world who goes vegetarian and gains weight."

"I'm not taking them home with me," Joey argued. "You live with two grown men who still eat like they're fifteen. I live alone."

"Fine. But I'm only allowed to have one more... tonight," Summer clarified.

They found the men checking out the fresh drywall on the second floor of the bright red barn next to the house.

"Gentlemen, we left fifty percent of the dishes for you to do. We didn't want you to miss out on your fair share of the cleanup," Summer said sweetly.

Jax looked like he wanted to argue, but Carter walked over to Summer and wrapped his arms around her waist. He lifted her off the ground and spun her in a little circle.

Gia felt her heart give a little thump when she saw the happiness in Summer's eyes.

What would it feel like to be loved like that? she wondered.

"Gentlemen, we're being kicked out and sent back to the kitchen," Carter announced, putting Summer back on her feet.

Grumbling, Beckett and Jax allowed themselves to be herded toward the door. Again, Gia felt the weight of Beckett's gaze on her, but he passed her without a word.

"Has anyone told you that you look like an angel?" Jax asked Gia with a sexy grin.

Gia blinked.

"She's not falling for that crap, Jackson," Joey warned him sharply.

"Guess I'll have to win the old-fashioned way," Jax said, stepping in on Joey. "With my physical prowess."

He smoldered, and Gia was surprised that instead of singeing, Joey fixed him with an icy glare. *A woman immune to the Pierce brother charm? Was that physically possible?* she wondered.

"Good luck with that. You're looking a little rusty," Joey told Jax coolly.

"Maybe you could help warm me up?" Jax ventured another half step closer before Joey slapped a hand to his chest.

"You're not getting out of the dishes. Go!"

Jax ambled out of the room but not before sending Joey a look that telegraphed exactly what he was thinking.

"That's better," Summer said once the men left. She twirled around the empty space. "I'm so excited about everything! It feels like all my dreams are coming true."

Gia couldn't help but smile at Summer's enthusiasm.

She gave them the quick tour pointing out the highlights of where her desk would be and the conference area as well as a small kitchen.

"Jax is Mr. Tech Geek, and he's hooking me up with video conferencing stuff so I'll be able to video chat with contributors and advertisers and interviewees all over the country." She hugged herself. "What do you guys think?"

Joey paced the length of the huge room. "I think it's awesome. How far along are you with the launch?"

"I'm launching my own digital magazine," Summer explained to Gia.

"I follow your blog," Gia admitted with a grin. "It took me a minute to realize you were *that* Summer Lentz. This is really exciting to see everything happening from this side."

"I'm over the moon," Summer said with a laugh. "I'm planning to launch in January. You know, the whole 'new year, new you' thing. I've got advertisers lined up and a couple of the features already in the works. I'm trying to focus on topics like wellness, food for your body and your soul, travel, community, and gardening."

"I think it's wonderful. It's just what the world needs, a magazine that helps you build a better life." Gia nodded.

Summer grinned at her. "Exactly. I'm amazed at how it's all coming together. Just a few months ago, I was determined to slave away in my cubicle for another two or three years before making the leap. And now here I am."

"Things sure have moved fast," Joey commented.

"You're not kidding," Summer agreed. "That's why I'm trying to slow things down and take my time. I fell for Carter so hard and so fast I sometimes worry that our foundation of hot sex and overwhelming events might be a little shaky. I want us to proceed down the right path at the right pace. We're in it for the long haul. We've got time to do things right."

Gia hid her grimace. It was the exact opposite approach she had taken, and her foundation had indeed proved to be too shaky.

"That's a wise life philosophy," she told Summer.

"Or she's just feeding her control freak tendencies," Joey said, smiling into her wine glass.

"I could say something about the pot and the kettle," Summer said, lifting her chin.

"You're calling *me* a control freak?" Joey's eyebrows rose.

"Everyone knows that you and Jax are meant to be together but you're determined to keep pushing him away until he meets your exacting standards." Summer crossed her arms.

"My 'exacting standards' require an apology for leaving town without a word to me eight years ago," Joey shot back.

"He never apologized?" Summer gasped.

Joey shook her head and took another sip of wine. "Nope."

"Team Joey," Gia announced.

Summer nodded. "Totally Team Joey."

"Can we please talk about something else?" Joey grumbled.

"How about what's up with Beckett and my father?" Gia offered.

Joey and Summer exchanged a long look.

"What's that mean?" Gia demanded. "I'm new here. I don't know what long, meaningful looks mean."

"It means that we're not sure what's going on there," Summer explained. "Beckett seems to have a problem with Phoebe and Franklin dating—"

"And moving in together," Joey added.

"And moving in together," Summer agreed. "But he's not talking about it to anyone. Carter and I ganged up on him about it this afternoon, but he wouldn't crack. He also refused to stay for dinner... until he realized you were here." She grinned innocently.

Gia couldn't hide the blush that tinged her cheeks. Nor could she dull the quick rush of pleasure she felt.

"Any comment on that?" Joey prompted.

"None at this time," Gia decided.

"Interesting," Summer mused out loud.

"So back to Beckett's potential issues with my father," Gia said, trying to redirect the conversation.

"I'll say this," Joey said. "It's out of character for Beckett to have an issue like this. He generally likes everyone, and Franklin fell into that category before Beckett knew he was dating his mother."

"I can't imagine my father would have done something to upset him," Gia said, tapping her fingers on her wineglass.

"Who knows what goes on in the minds of men," Joey grumbled.

8

---

*I*t was John Pierce's birthday.

Beckett's father should have been fifty-eight. But instead, his ashes were scattered on the low ridge that rose above the crooked creek that snaked its way through Pierce Acres.

His father had an eternal view of the best sunsets upstate New York had to offer, but he didn't have life. He didn't have a voice. He didn't have hands to slap his sons on the shoulder or stroke Phoebe's hair when he thought no one else was looking.

Beckett would have given anything to have just one more conversation with his dad. One more hug. One more look.

But there were no more chances. Just an emptiness where a great man had once been. And the shadow of a new man encroaching.

Was it his fault Phoebe was lonely? Should he have carved out more time for his mother? Was she being taken advantage of? Was the memory of his father starting to fade from their family?

The questions had plagued him all weekend. As had thoughts of a certain redhead, which he found frustrating. A run that morning had done nothing to cool his head or settle his heart.

Maybe an hour at the gym before his late morning appointments in the office would help.

∼

GIA PEDDLED her rubbery legs faster and cursed the need for cardio as the elliptical's cross-trainer program kicked up the resistance. She was definitely treating herself to a smoothie after this torture.

Monday morning classes—as well as Wednesday and Friday nights—at the yoga studio were covered by Destiny Wheedlemeyer. A free-range chicken raiser and founder of a very successful knitting store on Etsy, Destiny gave yoga students instructions in a breathy Marilyn Monroe-esque voice and dressed entirely in black.

Gia used Destiny's Monday class coverage to carve out a bit of free time for handling non-child-related responsibilities. After walking the kids to school—Evan had made her stop two blocks away from the junior high while Rora had a melt-down at drop off—she headed straight to Fitness Freak for a long cardio session to start the week off right.

Fitness Freak welcomed everyone regardless of physical ability. The front desk was usually manned by a woman named Fran, the coolest person Gia had ever met. Fran had a Mohawk, sleeve tattoos, and a wheelchair. She played bass in a garage band.

The weekday morning trainer at the gym bore a striking resemblance—in appearance and accent—to Dolph Lundgren. And the clientele ran the gamut from retirees in matching tracksuits to third shift semi-competitive body builders.

Her workouts here were a blissful window of responsibility-free enjoyment. No class to lead, no kids to watch, only a good sweat to work up. Fifteen minutes into the elliptical, Gia felt a presence over her shoulder. An irritated one.

"What are you doing here?"

She glanced over her shoulder at Beckett's frowning face.

"I'm baking cookies. What does it look like?" She mopped her sweaty forehead with her towel.

"You're everywhere." Beckett didn't sound happy about it. In fact, he sounded downright confrontational.

"It's a small town," Gia said, trying not to sound out of breath. "It's bound to happen, especially since I live in your backyard."

Gone was the charming, sexy Beckett that she'd had the pleasure of lusting after. And in his place was a crabby, snippy hot guy. His attitude was as confusing as it was unwelcome. She didn't get much time to herself. Sharing it with a grumpy neighbor—no matter how attractive—was irritating. And she didn't know Beckett well enough to warrant him taking out a bad mood on her.

After a long silence, Beckett climbed on the elliptical next to hers.

"You don't have to be my workout buddy."

"I might as well since there's no avoiding you," Beckett muttered.

"Excuse me?" Gia's stride faltered before she regained her pace. "Did I do something to upset you?"

He had the good manners to look slightly chagrined. "No. Everything's fine."

"Right. Because you sound fine." She sighed with relief as her elliptical clicked down to a less torturous resistance. "Do you want to talk about it?" she offered.

"No."

"My dad always says—"

"I don't need any fatherly advice from him," Beckett snapped. "I *had* a father. He was a great man, and some second-rate substitute isn't going to take his place."

"Is that what you think—"

Beckett cut her off again. His face was red, and it wasn't from exertion. "I also don't need to be analyzed by some kumbaya yogi who thinks we can all get along and that love will conquer all."

"Okay then. Message received. You don't like my father dating your mother."

"I don't like your father taking advantage of my mother," he corrected her, stabbing the resistance button on his machine.

"Taking advantage?" She felt the pulse in her head begin to thud, the sure sign of a headache blooming. "Beckett, I think you have the wrong idea."

"Is his restaurant in trouble? Maybe he's behind on his mortgage? He needs a little capital to keep things going, so he looks for someone with a nest egg. Maybe someone who's a little lonely. Lays on the charm. A few months later, and *bam!* He's moving in with her."

"I'm going to stop you right there before you go any further down this rabbit hole," Gia said. She took a deep breath and then another one, reminding herself not to take it personally. He was lashing out because he was hurting with a pain that was palpable.

And she needed to get out of there before she punched him in the face to give him some real physical pain.

"It sounds like you could use some time alone to work out your feelings," she said evenly.

"I could use some time without you and your father popping up everywhere in my life."

"Too bad about that year lease that I signed." She pressed the stop button on her machine and grabbed her towel and water bottle. "I hope you feel better."

BECKETT DIDN'T FEEL any better when Gianna left the gym. In fact, he felt worse. Now, a sick layer of guilt settled over the simmering anger in his belly. He got off the elliptical and wiped it and Gia's abandoned machine down before storming into the locker room.

So much for working off some of the mad before work.

Beckett headed into the gray tiled shower stall where he ducked his head under the water, willing it to wash away the sadness.

He was a mess. A mental mess. Obviously he had overreacted to Gianna. He hadn't expected to see her there in what he considered his space. The woman was everywhere. His backyard, his childhood home, and now his gym.

His attraction to her frustrated him to no end. He'd never felt so enamored with a woman before. Attracted? Yes. Interested? Yes. But this was different.

Gianna was different.

She wasn't his type. She was too spontaneous, too vivacious. There was nothing subtle about her, from the flaming red curls to the voluptuous curves and her throaty laugh. He preferred quiet confidence, the restrained beauty of sexy suits and impeccably styled hair. A woman he could discuss the law or the latest Wall Street news with, not someone who challenged him with arguments and teasing until he was lightheaded.

He didn't want to like her. Topping the list of reasons why was the fact that she was Franklin's daughter. There wasn't a scenario on earth that would make him friendly toward Franklin again.

Beckett twisted the faucet, cutting off the stream of water.

And there wasn't anything that could change the circumstances of his relationship with Gianna. She was his tenant, she had children. Both factors made the complications so steep that it should have only strengthened his resolve to swear off women for the rest of the year.

Trudy had been a mistake, one that he should have seen coming... and then run full-speed in the opposite direction. While Beckett considered them to be casually dating, the willowy brunette had been measuring his windows for new curtains and practically printing up business cards that said Mrs. Beckett Pierce.

Her biggest mistake had been assuming that being mayor of Blue Moon was just a stepping stone in his political career. She had actually started making inquiries into their district's congressional election. *"For you, darling. Isn't it time you look beyond this tiny town?"* she had asked, stroking a manicured hand down his chest.

She didn't understand why someone "with his education and drive" would want to stay in Blue Moon Bend. She told him he was wasting his potential. He told her they were over.

And in a move that he never saw coming, the erudite twenty-eight-year-old financial advisor set his welcome mat on fire and handcuffed herself to his staircase demanding that he reconsider ending their relationship.

Ellery had taken great pleasure in calling Sheriff Donovan Cardona to take care of the problem. "She was showing you her crazy all along," his paralegal had told him. "You just weren't paying attention."

Cardona had advised Trudy that it would be wise to never show her face near Beckett again, and she had pouted off in her Mercedes, tires squealing, presumably to line up a new victim.

It had been enough for Beckett to swear off women for a while. He was grateful that the recent attention from Summer's article was starting to die down without having reignited Trudy's interest in him.

Women. He shook his head.

The thought brought him right back to Gianna and her sexy sea-witch eyes.

What was it about her that had his blood and his ability to reason rushing right out of his head? She would be a mistake. *They* would be a mistake.

At least after the way he had bitten off her head, she wouldn't be open to making that mistake with him. He dragged a towel through his hair. It wasn't like him to snap like that. Instead of maintaining an aloof coolness, he had gone temper tantrum on her. He would have to apologize.

Just as soon as he could be sure he wouldn't lose his control again and yell at her or, worse, grab her and kiss her until they were both shaking.

Just as soon as he completely understood the out-of-control twin urges to push her away and claim her as his.

BECKETT WENT about his business the rest of the day and blocked out all thoughts of the redheaded temptress. He kept his office door closed and stayed focused on work. Both of his appointments went well, and he was able to squeeze in a return call to Bruce Oakleigh on the man's concerns regarding the proposed Halloween parade route. He considered it a success when the call only took thirty-two minutes.

A pop in by the Fincher brothers kept him occupied for

the rest of the afternoon. The flannel-clad siblings ran a camp-ground outside of town and were arguing about buying more property.

After the argument was settled and the Finchers were on their way, Beckett thought about texting his brothers to see if they would meet him tonight on the farm to drink a toast to their father at sunset but decided against it. It was an unofficial tradition that he and Carter had shared in the years since his brother came home from Afghanistan.

It would have been even better now that Jax was home again. But neither of his brothers seemed to be interested in the threat Franklin posed to their family. In fact, they probably weren't even aware that it was their father's birthday, and he wasn't going to be the one to remind them.

It was up to him to carry on his father's memory, and that's just what he would do.

Their mother had never joined them on the bluff, and Beckett wondered what she had done in years past to remember the husband she had loved so fiercely. He always made it a point to call her or take her to lunch on his father's birthday. Every year except this one.

He allowed that thought to eat at him until he closed the office down. He took off his tie and pulled on a lightweight sweater over his button down.

From his refrigerator, he grabbed a six-pack and avoided looking into the backyard from any of the windows.

Beckett took his time driving out to the family farm. As often as he visited, the drive today always held a special solemnity. It was a somber tradition cloaked in stubbornness. It was Beckett's way of refusing to forget, to let time mellow and dull his memories.

Tonight, he would drink a toast to his father, very likely alone. But with or without his brothers, he would remember.

He would carry on. Great men didn't just vanish from the world. They lived on in memory and tradition.

Beckett passed the farm's drive and instead turned onto the lane that wound around to the stables. It wasn't any faster this way, but at least he could avoid the farmhouse and its occupants. He followed the trail behind the barn and hung a right at the fork, bumping along the trail flanked by fence posts and fields.

When he rounded a copse of trees, he stopped, surprised to find three figures in his headlights.

Beckett turned off the ignition and slid out of the driver seat.

"About damn time," Jax called out.

His brothers were kicked back, beers in hand, in two of the four lawn chairs set up on the ridge facing west.

The third figure wandered toward him. Phoebe smiled sadly and opened her arms to him. What had been a dull throb in his chest bloomed into full-blown pain.

Beckett walked into his mother's arms, tucking her under his chin and holding her close. "Mom." It was all he could think to say. In all of his years observing this sunset ritual, his mother had never joined him.

"This is the first year I've been strong enough, happy enough, to come out here to remember him this way." She sighed into Beckett's chest.

"Where's Franklin? And Summer?" he asked.

"They're back at the house. They wanted to give us Pierces some privacy," she said, looking up at him, her eyes misty behind her glasses.

He was an asshole. An overgrown, immature, pathetic asshole, Beckett decided.

Maybe, just maybe, the man he'd been blaming for fading

his father's memory was actually somehow making it more vibrant for his mother.

And the brothers he'd thought had forgotten had beaten him to it.

He draped an arm over his mother's shoulders and walked her back to the chairs.

Wordlessly, Carter handed him a beer. Beckett took a seat between his brothers, and they all sat in silence, lost in their own memories as the sky went pink and orange.

"Remember that time Dad brought home the three-legged cat he found on the side of the road?" Jax asked, breaking the silence as the sun slipped behind the trees.

"Good old Tripod. He always did have a soft spot for strays." Carter grinned.

The sound of his mother's laugh was balm to Beckett's heart.

9

_____

*G*ia was feeling decidedly un-yoga-like. She'd considered pawning off her Pierce brother yoga competition judging to Destiny. But that was too cowardly.

Beckett's blow-up at the gym the previous morning had taken her by surprise. And, if she was being honest with herself, hurt. The last time they'd seen each other, he'd almost kissed her.

But it was a completely different Beckett Pierce that had coldly accused her—and her father—of essentially trespassing in his home, his town, his family. The volatility had seemed wildly out of character. Granted, she didn't know him very well, and he could very well be a closet temper-tantrum-thrower, but somehow she didn't think so.

Beckett was beloved in this town, and one didn't earn that esteem by lashing out and throwing hissy fits. She sighed. She didn't have time to crack the enigma that was Beckett Pierce.

It was just the universe's way of reminding her to stay focused on her kids and her new business, Gia decided.

She padded across the studio to roll out three mats for the Pierces. She'd put them in the middle row so they could follow what the front row was doing without hiding in the back.

She placed yoga blocks next to each mat and then inventoried the water in the little cooler against the wall. If Beckett's reaction to his first class was any indication, his brothers would need some serious rehydration, too.

She felt a wicked little smile play on her lips. It might be a little fun to torture the Pierces.

Gia checked that the heaters were cranked and the temperature in the studio was steadily rising. A glance at the clock told her she still had a few minutes before her early birds would show up, which meant Beckett wouldn't be far behind.

The nerves in her belly fluttered to life.

She, Gianna Rose Decker, was nervous about seeing a man. And not a sexy, intimidating Hollywood star-type man. Just a regular ol' normal hot guy next-door type. A regular ol' unpredictable hot guy next-door type.

Ugh.

A nice headstand sequence would calm her, she decided, bringing her hand to her unsettled stomach. She returned to her mat at the front of the room. Distributing her weight between her forearms and the top of her head, Gia let her legs slowly float up one at a time stretching toward the ceiling.

It was a graceful move that gave no hint at the core strength it took to achieve.

It had taken her a full year of relentless practice to nail this level of headstand. It was a solid reminder of what hard work and focus could bring to life. And that's exactly what she would do here in Blue Moon. Work hard and focus.

She let her body and breath lead her brain to quiet.

She could do this. She would do this.

The studio door opened, and Gia's eyes fluttered open. Even upside-down Beckett was a heartbreaker. She took her time lowering her toes to the floor and coming out of the pose, hoping the longer she stalled, the less time they'd be alone.

She came to her feet. Even though their height difference was comical, she didn't want to face him sitting down.

"I hope you don't mind that I came a little early," Beckett said, his hands shoved in the pocket of his hoodie. His dark hair was perfectly tousled; black gym shorts accented his long, muscular legs. Energy-wise, he was the opposite of the angry man in the gym yesterday. Calm and a little cautious today. He let his gym bag slide to the floor and nudged it with his foot.

Gia turned away from him and busied herself with rearranging the foam blocks on the shelving unit. "It's no problem. You can start warming up," she told him, pointing toward the empty mats.

"Actually, I was hoping I could talk to you for a—"

The studio door opened again, and Jax and Carter entered.

"I told you he'd weasel in here early and try to earn brownie points," Jax said to Carter.

"No one is weaseling anything," Beckett growled.

"Are you sure you want to put yourself in the middle of this mess, Gia?" Carter asked with a grin.

"Oh, I'm looking forward to this," she said with an easy smile. She felt Beckett's gaze on her and continued to ignore him. "I set you three up here next to each other. But if you can't behave, I'll separate you," she warned them.

"Why's it hot in here?" Jax asked.

"This is a hot yoga class," Gia said innocently. "You don't mind, do you?"

"Piece of cake," Jax said with a wave of his hand. His gaze

darted to Beckett. "Exactly how hot does it get in here?" he whispered to his brother.

Carter stripped off his sweatshirt and smiled at her. "I thought I'd ask you if you wanted to bring the kids by again soon to ride the horses. Franklin said they were pretty excited about seeing them this weekend."

"That's a very sweet offer," Gia said. "Is it bribery?"

"Yes, but you can still bring them over if I don't win." His drop dead gorgeous grin told Gia that Carter was used to getting his way.

"Here," Jax said, grasping her hand. "I brought you this." He dropped a shiny red apple into her palm.

"An apple for the teacher," Gia laughed. "You're a sneaky one."

He winked at her. "You're damn right."

"Gianna—" Beckett tried once again to get her attention, but he was elbowed out of the way by Jax as his brother headed toward his mat.

The rest of Gia's Tuesday night regulars began to trickle in and prevented Beckett from getting close enough to have that conversation he seemed to so desperately want. If he was as competitive as his brothers, she could only imagine the apology he had planned. Sincere with just enough flattery to give him a leg up in the competition.

It gave her a sinful tingle of pleasure to know that his plan wasn't working.

Bill Fitzsimmons scurried in and waved to her. He was a strange little man but an excellent student. Although, she wouldn't complain if he stopped wearing those tiny little shorts to class. He shook hands with each of the Pierce brothers and rolled out his mat next to Carter.

She watched Carter's face as Fitz took off his sweatpants with a flourish. Gia had to cover her mouth and look away

71

when the look of revulsion washed over his face. Carter slapped Jax on the shoulder, and both of them stared in horror as Fitz began his warm up stretches in his tiny yoga briefs.

"Dude," Jax hissed at Fitz. "You can't wear that here. There are ladies present."

"And people with eyes," Carter added.

Fitz chuckled and ignored them. He spread his legs wide for a stretch, and Jax gagged.

Gia bit her lip to keep from laughing. She glanced at Beckett and found him paying no attention to the Fitz show. He was watching her. She met his gaze and held it. The intensity in those gray eyes seared her to the bone. Want and frustration simmered between them in a silent, solid connection.

The spell was broken when the football players showed up, each giving her a fist bump as they passed.

When Gia dared spare another glance at Beckett, he had been dragged into a heated conversation with his brothers and Jax was gesturing wildly at Fitz.

Taneisha, stunning in purple capris and a filmy white tank, paused by Gia's mat. "Beckett's back?" she whispered, her perfectly groomed eyebrows winging up. "I thought he was going to need CPR after the last class."

"He and his brothers are settling some kind of competition here."

Taneisha rolled her eyes. "They do this periodically. Once in high school they battled it out to see who could eat the most tacos."

"Who won?"

"Jax with twenty-four."

"Impressive," Gia laughed. "Let's just hope they didn't do any competitive eating before this class."

She hid a chuckle when Taneisha set up her mat as far

away from the Pierces as possible. "Splatter zone," she mouthed to Gia.

After another few minutes, Gia got the class started with some gentle forward bends and easy rounds of sun salutation. She kept an eye on the Pierces, making sure they were keeping up and moving safely through the poses.

As she wandered past them in warrior one, she heard Jax mutter, "Piece of cake."

Gia grinned wickedly. "Okay, now that we're warmed up, let's flow."

She ran them through another dozen sun salutations. By the fourth one, Jax was sweating. By the sixth, all three of them had followed Fitz's lead and shucked off their shirts. On the next salutation, she had to step in to start making adjustments.

She squared off Carter's hips in warrior one and made Jax tremble when she made him bring his knees off the ground in the up dog flow. "Piece of cake, right?" She winked.

"Oh dear God," he whimpered as a bead of sweat dripped off his nose.

Beckett seemed to be faring a little better, so on the last sun salutation, she had the class hold chair pose. The groans were music to her ears. "That's right. Sink lower into your hips," she said, placing her hands on Beckett's hips guiding him to lower.

"Good," she smiled when she felt his legs begin to shake. "Now straighten your arms." She skimmed her hands up his arms until they reached straight for the ceiling. "Engage here," she said, dancing her fingers over his trapezius muscles.

His breath was coming in short gasps now. "Keep your arms reaching up but lower your shoulders." She tried to keep the smile out of her tone, but knew she failed when he shot her a glare around his shaky arm.

She heard a couple of groans echo around the room and knew they'd all had enough torture. "Great job. Let's fold forward and shake it out."

The groans of agony turned to sighs of relief, at least until she announced that hip openers were next.

~

CLASS ENDED with the Pierce brothers in sweaty heaps on their mats.

"I feel like I got hit by a meteor," Jax whispered into his mat. "A really hot one."

"I feel like a rubber band that was stretched until it tore in half and now it's completely useless," Carter sighed.

Beckett, still sprawled across his mat with his eyes closed, grinned. "I feel like a wet washcloth that was wrung out and thrown on the floor."

"I'm so glad we didn't let the girls come tonight." Carter rolled onto his side.

"Summer and Joey wanted to come?" Gia asked as she picked up the mat sanitizer.

"They would never let us live this down. They'd be looming over us taking pictures for Blue Moon Gossip or *The Monthly Moon*," Beckett guessed.

Gia thought it wise not to mention the fact that she'd seen both Fitz and Taneisha whip out their phones after class.

"How do people just get up and walk out of here?" Jax asked, opening an eye to watch the football players bounce out with as much energy as when they arrived.

Gia dropped a cold water bottle in front of each of their mats. "It gets easier," she promised.

Beckett dragged himself into a seated position and swiped

the bottle over his sweaty forehead. "Thank you," he said, before guzzling the contents.

"That Fitz is one flexible freak," Carter groaned, trying to work his way into a seated position.

"The image of him in that yoga diaper is going to haunt me for the rest of my life," Jax said, covering his eyes.

"Gia, I swear, next poker night we're going to talk to him about his yoga wardrobe," Carter promised. "I had no idea he was inflicting this kind of visual abuse on your class."

"And, Gia, I promise you that I'm going to clean this up, but I have to do this. I can't stop smelling myself." Jax promptly dumped the bottle of water over his head.

"Jesus, Hollywood," Beckett said, slapping his brother on the back of the head.

"He needed to do it," Carter argued. "I wouldn't have let him in the truck smelling like that."

"Get a freaking towel at least." Beckett threw his sopping wet sweat towel in Jax's face.

"That's disgusting. You smell worse than me!" Jax threatened to dump the rest of his water over Beckett until Carter punched him in the ribs.

"Get a fucking towel," he ordered.

Jax crawled over to the towel bin. "Do you have anything in a body-size?" he asked.

"Gianna, maybe now we could have that talk," Beckett suggested.

"Right. The contest," she said, purposely misunderstanding Beckett's overture. "I'm surprised none of you asked who won. So who feels like a winner?"

When none of them said anything, she smiled. "Good."

Jax paused his floor and mat scrubbing to look at her. "It was a three-way losers tie, wasn't it? Man, I had no idea yoga would be so..."

"Horrible?" Carter supplied.

"Painful?" Beckett offered.

"Amazing?" Gia interjected.

"Most of the above," Jax decided.

"Yoga has a way of highlighting both your strengths and weaknesses," Gia told them. "For instance, Jax, your flexibility is great."

"Thanks," he brightened. "I took a bunch of Pilates classes with this actress I dated a few years ago."

"The one with the..." Carter held his hands to his chest like he was clutching a pair of watermelons.

"No, that was Didi. I think those would have hindered her in any actual physical activity."

Gia rolled her eyes but continued. "Carter, you have incredible upper body strength. Those arm balances you did today aren't beginner's poses."

"What about my strengths?" Beckett asked, watching her closely.

"Aww," Jax cooed. "The middle brother's feeling left out."

Beckett gave Jax a boot with his foot and sent his brother sprawling across his soggy mat.

"Your endurance is great. You could do sun salutations all day."

"How about my weakness?" he asked. He looked at her like there was no one else in the room.

"Control."

His dark eyebrows winged up. "I don't have enough of it?"

Gia was certain Beckett Pierce had never been accused of not having enough control.

"No, you use too much of it. It makes you afraid to expand in your poses because you might fail or fall. You're so focused on doing everything exactly right you miss out on the fact that doing things wrong can teach you more or be more fun."

"I feel like this just turned into a yoga therapy session," Jax whispered.

"What about us?" Carter asked, curious now. "Besides Hollywood here being an asshole."

"Carter, you rely entirely on your strength to power through poses rather than bringing some flexibility to your practice. And you," she said, pointing at Jax, "get so focused on the competition that you pay too much attention to what others around you are doing and not enough to what you're doing."

"So, what you're saying is there was no clear winner," Beckett sighed.

"I'm saying that maybe instead of trying to kick each other's legs out from under them when you're in a balance pose—" she paused to glare at Jax, who looked away and whistled a little tune. "Or shoving each other over like dominos when you think I'm not looking—" she moved her glare to Beckett. "Maybe you should consider working together."

"So we come up with the inaugural beer together?" Carter ventured, stroking his beard.

Pleased, Gia nodded. "Together you might come up with something better than you would have individually."

"She's not only beautiful and strong, she's also brilliant," Jax announced.

Beckett shoved him again. "Quit kissing her ass. The contest is over."

"Your brother is just showing off his impeccable observational skills." Gia sniffed. "Now, if you gentlemen can peel yourselves off the floor, I've got to get home and make sure my kids haven't burned down the house."

Carter and Jax took the hint and, after using nearly the entire spray bottle of mat sanitizer, dragged a reluctant Beckett out the door with them. They decided to go to Shorty's to get a beer before heading home and were debating on how to spin the triple-loser situation to Summer and Joey when Gia locked the door behind them and laid her forehead on the cool glass.

It was only then that she allowed herself to laugh.

*B*eckett gave Gianna until the following afternoon to cool off before attempting his apology again. He knew she was avoiding him. That much was obvious from her skilled brush-off the night before. But the longer he waited, the worse he felt about it. Not only had he accused her father —a man she held in the highest esteem—of taking advantage of and intruding on the Pierce family, but he had then shown no qualms about dragging Gianna into the midst of a dispute with his brothers and making her settle it.

He thought about flowers as an apology accessory but decided it would send the wrong message. A houseplant, however, was an unromantic, friendly gift, wasn't it?

He swung his SUV into the parking lot of Every Bloomin' Thing after his last appointment of the day. The tiny florist shop, tucked between a hair salon and handmade pottery studio, worked in partnership with Gordon Berkowicz's seasonal garden center on the edge of town. While Blue Mooners flocked to the garden center for all their spring and summer landscaping needs, they came to Gordon's younger sister for year-round blooms.

Stepping inside the shop always made him think he was entering a rain forest. The air was thick with the scent of hundreds of blooms. A bubbling indoor water garden provided a peaceful backdrop of noise and color just inside the front door.

From the ceiling hung dozens of planters spilling over with greenery and color.

He found Elizabeth, wearing a lime green smock, behind the counter arranging orange roses and succulents into a glass vase. She wore her curly hair pinned up under a wide paisley headband. Chunky bronze earrings dangled from her ears.

Her make-up-free face brightened when she spotted him.

"Well, hello there, Mr. Mayor. What brings Blue Moon's fearless leader into my shop today?"

"Hey, Liz," he greeted her and leaned against the counter, content to watch her work. "I was in the market for a houseplant."

She efficiently snipped off the ends of the stems before tucking the shears back into her pocket. "Is this a green friend for you or a gift?"

"A gift."

He watched Liz snake a royal purple ribbon around the neck of the vase with deft fingers. "And what is she like?"

"How do you know she's a she?" Beckett countered.

Liz arched an eyebrow at him. "Would you buy a man-friend a houseplant?"

"Good point."

"So, what's *she* like? Classical, romantic, studious, serious, playful?"

Beckett brought the image of Gia collapsing out of her handstand and laughing to mind.

"Playful... and romantic."

"A free spirit?" Liz tucked a blank card into the arrangement she'd just finished.

"Definitely. She likes to laugh. She's very... warm."

"And what's the occasion?"

An apology for being an asshole, Beckett thought.

"Housewarming," he said instead.

"I've got the perfect thing," Liz said, wiping her hands on a towel. "Come with me."

She led Beckett through a tangle of hanging plants and potted ferns to a corner display of glass globes. "This is what I'm thinking," she said, holding up one of the globes. Tucked inside were tiny airy plants and mosses.

"A fairy garden," Beckett said, lifting the globe higher. "It's perfect. It's exactly her."

"We'll make one just for her," Liz said, collecting plants and opening drawers.

In the end, Beckett settled on an open globe that was flat on the bottom. They selected tiny tufts of moss and delicate stalks of greenery and tucked them into the globe on a foundation of rich earth.

"Any fairy accessories?" Liz asked.

After a considerable amount of deliberation, Beckett chose a delicate bench made out of twigs and two river rocks with the words *family* and *home* etched into them.

"You're very good at this," Liz said, leading him back to the cash register. "Any time you want to give up mayoring and the law, you come see me. I'll put you to work."

"Thanks, Liz. I'll keep that in mind next time the town meeting runs amuck," Beckett grinned.

∾

Prize in hand, Beckett didn't even bother going inside when he got home. He marched down the driveway and around the garage to the backyard.

He hopped up onto the front porch of the guesthouse and rapped on the door.

"Come in," he heard Evan and Aurora call out together.

Beckett pushed open the front door and stepped inside. Aurora was sitting on the stairs, her little chin in her hands. "Hi, Bucket," she said sadly.

A dejected Evan was frowning at the laptop on the dining table and reluctantly making notes with a pencil and paper.

The mood was definitely somber.

"What's going on?" Beckett asked.

"We're being punished," Evan sighed heavily.

"I'm in time out," Aurora piped up.

"And Gia's making me write a 100-word essay on the poetry of some guy named Rumi."

"Where's your... Gianna?" Beckett asked.

"In da shed," Aurora answered. "Can you ask her if I can be done in time out, Bucket? Please?"

"I'll see what I can do," he promised. "Evan, if your essay goes by word count, make sure you copy and paste some of the poems. That'll make it longer."

Evan perked up. "Nice! Thanks!"

Beckett headed back outside to the shed in the corner of his fenced in lot. He'd never used it and had thrown it in with the rental of the guesthouse for additional storage. He was a little curious to see what Gia was storing in the shed. She didn't seem like the years of paperwork kind of woman. Maybe she had a secret crafting hobby. Scrapbooking, perhaps?

Nope.

A wooden tug on the door revealed his little redheaded fairy whaling on a heavy bag.

She was still dressed for class in a tank top and tights. He watched the muscles in her shoulders and arms ripple with each punch.

Gianna was in the beat down zone. Her hands were wrapped, her feet were bare, and earbuds prevented her from hearing him open the door.

The bag, suspended from one of the shed's rafters, was the only item inside the shed.

Beckett crossed his arms and watched. The longer she beat on the bag, the madder she looked.

She spotted him as she swung around for a spin kick and bared her teeth.

Spoiling for a fight, he thought. Gianna yanked the buds out of her ears and rounded on Beckett. "I suppose you're here to pile on, too? Maybe tell me what a horrible man my father is again? Or accuse me of stalking you? Or how about you just jump on the bandwagon and try to drive me insane, too?"

He instinctively put his hands up. "Whoa."

"I am not a horse!" She drilled a slim finger into his chest and glared up at him. She let out a hiss of exasperation and turned back toward the bag. "Get out!" Her small fist plowed into vinyl, making the chains above jingle.

Beckett decided to take his life in his own hands. He stepped further into the shed and nipped her around the waist.

Swinging her around, he pushed her back against the plywood wall and held her in place by the shoulders. "Take a breath," he ordered.

"I'm a yoga instructor. I know how to breathe," she hissed.

She was spectacular. Her flaming curls escaping their confines to frame her face. Those green eyes crackled with energy and anger. A flush tinged her ivory skin. Her chest heaved with every breath.

"Now I know what 'she's beautiful when she's angry' means."

She growled at him.

Beckett had meant to keep those words to himself. But having the spitfire in his arms was making him careless.

Gianna tried to shrug out of his grasp, but he merely tightened his hold. When he saw the glint in her eyes, he stepped in closer so she couldn't kick him.

"Talk," he said.

"Why should *I* talk to *you*? Dr. Jekyll Mr. Pierce." She struggled against him and then stomped her foot. Gianna closed her eyes and took a deep breath and then another one. "I'm sorry. That was uncalled for. I shouldn't be taking my mood out on you."

"I came here to apologize to you. Not the other way around."

"Still, I shouldn't be venting negativity on anyone." She paused and frowned up at him. "Even you."

He thought it wise to contain his laughter. "That's very kind and mature of you. Now, I'd like to apologize for being a horrible ass the other day at the gym. I was upset, and I targeted you unfairly. I'm very sorry for what I said and the way I treated you."

"Apology accepted."

"Just like that?" Most of the fight seemed to have left her. But it had been replaced with resignation.

Gianna tried to shrug her shoulders under his hands. "It's fine. It happens."

"It's not fine, and it shouldn't happen. And I want you to know that I've felt like crap about it since Monday morning."

Her lips quirked. "That does make me feel slightly better."

"I also want you to know," Beckett said, leaning in slightly to look into her eyes, "that it was completely out of character for me."

"I know," she sighed.

"How?" he asked, brushing a curl back from her face and tucking it behind her ear.

"I know you."

"We just met," Beckett argued.

"That doesn't mean I don't know you," she said, rolling her eyes. "Are you trying to convince me that you're not the good, solid, thoughtful man I thought you were?"

Beckett frowned. "No. I just expected that I'd have some proving to do to make you believe me."

"What does it matter what I think of you?" Gianna asked, tilting her head to the side. The skin of her neck was dotted with tiny beads of sweat. Some joined together to trickle lower, winding their way down her chest to the valley between her breasts.

"I don't know, but it does," Beckett told her. He gave in and traced that delicate line from her neck to her shoulder before brushing a finger over her collarbone.

She didn't stop him, merely watching him curiously.

"I knew something—besides me on an elliptical—must have upset you Monday," she said, drawing his attention back to her face, her mouth.

"It was my father's birthday, and, at the time, I thought I was the only one who remembered."

He saw it then, the rush of compassion in her eyes, the softening of her face. "Oh, Beckett. I'm so sorry. That must have hurt."

"It was a false assumption that had me remembering how lucky I am to have my family. Now, let's talk about you. What brings you to the shed today? And don't think that I'm going to

85

let the irony of the yoga instructor beating the shit out of a punching bag slide by."

Gianna sighed again. "If I were a camel, I'd be covered in straw."

"An interesting way of saying lots of little things upset you?"

"Leading the witness," Gianna teased. Her wry smile loosened some of the knots he'd carried in his gut for the past few days.

"I'm a good listener. You can tell me, and I won't judge—because I can't, I'm just a lawyer. I won't tell anyone either because I think this counts as attorney-client privilege."

She took another deep breath, and he thought she might be brushing him off again, but she surprised him by relaxing in his arms.

"I was upset already by a conversation with the kids' dad this afternoon. And when I brought them home, Aurora announced that So-and-So's mommy lets her have a cell phone and an iPad, and by that logic, I'm mean, and she hates me because I'm not running out to the store to buy expensive technology for her five-year-old self. Then I get an email from Evan's teacher who tells me he hasn't bothered turning in his homework two days in a row. And this is after he's told me that he finished it in school and that 'everything at school is going fine.'"

"Monsters," Beckett said, shaking his head. She rewarded him with a small smile.

"So I put Aurora in time out and gave Evan a homework assignment that he has to do for me before he can start on his school work, which I will now be checking every night. And then I came out here to release my aggression so I don't maim my children."

"Do they know they have a heavy bag to thank for a life free of maiming?"

"They think I'm meditating."

Beckett chuckled. "Do you want to talk about your conversation with your ex?"

Gianna shook her head. "It will all work out. It always does."

She closed her eyes and took another slow, deep breath. Beckett was so close he could see the freckles sprinkled across the bridge of her nose.

"Ready to go back in?" he asked her.

She shook her head again and kept her eyes closed tight. "No."

"What if, as part of my apology, I order pizza and you and the kids can join me for dinner?"

He glimpsed green through her lovely, long lashes as she opened her eyes and studied him. "You're lucky that I'm avoiding complications for the foreseeable future because you're very tempting right now," she told him in a husky whisper.

"Temptation is bad," Beckett said, stepping in until his shoes brushed her bare toes.

"This would be such a bad idea," Gianna said, bringing her hands to his chest. But instead of pushing him away, her fingers gripped the lapels of his jacket. "I have kids."

"I'm your landlord." He lowered his face to hers stopping just a millimeter above her full, rosy lips.

"Our parents are—"

He cut off her reply by bringing his lips to hers. Softly, sweetly, he felt her mouth come to life under his. Experimenting, tasting, teasing.

Beckett brought his fingertips to her neck. Cupping her face, he tilted her head back. She opened her mouth for him on a sigh, and he took advantage of the invitation. His tongue swept in to taste her, and the second it touched hers, the playfulness disintegrated.

He was hungry for her. Starving. Beckett didn't realize he was shoving her back against the plywood wall, didn't know that the hands that gripped her slim, strong arms were bruising.

Those sexy little whimpers Gianna was making had him fully hard in the space of a heartbeat. She tasted exotic, dangerous. Addicting. He flexed his hips into her and groaned as she instinctively pressed back against him.

Beckett felt a growl rumble low in his throat and pulled back. He had to hold Gianna against the wall to keep her from following his mouth. Her hands were fisted in his jacket. Her lips were swollen from the aggressive assault on her mouth. And those eyes with all the depths of the oceans were glassy and dazed. Even more tendrils had escaped the hair band to hang down, tempting him.

He was honest enough to admit that he wanted her more than he could ever remember wanting any woman.

"What was that?" she whispered, trying to catch her breath.

"That was a mistake," he said, dropping his forehead to hers. A shed. He'd kissed her in a shed. Where had his moves gone? He was king of the seduction. But with Gianna, he was dissolved into a man with a hard-on in a garden shed.

A man with a hard-on in a garden shed kissing a woman he had no intention of seducing, he reminded himself.

"We can't do this," Gianna said, shaking her head to clear it.

"No. We can't."

He would have stepped back, would have released her from his grip, but she brought her mouth to his. Again, twin passions ignited and flared. His hands traveled from her shoulders to her hips. Cruising over those dangerous curves, they moved higher, skimming her ribs to rest under her soft breasts.

He was losing himself in the heat. "Baby," he whispered against her busy lips. "We have to stop."

"Mm-hmm," she murmured, stealing his breath without backing off.

"Gianna." Beckett brought his hands to her face and gently forced her back.

"I'm sorry. What were we talking about again?" she asked breathlessly.

Beckett yanked her against him for a hug, crushing her to him. "We were talking about how we aren't going to do this."

"Right. I forgot," she said, snuggling into his chest. "I have kids that I need to think about. I've made too many mistakes already, and they're depending on me to make this work."

"Too many complications for both of us," Beckett agreed, dropping a soft kiss on the top of her head. Her hair smelled like eucalyptus and lavender. "I'm not looking for anything serious."

"And two kids means serious. They'd get attached."

"The town would be booking wedding space if we started dating. Blue Moon would take it harder than the kids if we didn't work out," Beckett sighed.

"And it wouldn't work out. I'd do something stupid or—"

"I would say something stupid, and then we'd end up seeing each other all the time, and it would be horribly awkward, and—"

"I'd have to break my lease with you so I wouldn't have to watch you mow the lawn shirtless because that's what you do in my fantasies. Plus, you don't like my father, and that's a deal breaker."

"I may have slightly misjudged your father, but that doesn't mean I like him dating my mother."

"That makes us practically brother and sister," Gianna said. "That's gross."

"Really gross," Beckett agreed.

She sighed and tilted her head back to look at him. "This doesn't mean I'm not insanely attracted to you," Gianna clarified.

"Right back at you, Red. If those two kids weren't next door, you'd already be naked."

"Well, that'll keep me up tonight."

Beckett leaned down and gently kissed the tip of her nose. "You should probably get back in there before they decide to see who can fit in the microwave. They looked pretty miserable when I stopped in."

"It's a trick. Don't fall for the puppy eyes. Especially Rora's. She's got them down to a science."

"I'll say. I felt like my guts had been ripped out and then trampled."

"I'm suddenly in a much better mood," she said with a slow grin.

"Happy to help. I'd say anytime, but if we do this again, it won't stop at kissing." It was a dark promise.

He turned her around and pushed her through the door in front of him.

"What's this?" she asked, spotting the glass globe on the ground.

"I forgot. It's your housewarming slash apology-for-being-an-asshole gift," Beckett said, picking it up and handing it over.

"Beckett!" She peered through the glass. "It's a fairy garden. I've always wanted one—how did you know?" She looked up at him, wonder and surprise written all over her beautiful face.

"Stop looking at me like that," he said gruffly.

"Like what?"

"Like you want to go back in the shed."

Her face transformed to a wicked temptress. "Oh, but I do," she said with a slow wink.

"Gianna, get in your house, now," he ordered.

"Thank you, Beckett. For everything."

"Bring the kids over in half an hour. And for God's sake, please wear something baggy."

11

----

*G*ia decided not to tempt fate, or Beckett, and wore yoga pants and a long sleeve wrap sweater in a safe, bland gray to dinner.

When she announced they were having dinner at Beckett's, Evan had shot her a skeptical look while Aurora immediately ran upstairs to find her shoes.

They trooped across the stretch of grass from their front door to Beckett's back. He was waiting for them in the kitchen and let them in before Gia had a chance to knock. He'd changed too, she noticed. Gone was the dark suit she'd been tempted to wrestle him out of, and in its place he'd donned a pair of chinos and a lightweight sweater with the sleeves shoved up to his elbows.

He sent her a warning look when he caught her studying the way the soft navy fabric stretched across his broad chest and shoulders. Gia gave him an embarrassed smile and slipped off her shoes inside the door.

"Thank you for having us over for dinner," she said, politely. As her lips quirked, she was painfully aware of what her mouth had been doing half an hour earlier.

Beckett sent her another smoldering glance before answering. "Thanks for coming over. I needed help eating all this pizza."

Evan perked up. "Pepperoni?" he asked.

Beckett's eyebrows rose. "Is there any other kind?"

"There's cheese," Evan reminded him, toying with the dishtowel on the counter he leaned against.

"I got one of those, too."

"I want cheese, Bucket," Aurora said, wrapping her sweet little arms around his legs.

Beckett leaned down and picked her up. "Are you vegetarian?" He frowned.

Evan snorted, and Gia let Beckett explain an admittedly slanted view of vegetarianism while she scoped out his kitchen. The daughter of a restaurateur was required by DNA to place great value on that particular room in the home. Gia considered herself to be a creative, reliable cook. The kids only really complained when she went too far toward the creative side. Like with last week's Thai coconut soup.

It was a large, airy kitchen, most of which had been modernized, but one wall of original glass-fronted cabinetry stoically stood the test of time. He'd gone with dark cabinets and glossy marble everywhere else. The upper cabinets, that at one time hung above the sink, had been removed to allow for a large window overlooking the backyard.

A worn butcher-block island, lit by a pair of oil-rubbed lanterns that hung from the tin tiled ceiling, dominated the center of the room. Judging from the stack of law journals and other mail, she imagined it was where Beckett took most of his meals.

The mosaic tile floor extended into a cozy breakfast nook on the other side of the back door. There he'd chosen a round pedestal table in black surrounded by armless chairs covered in a creamy white upholstery.

Gia made a mental note not to let Aurora and her pizza fingers anywhere near those chairs.

Beckett enlisted their help in carting plates, glasses, and utensils into the dining room. Gia tried not to gape, but every room she walked into was more magnificent than the last. The dining room had high ceilings and glass-front built-ins in two corners. A small fireplace with marble surround occupied the space between the room's two windows. An honest to goodness chandelier hung over the long, rectangular table.

"How many fireplaces do you have?" Gia asked.

"A lot. Would you like a tour?" Beckett offered.

"Yes, please," she said, clasping her hands together.

As he led the way from the dining room into a parlor at the front of the house, Gia tried not to admire how well his pants fit from the back or remember how solid his chest felt under her hands.

The parlor had tall windows with built-in seats on two walls. There was another fireplace in the same marble. The spectacular wood trim here was painted a dark navy and complemented by blue and gold fleur de lis wallpaper. Beckett had filled it with small, comfortable couches that flanked the fireplace. A wide, cozy chair was tucked into the round turret in the front corner. Several houseplants took up residence on shelves and tables.

It was a romantic room. One she could imagine whiling away the hours with a good book and hot chocolate while snow fell outside.

They wound their way through the first floor, moving on to the three-story staircase in the foyer and then the main living room, a mirror of the parlor. Yet another fireplace here, but Beckett's big screen TV and entertainment center were the focal point. Through the door on the far wall, Beckett showed them his office area with library and waiting room.

Gia could tell this was the heart of his home. In these rooms he served his community and his clients day in and day out, hoping to make all their lives a bit better. It was part of her attraction to him, she admitted. The pure goodness in him was turning out to be as intriguing as the bad boy vibe she'd fallen for years before.

"Pizza should be here in a minute, but I have something else I can show you upstairs," Beckett offered. "It's kind of awesome," he warned Evan.

Gia bit the inside of her cheek. Going anywhere near Beckett's bedroom would spell disaster. "How about I wait down here for the pizza and you can take the kids up?" she suggested.

Beckett's heated gaze bored into her. He knew exactly what she was avoiding.

"Money's on the table by the door," he said with a wink. "You guys want to see what's upstairs?"

Evan was already halfway up the stairs. "Is it an arcade?"

"Do you have a room for me, Bucket?" Aurora asked, grasping his hand as she took the stairs one at a time.

Right on cue, the doorbell rang. Gia was surprised to find one of her yoga students clutching a tower of pizza boxes and bags.

Ruby was a gangly seventeen with choppy auburn bangs and a tiny stud in her nose. She helped out on her family's farm in the mornings before school and could nail some incredibly advanced yoga poses.

Ruby's brown eyes widened. "So you're the reason Beckett ordered enough food to feed an army," she said. "We thought he was having his brothers over."

Gia grinned. It was probably a bit of a disappointment

for Ruby to not be delivering to three of the best-looking men in Blue Moon. "Beckett's feeding me and my troops tonight."

"Interesting," Ruby said, raising both eyebrows.

"Are you coming to class Saturday?" Gia asked, sensing the interest and changing the subject. "I'm thinking about throwing in some forearm stands."

"I'm so there!" Ruby said, trading food for cash. She started for the porch steps. "Have a good time with Beckett tonight," she called over her shoulder and winked.

Gia sighed and wondered what kind of gossip tornado had just been stirred up. Juggling the tower of food, she shut the door behind her and headed into the dining room.

"Gia!" Evan called excitedly from the stairs. "You've gotta come see this."

She put the food down on the table and jogged up the stairs. "Marco?" she called when she reached the second floor.

"Polo!" Evan and Aurora's voices sang from a bedroom at the front of the house.

Gia found them standing with Beckett in front of a book-case. A few dusty volumes took up residence on the otherwise empty shelves. She raised an eyebrow. "You're not usually so excited about reading, Evan," she commented.

Evan rolled his eyes. "Not the books. Show her Beckett!"

Beckett grinned and shook his head. "Go for it, kid."

With gleeful enthusiasm, Evan pressed a knob that was carved into the molding around the shelves. She heard a metallic click and the entire bookcase silently opened out.

"It's a secret passage!" Evan announced.

Aurora grabbed Gia's hand and dragged her toward the dark opening. "Come on, Mama! Let's hide!"

"Here," Beckett said, handing Evan a flashlight. "Let your brother go first, and we'll follow him."

Evan grabbed the light and ducked behind the shelves. "Come on, Gia!"

Aurora slipped her hand out of Gia's and hurried ahead. "I walk with Van," she announced and danced after her brother.

The passageway was narrow and black as night once Beckett pulled the shelves back into place behind them. The beam of Evan's flashlight was the only sliver of light cutting through the darkness.

Gia saw the light climb higher in front of them. "Watch your step," Evan warned from above.

"It's a staircase," Beckett said softly, coming up behind her.

He wasn't touching her, but she was so aware of his presence she felt him as distinctly as if he had his hands on her.

The stairs were steep and narrow, only wide enough for one person at a time. As if she conjured them, she felt Beckett's hands come to rest on her hips. A low hum escaped her throat, and his fingers flexed into her flesh.

"We'll wait for you outside," Evan called down.

"Wait! You have the light," Gia yelped.

"Beckett's got another flashlight," Evan assured her. "Come on, Rora. We'll surprise them on the other side."

Above them, Gia heard a click and saw fading daylight filter into the passageway, and then it was gone. The darkness stopped her dead in her tracks. Beckett came to a halt on the step below hers. He was still taller than she was. She could feel his breath in her hair.

"Tell me you really do have another flashlight," she whispered.

"I do."

His lips brushed her ear, and Gia let out a little gasp. She was so aware of him, so ready to be touched.

"The things I want to do to you right now," Beckett whispered grimly against her neck.

Gia leaned her head back against his shoulder to give him better access. The scrape of his teeth behind her ear drew a purr from her. "Forbidden fruit," she whispered. It was a reminder to them both.

"Gianna, I need you to get up these stairs before I take you right here."

"Beckett." She breathed his name as if it belonged to a deity.

His hands came around her, palms to her shoulders. And while his mouth delicately dined on the skin of her neck, he stroked down to cup her breasts through her sweater. Through the layers of fabric, Gia felt her sensitive peaks harden. Boldly, she grasped his hand and led it under the neckline of her sweater. His palm slid over the thin lace of her bra, and she gasped at the pleasure that erupted when his fingers gently tugged at her hardened nipple.

"Red," he growled in her ear. "Move. Now." His hand slid out from her sweater and slapped her on the butt.

Gia sprang to life, taking the rest of the stairs quickly even as Beckett fumbled with the flashlight.

She pushed through the door at the top of the staircase and found a grinning Evan and Aurora.

"How cool is this?" Evan asked. "We're on the third floor!"

Gia barely spared the cavernous room a glance. Guiltily, she put on a cheerful face. "That was pretty cool. Are you guys hungry? The food's here."

At her insistence, they trooped back downstairs using the actual staircase instead of the passageway. Gia pointedly refused to look at Beckett until her racing heart beat was under control again.

They dove into the food in the dining room, talking and laughing and staging a mock fight over breadsticks.

She was impressed with how relaxed Evan seemed here.

Rather than the sullen, quiet kid who'd moved to Blue Moon Bend, here was the chatty, carefree boy of old. He and Beckett compared teachers at Blue Moon Middle School, finding a number that they had in common. Evan's comments of "he must be like a hundred years old" were punctuated by Beckett's advice on how to stay on the good sides of certain faculty.

She hoped it was a sign of things to come with Evan. The reemergence of the happy boy with boundless curiosity.

So many mistakes had brought them to this point, she thought.

But perhaps, in the long run, they wouldn't be considered mistakes. After all, falling for Paul had brought her Evan and Aurora and she couldn't imagine her life without either of them.

She hoped she could teach the kids the lessons she had learned from her own mistakes. She would help Aurora grow strong and confident. She wouldn't get swept away by the thrill of attention from a man who could never fully commit. Instead, she would teach her daughter to wait for someone with a beautiful soul who wanted the same things out of life. A partner.

And Evan. How many times could a child be disappointed and let down before it permanently dimmed his spirit? Evan's father loved like he lived. Carelessly. He had assumed that Gia would take the kids. She'd been prepared to fight for Evan in the divorce. Late night shows in dive bars were no life for a kid, but she'd still been sadly surprised when Paul didn't even try to change his life to maintain custody of Evan. Instead he'd helped them pack and waved them off.

Gia's heart broke for Evan, but she was determined to make things right for him. Two shitty biological parents didn't mean he didn't deserve a wonderful life.

After the divorce, he'd stopped calling her 'Mom.' Now, she was Gia, his ex-stepmother. She understood his need to push her away, just as she understood that it was only to make sure she stuck. And stick she would. Blood or no blood, Evan was her son.

Gia mopped Aurora's face with a napkin and tuned back into the conversation. Beckett and Evan were hotly debating The Rolling Stones versus The Grateful Dead. After a particularly impassioned exchange, Beckett frowned. "You ever think of law school?" he asked Evan.

The boy grinned and reached for another slice of pizza. "It's nice to have a logical discussion for a change," Evan said, nodding in Gia's direction.

Gia winged a piece of breadstick at him.

"Freeze!" she ordered Aurora, who had just picked up her crust to throw. "Only people over the age of twelve can throw food."

"Mama! That's not fair! What can I do?"

Gia looked thoughtful. "Hmm, how old are you again?"

Aurora giggled but didn't release the pizza crust. "Five!"

"Five? Wow, you are getting old. Five-year-olds are allowed to eat an entire piece of pizza without using their hands."

Evan feigned skepticism. "I don't know, Roar. Think you can do it?"

Aurora nodded seriously, accepting the challenge.

Gia cut a slice of cheese into bite-sized pieces and slid it onto Aurora's plate. She grinned at Beckett as her little girl squished her face into the plate like a champ at a pie-eating contest.

Gia and Evan air high-fived each other across the table drawing a laugh from Beckett as he reached for the salad.

"Just like Summer and Carter's piggies," Aurora announced, lifting her head and proudly showing off her pizza-stained face.

"I'm really impressed, Rora." Beckett's praise had the little girl giggling.

Gia winked at him. "Okay, my little piggy, let's get you cleaned up before you smear pizza sauce all over Beckett's nice house."

"I got her," Evan said, pushing back his chair. "Come on, Roar."

"You forgot to 'fro pizza at Mama," Aurora reminded him as they pushed through the door to the kitchen. "You're twelve."

"I'll get her next time," Evan promised his sister.

"Sorry about that," Gia apologized to Beckett. "Sometimes Evan and I have to get a little creative to make sure she eats enough. She's easily distracted."

"They are great kids," Beckett assured her.

"They really are. For every time I want to lock them in the basement, they've made me laugh until my face hurt five times."

"Sounds like extreme highs and lows," he commented.

"The bipolar experience of parenting. Is it a pool you plan to dip your toe into someday?" Gia asked.

"I haven't really given it much thought."

"A man doesn't buy a five-bedroom house without giving it a little thought," Gia countered, nibbling on the rest of her breadstick.

"I bought a one-bedroom house with a man cave, a home gym, a second office, and a sex room."

Gia laughed. "Oh, I like you, Beckett. And under different circumstances I'd really like to see your sex room."

She enjoyed his groan. "You're making me regret doing the right thing."

"Mission accomplished. Now, the least I can do is your dishes." She got up from the table and collected the plates.

Beckett followed her with the glasses and utensils. They

found a damp Evan mopping up a lake-sized puddle on the floor.

"Sorry, Bucket," he said. "She got a hold of the sprayer." Aurora was gleefully dancing around the edges of her self-made water park.

"Say you're sorry, Aurora, and clean up your own mess," Gia said sternly.

"Sorry, Bucket," Aurora chirped with a happy grin, obviously not the least bit apologetic. She took the towel from Evan and sloshed it through the water.

"I promise I'll actually clean that up," Gia whispered to Beckett as Aurora splattered water over the bottom cabinets. "Aurora, you owe Evan five minutes of peace and quiet."

"Yes!" Evan pumped his fist in the air.

"What does Rora get when Evan's in trouble?"

"Five minutes of playtime," Evan answered, rolling his eyes.

"Usually tea party or dollies," Aurora said conversationally as she swiped the sopping wet towel through the puddle that had now spread to the refrigerator.

"Okay. Thank you for cleaning up your mess, Aurora. Can you guys thank Beckett for dinner?"

"Thank you, Bucket."

"Yeah, thanks, Bucket."

Beckett ruffled Evan's hair. "No problem. See you around."

Gia shooed them out the backdoor. "I'll be right over," she told Evan. When the door closed behind them, she grabbed the roll of paper towels on the counter and went to work sopping up the puddle.

"You don't have to do that," Beckett said, his voice strained.

Gia scrubbed hard at a stubborn stain she found, a flyaway curl tumbling free. "I don't think my security deposit covers damage to your home caused by my kids."

"Seriously, Gianna. I need you to get up." His voice was low, rough.

Gia sat back on her heels and looked up at him. He was looming over her, and he was hard. She could see the impressive length of him as his erection strained against his chinos. "Oh," she said again.

He grabbed her by the elbows and hoisted her to her feet.

"You should go now," he said quietly.

But he didn't let go of her arm.

Gia's body was on high alert. Every thump of her pulse, every shaky breath, was magnified. She felt like prey. Prey willing to be sacrificed in the heat of the chase.

"Red, if you don't go now, I'm going to pick you up and put you on the counter there." He nodded toward the space next to the pantry. "Then I'm going to put my hands and my mouth on you until you're screaming my name."

Her indrawn breath was a squeak. Never had any man made her feel so desired, so craved, so hunted.

She moved her mouth to speak, yet no words came out.

"Gianna." He said her name like a threat. "I'm trying to do the right thing."

"Sorry," she stammered. "You still have my arms. If you want me to go, you're going to have to let me."

Beckett loosened his grip and dropped his hands to his side. She felt his eyes on her as she slipped out the door. She didn't dare to look back because if she did, Gia knew she'd beg him to touch her.

She waited until she got to her own front door before turning around. He was there in his open doorway, watching her with an unreadable expression on his perfect face.

Gia brought her fingers to her lips and blew him a kiss before darting into the safety of her home.

12

*G*ia tiptoed barefoot into Beckett's office late the following morning and waved a greeting to Ellery.

"Morning, El," she said, taking in Ellery's pink skull cardigan.

"Hey, Gia," Ellery greeted her. "What's up?"

"Is Beckett around?" She pointed down at her feet. "I think I left my shoes in his kitchen last night."

"You did," Beckett said, stepping into the reception area from his office holding her sneakers in his hand.

"Oh, thank God!" Gia sighed with relief. "We got a late start today. I couldn't sleep last night and forgot to set my alarm. So I had to drive the kids to school, and we got all the way to drop-off before I realized that Rora's lunch was at home and Evan's gym clothes were still in the dryer. So I had to run back home and—oh, never mind." She took a breath.

She was babbling. But she couldn't help it. She'd spent all night tossing and turning, thinking of how it felt to have Beckett's hands and mouth on her. The lack of sleep had left her a scattered mess. And now he stood before her looking perfect and well rested in another sexy suit.

"Why aren't you wearing shoes?" he asked.

"Because you're holding them in your hand."

Beckett frowned. "These are your only pair of shoes?"

"Of course not!" Gia was indignant. "I just can't find any of the other ones."

She was becoming vaguely aware of the fact that Ellery was following their exchange with marked interest and a big grin.

"How messy are you? Do I need to do a walk-through of your place?" Beckett teased.

"Very funny," Gia said, glaring at him. "I packed them in a box marked 'shoes' and haven't seen them since. I'm hoping they're at my dad's house. It's on my list."

"Can you find your list?"

"You're hilarious for an attorney. Ellery, I don't know how you get any work done with all the laughing you must do here," she said, snatching the shoes out of Beckett's hand. She hurried over to the faded couch against the window and sank down to put on her shoes.

"It's a laugh a minute around this place," Ellery quipped.

"Thank you for finding them for me, Beckett. I've gotta run. I have a class at noon. El, will I see you tonight?" The words tumbled out in a stream. Apparently knowing what it was like to kiss Beckett had made her even more nervous around him. Great, and now she was blushing furiously.

"I'll be there," Ellery said, putting her chin in her hand and grinning.

"Great!" Gia jumped to her feet. "See you then." She dashed out the door only to pop her head back in a second later. "Bye, Beckett," she said softly.

BECKETT WATCHED GIANNA LEAVE. And then watched her hustle off the porch, her red curls streaming behind her.

Ellery cleared her throat twice before he turned back to look at her.

"Sorry. Did you say something?" he asked, snapping back to reality.

"Keys."

"What?"

"Gia left her keys," Ellery said, pointing at the couch.

Beckett picked up the Om symbol key ring and twirled it on his finger. "How about I pick up lunch today?" he offered.

"Righteous Subs?" Ellery asked hopefully.

"The usual for me," he nodded. "Call it in, and I'll be back shortly."

He missed the curve of Ellery's black lipstick as he grabbed his wallet and hustled out the door.

Beckett made a quick pit stop at Blakeley's Hardware before continuing down the block to the yoga studio. As he approached, he spotted a small crowd of people clutching rolled up mats gathered at the front door.

Gianna was on her cell phone frantically pacing in front of the building. She stopped mid-step when she spotted him. Wordlessly, Beckett held up the keys, and the smile that bloomed on her flawless face was like sunshine.

"Never mind," Gianna said into the phone before hanging up. She launched herself at Beckett, wrapping her arms around his neck and planting a smacking kiss on his cheek.

He chuckled and lowered her carefully to the ground.

"Thank you, thank you, thank you," she chanted. "Mr. Mayor saves the day," she announced to the crowd. He gave a mock bow, acknowledging the cheers and whistles.

Gianna unlocked the front door and started herding students inside.

"Isn't that lucky that you found Gia's keys?" Willa said sweetly. Her waterfall of pale blonde hair was pulled back into her trademark braid, and she was wearing a Blue Moon Boots tank top.

"I must have left them at his office when I stopped by," Gianna said cheerfully.

Willa's curious expression was making Beckett sweat.

"Oh," Willa smiled. "Were you there on business?"

"Oh, no. I just left my shoes there last night," Gia answered, holding the door for Willa.

Gianna obviously had no idea the train wreck she was setting into motion, Beckett thought as panic gripped him. It had been funny when it happened to Carter, hilarious even. But to be in the sights of Blue Moon's diabolical Beautification Committee himself? To be a target of their overt and ridiculous matchmaking attempts?

It was no longer a laughing matter.

"I see," Willa said, eyes glittering.

"It was just dinner," Beckett said quickly. "Pizza. We had pizza." He was babbling. Lawyers didn't babble. At least not good ones.

"The kids loved it," Gia said, beaming up at Beckett.

Beckett wished Gianna would just go inside instead of looking at him like he was some kind of Greek god.

"How sweet," Willa said. Her phone was already out, and he had a sneaking suspicion she had captured Gianna's greeting on camera. "I guess I'd better get inside. Have a great day, Beckett," she called over her shoulder.

Beckett felt his blood pressure spike and was about to stop Willa to set the record straight when Summer and Joey jogged down the sidewalk.

"We're not late, are we?" Summer asked, gasping for air.

"I didn't know you two were coming!" Gia said. "What a

nice surprise! You're right on time. Just go on in and pick your spots. If you need a mat, they're on the shelves along the wall."

"She bribed me with lunch," Joey said, glaring at Summer's departing back. "You should come, too."

Gianna blinked. "Well, sure. I'd love to."

Joey glanced up at Beckett. "You coming?"

He shook his head rapidly from side to side.

"Beckett's had his fill of yoga for the time being," Gianna explained, winking up at him. "He suffered through two hot power classes."

"Hot power yoga?" Joey looked scared.

"Don't worry," Gianna reassured her. "Lunch Hour Yoga is a relaxing vinyasa class." She gently prodded Joey through the door.

"Vin-what-a?"

"Thanks again, Beckett." Gianna shot him a sweet smile over her shoulder. "You're my hero of the day."

He stood rooted to the spot, staring at the glass and feeling a mixture of panic and defeat. His phone signaled in his pocket.

"What?"

"That's not a very Mr. Mayory way to answer the phone," Carter answered.

"Sorry. I just had a... conversation with Willa."

His brother's gleeful chuckle further rankled Beckett. "She works fast. I take it you haven't seen Facebook yet?" Carter asked.

Beckett swore and pulled the phone away from his ear.

"What am I looking for?" he asked, switching to speakerphone.

"You'll know it when you see it," Carter returned cryptically. "I gotta go. Good luck."

"Good luck?" Beckett muttered. *Good luck with what?*

Shit.

Blue Moon's Gossip Group was faster than a Ferrari on the drag strip. Two minutes ago, someone—presumably Willa—had posted a picture of Gianna in his arms exactly where he stood.

Could Blue Moon have a new first lady? It looks like Beckett Pierce might finally be off the market.

The previous post from the night before announced that Beckett and Gianna were sharing a "quiet family dinner."

His phone rang again, and he bobbled it.

"I didn't interrupt you two working on your wedding registry, did I?" His younger brother snickered.

"Fuck you, Jax," Beckett growled. He stalked down the street.

"Now don't tell me the gossip group got it wrong."

"There is nothing going on between Gianna and me."

"Oh," his brother said innocently. "So you didn't have dinner last night?"

"It wasn't a date. The kids were there."

"A nice, 'quiet family dinner,'" Jax quoted.

"I wish you were here so I could punch you in the face," Beckett muttered. He crossed the street to cut through the square.

Was it his imagination, or was everyone looking at him? he wondered.

His brother's laugh told Beckett that his threat wasn't being taken seriously.

"So if nothing's going on, what were you doing making out with her on Main Street?" Jax asked.

"She was thanking me for dropping off her keys."

"That's a really friendly thank you. I'm starting to feel

shorted. Fitz didn't thank me like that when I picked up the twenty he dropped at Karma Kustard yesterday. How did you end up with her keys?"

"She left them at my place when she stopped to get her shoes," Beckett snapped.

"She left her shoes at your place?" Jax's gleeful tone grated Beckett's last nerve like lemon juice in an open wound.

"Ask him if they're going steady!" Beckett heard Carter yell in the background.

"Don't you assholes have farm things to do?"

"We're multitasking." Jax snickered.

"Yeah, well, why don't you multitask someone else? I'm busy."

"Busy making out in front of a crowd."

"Nothing is going on!"

"Uh-huh. So you haven't kissed her?"

"How did you—"

Jax whooped on the other end of the line.

"I hate you both," Beckett snarled and hung up.

13

_____

*B*lissfully unaware that nearly every conversation in town was about her, Gia led the class through another slow sun salutation. She padded between the rows of students, adjusting shoulders here, tweaking foot position there.

"Inhaling and lifting into up dog," she instructed and breathed with her class. "Keep those glutes tight, Joey."

She didn't bother hiding her smile as Joey shot her a glare. Gia loved reluctant yogis.

"With an exhale, roll back on the toes and push those hips back, back, back for down dog. Let's take a few deep breaths here and settle into the pose."

She had a dozen students today. Not bad at all for the lunch hour class. Attendance had been better than she'd hoped right off the bat. A benefit of purchasing an existing studio.

She would grow it. She already had ideas. New classes and time slots, private lessons and parties. Blue Moon would be her home, and her students would be her neighbors and friends.

She thought of Beckett. Tall, smoldering, with a dry wit and wicked eyes. Where would he fall? Neighbor or friend? As exciting as it would be to explore that attraction, it was a line neither should cross. She had Aurora and Evan to focus on. And Beckett's distrust of her father added another layer of confusion to the mix.

Maybe someday she would find the partner she always desired. And maybe she would find him here.

"Let's come into tree pose," Gia told the class. "In tree, we root down so we can lift up." She returned to her mat and joined the students in the balance pose.

While some proudly stretched their arms overhead, others —including Joey—wobbled and toppled.

"Don't worry if you're shaky," Gia told them. "Wobbling and even falling is part of the process. If you never fall, you aren't going far enough."

She spotted Summer sinking down to her mat to sit.

Gia had everyone else switch the pose to the other side before approaching her. "Everything okay?" she asked Summer quietly.

"I was seeing spots," she said grimly. She brushed an imaginary speck of dirt from her lavender tank top.

Gia handed her a water bottle. "Do you want me to call Carter for you?"

Summer shook her head. "No. It's nothing. I'm just feeling a little off today."

"Sometimes our bodies have uncomfortable ways of telling us to take a break," Gia said. "Make sure you're listening."

"Loud and clear. I think I'll just sit here for the rest of class," Summer decided.

"Good call," Gia nodded. "We're almost finished."

She moved everyone to the floor for a few deep stretches

and ended class the way she always did, with everyone resting in corpse pose. A morbid name, but it was the best way to send everyone back into the world—fully relaxed and aware of their own mortality.

She chatted with her students as they exited, making sure to spend a moment with each one to catch up on their lives and to thank them for coming. By the time the studio cleared out, Joey had scooted over to Summer's mat, and the two were deep in conversation.

"Are you feeling any better?" Gia asked, joining them.

"I am." Summer's blonde ponytail bounced emphatically.

"We can always take a rain check on lunch if you want to go home and rest."

"Actually, lunch sounds really good," Summer countered. "Joey, can you still spare some time for food?"

"I suffered through an entire yoga class. You have to feed me," she announced. "Just as soon as you call Carter."

Summer made a face. "I have a complicated health history," she explained to Gia.

"As a fan of your blog, I'm aware. Do you think this is anything to be concerned about?"

Summer shrugged her slim shoulders. "I don't think so. When I was diagnosed with adult Hodgkin lymphoma, I was tired. So tired all the time. I just thought I was overdoing it at work. But then the weight started to come off, and there was this weird swelling in my neck and armpits." She sighed. "Oh, and then what *really* freaked me out was drinking wine and feeling a stinging in my lymph nodes."

"That's a good indicator of something being really wrong," Gia agreed.

"This is different. Definitely tired, but I feel more like I'm coming down with a bug."

Joey shushed her and slapped a hand over Summer's

mouth. "Don't say that around here," she hissed. "You haven't lived through flu season in Blue Moon. Every second-generation hippie and their mama tries to pour lemon ginger tea down your throat. They put up public hand sanitizing stations all over town with homemade cleansers that make you smell like licorice and cow shit."

Gia could just imagine.

"Natural cold and flu remedies! Great idea, Joey," Summer said. Gia could see her wheels turning.

"Always on the lookout for article ideas," Joey told Gia. "Watch out or she'll drag you with her."

"Joey, you're on a roll," Summer said, eyeing Gia. "I bet you have a ton of them for health and fitness. I'd love to pick your brain sometime."

"Sure," Gia agreed. "I'm happy to help."

"Great. Let me text Carter because I'm an open and communicative girlfriend now," she said, looking pointedly at Joey. "And then we can go for lunch."

"Good. Now that that's settled, where are we going?" Joey demanded.

AFTER SUMMER TEXTED CARTER, answered his phone call, and scheduled an appointment with her doctor in the city, they settled on Franklin's restaurant, Villa Harvest, for lunch.

Summer was still muttering about everyone overreacting while they perused their menus.

"So what does a yoga teacher eat?" Joey asked Gia. "This one over here went vegetarian as soon as Carter got his hooks in her."

Gia laughed. "I've got two growing, picky kids at home. We

follow the eighty-twenty rule and throw in one pig-out fest a week."

"Eighty percent meat, twenty percent cheese?" Joey asked hopefully.

"Uh, no."

"Don't mind her," Summer said, closing her menu. "Joey carries beef sticks in her glove box for emergencies."

"Speaking of beef sticks..." Joey's eyebrows winged upward.

Summer choked on her water. "Real smooth, Joey. Well, we're committed now."

"What Summer is beating around the bush about is we want to know if you've been enjoying Beckett's beef stick."

It was Gia's turn to choke. "My, you all sure are friendly around here."

Summer snickered. "It goes with the territory. Have you been added to the gossip group on Facebook yet?"

"Gossip group?"

Joey slid her phone across the table to Gia. Facebook was open to a picture of her with Beckett when he dropped off her keys at the studio. Gia blushed crimson to the roots of her hair.

"First lady? Off the market?" Gia dropped the phone. "The whole town can see this?"

"Not the whole town," Joey said, taking pity on her. "Just any adult who's a Blue Moon resident past or present."

"So my father? Phoebe? *Beckett?* This is not how I wanted to make a fresh start," she groaned, covering her face with her hands.

"Soo...?" Summer looked at her expectantly.

"Soo...?" Joey asked as she chewed an aggressive bite of breadstick.

"What?" Gia asked through her mortification.

"Is it true?" Joey rolled her eyes.

"No! Beckett and I are not secretly dating. He and I already settled this."

"And by 'settled this,' you mean?" Summer snagged herself a breadstick from the basket on the table.

"Neither of us is looking for a relationship, and we agreed that getting involved with each other would be a disaster."

Joey's eyes narrowed. "That seems like a pretty heavy conversation to be having with someone who's just your landlord."

"Unless it wasn't just a dinner," Summer speculated. "Maybe something besides a discussion about pizza toppings happened?"

Gia looked from Summer to Joey and back again. "Have you two ever considered starting your own interrogation service?"

"Quit dodging our thinly veiled insinuations," Joey said, tapping her menu on the table.

"We're all friends here," Summer said, smiling sweetly.

Gia groaned. "Fine. We kissed."

Summer squeaked and grabbed her hand. "I knew it!"

"And then we talked about why it would be a terrible idea to pursue anything together."

Unimpressed, Joey crossed her arms. "Lame."

"And then we kissed again, and it was super hot, and he ended up kicking me out of the house after dinner, and I forgot my shoes because I've never had the bejesus kissed out of me like that before. And I was married to a musician."

Joey watched her thoughtfully for a moment. "I like her," she finally said to Summer.

"Me, too," Summer agreed. "So tell us more about this super hot—"

"Well, this just makes my whole day," Franklin announced,

swooping in from behind the bar in his green Villa Harvest polo. His salt and pepper hair was neatly combed, and his smile was wide. "I heard there were three beautiful women here for lunch."

"Hi, Dad," Gia said, standing to greet him with the Merrill double kiss. "Looks like you've got a nice late lunch crowd in here today."

Franklin nodded, looking around the dining room. "Business is good," he said with satisfaction. "How's the studio?"

"It's going great. I think you were right about making the move here," Gia said.

"Always listen to your father," he advised with a wink. "Now, if you lovely ladies will excuse me, I need to get back in the kitchen."

Summer and Joey waved him off. "Your dad reminds me of a giant teddy bear. I just want to hug him all the time," Summer said, watching Franklin hurry out of the dining room.

"He's great," Gia agreed.

"Yeah, yeah. He's adorable. Now back to the super hot kiss," Joey said. "I believe you said something about bejesus?"

Gia stalled, and the blush returned to her cheeks.

"Come on," Summer said cajolingly. "We're practically family. Franklin is almost the stepfather of the man I live with, who happens to be the brother of the Pierce you made out with. And Joey here has had the pleasure of kissing your Pierce and doing many other exciting things with Jax."

"See? We're practically related," Joey nodded.

Gia glanced over her shoulder to make sure her father hadn't returned. "Fine, but don't even think that we're going to gloss over that whole 'Joey made out with two Pierce brothers' thing," Gia said, pointing a finger at the brunette.

"Deal," Joey agreed. "Now spill."

Their meals arrived, and the conversation paused until the server left.

"So, was Beckett super sweet and proper?" Summer wondered, spooning up some minestrone. "He seems like he would be romantic."

"Not proper, very little romance, and so much heat I was worried about spontaneous combustion," Gia said, diving into her salad.

"Was it all mouths, or did his hands go roaming?" Joey demanded over a bite of her chicken parm sandwich.

"Roaming. Do you two always talk like this?"

"It's her fault," Summer said, pointing her spoon at Joey. "My first actual conversation with her, she asks how the sex with Carter is."

"And how is it?" Gia smiled, happy to be on the asking end.

Summer's eyes rolled heavenward. "If you could combine amazing, incredible, and earth-moving into one word, it still wouldn't do Carter and his skills justice."

Gia fanned herself with her napkin. "Wow."

"So your musician ex can't compete with that?" Joey asked.

Gia shook her head. "Nope. But he was great at disappearing when things got sticky." She winced at the flippant comment. "That's not fair of me. Paul's a great guy, and I knew what I was getting into when I married him."

"How great of a guy is he that he lets you move his two kids away from him?" Joey countered.

"He just doesn't like to be tied down. Didn't even try to talk me out of leaving," Gia said, digging into her pasta.

"He didn't put up a fight for his family," Summer sighed. "That's just sad. And it makes me sad for him. He doesn't know what he's missing out on."

"Exactly," Gia agreed.

"But you're here now, starting your own business, raising

your kids in a great town, and—in your spare time—making out with the mayor in his house," Joey reminded her.

"And in his shed," Gia joked. "But you're right. This is where I'm meant to raise my family. I think we're all going to be happy here."

"I think so, too," Summer said, patting her hand again.

"Speaking of families," Joey interjected. "What's the story with Evan's mom?"

Gia saw Joey jolt in her chair.

"Ouch! You didn't have to kick me," she said to Summer, rubbing her shin under the table. "Gia is perfectly capable of forming the words 'none of your damn business.'"

"So dragging details of my near-tryst out of me is fine, but asking about my ex-husband's ex-wife is crossing the line?" Gia was amused.

"I see your point," Summer conceded. "My apologies to you both."

"You're *not* forgiven. I need this leg for stuff." Joey sulked.

"Would it make you feel better if I told you about Evan's mom?" Gia offered.

"Yep," a fully recovered Joey said.

"I never met her," Gia began. "She was long gone before I came into the picture. Paul was a few years older than me. Evan was six and the cutest little boy. I loved him before I loved Paul. Never could understand how she walked away from him." She shook her head sadly.

"She just left?" Summer asked.

"She was a singer. That's how she and Paul met. He said one day he came home, and she was packing. Told him she got some gig on a cruise ship and that he had to keep Evan because she didn't know when she'd be back."

"Bitch," Joey said succinctly.

Gia nodded. "No argument here. I met Paul shortly after

that. We'd been married about six months when he learned that she'd died."

"Someone shove her overboard?" Joey asked.

"Let's just say that she considered her body to be more of a Dumpster than a temple."

"Does Evan ever talk about her?" Summer wondered.

"No."

But he did talk about his father and made sure to remind Gia that she wasn't his real parent. She could have been had she pushed harder. She should have. Everyone deserved to have someone fight for them.

"So can we talk about someone else now?" she asked.

"You and Joey can compare notes on kissing Beckett," Summer suggested.

14

 $\mathcal{I}$ t was after seven on a Wednesday when Gia had to extricate herself from crow pose to answer the knock at the door. She tagged Aurora to take over for her in the yoga competition with Evan on his gaming system.

Her heart rate kicked up a notch when she glimpsed Beckett through the glass. *Off limits*, she reminded herself.

"Hi," she said, opening the door.

He was dressed casually in jeans and a long sleeve Henley that matched his eyes. His hair, just turning to curl on top, looked like it had been styled by a professional. "Hi," he said, shoving his hands in his pockets.

She'd wanted to ask him if he'd seen the post in Blue Moon's Facebook group—the group that she joined as soon as she realized it was speculating about her future—but decided it would be opening a can of worms that didn't need to be opened.

"Come on in," she said, holding the door for him.

"Hey, Beckett," Evan called from his downward facing dog in front of the TV.

"Hi, Bucket," Aurora chirped, trying to mimic her brother's pose.

"Hey, guys. Is this some kind of child torture?" he asked, feigning concern.

"It's gaming night," Evan announced. "Gia and I battle it out in two events. I let her win at yoga, and then I destroy her in baseball or bowling."

"I win, too," Aurora interjected, her red curls bouncing emphatically. "I win at ponies with Mama!"

"Ponies?" Beckett asked.

"It's this god-awful glitter bomb game with horrible music," Gia whispered.

"Want to play ponies with me, Bucket? I can show you how." Aurora danced over to them.

"Uh..."

"Beckett's really busy, Rora. Maybe some other time," Gia told her daughter.

Aurora's lower lip popped out. Her green eyes widened and began to water.

"What is this? What's happening?" Beckett asked in a panic.

"She's just playing you," Gia warned him. "Stay strong."

"Please, Bucket?"

Gia rolled her eyes at her daughter's faux devastation.

"I guess I could play one game?" Beckett said, the words tumbling out.

Aurora's watery gaze cleared immediately. "Yes!" She punched her little fist in the air. "Van, me and Bucket are playin' ponies."

"Fine, but then he has to play baseball with me," Evan bargained.

"'Kay. Me first though, right?"

"Sucker," Gia coughed.

"You can't tell me you can say no to that," Beckett protested.

"I'm a parent. It's my job to say no to that," she countered.

"I'm not buying it."

Gia turned to face him. She tilted her head to the side and poked out her lower lip making it tremble ever so slightly. She furrowed her brow and gazed up at him with all the sadness she could muster.

Beckett grabbed her by the shoulders. "Don't ever look at me like that again. I'm begging you."

Gia grinned, enjoying his discomfort. "I invented that look. That's why I'm immune to it. Wait'll you see Evan's disappointed face. That one's a killer."

Beckett shuddered and dropped his hands. "I hope to God I never see it."

Aurora grabbed him by the wrist. "C'mon, Bucket! It's time for ponies!"

"Do you like apple pie?" Gia called after him, laughter ringing in her voice.

BECKETT HAD apple pie with ice cream and played video games. And spent the evening feeling grateful for the fact that Gianna lived in his backyard safe from the prying eyes of Blue Moon.

Just a neighborly visit.

It wasn't a bad way to wrap up his day, he thought as he chased after Evan's long drive to centerfield. Aurora had killed him at *Pink Rainbow Ponies*, and he was determined to give her brother a run for his money.

He wasn't sure if it was the homemade apple pie, the giggles from the kids, or the constant music that flowed from a stereo in the corner, but Gia had made his guesthouse feel like a home.

The living room furniture was worn but comfortable. Mismatched frames held pictures of the kids, the kids and Gia, even Franklin. The framed images told the story of their family. There were two pictures of the man Beckett assumed was the kids' father. In the first, he was on stage behind a drum kit, the stage lights painting him in blue.

The other showed him sitting at a bar, drumsticks in his back pocket and sunglasses on his face. Beckett could make out just enough of Evan in the man's jawline and nose.

There were no pictures of him with the kids or with Gianna, and he wondered if that was selective editing or, more likely, he hadn't been around to be in any of the pictures.

He noticed she'd hung soft, colorful tapestries from the walls and tucked candles into nooks and crannies, adding bits of color and texture to the living space. They ate off simple white dishes that Gianna washed by hand, though not without telling Beckett the charm of the house had only barely offset the lack of a dishwasher.

It was a tidy and cozy home full of life and laughter.

At eight, Aurora argued and bargained her way upstairs to bed. At nine, it was Evan's turn. He didn't put up the fight that his sister had but hugged both Gia and Beckett before forlornly shuffling up the stairs.

"A voluntary bedtime hug," Gia sighed, sliding onto the arm of the couch. "That's a good day."

"That's not an every night occurrence?" Beckett asked, leaning back against the cushions.

"Sometimes I have to chase him upstairs and threaten to hold a pillow over his face first."

"You're really good at this, Gianna," Beckett said, studying her.

"Thank you," she said softly. "I try hard. It's a constant balancing act, and a lot of times I feel like I'm failing."

Beckett reached out and grabbed her foot, tugging her down onto the cushion beside him. "You're not failing."

"Oh, I'm getting very close. Do you want to see my dirty little secret?"

"More than anything in the world," Beckett said, stroking his thumb across the bottom of her bare foot.

She bit her lip, and he felt his blood rush south so fast he saw stars. She had the power over him to make him hard in a second. It was disconcerting, yet not enough to make him leave her alone.

"Come here." She rose and pulled him with her to the glass doors that led to what had been a sun porch.

She was taking him to her bedroom. Panic spiked in Beckett's veins. He wasn't prepared to be strong enough for the both of them. Especially not if a bed was in view.

"I don't know if this is a good—"

"This is my dirty little secret," Gia announced, pushing open one of the doors.

The gauzy curtains on the other side of the glass had blocked the nightmare beyond. There was indeed a bed set back against the far wall, but in order to get to it, one would have to weave through dozens of boxes, piles of clothing and books, and a tangled mountain of home décor and yoga accessories. In the corner opposite the doors, a yoga mat was rolled out.

"What is this?" Beckett winced.

"My bedroom slash office slash studio," she said with resignation. "It's awful isn't it? I just wanted to get the house together for the kids. You know, make the transition a little easier?"

"So everything that didn't have a place landed here?" He

caught a sweatshirt that started to tumble off the mirror of a dresser that was buried under boxes. A swatch of lace floated out of the hood. He picked it up before realizing it was a pink thong.

"It looks like a hoarder lives here," he said.

Gia nodded looking at the chaos. "Come to think of it, we did have a cat when we moved in."

Beckett felt the color drain from his face.

"I'm just kidding," she said, smacking him in the chest.

Distracted, Beckett wrapped the lace around his fingers. "Gianna, you can't live like this."

"I know," she said, pushing him back out the door and closing it behind her. "I just haven't had time to fix it. If I'm here, I'm with the kids making sure they stay alive, eat, go to bed, do their homework. And if I'm not here, I'm at the studio. When I finally have some time, I'll take care of this. I'm just starting to worry that I'll never find the time."

"Did you at least find your shoes?"

She nodded. "I found the box."

"And?"

"And it's in there somewhere."

"My God, Red. I'm breaking out in hives just thinking about you going in there at night. What if there's a stuff avalanche and you get buried alive?"

She was staring up at him with an odd mixture of amusement and sadness. It tugged at him and made him want to reach out to touch her. Pull her in close and tell her that everything was going to work out. But he didn't.

"See? My balance isn't so great."

"Gianna, you don't have to do everything yourself," Beckett reminded her. "You have... family."

She shook her head. "My dad has given me so much in my

lifetime. It's not fair to ask him to help me clean up my own literal mess."

They were quiet for a few moments. "I should go," Beckett said finally.

Her expression went a little sadder. "Thanks for coming over. It was really nice."

"It was." He meant it, too. "Thanks for the pie."

She lifted onto her toes and placed a chaste kiss on his cheek. "Thanks for the company."

He let himself out, using all his will not to look over his shoulder at Gianna. If he did, he was afraid he'd end up dragging her back to her bedroom and spend the night making love to her or helping her organize the mess. He wasn't sure which urge would win out.

He'd made it halfway across the yard before he realized he hadn't gotten around to telling her the reason for his visit. Beckett briefly debated just going home and talking to her tomorrow. But once he realized he still had her skimpy little thong wound around his hand, he reconsidered.

He knocked softly on her front door and saw her turn away from the sink. She padded over to the door and opened it.

"Miss me already?" she teased.

He held up her underwear between his fingers. "I accidentally took these."

Gianna pressed her lips together and grabbed the thong out of his hands. Her green eyes danced with humor and heat. "Thank you for returning them. They're one of the only pairs that I can find."

Great. Now he was going to think about her running around town without underwear. He shook his head, trying to rattle that thought out of his mind.

"I also forgot to tell you why I came over in the first place."

"You weren't just being neighborly?" she laughed.

"There's a town meeting tomorrow night. It's always good for business owners to attend, and we'll be talking about the Halloween carnival, too, in case you were thinking about taking the kids."

"Thanks, Beckett. I'd like to come."

Yes, he'd like her to as well, he thought darkly.

15

There were so many people out on the streets of Blue Moon when she locked up the studio that Gia wondered if the Pope or Pink Floyd had come to town. But as she watched everyone funnel into the second-run movie theater on the far end of the square, she realized they were all there for the town meeting.

Apparently the theater was the only venue large enough to handle the attendance.

Gia hustled through the park to the well-worn theater. The smell of fresh popcorn teased her when she opened the heavy door. She was delighted to see that the concession stand was open. She treated herself to a box of malted milk balls and stepped into the theater. The Art Deco-style theater boasted romantic frescos and hand-painted pillars that held up the fading, muraled ceiling. On the weathered stage in front of them was a podium flanked by a handful of metal folding chairs. A heavy velvet curtain covered the movie screen behind the chairs.

She found a seat on a worn velour cushion in the middle section next to Beverly from the HVAC place in town.

Beverly was working her way through a tub of popcorn the size of an ottoman. "They always get me with the 'you can full-moon-size that for just a dollar more,'" she said, shaking her head. She tilted the greasy bucket toward Gia. "Want some?"

Coming straight from her last class of the day, Gia was ravenous. "Thanks," she said, helping herself to a handful. "This is my first town meeting. So far I'm a fan."

"You're in for a treat," Beverly predicted.

Gia craned her neck to get a look at the crowd around them. She recognized several familiar faces. Evan's science teacher was there with her husband. The rat-tailed Fitz was chitchatting with Donna Delvecchio, who was still wearing her scrubs. She spotted her dad—using his trademark expansive hand gestures—and Phoebe standing in a small knot of people toward the back.

The lights flickered and the standing stragglers took their seats. Once everyone was settled, Beckett and four others took the stage. All business, he strode toward the podium in his suit and tie, hesitating only for the briefest of seconds when "Hail to the Chief" crackled over the speakers.

A smattering of applause rose up from the audience and Beckett shot a frown over his shoulder. The man behind him in the argyle sweater vest strutted unconcernedly to his seat.

Beckett shook his head and took his place behind the podium. He made a slashing motion over his neck and the music cut off abruptly. "Well that was a... surprise."

Gia grinned at his obvious embarrassment.

"Thanks for coming out tonight, everyone. We've got a few agenda items to move through at the top of the hour," Beckett announced. "On behalf of our residents and council members I'd like to remind everyone that we set aside exactly sixty minutes for these meetings."

Beverly leaned over to Gia. "That's a warning to Bruce,"

she said, nodding toward the bearded man in the sweater vest. "He's a bit verbose."

"Any issues not settled in those sixty minutes will be addressed at the next town meeting," Beckett continued. "So without further ado, let's begin." He reached over and slapped the button on a digital clock that began counting down from sixty minutes.

"The council would like to report the results of our public vote on the following awareness topics for November. In addition to National Diabetes Month, Blue Moon will be observing Green Friday, Clean Up After Your Dog Week, and..." he trailed off and cleared his throat before continuing. "And November Awareness Month."

Gia looked around as the audience applauded with enthusiasm. "November Awareness?"

A man in a blue fleece jacket shirt stood up. "I move that we observe November awareness with a month-long $5.99 hot turkey sandwich special at the diner," he announced.

A woman wearing a fuzzy poncho rose. "Second that."

"I appreciate your appetite for hot turkey sandwiches, Mitch... and Brenda," Beckett said, clearing his throat. "But the town council can't just order a business to provide a special."

"Okay, fine." Mitch was unconcerned. "I move that we petition the diner to serve a month-long $5.99 hot turkey sandwich special," he amended.

"Seconded," said the poncho lady.

A man in the row behind Gia stood up, his hands were tucked into the pocket of his Blakeley Diner sweatshirt. "Yeah, okay. We'll do the special. But I'm thinking more like $8.99," he said, his accent thickly seasoned with Jersey.

A spirited bidding war broke out that ended with Mr. Blakeley agreeing to $7.50 and throwing in a side of sweet corn. "As long as Mrs. Blakeley okays it," he cautioned the crowd.

Beckett pounded his gavel. "Sold for $7.50 and corn with Mrs. Blakeley's approval."

"If anyone has any questions on how else to appropriately observe November Awareness, please see Fitz from the bookstore since it was his suggestion." Beckett moved on. "The first item on the agenda is our Halloween carnival. Bobby, you have the floor."

Bobby, the silver dreadlocked proprietress of Peace of Pizza, moved to take the podium. "Okay, Mooners." Her voice was like a mellow jazz singer, and Gia wondered how she ended up in pizza. "We're finalizing the details for our annual Halloween bash."

Beverly leaned in again. "We do a Halloween carnival instead of trick or treat," she whispered. "The kids love it, and it's so much easier on the parents."

Gia had a feeling Evan and Aurora would enjoy it. Finally, her family was settling into a town where they could know their neighbors and make all those memories that childhood is built upon.

She felt an awareness skim over her. A heat sliding over her skin. Glancing up, her gaze connected with sterling eyes watching her from the stage. Beckett winked at her, and she smiled back.

It was a shame he wasn't hers to explore. She liked Beckett Pierce on principle and in reality. Gia knew from experience how hard it was to find a good, solid man. Not only was he dedicated to his family and his clients, but Beckett put just as much of his time and energy into his town. He had a big heart and a level head, not to mention a spectacular physique and sexy face.

And he would remain firmly out of her reach, Gia reminded herself.

While the council members hustled through agenda items —yes, the carnival would end at nine, and, no, they would not enforce a Star Wars theme—Joey slid into the empty seat next to Gia.

"What'd I miss," she whispered, reaching over Gia for Beverly's popcorn tub.

Beverly gladly shared. "No on the Star Wars proposition," she said.

"Damn. I guess that means we won't see the Jabba the Hut costume Big Ben's been threatening to wear," Joey sighed, sliding her long, denim-clad legs under the seat in front of her.

Gia offered her some candy which Joey accepted in her empty hand.

"Do you come to these often?" Gia gestured toward the stage.

Joey shrugged. "When I need entertainment. I wasn't planning to tonight, but Summer texted and asked me to meet her here."

"Is she here?" Gia asked.

"Not yet. Said she'd be here right after the meeting." Joey was quiet for a few moments. "She and Carter were on their way back from the city," she said, finally.

Summer's doctor's appointment, Gia realized. She glanced sideways at Joey, but the only clue to her state of mind was the drumming of her fingers on the screen of her cell phone.

"Any punctuation or smiley faces in her text?" she asked.

Joey swiped the screen and showed Gia the text.

Summer: On our way back. Can you meet Carter and me at the town meeting tonight?

"Hmm," Gia said.

"I know. Jackson's coming, too. He and Colby were trying to finish up a few things on the farm with Carter and Summer in the city."

"Are you worried?" Gia asked.

"Let's go with mildly concerned."

Gia watched the clock tick down to forty minutes. "Well, you don't have long to wait before you find out what's going on," she said, patting Joey's leg.

Joey heaved a sigh and shoveled more popcorn into her mouth.

Beckett wrapped up his announcement that the council would be surveying the borough's sidewalks in the spring to see which ones needed to be replaced.

"Before we get to the open forum portion of the evening, the town council would like to formally recognize Bucky Quan. Mrs. Quan, if you could bring Bucky to the stage, please?"

Gia watched in amazement as a small woman with a jet-black blunt bob carried a bundle of fur to the stage.

"What is that?" she whispered to Joey.

"A rabbit. He was raised by the 4H program and adopted out after the county fair."

"With the death of his brother Winston last week, Bucky is officially the oldest lop-eared rabbit in Blue Moon Bend. And while our condolences go to Winston's family, we would like to honor Bucky and his eleven years with this plaque."

Gia found herself applauding with the rest of the crowd as Beckett presented Mrs. Quan with a small, engraved plaque and posed for a picture taken by the same skinny young man in glasses who had shot her ribbon cutting. Anthony, she reminded herself, Rainbow and Gordon's son.

"This is the most amazing way to spend a Thursday night." Gia grinned.

"Now comes the real entertainment," Beverly said, raising her chin toward the stage where Beckett was introducing the final portion of the evening's meeting, the open forum.

"I'll turn the podium over to Bruce Oakleigh for the conclusion of his argument."

The bearded man stood and gave a formal bow to Beckett and then the crowd.

"Before I begin my conclusion on why it is important for your town leaders to don period powdered wigs, I'd like to recap my previous points."

The crowd groaned.

"Again?" Joey moaned.

"He's been arguing this during open forums for the last four months," Beverly explained. "The last three meetings have been recaps of the points he made in the first meeting. He never gets to the conclusion."

"The council has to vote on that?"

"No, it's a town vote. We're all set to vote yes because, I mean, *come on*." Joey held up her hands. "Beckett in a powdered wig? But Bruce never shuts up long enough to call a vote."

"I think I'm in love with this town," Gia decided.

Bruce argued mightily in favor of powdered wigs but once again went to the last second with his argument leaving no time for the public to vote.

Beckett looked decidedly relieved as he adjourned the meeting.

As the crowd began to disperse, Joey unfolded herself and stood up.

"I'm going to see if I can find Carter and Summer," she told Gia. "I'll see you around."

"Good luck," Gia called after her.

She thanked Beverly for the popcorn and the commentary and decided to stop by the stage and say hi to Beckett. *Just a friendly hi between neighbors,* she reminded herself.

BECKETT WAS TRYING to pay attention to his conversation with Mrs. Nordeman but found himself distracted by Gianna as she approached. She was wearing gray patterned tights that ended just below her knees and a hooded sweatshirt. Her hair was piled up in a knot on her head. With siren-red hair, the woman could never blend in in a crowd.

She reached his side just as Mrs. Nordeman wrapped up her complaint about the public library not expanding its erotica section.

Beckett resisted the urge to close his eyes and instead nodded thoughtfully. "I'll do some research on that, Mrs. Nordeman."

"Great!" she said, breaking into a smile. "I'll email you a list of titles for your consideration." Mrs. Nordeman dashed off, her bell sleeves billowing behind her.

"You look like you have a headache," Gianna told him with a sunny smile.

Beckett brought a hand to his brow. "Does it show?"

"I'd have a headache at the thought of having to wear a powdered wig, too," she said sympathetically. "But if you need any help researching the library's erotica collection, I'm willing to volunteer my services."

"I appreciate that." Beckett looked her up and down. "Did you come straight from class?"

She nodded. "Evan's watching Aurora for me. In fact, I

should be getting home to them to make sure she didn't somehow talk him into letting her destroy the house."

"I'll walk you out," he offered, putting his hand on her shoulder. The words were out of his mouth before he knew they were in his head. The last thing he should be doing is be seen lusting after Gianna in front of the entire town. Willa and the rest of the Beautification Committee would be on them like Mrs. Nordeman and a new erotica novel. After the social media speculation about the two of them, he should be avoiding her like summer school.

"Thanks, but I think you have a family meeting," Gianna said, pointing at the group approaching them. Summer and Carter led the way down the aisle followed by a worried-looking Phoebe, Franklin, Jax, and Joey.

Beckett tightened his grip on Gianna's shoulder.

Shit. "Summer's appointment," he said half to himself.

Gianna reached up and squeezed his hand. "It's going to be fine. No matter what it is, she has all of you."

"Hey," Carter said by way of a greeting.

"Hey," Beckett heard himself respond over the thudding in his chest.

"I should get going," Gianna said, trying to pull free.

Beckett merely clamped down on her shoulder holding her in place.

"If you have a minute, Gianna, we've got some news we wanted to share with everyone," Summer said. "Including you."

"Um. Sure." Gianna darted a glance at Beckett, and he squeezed her shoulder.

Carter hauled Summer up against his side.

"So, we got some news from the doctor today, and it was a little unexpected," Summer began.

Beckett felt his heart climb into his throat. If there was

anything wrong with Summer, he didn't know what they'd do. It made him feel helpless, useless. The tension hung thick in the air like a fog.

He watched his brother take a deep breath. "We're pregnant," Carter announced.

The response was immediate. Beckett was so relieved he doubled over to catch his breath. He felt small Gia's hand gently stroke his back. His mother gasped in delight and burst into tears. Joey's jaw dropped.

Jax's response was the most succinct. "Holy shit."

"With twins," Summer added.

"*Twins?*" Everyone shouted the word at once.

Summer's face glowed, and her eyes gleamed with unshed tears. Carter looked happy and shell-shocked.

"You scared the shit out of all of us," Joey said, finally regaining her voice.

"Scared? I'm more scared *now*. We didn't even know if kids were possible, and now twins?" Summer said, the hysteria rising in her voice. She seemed like she couldn't quite catch her breath. "Oh, my God. Carter! We have to get married."

Beckett nudged Carter. His brother slyly tapped the front pocket of his jeans.

"I thought you didn't want to move too quickly," Carter said innocently.

"Twins, Carter. *Twins.* Two babies," Summer yelped. "There's no slowing down this crazy train."

"Well, in that case," Carter began. He shoved his hand into his pocket and started to sink down on one knee.

"What?" Summer gasped. Her hands flew to her cheeks, and she shook her head slowly from side to side. "This... I..."

Carter pulled out the ring and held it up. "I bought this weeks ago. The same day that you told me things were moving so fast you just wanted to sit back and enjoy them for a while.

But I knew that there was nothing I wanted more than to have you as my wife, my partner."

Summer pressed her fingers to her mouth.

"I know you wanted to wait, to get comfortable, to figure things out. But honey, the second I saw you, everything fell into place the way it was meant to be. We're crazy if we put it off a second longer. I may be scared shitless right now, Summer. But there is nothing more that I want in this world than to spend the rest of my life with you. I want to marry you, to have babies with you, to follow dreams with you. Together we can handle it all. Will you be my wife?"

Summer couldn't answer. She was crying too hard. But so were all the women.

Phoebe was sobbing in utter joy into Franklin's chest. Joey swiped at a stray tear and didn't even punch Jax when he leaned in and kissed her on the top of the head. Gia clasped her hands together under her chin and grinned through happy tears as she watched Carter sweep Summer up in his arms.

Thunderous applause rose up, and Beckett looked up to see dozens of the town's residents still standing at the back of the theater.

"We're getting married!" Carter yelled, gently lowering Summer back to the floor.

"And having twins," Summer added.

The crowd hooted and hollered all over again.

Carter hyperventilated and doubled over.

"We are so screwed." Summer grinned, resting her cheek on her fiancé's heaving back.

∾

A CELEBRATION WAS DEFINITELY in order. It was determined that both Gia and Beckett had chilled bottles of champagne in their refrigerators, so the party would proceed to Beckett's house. While Summer and Carter were waylaid by congratulations from the crowd, Gia hurried home to get the kids and the champagne.

She had texted Evan after her class, before the meeting, during the meeting, and then immediately after the meeting. At which point he had replied, *Stop smothering. We're fine.*

That had her cracking a smile. They may not have shared blood, but he definitely got his dry wit from her.

When she opened the front door, Gia found both her kids alive and well and engaged in a heated argument.

Aurora was in the middle of explaining exactly why her bedtime was too early for a kindergartner while Evan was passionately suggesting she take it up with her mom because he wasn't "falling for her cute crap."

Her heart still full, she wrapped them both up for a hug before demanding to know why Aurora had ignored her bedtime.

"Well, Mom, I was jus' telling Van that it's not fair that I hafta go to bed at eight," her daughter said earnestly.

"I tried to make her go," Evan said, giving a shrug of his skinny shoulder.

Gia released them to inspect the house. "Well, I see the roof is still attached. The walls are still standing." She sniffed the air. "I don't smell any gas leaks."

Evan and Aurora waited, watching her for her reaction.

She crossed her arms and let them sweat a little bit. "Evan, good job tonight. Aurora, we'll talk about a later bedtime at another time. For now, I need you guys to get your shoes on."

Evan looked down at his pajamas. "But we're dressed for bed."

"We're running over to Beckett's for a few minutes."

"Yay! Bucket!" Aurora charged up the stairs in her little pink elephant pajamas on a quest for shoes.

Her brother was not as easily convinced. "Why are we going to Beckett's?"

"The Pierces are celebrating some good news, and they invited us over."

"Summer and Joey, too?" He tried to look disinterested.

"Yep. Both of them."

"I guess we can go. For a little bit." He started up the stairs and paused. "Are you mad that Roar didn't go to bed?"

Gia shook her head. "You did a great job tonight—as long as you did your homework." She gave him the evil eye until Evan nodded. "Good. You being so responsible really helps me out."

"It's not your job, you know."

"What's not my job?"

"Taking care of me. You don't have to."

"Of course I do, Evan. It's illegal to let your kids live in cardboard boxes and fend for themselves. Trust me. I looked it up."

Evan shook his head and pretended he wasn't smiling. "You're so weird."

"Where do you think you get it, kid?" she called after him as he hustled up the stairs.

Evan changed out of his pajamas into jeans and a button-down, confirming to Gia that he was suffering from a massive crush on both Summer and Joey. She hoped he wouldn't be too devastated by Summer and Carter's announcement.

Guilt drove her to let him have a soda—a decision she knew she'd regret—for the toast. Aurora toasted Summer with apple juice and bounced from Pierce brother to Pierce brother showing off the "efelants" on her pjs.

Beckett's living room was overflowing with happiness and people. Gia ducked out into the hallway to catch her breath. It was a beautiful, overwhelming thing to see so many people so happy.

Summer stepped out of the kitchen, flushed and beaming. She raised a finger to her lips and beckoned to Beckett's rarely used parlor off the stairs.

Gia followed her in, and Summer grabbed her hands.

"I just wanted to thank you for being here, Gia," she said in a rush.

"Thank you for inviting us to be part of the celebration," Gia said, squeezing Summer's hands.

"I have an ulterior motive." Summer's cornflower eyes were wide.

"And what's that?"

"I am scared to death," she confessed. "I don't know anything about parenting. I didn't think it was possible, let alone probable. What am I going to do with *twins*?"

Gia put her hands on Summer's shoulders and took a deep steadying breath. "Deep inhale," she ordered. Summer took a gasping breath.

"Summer, you've had less than a day to digest this amazing news. You have nothing to worry about. You and Carter are good people. The best. You are responsible, healthy, fun, kind, generous, smart people. Your babies are the luckiest unplanned kids in the world."

"See? This is why I need you. You're going to be my new best friend, okay?" Summer said, her eyes still huge. "I need you to show me how to be a mom."

Gia did laugh then. "I will be here to help in whatever way I can, but you've got this. You're going to be amazing."

"At best I hope to be mediocre to average and not emotionally scarring," Summer said. "And with your help, I think I can get there. You're an incredible mom. You have all this stuff figured out already. You can help me catch up."

Gia was at a loss for words.

"I mean it," Summer nodded earnestly. "You're amazing. Your kids are amazing. And you're doing this on your own. You make it look so easy."

"Remind me to show you my bedroom soon," Gia quipped. "But seriously, you can do this. You and Carter can absolutely do this and it's going to be one of the most amazing things you share in addition to a kick-ass marriage."

"It is going to be kick-ass, isn't it?" Summer glanced down at the sparkling promise Carter had put on her finger.

"It's *all* going to be kick-ass."

"And you'll be there to help me?"

"I'll be there," Gia nodded. "How do you feel?"

"So very happy and grateful and scared."

"Welcome to motherhood."

16

*G*ia ushered the kids through the front door and dumped the groceries on the table. "Okay, you," she pointed to Aurora, "Go change for your party. And you," she pointed at Evan, "Go find Brian's birthday card."

She could barely recall the days when a Saturday meant relaxation. She'd gone from Saturday morning hangovers and brunch in college to pregnant and married in the blink of an eye.

Now her weekends were a blur of kid birthday parties, frantic trips down the grocery aisle, and yoga classes.

She'd planned to tackle at least a small portion of the hot mess that was her bedroom today, but two birthday invites and an impromptu dinner party later and she would be lucky if she saw the inside of her room before ten tonight.

Not that she was complaining. Seeing Evan get excited about a party invitation from a classmate was an awesome sign that he was making new friends. Because he was quiet and a little reserved, it usually took him longer to make friends than the gregarious Aurora. And in the leapfrog moves they'd made to follow Paul's dreams, he'd had to start over too often.

But in Blue Moon, no one was a stranger... or strange.

Gia grabbed the grocery bag and hauled it into the kitchen. She'd throw together grilled cheese sandwiches before hitting two parties on opposite ends of town that started at the same time. She could drop off Evan at the Lord of the Rings themed party, but it was probably frowned upon to abandon a five-year-old at a party with a bunch of strangers.

At least she had dinner to look forward to. She'd invited her dad and Phoebe over for a nice quiet dinner. Part of the reason for moving here was to spend more time with her father. And that also meant his girlfriend.

She quickly assembled sandwiches—with three different combinations of ingredients—and was getting ready to toss them in the pan on the stove when her tablet signaled an incoming call.

Her older sister's face grinned up at her from the screen. Emmaline was an auburn-haired beauty with a head for business and a smart mouth. Their weekly video chats were always entertaining.

"Hey, sis," Gia answered, deftly transferring a sandwich to the pan.

Emma wrinkled her nose. "What are you making?"

"Grilled cheese. It's no broiled chicken breast and celery stalks, but it'll do."

"Smart ass," her sister said, sticking her tongue out.

"So what's up? How's the life of a big, important five-star restaurant manager?" Gia asked.

"Oh, you know," Emma answered, adjusting her tailored suit jacket. "The usual. Wining and dining celebrities, jetting off to Tuscany to woo a potential new head chef. Nothing special," she winked.

"Give me a hint on the celebrities," Gia said, flipping the sandwiches over.

"Hmm, okay. One very good-looking secret agent in the box office joined us for lunch with his very famous wife and then returned for dinner with an unknown, huge-breasted aspiring actress."

"Gross."

"Players are pigs." Emmaline shrugged. "Always have been always will be."

"You'll meet a non-player someday, Em," Gia told her.

"Maybe if I get myself out of a city crawling with celebrities and athletes. How's Blue Moon? Maybe I should move in with you."

Gia tried to imagine her urban chic, balance-sheet-loving sister finding passion in rural paradise.

"There's always room for you here. You might have to sleep in the bathtub or the shed, though."

"I'm reconsidering my rash decision to throw away my nice, fat salary and apartment with its squishy king-sized bed."

"Yeah, I'd put some thought into that if I were you," Gia teased. "So what do I owe the pleasure of your face today?"

"I'm calling on behalf of Eva and myself with orders for you to get the dirt on Dad's girlfriend. Since you're on the ground, we're depending on you to give us a full report on this Phoebe Pierce."

It was hard for her sisters to be so far away from their father, especially since Franklin was often less-than-forthcoming about the details of his life. But now that Gia was close by, Emmaline and Evangeline had a direct line for information.

"I mean, it's great that he's getting out there and dating. But what do we really know about this woman?"

"They're not just dating, Em. They're moving in together. They've been house hunting together."

Emma sat forward. "What?" she demanded icily.

"You're using your manager voice," Gia reminded her.

"Sorry," Emma said. She leaned back and fixed a phony smile on her face. "What?" she asked through unmoving lips and clenched teeth.

"Yeah, Beckett spilled the beans on that one. I guess Dad wasn't ready to share that particular piece of information."

"Who's Beckett?"

"My... landlord. And Phoebe's son."

"Interesting." Emma pursed her lips together.

"What's interesting?"

"The way your face gets all soft and dewy when you say his name."

Gia fumbled a sandwich, dumping it on the counter instead of the plate.

"Very interesting," her sister reiterated.

Gia was about to argue when there was a knock at the door.

"I got it!" Evan shouted, hurrying down the stairs. "Hey, Aunt Em," he waved as he raced by Gia's screen, dropping a crumpled envelope on the table.

"Hey, Van Morrison," Emma returned.

Evan rolled his eyes at the nickname and missed Gia sending his aunt a wink. Emma's eyes widened at something behind Gia. "You've got company."

Gia glanced over her shoulder and proceeded to burn herself on the hot pan when she spotted Beckett coming through her front door.

She yelped and swore, bringing the flesh of her palm to her mouth. Evan snickered at her language.

"Are you okay?" Beckett asked, backing through the door handling his end of a large cardboard box.

"I gotta go," Gia hissed at Emma. "I'll call you later."

"Don't you dare hang—" Gia cut off her sister's threat and disconnected.

"What's all this?" Gia asked, moving the frying pan to the safety of a cool burner.

Jax shuffled in after his brother hefting the other side of the box. "Just go about your business. Don't mind us," he said with a wink in her direction.

They moved past the table and stopped next to the island. "Here's good," Beckett decided. They let the box slide gently to the floor.

"A dishwasher?" Gia eyed up the box. "You brought me a dishwasher?"

Beckett swiped his hands on his jeans and turned his attention to her. He grabbed her wrist and examined the burn before turning on the cold water in her sink and shoving her hand under the stream.

"Better?" he asked, still holding her wrist.

Gia craned her neck to look up at him. She was still staring into those concerned gray eyes when Phoebe and her father walked in.

"Grampa!" Aurora shouted from the top of the stairs. She thundered down the skinny staircase and threw herself into Franklin's outstretched arms.

Gia's heart was thumping in her head, and she wasn't sure if it was stress or Beckett, who was still holding her hand.

She shut off the water and tugged out of Beckett's grasp but not before sensing Phoebe's knowing gaze.

148

"This is a nice surprise." She greeted her father with a kiss and offered Phoebe a hug.

"Mama, I'm hungry," Aurora announced, wiggling out of Franklin's arms.

"Well that's perfect timing because lunch is ready. Can I get you guys a drink?" she asked as she skirted around the island

Gia studied the outfit her daughter had chosen. Aurora was wearing black leggings under a purple and pink striped dress with little green Crocs. *Good enough*, she decided.

"I'd love a water," Phoebe said. "Can I help with anything?"

Gia stepped over Beckett who was kneeling next to the sink and wished to God she'd had time to grab a shower before her house was overrun.

"I think everything is under control for now. We actually have to head out for some birthday parties in a few minutes." She grabbed a bottle of water and two baggies of sliced vegetables out of the fridge. She passed Phoebe the water and tossed the baggies onto the plates.

"Evan, lunch."

He was on the floor between Jax and Beckett frowning at a tape measure with them.

Gia deposited the plates on the table. Franklin sat next to Aurora and pretended to eat her sandwich. "No, Grampa! That's mine," she giggled.

Evan strolled over and slid onto his chair. "Vegetables again? Jeez, Gia. Haven't you ever heard of chips?"

"You're going to a party where you'll stuff your face with pizza, chips, cake, and ice cream. You can suffer through some cucumbers and carrots now."

He grumbled but opened the bag.

Gia ignored her own sandwich and grabbed one of the juices she'd picked up at OJs by Julia. A glance at the microwave clock told her she only had ten more minutes before she needed to herd everyone out the door. Not enough time to change or eat. She unscrewed the lid and drank deeply.

Jax laid a hand on her shoulder. "That's not Jolly Green, is it?"

She shook her head. "No. It's a new juice Julia's doing for fall. I think she calls it Harvest. Why?"

"I had a bad experience," he said and shuddered.

"Want to try this one?" she offered.

He shook his head. "I think I'm still too traumatized."

"So you two are a little early for dinner," Gia said, sliding into the chair next to Evan.

"Well, we had a free afternoon and wondered if we could help out," Franklin said, taking a bite out of the baby carrot Aurora offered him.

"Help out with what? Dinner?"

"I'm offering up my chauffeur and chaperone services, and Phoebe here happens to be an excellent amateur organizer," her dad said waving his hand in the direction of Gia's bedroom.

Phoebe smiled. "Beckett told me you have a bit of a situation," she said nodding toward the room. "If you're okay with it, Franklin can take the kids to their parties this afternoon, and I can help you go through some boxes."

Gia blinked.

Beckett had ratted her out, and now everyone knew her dirty little secret. She was going to murder him... after he was done installing the dishwasher.

"It can't be easy making such a big move. Getting your kids settled while starting a new business. But it doesn't have to be on your own. You have us," Phoebe said, smiling cheerfully.

"Besides, it'll help feed my sickness for personal organization."

"I see," Gia said primly. "Beckett? Can I see you outside for a minute?"

His head popped up on the other side of the island. "Now?"

"Now."

She shut the front door behind them and fixed him with her best suspicious mom look. "What are you doing?"

He ran a hand over the back of his neck. "I'm trying to install a dishwasher."

"Why?" Gia crossed her arms.

"A dishwasher would make your life easier. And so would a little time and help to organize the rest of your crap," Beckett said, sounding annoyed now.

"What if I weren't your tenant? What if it was someone else?"

"Are you asking if I'd be doing this for someone else?"

"Yes, that's what I'm asking. You say I'm not your type. We decide we need to keep this professional, and then you show up here with kitchen appliances and my father, who you don't even like—"

"It's what we do, Red. We're fixers. Smotherers. I talked to my mom. She talked to Franklin. We devised a plan. It's the Blue Moon way."

"So you, as a Blue Mooner, see a way to improve someone's life, and you just jump on in and force your help on them."

"Exactly. The only difference this time is I also have an irrational and completely unrelated desire to sleep with you while I help you."

A small smile played across her lips. "I can't peg you, Beckett. Just when I think I have you figured out, you surprise me. A steamy make-out session, and we both know we're not right for each other. Then you go and blab about my failings to your family and mine. Then you show up here with a dishwasher and the cavalry and tell me you want to sleep with me. I'm confused. Annoyed and confused."

"Is that all?"

"And hungry," she added. "Are you helping me because you think I'm doing a bad job?"

Beckett looked genuinely surprised and a little offended. "Of course not. I'm buying you an afternoon of your life back and twenty minutes a day of dishwashing."

"Okay. Then I am annoyed, confused, hungry, and grateful," Gia revised.

"Yeah, well, join the club. Now, can I get back to installing your dishwasher while fantasizing about you doing yoga naked?"

"Just one more thing. If I ever trust you with a secret again —no matter how silly it may seem to you—I expect you to keep it to yourself."

"You got it, Red." He glanced over her shoulder to make sure no one inside was watching. "You look really sexy in this shirt," he said, hooking his index finger in the scoop neck of her tank.

"Beckett, behave yourself," she said, slapping his hand away and tugging her cardigan tighter around her.

"Really sexy," he said again, tapping her nose before heading back inside.

She should be annoyed. Should be furious with Beckett for outing her and then riding to her rescue. She took pride in being able to provide for her kids, to run a business and a house. In never asking for help.

She was independent, first by chance and now by choice. She had Paul to thank for that. While he had chased his dreams, dragging the rest of them along like luggage, Gia had turned herself into a strong, capable woman.

She didn't do everything perfectly. Obviously, she thought, cringing over her bedroom. But damn it, she was good at being a mom and good at running a business. And someday she hoped to be great at it all.

She let herself back inside. "My friend Walter has two moms," Aurora was saying conversationally to Franklin and Phoebe. "Van, can I try yours?" she asked, eyeing up his grilled cheese.

Evan pulled off a piece of his sandwich. "Trade?"

"Are you sure it's okay with you, Dad?" Gia asked, looping her arms around his neck. "You'll actually have to stay with Rora. That's ten screaming five-year-olds hopped up on sugar and crowd mentality. And Phoebe, I don't know if Beckett explained just how serious my 'situation' is."

"I'd be happy to spend some time with my grandkids," Franklin announced. "Phoebe and I were talking about how we're hoping to spend an evening a week with the kids. Plus, Walter's moms are going to be there, and I'm hoping to pin them down on a catering gig."

"We both miss having little ones around," Phoebe said wistfully. "Not that Evan isn't practically an adult," she said, winking at the boy.

Jax chose that moment to shove Beckett out of his squat on the kitchen floor. Beckett's foot lashed out to catch his brother in the gut. They grunted and wrestled, slamming into the cabinets.

"Or that my boys are remotely grown up," Phoebe amended. She stood up, turned on the sink faucet, and calmly hosed her sons down with the dish sprayer. "Just in case you ever need to know how to break this up." She winked at Gia as Jax and Beckett sputtered under the stream of water.

"Now clean up that mess and pretend to act like adults," she ordered them.

Gia felt a tickle in her throat. Family. Help. A few hours a week all to herself. It was a Blue Moon miracle.

"Would you guys like to hang out with Grampa and Phoebe?" she asked Evan and Aurora.

"Can we go back to the farm?" Evan asked.

"Definitely," Phoebe said. "Carter wants you to come out for a riding lesson soon."

"With Joey?" Evan was trying to sound nonchalant.

"Probably," Phoebe nodded.

"Sounds okay," Evan said with a shrug.

"I can ride a pony?" Aurora gasped. "Do you have any pink ones? Bucket likes pink ponies, right Bucket?"

Beckett's head popped up over the kitchen island. "Sure do, shortcake."

"We don't have any pink ponies, but we do have a little white one named Princess," Phoebe said.

"Princess?" Aurora's little mouth formed a perfect "o."

"I think you just made her day," Gia laughed.

_____

17

With the kids packed off to birthday parties and Beckett and Jax systematically ripping apart her kitchen cabinets, Gia led Phoebe into the battlefield that was her bedroom.

"I know it looks bad, but it's actually probably worse than it seems," Gia confessed.

"That's very comforting," Phoebe said, taking stock.

"You really don't have to do this," Gia reminded her. "I think with three free hours I can make some headway on my own. I'm sure you have better things to do than go through mislabeled boxes and piles of things that should have been thrown out or recycled years ago."

Phoebe smiled. "Not only do I enjoy digging into projects like this, it'll give me the chance to spend a little time with my handsome boyfriend's daughter. And—" she glanced over her shoulder at the kitchen. "The woman who makes my son's face light up."

Gia blushed. "I don't know what to say to that. Beckett and I aren't... pursuing a relationship. We're not exactly a good match on paper and prefer to keep our relationship professional."

"I see Facebook, and I see the way you two look at each other," Phoebe said knowingly. "Just because you don't like the way it looks on paper doesn't mean it wouldn't be a worthwhile adventure."

"I appreciate the sentiment, but right now I've got a lot on my plate... and my dresser and my bed. A boyfriend is pretty low on my To-Do list. And even if it wasn't, a man who takes over and makes decisions for me wouldn't make my list."

Phoebe patted Gia's arm. "Well, maybe we can take care of a few of those higher priority items, and then you can spend some time figuring out what kind of a man does belong on your list."

WHILE HIS MOTHER and Gianna dug into the debris in the bedroom, Beckett measured, cut, and ripped his way through the dishwasher installation.

"You must really like this girl," Jax puffed as he shoved the dishwasher back so it was flush with the cabinets.

"It's a kitchen. It needs a dishwasher," he said mildly.

"Bullshit." Jax opened a bottle of water and drank deeply. "You like her."

"Of course, I do," Beckett said, annoyed. "What's not to like? She's the perfect tenant."

Jax grinned. "I bet you spend a lot of time looking out your kitchen window, don't you?"

"Shut up, Jax," Beckett warned his brother.

"What? I've got eyes, don't I? I see the way you look at her. You're like the big bad wolf just waiting to get the jump on Little Red. Hey!" His brother's gray eyes lit up. "Have you two picked out your couples Halloween costume yet? Because that would be perfect."

Beckett shoved Jax. "I liked it better when we were busting on Carter for Summer."

"Yeah, but picking on him now when he's all gooey like this is pointless. He doesn't even know we're making fun of him. You, on the other hand..."

Beckett wiped down the countertop. "Hold on. Let's talk about you for a second. If Joey would bother giving you the time of day, you'd be gooier than Carter. You've been back since June. Why the hell haven't you made a move on her?"

"You think I like sitting back, letting her ignore me?" Jax tossed his empty water bottle into the sink with enough force to have it ricocheting back out. "I'm taking Summer's advice. I'm giving Joey time to get used to me being back."

"You're taking love life advice from Summer Lentz?"

Jax shrugged. "What's wrong with that?"

"Look, I love Summer. But the woman refused to tell anyone she had cancer. Then she falls in love with Carter, and what does she do? She runs for the hills."

"Yeah, but she came back. She's happy now."

"Jax, Jax, Jax." Beckett shook his head. "You already had Joey, and then you ran away. Don't you think it's time for something besides sitting on your ass waiting for her to fall for you again? Is that how you'd write one of your screenplays?"

Jax frowned. "Don't take this the wrong way and get a huge, bloated head, but you may have a point."

"Pierces don't wait around and hope for the best. We get in the way, and we make sure we stay on their mind," Beckett said, poking his brother in the chest.

A slow grin spread across Jax's face. "We install dish-washers when they didn't ask for one."

Shit. He'd walked into that one.

"Shut up, Jax."

"You shut up. You set yourself up."

"Don't you have a woman to hide from or something?"

~

EYES CLOSED, Gia sighed blissfully and rested her head against the back of the couch. Her house actually *smelled* clean. And organized, too, if that was possible.

After dinner, she loaded the dishes into the newly installed dishwasher, packed the kids off to bed, and was now enjoying a second glass of wine and some exquisite quiet time.

She spent the afternoon purging and organizing. And when her bedroom was spotless—she'd had to secede some territory in the shed—she'd enjoyed herself in the kitchen making chicken panzanella for her family. She'd invited Beckett and Jax to stay for dinner but was relieved when they both declined.

She could use some space from Beckett, she decided. Her resolve wavered every time she looked into those deep, searching eyes of his. In fact, her desire to stick to her resolve was practically non-existent by this point. He was a good man. A kind-hearted one who was a protector and a provider by nature. Family was so important to him, and that was part of the attraction.

Gia had fired off an email to her sisters after Franklin and Phoebe left. She liked Phoebe. The woman was smart and sarcastic, full of energy. The way she paid attention to Evan and Aurora made them feel important and interesting. She never once flinched at Aurora's unending questions or Evan's pre-teen smirks.

Phoebe was a solid match for Franklin. They seemed comfortable, yet still flirtatious with each other. And it was great seeing her father so happy after so many years. He deserved this. Her sisters were going to get quite the detailed report this weekend. She hoped that Beckett would come around sooner rather than later. It didn't make sense to fight something that was so obviously good for both his mother and her father.

Gia took another deep breath and relished the fact that she didn't have to do anything in that particular moment. The house was clean, the dishes were done, groceries were bought, and she had a whole day off tomorrow to spend with the kids.

Life was starting to look pretty perfect.

18

It had been six long days since he'd seen her last. Sure, Beckett had caught glimpses of Gianna hustling the kids out the door in the morning and one night had the unfortunate timing to witness her shucking off her yoga clothes in her curtain-less bedroom.

That had been a long, sleepless night for him. To be honest, he'd been missing a lot of sleep lately thanks to Gianna. He was starting to wonder if avoiding her since he showed up unannounced with a kitchen appliance was making him think of her even more often.

He'd wanted to get some space, some perspective. Every time he was near her, his judgment clouded. He was distracted to the point that Ellery had suggested that perhaps he needed another vacation. The woman didn't just occupy his backyard. She occupied his mind. If he wasn't thinking about how much he wanted her, he was analyzing why he wanted her more than any other woman to date. And he'd been pretty damn excited about Moon Beam Parker at sixteen.

It felt unhealthy. He was used to dating and enjoying women who didn't run in an obsessive loop in his head all day, every day. But Gianna? She was on his mind on his morning run, in the shower, during conference calls. He'd even had a few colorful dreams about her that left him disappointed when he woke to find himself alone in bed.

He briefly considered confiding his confusion in his brothers but immediately rejected the idea. They'd only tell him to embrace the attraction... and then tease him mercilessly.

There were two choices. One, stay the course and leave Gianna as just a tenant and neighbor. Or two, explore the attraction that kept growing while risking it all. If it didn't work out, there were the kids, the town, and a year's lease to think about.

All weighed heavily on his mind.

Beckett was still pondering his options over the sink as he washed his lunch dishes when he caught a glimpse of Gianna walking from the driveway to her front porch. Even with her head down, he could tell she was crying.

He was out the back door before she even made it to her porch.

"What's wrong, Red?" he asked, climbing the steps behind her.

She hid her face as she dug through her bag looking for her keys. There was a definite nip in the October air that would transform to a real chill by the carnival that night.

"Nothing's wrong. I just can't find my key."

Beckett reached up to the porch rafter and slid the spare into his fingers. "Here."

Gianna finally looked up at him and frowned. "Where did you find that?"

"I had a spare made when you left your keys in my office. There's a spare for your studio, too."

"Do you think I'm some bumbling idiot who can't survive on her own?" She sniffed indignantly.

"No, Red. I think you spend all your time taking care of others, and you don't leave any room in that brain of yours for yourself. You feed the kids lunch and forget to have any yourself. You stay late after class to listen to a student who needs to talk and forget where you put your keys. You prioritize your day by what's important to you, and that's other people, not things like keys and lunch and probably your cell phone."

Gianna glanced down in her bag and frowned. "Shit."

"It's probably with your keys."

"Did you lock your studio?"

She winced. "I can't remember."

"Baby, this is Blue Moon. We could leave the bank vault open and send everyone out for lunch, and no one would think to walk in and help themselves."

She was tearing up again.

"Okay. Let's get you inside." Beckett took the key from her and let them in.

He put her bag on the floor by the door and pulled out a chair from her dining room table. "Come here, Red."

He sat and pulled her into his lap.

Sitting stiffly against him, she sniffled. "That was a really nice thing to say rather than calling me flighty and scatter-brained or stupid."

"Gianna, anyone who would call you stupid is a fucking idiot." He stroked a hand down her back.

She laughed.

"Now talk. What's wrong?"

As the tears came back, she sank into him. Beckett grabbed the tissue box off the table and handed it to her.

She buried her face in a tissue and took a shaky breath.

"It's mostly good. Mostly happy tears."

"Tell me."

She rested her head against his chest and hiccupped. "Evan's teacher emailed me at lunch. She said there's a new girl in his class who's been having a hard time at home, and today Evan brought her flowers and a homemade card to cheer her up. And then he and his friends invited her to sit with them at lunch."

She ended her explanation on something close to a wail.

Beckett continued to stroke her back. "That's very thoughtful and considerate."

Gianna nodded against his jacket. "You'd better check your mums. I think I have a feeling I know where he got the flowers."

Beckett chuckled.

"To know that the boy I'm raising has that much compassion and empathy is just incredible. He's going to grow up to be such a good man. Despite everything."

"It's not *despite* everything. It's *because* of how you're raising him," Beckett said softly.

"Just when I think I'm doing everything wrong and turning them into monsters, they go and do stuff like this. And just when they go all awesome on me, I fail them spectacularly."

"How did you fail?" He let his hand slide up to the back of her neck where he gently rubbed.

"Paul called. Said he's losing his job. Again. He asked if I could put Evan on my health insurance." Gianna hiccupped again.

"But because he's not your biological son..." Beckett filled in.

"Exactly. And even if he was, the premiums are astronomical. I need to think about a part-time job. The studio is too new to start pulling money out of it."

Beckett frowned. Gianna was the hardest working businesswoman and mom he knew. She didn't have enough hours in the day to do it all alone.

"What about your ex? Can't he contribute?"

Gianna wiped her eyes. "He's not exactly reliable. The support he's supposed to pay for the kids is either late or light. And now that he doesn't have a job, I don't see how I can count on him for help. Not that it even matters since Evan isn't technically mine. He should have been. I asked Paul about adopting him when we found out his mother died. But I just let it go when Paul said he'd look into it. So stupid."

"Now *that* I can help you with."

She dabbed at her eyes. "Really? How?"

"Do you think Paul would be open to making you Evan's legal guardian?"

She frowned, considering. "Would he have to give up his parental rights?"

Beckett shook his head. "A legal guardian is kind of an additional 'parent' in the eyes of the courts. It can be a tricky process, especially if the biological parents aren't open to the idea," he cautioned. "But it would allow you to put Evan on your insurance and make schooling and medical decisions for him."

Gianna perked up. "That sounds perfect! I can't see why Paul wouldn't go for it."

"Some parents aren't open to other people being legally responsible for their kids," Beckett warned. "Even though they still have rights, it can get sticky. And if he fights it, the courts often side with the biological parent. If he is on your side, it would make the whole process a lot easier."

"What do I have to do to start the guardianship process?"

"Talk to your ex first, and talk to Evan, too. Make sure he understands that his dad isn't just signing him over to you. Then come see me, and I'll get started with the paperwork."

She reached up and held his face in her hands. "Beckett, I don't know what to say. This would mean so much to me."

Her tear-stained face was doing something to his chest. Something painful. He shoved her head back down against his shoulder so he didn't have to look into those watery green eyes.

"Are you and the kids going to the Halloween carnival tonight?" he asked, changing the subject.

She nodded against him. "Will you be there?" Her fingers were toying with the lapel of his jacket.

He dropped his chin to the top of her head. "I'll be there. As mayor, it's my duty to judge the parade floats."

"Are you dressing up?"

He heard the smile in her voice.

"I am not."

"Party pooper. Aurora will be devastated."

"I take it that means you'll be in costume?"

"One cannot escort a doctor and a ninja to a carnival in regular everyday clothes," she told him.

They were quiet for a minute before Gianna spoke again. "Beckett?"

"Hmm?"

"Why am I sitting in your lap telling you why I was crying?"

"Because you like me."

She nodded. "I do like you."

He sighed heavily. "And I like you."

"Things are going to get complicated, aren't they?" Gianna asked.

"Very."

BECKETT HAD LEFT her with a kiss on the forehead and a head swirling with thoughts. He'd given her hope. For Evan and herself.

After he headed back to his house, she'd taken out her laptop and opened up the yoga studio financials. She was doing well, better than she'd hoped at this point. But, as she'd thought, it was still too soon to start pulling any extra cash out of the business. She'd find something part-time and flexible. It was important to her to be there for the kids as much as possible. So that left a few hours here and there during the week, at least until summer.

She would make it work.

"Aurora! Wait for me, please," she called. She'd gone old-school witch in a long sleeve black dress over spider web stockings and knee-high boots. It wasn't creative, but it was comfortable, and the cloak and pointed hat pulled the outfit together.

Her five-year-old ninja danced at the corner, swinging her orange pumpkin impatiently.

"Hurry, Mama! The parade."

"They won't start without us," Gia promised, shouldering Evan's backpack for his sleepover at a friend's that night and pulling Aurora's pony suitcase for her overnight with Grampa and Phoebe behind her.

A night without her kids. The prospect both excited and terrified her.

"I think Roar gets more excited about Halloween than Christmas," Evan commented through his surgical mask. The scrubs Gia had hemmed for him were smeared with fake blood, and he carried a plastic scalpel that looked more like a butcher knife than a surgical instrument.

Gia laughed. "It's the candy. If Christmas presents were made entirely out of sugar, she'd be more excited about it."

"The last thing that kid needs is more sugar," Evan shook his head sadly.

"Oh, like you aren't going to fill up on energy drinks and five-pound bags of sugar the minute my back is turned," Gia teased.

"Yeah, but I can handle my sugar. Roar just goes crazy and then passes out. Remember the wedding cake incident?"

"Who knew four pounds of cake could result in so much damage?" Gia shook her head. "At least the bride and groom will have the memory of a three-year-old spewing projectile vomit under their gift table forever."

"Just try to keep her away from any cake tonight," Evan warned. "I won't be around to help Grampa and Phoebe wrangle her."

"I'm picking you up at ten tomorrow, right?" Gia asked.

"Yeah. I left Lance's address, phone number, and his mom's name on a sticky note on the fridge."

"You're like the best twelve-year-old surgeon in the world." Gia sighed.

"They don't call me Dr. Awesome for nothing."

They trooped to the yoga studio where Gia stashed the backpack and suitcase inside. She planted the kids on the curb with bottles of water and enjoyed the show around them as the residents of Blue Moon converged on the street and square claiming their spots for the parade.

Her neighbors at McCafferty Farm Supply on the next street over had set up temporary grandstands for the parade judges. Gia could just make out Beckett in jeans and a gray wool coat helping to set up the judge's table.

"Mind if we join you?" Carter and Summer strolled up arm in arm, glowing with happiness in the falling dusk.

"Sure," Gia smiled. "We've got room for the four of you."

"Four?" Summer's hand flew to her belly. "Oh my God. I

was just getting used to being part of a two-some! Are we going to need a minivan, Carter?"

"And get rid of the Jeep? Serves me right for keeping expired condoms in my house," Carter quipped, shooting a belated glance in Evan and Aurora's direction.

Summer elbowed Carter in the gut. "Too much information, Pierce," she teased.

Gia laughed and ushered them to the curb where the kids greeted them enthusiastically. She bit her lip when she saw Evan slide just an inch closer to Summer. She guessed the baby and engagement news hadn't been much of a deterrent to the twelve-year-old.

"So, Gia," Carter began, slinging an arm around his fiancée. "Are you a good witch or a bad witch?"

"It depends on the day," Gia winked.

"Speaking of days, what are you guys doing for Thanksgiving?"

"I have no idea. Presumably eating too much," Gia said. She hadn't given the upcoming holidays much thought and realized that for the first time in too many years she would get to spend them with her father.

"We were hoping you'd spend the day with us," Summer said casually, but her sparkling eyes gave her away.

"Thanksgiving with the vegetarians?" Gia asked.

"Well, Thanksgiving and a wedding." Summer grinned.

"Are you serious? You're getting married on Thanksgiving?"

Summer giggled. "We want something small, but I want to still be able to wear a spectacular dress, which means the sooner the better," she said, patting her still-flat belly again.

"We would be thrilled to spend Thanksgiving with you. We've all got a lot to be thankful for this year," Gia said happily.

"Good, because now you can't say no to the next thing."

"What's the next thing?"

"I want you to be a bridesmaid," Summer stated firmly. "Now, I know what you're going to say," she said holding up a hand when Gia started to speak. "We haven't known each other long, but I like you more than any 'friends' I had in the city and you're practically family... Because of Franklin," she added, darting a glance at Carter.

"I don't know what to say," Gia told her. She was touched. She liked Summer and admired the life she and Carter were forging together. To be asked to be a part of it was sweet and exactly the kind of relationship she'd been looking to build here.

"Say yes," Summer urged. "Besides, with your hair and coloring, you'll look amazing in the bridesmaids dress I picked out."

"Well, when you put it that way, how can I say no?" Gia laughed.

"Perfect!" Summer winked and snuggled into Carter's side. "It's you and Joey for bridesmaids and Beckett and Jax are groomsmen. Beckett will be your escort."

19

*T*he parade was an undisputed hit. Gia especially enjoyed the showing of the Higgenworth Communal Alternative Education Day Care. Three- and four-year-olds dressed as farm animals ran amok on the street as their adult chaperones attempted to shoo them back into formation.

Next to her, Carter shuddered when the ringleader, a woman dressed in overalls and a straw hat, waved to him. He gave her a weak smile, and Gia swore the hand he raised to return the greeting was shaking.

"Remember your promise to me," Summer said through gritted teeth and a pained smile.

"Our children will never behave like that," Carter recited. "And if they do, we're going to drop them off at HCAEDC and run for our lives."

A little girl with pigtails and a rubber chicken beak paused mid-skip and vomited what looked like a dinner of cotton candy onto the asphalt. She wiped her mouth on her little sleeve and cheerily skipped on.

"Katie Bell," Carter and Summer sighed together.

The parade came to a spectacular end as the Blue Moon High School Marching Band playing "Monster Mash" ushered off the last float.

Gia's little crew marched across the street to the square where the smell of popcorn and fried pickles wafted. The park was done up in Halloween fashion. Orange lights were strung overhead and wrapped around tree trunks, and giant bushels of mums were clustered around park benches. Carved pumpkins entered in the contest were showcased on bales of hay. As she'd learned from the town meeting, the fake spider webs had been vetoed this year given the impossible cleanup they'd posed last year. The two dozen food and craft stands were decked out with orange and black bunting, and nearly everyone had donned festive costumes.

Evan dashed off with his friends, ten dollars, and strict instructions to meet her back at the studio in an hour so she could say goodbye before his sleepover. She valiantly tried not to imagine the number of preservatives and energy drinks he was going to enjoy until morning.

She and Summer were waiting in line for French fries when she felt a tingle zip through the space between her shoulder blades. Beckett.

He was talking to Carter who was on Aurora duty, at least until she twirled over to Beckett and wrapped her arms around his legs. Beckett hoisted her up, mindful of the plastic swords strapped to her back.

Gia felt her throat tighten a degree.

"The Pierce men are meant for fatherhood," Summer said, noting the direction of Gia's stare.

"Yeah, well, one of those men is going to find out sooner than the others," Gia teased.

"Only one?" Summer raised a perfectly groomed brow.

"Just what are you getting at, Cryptic Cindy?"

Summer shrugged daintily. "Oh, I just have a feeling. About you. And about Beckett."

Gia rolled her eyes. "You and the rest of Blue Moon. I hate to disappoint the hopes of an entire town, but I don't think I'm going to have time for any relationships, real or imagined."

"Business booming?"

"It's going well, but I ran into a surprise expense, and I'm going to have to take something on part-time—and hopefully very flexible—to get us through until the studio is making a bit more."

Summer's fingers gripped her arm. "Oh. My. God. Gia!"

"What? Are you okay?" Gia asked, panicked and expecting a medical emergency.

"I'm better than okay!" Summer released her death grip on Gia. "How are your writing skills?"

"Are you two in line?" An impatient Mrs. Nordeman dressed as Scarlet O'Hara in draperies peeked around them at the growing gap in the line.

"Sorry, Mrs. Nordeman." Summer offered her a bright smile. They stepped forward.

"My writing skills?" Gia asked.

"So today I landed a very large, very enthusiastic advertiser for *Thrive*," Summer began.

"Congratulations, Summer! That's fantastic."

She waved away her praise. "What this means is I'm looking for a very flexible, very part-time assistant editor. Preferably someone with a background in health and wellness." She looked pointedly at Gia.

"Are you offering me a job?" Gia squeaked.

"I'm offering if you're accepting. Oh my God, your education in plants means we could beef up the gardening content, too!" Summer clapped her hands together. "This is too perfect.

I'm thinking between ten and fifteen hours a week would do it, and we'll work around your schedule. What do you say?"

Gia felt shell-shocked. "This is the second time in one night you've given me an offer I can't refuse."

Summer grabbed her in a tight hug. "Thank you, thank you, thank you," she chanted.

"I should be thanking you," Gia gasped as the oxygen was squeezed out of her by Summer's surprisingly strong grip. "You have no idea what this means to me and my family."

"Hey, you girls want fries?" the man behind the stand barked.

Mrs. Nordeman grumbled past them in her full skirt to order.

"Sorry, Mrs. Nordeman," Summer and Gia said.

When they finally returned bearing greasy dishes of fries, Carter demanded to know what all the fuss in line had been about. "What's with all the jumping and hugging?"

"Don't tell me you're *that* big a fan of French fries," Beckett said, fishing one out of Gia's vinegar-sodden dish.

"Gentlemen, and Aurora, say hello to my new assistant editor," Summer announced, waving expansively at Gia.

"Hello, Mama," Aurora chirped.

"We're going to need another desk," Summer winked at Carter.

"I'd better get building," he said, stroking a hand through his fiancée's glossy hair. "Hey, how do the twins feel about milkshakes?"

"I like milkshakes," Aurora said, tugging on his hand. "Ninjas love milkshakes, right, Bucket?"

Beckett grinned at her. "They sure do, shortcake. And I bet if you give Carter that sad face of yours, he'd invite you along to the milkshake stand."

Aurora spun around to face Carter, her sweet face morphing into wide-eyed, lip-trembling devastation.

"What the hell is that?" Carter asked in horror, picking her up.

"Mama, Carter said 'hell.'" Aurora said in a loud whisper, her faux sadness forgotten in the thrill of a tale to tell.

"Jesus," Carter said, rubbing his free hand over his heart.

"See what you have to look forward to?" Gia said sweetly.

Beckett grinned.

Summer covered her belly with her hand. "Please don't be two girls," she whispered.

"What do you say, Rora? Want to come with Summer and me and get a milkshake?" Carter asked.

Aurora nodded earnestly and stroked her little hands through Carter's beard. "Yes, please."

"Mama, is it okay with you?" Summer winked at Gia.

"Sure, just please don't let her order a large. I'll catch up with you after the fried cauliflower stand."

Gia sighed as she watched her little girl dance off between Summer and Carter holding their hands.

"What are they going to do with two of them?" Beckett asked.

"Never sleep again?" She turned to face him. "You know, we probably shouldn't be seen alone together in front of the entire town," she reminded him.

"I'm just a mayor having a friendly conversation with a witchy constituent." His gray gaze was warm on her face. "I like your costume. Very fitting."

Gia glanced down.

"Thank you. This is my standard Friday night outfit. I'm curious about your costume. What are you, exactly?"

"I'm a man trying to hide his attraction to a very sexy

witch." He reached out and fingered the tassled tie of her cloak. "I don't understand it," he murmured.

"Don't understand what?"

"Why I find you so irresistible."

"Beckett!" His name crossed her lips on a hiss. "Your logic is the only thing saving us from a mistake right now. I need you to resist."

"What about your logic? Your resistance?" His voice was low, skirting toward dangerous.

"They both disappeared when you brought me a fairy garden."

He took a step closer. "Don't say things like that."

Gia's gaze darted around. Was it her imagination, or did everyone in line for cotton candy have their cell phones pointed in their direction?

She grabbed his arm and dragged him off the sidewalk and behind one of the giant oaks that stretched toward the twilight heavens.

Out of the lights, away from the prying eyes, she decided to put it all out there. "Beckett, I need to be clear. I'm very, very attracted to you." Her gaze skimmed down his body and back up again. "Very," she said again.

"The feeling is mutual," he said, bringing his warm hands to her hips.

"But I have two kids. I can't just have a fling any more than I can jump into a relationship."

"I know that, Gianna. They're great kids. I don't want to jeopardize anything for them or for you. But I can't get you out of my head."

"So what are you suggesting?" She let him pull her a little closer, let her hands slide under his jacket.

"I don't know." She could hear the frustration in his tone.

His fingers dug into her flesh with it. "I guess, curtains for one."

"Curtains?"

"You need some curtains for your bedroom. I spend way too much time staring out of my windows into yours. It's creepy. I feel like a stalker. And you don't have curtains, and I can't look away."

Gia knew she should be mortified. But the heat that swept through her wasn't embarrassment.

"You're so unbelievably beautiful. You just pull me in, and I'm powerless to fight it. I don't want to fight it. I want to know what it's like to be with you, in you."

His lips were a breath away, and her legs went boneless.

"Tonight." She whispered it, unsure if he heard it over the pounding of the blood through her veins.

"Tonight what?" His grip tightened on her.

"Be with me tonight," she breathed. "And then we'll see... Maybe once it's out of our systems, a set of curtains will be the answer."

"And if curtains aren't the answer?" He asked the question she was most afraid of, the one she already knew the answer to.

"If they aren't, then we'll find the answer. Together."

His hands moved to her arms, gripped until her skin stung. "What about Evan and Aurora? We can't just have a sleepover. They'll be scarred for life if they had to listen to all the things I want to do with you."

She could see the fire in his gaze. Desire warred with trepidation. He cared about her kids, and that was the most important thing. That was the only thing. She smiled and brought a hand to his face.

"They're the ones having sleepovers. Your mom and my

dad are taking Aurora for the night, and Evan is staying over at a friend's house."

"Tonight?" He said the word with hope and fear.

"Tonight."

"Are you sure?"

Gia nodded. "No."

"Your head is saying yes, but your mouth is saying no."

"Maybe you can change my mouth's mind?" she whispered, brushing against his lower lip.

Beckett groaned and pulled back an inch. "Gianna, I want this so badly. But only if you're sure. There's a lot at stake."

"I really like you, Beckett. If you're a mistake, I have a feeling you're going to be my favorite one." She ran her hands through his hair, tugging him down until her lips met his.

20
---

*B*eckett let them in the front door of his house. He took his coat from her shoulders and hung it in the foyer closet.

Gia clasped her hands in front of her and tried to smooth out her breathing. Her nerves were spiraling out of control inside her. She had told him she'd meet him here, but he'd waited for her outside the studio until the kids were packed off and goodbyes said. She'd wanted the quiet of a solitary walk, maybe she would have taken a few moments at home to check her makeup, give herself a pep talk.

But here she was. In Beckett's foyer, trying to not have a heart attack.

"Do you want a glass of wine?" he asked. His voice was soft, low.

She surprised them both by shaking her head. "I want you."

His reaction was swift, instantaneous. He crossed to her and buried his hands in her hair. Beckett's mouth captured hers in a demanding blaze of need.

She whimpered against his lips and dove into the fire after

him. Her fingers dug into his shoulders. Her back met the front door with an unceremonious thump, and she yelped.

"Sorry," he whispered against her mouth, stealing her breath. But he didn't move back an inch. She was sandwiched between the door and the unyielding weight of his body, and she wanted more.

His hands chased her curves, and Gia melted under his touch. She felt him, achingly hard, against her stomach. He groaned when she slipped a hand between their bodies to touch him through his jeans.

"Wait, wait," he commanded when she opened the button of his pants.

He grabbed her hand and stilled it. "Just wait," he said, his breath ragged. "Birth control?" he asked.

"Pill. We're good," she assured him. When she rose up on her toes to take his mouth again, he gripped her shoulders.

"Wait," he said again. His hand held her firmly against the door. "I've thought about this for... a long time. I don't want to just rip your clothes off in the foyer."

"What do you have in mind?" Gia said, her chest rising on short sharp gasps of air.

"Give me five minutes, okay?"

"I live with kids," Gia reminded him. "I don't care if you have dirty underwear on the floor."

He grinned. That quick, charming smile that went to her gut like a shot of whiskey. "Stay here. Don't move." Beckett took the stairs two at a time.

As soon as he was out of sight, Gia brought her hands to her flushed face. She took several deep breaths to steady herself. She and Beckett Pierce were going to...

It had been so long for her. What if she'd forgotten what to do? What if the sex was terrible?

She immediately shook that fear from her head. If the

kisses were that devastating, sex was guaranteed to be better than good. She brought her fingers to lips swollen from his kisses. Way better.

"Gianna?" Beckett appeared at the top of the stairs.

She climbed the stairs, taking her time, her gaze never leaving his face. She wanted to commit this moment to memory. Her choice to go to him, the anticipation of all that was to come. She saw want and need in his eyes and something else that simmered just beneath the surface.

He held out his hand, and she laid her palm in his.

"Mine."

She thought she heard him whisper the word but dismissed it when she realized she couldn't hear anything over the thudding of her heart in her chest.

Gia was shaking with nerves, with need, with anticipation. In her head, there was only room for the now. No doubts, no to-do list, no responsibilities. There was only Beckett. Only her.

He drew her down the hall to the front of the house and the empty bedroom she'd visited once before. The bookcase was ajar, light flickering from beyond.

"Beckett," she breathed as he led her inside.

There were gas sconces built into the wall that she hadn't noticed in the dark. They were lit now and joined by a dozen candles that flickered on stairs.

He brushed her hair away from her neck and over her shoulder. "I've thought of you here like this since that night."

Her eyes fluttered closed as his lips fed on the flesh under her jaw. "I bet I wasn't dressed as a witch in your fantasies."

"You'd be surprised," he said darkly.

He worshipped her with his hands, stroking and caressing, sending shivers of need down her spine. She gave herself over to the tidal wave of sensations. His fingers tugged at the tie that fastened her cloak. It fell from her shoulders in a fluid swoop, puddling on the floor between them.

Beckett abandoned her neck and sank to his knees. His hands trekked down her body lower and lower, refusing to miss an inch of flesh. When those warm palms reached her knees, they traveled back up swiftly, drawing her dress with them. Beckett's lips blazed a trail north.

Gia raised her arms overhead and let him pull the material from her body. He tossed the dress behind them and slowly turned her to face him. His shaky inhalation made her grateful she'd sprung for the spider web thigh highs. They added a little drama to the simple black bra and briefs she wore.

"Were you hoping for the pink thong?" she teased, her voice breathless.

"Next time." His whisper was a promise.

She reached for him, but Beckett intercepted her hands. "Wait. Just let me look," he breathed. "You are stunning. You are more than beautiful, Gianna."

His words, like his hands, had her weak in the knees and trembling. She felt the prickle of tears in her eyes and didn't know why.

He pulled her to him, rough palms skimming skin. His breath was warm on her face. Gia looked up at him, into him. She could see them, the thin, tight wires of control that he held on to so desperately. She could feel the tension in him, humming beneath her hands.

"Are you sure about this?" Gia asked him.

Beckett's laugh was strained. "I'm the one who's supposed to ask you that." His thumb grazed her full lower lip.

Gia nibbled at the flesh. "Oh, I'm sure. I just don't want to be a regret to you."

He dropped his forehead to hers. "My only regret is waiting this long."

"I haven't even known you a month yet," she said, her tongue darting out to taste him.

The noise in his chest was something between a groan and a growl. Primal, dangerous.

"Too long," he told her. "Be with me, Gianna."

"I'm yours."

Their mouths met in a furious eruption of desire and power, each wanting to consume. The battle waged, and Gia felt herself losing ground. She was too vulnerable, too raw.

Her fingers struggled with the buttons of his shirt, fumbling them free until he shed the fabric from his shoulders. Her hands flew to his jeans, freeing him from the confines of denim. She felt him strain against the soft cotton of his underwear. He groaned against her mouth when she boldly stroked over his thick erection. A tiny damp spot on the fabric told her exactly how much he wanted this, wanted her.

Their breath came in pants now. Beckett hastily toed off his shoes and stepped out of his pants, never breaking contact with her mouth. But when Gia slid her hand in the waistband of his briefs, he stopped her.

"If you touch me now, this is going to be over too fast," he murmured against her bruised lips. "Trust me?"

Heavy-eyed, she nodded. She didn't know what he planned to do, didn't care as long as his hands were on her.

Beckett spun them around until her back was to the wall. Using his hand, he cuffed her wrists overhead. He pressed his knee between her legs until she opened her thighs for him. His knee met the wall behind her ensuring she couldn't close on him.

Exposed and at his mercy, Gia felt the flutter of nerves.

His free hand skimmed down, leaving a trail of fire to the

front clasp of her bra. He paused, only for the span of a heart-beat, before deftly releasing her breasts from their lace-bound prison.

He sighed, the hot cloud of his breath tickled her neck and sent a shiver down her spine. His hand paused on her ribs, just under her breast. "I want you so badly, I'm almost afraid to touch you. Afraid I won't survive." His lips murmured the words over her jaw and lower to where her pulse fluttered frantically.

Gia felt her legs give, thankful that he kept her from falling. He was seducing her, methodically, absolutely. She wasn't prepared to defend against it. She couldn't protect her heart from the imprint of the words he uttered or her body from the branding of his hands. In this moment, she was his.

He brought his lips to hers once more, his palm sliding over the heavy curve of her breast to cup it. Gia gasped against him, and he used the opportunity to deepen the kiss.

He released her mouth in a bid to taste more. Her hands flexed against their restraint, but he held firm. He cradled her breast and brought his lips within an inch of her sensitive peak. Her nipple strained toward his hot breath, and a cry tore from her throat as he finally took it in his mouth.

She wanted to fight the sensations that swamped her, rocking her equilibrium. But she could only whimper as he latched on and drank her in. His hand slid down across her stomach until his fingertips toyed with the waistband of her underwear.

Gia reflexively tried to close her legs and only succeeded in squeezing his thigh between hers.

Beckett released her breast and straightened. His fingers slid beneath the black cotton, smoothing over her soft folds. Gia let her head drop back against the wall. Her eyes fluttered as he parted her lips slick with desire but didn't close. They couldn't. Not with Beckett's gaze piercing her as his fingers did, sliding in and up.

Gia's hips flexed against him, and he obliged her, withdrawing his fingers slowly before thrusting them back into her center. Again and again, harder, deeper. She was falling now. Falling into the waves that threatened to carry her away, but she still couldn't close her eyes.

The stormy gray of Beckett's gaze held her where she was. Anchored her as the waves crashed over her, in her. She came in the storm, lightning electrifying her body, her muscles quivering around his fingers.

"My God, Beckett." Her breath came in shallow bids for oxygen.

He released her arms from their restraint, and they tumbled to his shoulders. "Hold on to me," he ordered.

Gia did her best to wrap her shaking arms around him as he lifted her up, his hands cupping her. He used a hand to wrench his cock free and yank her underwear to the side. The broad crest of his penis nestled at her entrance, and Gia gasped.

She cupped his face in her hands. "I want to see you—" The words were wrenched from her when Beckett thrust into her—triumph burning in those smoke-gray eyes—impaling her against the wall. The thinnest slice of pain wove its way around the pleasure she felt from finally being stretched full. She had to adjust her legs around his waist before she could fully accommodate his length.

But there was no time to adjust because Beckett had lost himself to a rhythm as old as time. Taken over by need and greed, his body dictated a wild pace.

Her nipples grazed his chest with every thrust, heightening their sensitivity to epic proportions. Already her delicate muscles inside were starting to tremor. The wall bit into her back as he rammed into her again, but she didn't care. Gia wanted more. Everything that he had to offer, she wanted.

Holding her with one arm, he brought his free hand to cup her other breast, tugging her nipple with strong, insistent pulls that drove her mad.

She gasped out his name and exploded around him violently. He slowed his thrusts by degrees to match the ripples of her orgasm, letting her core milk him while she shattered.

He rode out her climax before carefully lowering her to the floor. Gia's legs couldn't hold her, so he carried her to the stairs.

He gently turned her away from him and down until she was kneeling on a tread.

"Are you okay with this?" he asked, kneeling behind her and stroking her hair.

She glanced over her shoulder. His face was tight with need. His erection stood at attention just behind her. "God, yes," Gia whispered. She planted her hands on the step in front of her and braced her knees apart. "Please, Beckett."

He guided his cock between her legs and ran it over and around her opening. "This is what I wanted to do to you that night," he whispered. "This is what I've fantasized about every night since."

He entered her slowly with aching precision. A low growl rumbled in him as Gia wiggled her hips to allow the last inch of him to slide in. His hands gripped her hips to control the pace. "Gianna." He slowly withdrew inch by inch.

She moaned as he filled her again, this time faster. He had to be desperate for release, she thought, but Beckett held back with smooth, measured thrusts. His size left her aching as he filled her and then again with emptiness when he left her.

She wrapped her hands around the spindles of the staircase and leaned a little lower. Beckett's hands came to her breasts, cupping them gently. It was here, with her hardened peaks grazing his palms with each thrust that he began to lose control.

He grunted softly when she shifted her hips back against him and again when he felt her start to tighten around him. He brought one hand to her hair, fisting in the wild wonder of it. His other hand left her breast and slid between her legs.

"Again, Red."

She didn't think she could. There was nothing left to give, was there?

But as she felt him get impossibly harder, as he began to grunt on every thrust her body gave her answer, she realized there was more. So much more.

Beckett's hips flexed violently as he came, releasing his seed into her with a shout. "Gianna!"

His orgasm sent her over the edge once more, ripping a climax from her as he arched against her. Once. Twice. Three times. "Mine. Mine. Mine," he whispered as he filled her with his release.

---

21

*B*eckett wondered briefly if he was dead and then decided he didn't care. It had been worth it. He'd never felt anything like it. The possession that choked him when he made Gianna come, the wrenching release of his own orgasm.

He was afraid he'd just had a religious experience. With a witch. In a secret passage.

He shifted to bury his face in Gianna's hair. Maybe she was a witch? A spell had obviously been cast. She had bewitched him. It was the only explanation for what had just happened.

"Can you breathe?" he asked, nuzzling her.

"Mm."

"I can't tell if that means I'm smothering you or you just can't form words yet."

"No words," she mumbled, snuggling back against him.

Beckett brushed her hair out of her face and fanned it out over the stairs. "Is that better?"

"My ears are ringing," she sighed, finally opening her eyes. "I think it's from me screaming your name."

He grinned. She had shouted his name as they came together.

"I still feel the need to ask you if that was okay." He brought her hand to his mouth and kissed her fingers one at a time. "I think I got a little rough, and I didn't mean to."

She smiled smugly. "Better than okay. I think all the cells in my body are singing... or weeping with joy."

Beckett felt a quick wash of relief. He'd lost control, let go. He'd never done that with a woman before. Gianna's words at yoga came back to him. She'd accused him of being too in control, afraid of falling. If this was falling, he wanted to do it again.

"I think we need to get off these stairs," he decided.

"Okay," Gianna sighed. "Which one of us is carrying the other one back downstairs?"

"Why downstairs?" Beckett asked, envisioning the soft expanse of his bed.

"That's where your kitchen is, and I need you to feed me."

A quick detour to his closet yielded a pair of pajama pants for himself and a t-shirt for her, and together they staggered down the stairs to the kitchen.

Gianna ducked her head into his refrigerator while he rummaged through the pantry. Beckett wrestled a box of Frankenstein-shaped macaroni and cheese from the back of a shelf. It must have been Ellery's. He hoped she wouldn't mind donating it to the cause.

"How about this?" he asked holding up the box.

Gianna grinned. "It'll go perfectly with these." She held up a bowl of raspberries and a bag of sliced cucumber.

"You have an interesting post-sex appetite," he told her, pulling a pan out of the cabinet and filling it with water.

Gianna tossed him a saucy look and began plating the berries and cucumbers in a rainbow across the plates. "The handful of French fries I nervously inhaled did not sustain me," she told him.

"Nervously?" Beckett looked up from the simmering water.

Gianna hopped up to sit on the island. "You weren't nervous?" She poked him with her foot.

"I'm a man. Men don't get nervous. We get focused on whether or not we will be able to provide appropriate amounts of reciprocal pleasure."

She rolled her eyes in a way he found utterly sexy. "You are such an attorney."

He stepped between her legs. His hands skimmed under the t-shirt to pull her closer. "And you are so irresistible." He nibbled along the line of her neck until he felt goose bumps rise on her skin. "Why were you nervous?"

Her eyes were still closed, and she angled her jaw to give him better access. "Because I was afraid you wouldn't be any good at it." She sighed.

Beckett's teeth sank down. Hard.

She yelped.

"Not funny, Red."

She was laughing now, and it sounded like music.

He shoved a cucumber slice in her mouth. "Enjoy your snack. It looks like we're not going to eat for a while." With that, he turned off the stove, tossed her over his shoulder, and marched upstairs, smacking her once soundly on the bare flesh of her ass when she struggled.

Gianna bounced when he pitched her on to the bed and he fully expected her to jump back up. But instead, she rose up on her knees and beckoned him with a finger. A siren's song couldn't have had a more immediate effect. He found himself painfully hard and diving across the mattress to her and those sea-witch eyes that called to him.

Beckett met her in the middle on his knees with a kiss

meant to brand her. She was his for tonight. And he belonged to her. They tangled and tumbled, rolling over the expanse of sheets sending pillows and clothing flying to the floor.

He wanted—no—he craved her with an ache that hollowed him out. *This wasn't how it was supposed to be*, he thought, as his mouth cruised over her shoulder and then lower to feed.

She fell back on to the mattress, hair fanning out like wildfire. Beckett used the opportunity to gain the upper hand. When his mouth closed over a taut nipple, her fingers closed around his shaft. She stroked him with something that skirted the ragged edge of violence and almost sent him tumbling over that cliff.

A last lap of his tongue and then he was sliding down her body, out of her grasp. He tasted his way down her taut stomach and around the lush curve of her hip. Her breath was coming in gasps, and Beckett wanted to push her further.

He nibbled the delicate flesh of her inner thigh and was rewarded with her gasp when he ventured higher. There, Gianna's fiery core welcomed him home. He used his palms to spread her thighs, leaving her bared to him. She trembled against him, her thighs fighting his grip.

"Hang on, baby," Beckett whispered. His tongue dove into her slick folds, teasing and tasting. She bowed back, hips pumping with frantic energy. Her response frayed his control, and when she moaned his name, Beckett felt his cock go impossibly harder.

He paused just long enough to stretch two fingers into her tight channel. She was sobbing out his name now. His tongue found that most sensitive bundle of nerves and, with a single stroke, sent her hurtling off into the darkness.

Her fingers locked in his hair, and her hips bucked wildly as she rode out the orgasm. Gianna had barely started breathing again when Beckett ranged himself over her. Her eyes fluttered open, misty green and dazed. "We're not even close to done, sweetheart." He made the promise as he buried himself in her. Fully sheathed in her heat, Beckett saw stars and fought to restrain himself.

Gianna's fingernails dug into his shoulders, and he held himself perfectly still for a heartbeat and then another. When her gaze—wide and hungry—met his, he began to move. He wanted to give her everything. Everything that was inside of him, locked up under layers of restraint and control.

He didn't see her next move coming. Gianna used those strong, perfect legs of hers to lever him onto his side. They rolled, still joined until she gained the top. She stared down at him triumphantly and began to ride.

She set a reckless pace, and Beckett understood her goal then. He wasn't going to give her everything. Gianna was going to take it.

His hands found her hips and gripped as she rode. His jaw clenched, teeth bared, he tensed for the raging battle. He wouldn't lose. He couldn't lose. Gianna brought a hand to the base of his throat and held lightly just over his thundering pulse.

He stared into the face of the woman who had bewitched his body and quite possibly his soul. Her color was high, and as she leaned forward to capture his lips, her hair tumbled over them in a curtain of fire.

"My Gianna," Beckett heard himself whisper against her mouth.

She rose up again, a flawless goddess with her milky smooth arms reaching for the sky. She didn't stop moving, bowing back, back, back until Beckett thanked God for yoga.

His hips took over the impossible pace, thrusting again and again until it didn't matter who came first. That first quickening, a tightness in her, was more than he could handle. He couldn't hold back the orgasm that churned for release. And the second he spilled inside her, Gianna's own climax echoed until they became one.

Seared to the soul, Beckett gathered her to him and buried his face in her hair. Their hearts beat together, too fast and a little unsteady. Gianna was everything: brave, beautiful, bewitching.

GIANNA WOKE to sunshine and the delicious heat of the perfect male form next to her. And partially on top of her. She was locked in the cage of Beckett's arms and had absolutely zero desire to escape.

She kept her eyes closed, but her lips curved in a feline smile of satisfaction.

"Good morning, gorgeous," Beckett murmured against her ear.

"Mmm. Good morning," she said, rolling in his arms to face him. "How did you know I was awake?"

"I saw you smirking." His finger traced her full, rosy lips.

She bit his finger lightly. "I wasn't smirking. I was basking in the many, many orgasms of last night."

Beckett forced a frown. "Many, many? I feel like you're missing a many."

She felt him hard against her thigh and moved to cuddle his erection to her. "Beckett, darling, if you don't feed me immediately—and make it the biggest breakfast either of us has ever seen—I'm going to faint from hunger and forget all about those many, many, *many* orgasms."

"And after breakfast?"

"I'm picking up my children from their respective sleepovers and trying not to look guilty and smug for the rest of the day."

Beckett lifted his head and squinted at the clock on the side table. "If I cook fast and we eat fast, we could still manage a very *friendly* shower before you leave." He nibbled her neck and earlobe.

"You forget. I've seen the inside of your refrigerator, and it's sadly lacking in breakfast carbs," Gia teased. "Why don't we sneak out the back door, and I'll make you breakfast at my place, and we can shower there with all of my nice shampoos and shower gels."

"I think I could be convinced."

They laughed and stumbled their way from Beckett's back door to Gia's front in a state of undress that would have scandalized all of Blue Moon, the rainbow of fallen leaves providing a colorful carpet for their bare feet as they scurried over the frost-scarred grass.

She made him pancakes in the sunny little kitchen while he started coffee and poured juice. They ate and laughed at her kitchen table, seeking touches or kisses between bites.

She sighed contentedly after Beckett fed her a piece of bacon. The only thing that would have made life more perfect at that moment is if Evan and Aurora were at the table eating and arguing. But the timing for that little fantasy needed to wait. She and Beckett weren't in a relationship, no matter how tied to him she felt with a shiny chain of orgasms and sweet feelings.

And no relationship meant no public declarations of affection. No family breakfasts, no sleepovers.

Gia glanced at the clock and sighed. "Our window is almost closed."

Beckett took their plates into the kitchen, rinsed them, and stacked them neatly in the dishwasher.

"I think we've got just enough time for a shower," he said with a smoldering look.

Beckett Pierce stood in all his shirtless glory in her kitchen after loading the dishwasher, and Gia knew she was a goner. There was no way she was going to come out of this unscathed, and somehow she just didn't care.

She stood up, a wicked sparkle in her eye. She had no idea how the two of them would fit in the tiny tub, but they would find a way and she could put her hands on him one more time. "Race you upstairs?"

He grinned, a heartbreaker of a smile.

Gia's phone rang on the table. She hesitated for just a second, debating, before answering it.

"Hi, Dad. How did everything go last night?" She watched Beckett cross his arms and lean against the counter.

"Everything was great," her father assured her. "Aurora had almost as good a time as Phoebe and I did. We were calling to see if you wanted to pick up Evan and join us for brunch."

"Brunch?" Gia repeated.

Beckett hung his head in mostly mock disappointment.

"Brunch sounds great. I'll go get Evan now."

"Phoebe suggested seeing if Beckett's available to join us since you're neighbors and all," Franklin said. Gia could hear Aurora's giggle in the background.

"I'll see if Beckett's around and hungry," she said.

"You just ate three pancakes," Beckett pointed out when she hung up.

"I can't not go. I have to pick up Rora, and if I don't eat, they're going to get suspicious."

"Suspicious of what? That you already had breakfast?"

Gia went to him and laid her head on his chest. Her fingers

trailed over the ridges of his abs. "Want to come with me? You're invited."

He stilled her fingers with his hand. "Red, you see what's happening with just a little touch." He brought her hand to his barely contained erection. "If you look at me the wrong way across the breakfast table, everyone's going to get an X-rated show. I'm not going to be able to keep my hands off of you. They're going to take one look at us and know."

"Know what?" Gia whispered, her hand sliding under the waistband of his pajama pants.

His inhale was a hiss when her fingers closed around his thick shaft.

"That we spent all night naked, wrapped around each other?" Her hand stroked up from the root to the crown. Beckett's knuckles went white on the countertop.

"We don't have time for another round, Red," he groaned.

"You know, a lot can be accomplished in five minutes," Gia said, slyly freeing him from his pants.

His eyes closed on a growl as her ripe lips encircled the crown of his cock and she proceeded to show him exactly how much could be accomplished.

22

*B*eckett whistled his way into the office on Monday morning with two steaming mugs of coffee. "Good morning," he said, greeting Ellery.

It was a beautiful fall morning with just the slightest chill in the air demarking the arrival of sweater weather. The leaves were at their peak of color painted in bright reds and golds against the denim sky. He'd found himself hopping out of bed with a smile on his face that remained fixed there during his six-mile run before a shower, shave, and work.

"Morning," she said, eyeing him suspiciously.

Today she was decked out in a relatively sedate black sweater and skirt with what he affectionately referred to as her Frankenstein shoes. Her black tights had an argyle skull pattern with crystals for the eyes.

"How was your weekend?" he asked, settling in the chair in front of her desk.

"Just dandy. How about yours? You look like you won the lottery." She took a sip of coffee and leaned forward.

Beckett knew he was grinning like an idiot. He had been all weekend long. And he hadn't seen Gianna since they parted Saturday morning with rug-burned knees and sore, well-used bodies.

He'd still been grinning like a fool Sunday when he'd checked in on the farm. His brothers had accused him of glowing like Summer. Their concern grew when he agreed to check out a house with his mother later that week.

He played it off as being refreshed from vacation until they were only mildly suspicious and escaped the brewery after helping set up the rest of the equipment before they could interrogate him further.

After this weekend, he was certain of two things. One, he was nowhere near done with Gianna Decker. And two, he didn't want to drag her through the unflinching Blue Moon spotlight, which also included his family. Until he and Gianna figured out what they were and where they were going, it was no one else's business.

"My weekend was good. Quiet. Got some work done." He felt his lips curving into a smile again. People were going to think he had developed a drug habit on vacation if he couldn't regain control of his facial muscles. "So what's on the agenda for this week," he asked gruffly.

Ellery was still eyeing him as if he had started casually shaving his head. Temporarily putting aside her suspicions, she began to run through the schedule.

"And then today I squeezed Gia into your schedule before lunch. She wants to talk about a legal guardianship."

Beckett caught himself before he appeared too interested. But the flicker in Ellery's coffee brown eyes told him he hadn't been careful enough. He wiped the smile off his face and frowned intently. "Okay, that's fine. I'm going to go catch up on some emails before Mrs. Eustace comes in at nine."

He was already reaching for his cell phone and didn't see Ellery's smirk.

He fired off a quick text to Gianna.

Beckett: I see I have a beautiful redhead on my calendar today.

Her response was immediate.

Gia: Hope you don't mind. It's not an excuse to see you. Or, at least, not just an excuse to see you.

Beckett: My door is always open. Literally. I never lock the back door. Anytime you want to sneak on over here I'd be happy to see you. Naked or clothed.

Gianna responded with a winky face that had him grinning like a damn clown. He needed to pull it together and before the entire town thought he lost his mind.

He counted down the seconds to 11:30 and was already halfway out of his chair when he saw her glide across the porch outside his window. Beckett had to force himself to sit back down and not hurdle his desk in his hurry to see her.

He waited until he heard Gianna and Ellery chit-chatting before casually exiting his office.

She wore cement-colored capris with a dizzying pattern. Whatever strappy tank top she wore was hidden under a fitted, zipped jacket. Her hair was up in a sloppy knot on top of her head. She smiled at him as if he were the sun and she an exotic bloom.

"Good morning." Her voice was a little husky and full of energy.

"Morning," he answered.

They both stood there grinning at each other until Ellery cleared her throat. "Can I get you something to drink, Gia?" she offered.

"Oh, uh, sure. Coffee?"

"No problem," Ellery smiled. "I'll bring it in. Sugar?"

Gianna couldn't seem to take her eyes off Beckett, and he liked it. "Yes, please."

Beckett waited until Ellery headed for the kitchen before pulling Gia into his office. "Kiss me quick before she comes back," he ordered.

Gia melted against him, her lips finding his in a spicy sizzle of heat.

He pulled back and studied her face. "I thought about you all weekend," he told her.

She smiled, slow and sweet, and took a chair in front of his desk. "You may have crossed my mind a time or seven thousand, too."

"We didn't really get to talk... after." Beckett rounded his desk and sat down.

Ellery bustled in with a mug. "Here you go," she said, setting it down in front of Gia. "Anything else I can get you?"

"I think we're good," Beckett said. "But do you have the draft—"

"Of the motion? It's in your email."

Beckett glanced at his computer screen. "Perfect. And how about the—"

"Summary on Yeskovik vs. Yeskovik is done, but I found another more obscure case. Same custody issue, same outcome. So I'm adding that to the summary this afternoon."

"Great. I also need to have the Yukon inspected and an oil change. Can you—"

"You're on Ernest's schedule for Thursday at 1:30. He said half-price since you helped his mom with the family trust."

"You're the best, El."

She waved pistol fingers at them on her way out and shut the doors behind her.

"Where can I get one of those?" Gia demanded the second the doors were closed.

"Ellery? Hands off. She's mine. I can't live without her."

"I can see why," Gianna sighed. "She'd make life so much easier."

Beckett grinned at her.

"What?"

"Nothing. I just like having you here. In my office. Alone."

"Beckett Pierce," Gianna teased. "Are you flirting with your client?"

"A. Since this is a consultation, you're not technically a client yet. B. Since our—" he paused and glanced over his shoulder before continuing in an exaggerated whisper. "Sexual relationship began before you were a client, I'm not being unethical. And C. Yes, I am."

Gianna's smile lit up her face. "In that case, after we're done consulting, I was wondering if you'd care to join me for lunch. At my house. Clothing optional."

Beckett was glad he was sitting behind a desk so Gia couldn't see his immediate and very noticeable physical reaction. "I think that sounds do-able."

"Great, then let's get this consulting nonsense over with so I can take your pants off."

Beckett blinked. His mouth was open, but no noise came out.

Gianna was grinning at him in his visitors chair. "Unless of course, you'd like to test out how sturdy your desk is now and then consult later?"

"You're evil. You stay on your side of the desk, and I'll stay on mine for the next fifteen minutes."

She pouted, and Beckett wanted to bite her bottom lip. "Behave yourself, Red," he warned.

"Fine," she sighed with an exaggerated eye roll. "Go ahead and consult me."

"Did you talk to your ex-husband about legal guardianship?"

She leaned forward and grabbed the coffee. "I did. He seems to be in favor of it."

"Seems to be?"

"It's hard to get Paul to focus on the details, but he seemed enthusiastic about any solution that would free him of the burden of health insurance."

"Okay. We'll get started, but I do want you to try to make him understand all the implications. You don't want him thinking that you're taking his son from him *or* that this means he's free from obligations such as child support and visitation."

Gianna nodded. "I'll make sure he understands."

"Good. Then I'll start the paperwork. We'll file a Petition for Appointment of Guardian in family court. Paul will need to give his consent, which will make the process less complicated. Then there will be a court hearing."

Gianna blanched. "A hearing?"

"It's much less scary than it sounds. In a case like this, the judge will likely review the filing and ask you and Paul why Evan should be with you before approving the guardianship."

"Evan won't have to testify, will he?" Gianna asked wide-eyed.

Beckett shook his head. "Since Evan's under fourteen, the judge won't ask for what they call 'informed consent.' And as long as you and his father are in agreement, it should go smoothly."

Gianna nodded. "Okay. Then let's get started."

"We'll get the papers drawn up this week."

"So that leaves the issue of payment," she said, pulling her checkbook out of her jacket pocket.

"Actually, I was wondering if you'd be willing to work out a trade?"

Her eyes narrowed. "Exactly what kind of a trade?"

"Mind out of the gutter, Red. Ellery's birthday is next month, and I've been racking my brain for a gift. She loves your studio. Would you be willing to trade, say, six months of classes?"

"Of course. As long as it's an equitable trade. I don't want you doing me any special favors here. Evan's mine, and I'd pay anything to make sure he has what he needs."

"Understood. And the only special favor here is you're saving me from mangling wrapping paper."

"As long as that's the case and you're not trying to cut your secret lover a special deal in return for secret lover favors."

"Those favors will remain completely separate from our attorney-client relationship."

A smile bloomed on her pretty face. "Good. Thank you for your help, Beckett. It means a lot to me that you're willing to help my family."

"Just doing my lawyerly, landlordy duty."

She cocked her head to the side. "Who knew?"

"Who knew what?"

"That goodness was such a turn on."

GIA STRETCHED like a cat and then flopped back down on her mattress. Beckett was face down, his arm anchoring her to his side. "Well that sure beats a mid-afternoon cup of coffee," she sighed, snuggling in.

The afternoon light filtered through the windows of her

bedroom. New gauzy sheers that she still neglected to close at night hung from the corners of the room.

The house was blissfully quiet, and her heart rate had returned to normal after two adrenaline-spiking orgasms.

Beckett nuzzled her hair. "What kind of shampoo do you use?" he sighed. "I like it."

"It's a fancy organic kind you can only get online."

"It smells like a rainforest."

Gia lightly trailed her fingers down his back. "You, Mr. Pierce, are a fine specimen." She pinched his very firm butt cheek.

He grunted and flexed under her hand, teasing a laugh from her.

"Baby, don't you think we should talk?"

"Are you talking to me or the pillow," Gia asked.

Beckett rolled them both to the side and tugged her hips back against his. He was already hard again, and Gia wondered if he had a genetic mutation that had him walking around with an erection all day every day.

Whatever it was, she thought as he guided his shaft between her legs, she was profoundly grateful for it.

He positioned himself against her entrance and slowly, inch by inch, eased inside her.

She sighed out her breath as he filled her. The angle didn't allow for deep penetration, but it was enough to have her blood singing again. She moaned softly.

"Now, let's talk," Beckett said, whispering in her ear.

"Now?" she gasped as his hand traveled north to cup her breast.

"Now," he said, his hips moving slowly, steadily.

"What do you want to talk about?" The words came out strangled.

"Us."

"Beckett, you can't seriously be trying to have a... conversation." Her sentence ended in a gasp.

He nuzzled her neck and continued his onslaught on her senses. "What are we doing?" he asked, nibbling at her ear.

Gia tilted her head to give him better access to her neck. "Making love," she whispered.

"And what are we?" His breath was hot on her throat.

She paused, lost in sensation. She waited too long, and he pinched her sensitive peak.

"What are we?" he asked her again.

Her gaze focused on the fairy garden she kept on her nightstand. *Home* and *Family* stared back at her. "Lovers." She sighed out the word.

The growl low in his throat told her he liked her answer.

"Is that enough?" he asked, quickening his pace ever so slightly.

For now, she thought. "Yes. Please, Beckett," she begged.

His hand slid from her breast across her belly to nestle between her thighs where he teased her to her end. As she began to come, she sobbed out his name and felt her release force his.

They lay in silence for several minutes, Beckett's lips softly murmuring words too quiet to hear.

"Why do you call me Gianna?" she asked, finally breaking the silence.

She could feel his lips curve against her. "It's your name, isn't it?"

"Yes, but everyone else calls me Gia." She rolled over in his arms to face him.

"I'm not everyone else. And Gianna is a beautiful name. You're a beautiful woman." He circled the silk of her throat with his hand. "Bewitching. Sexy. Breathtaking." He kissed her with each word.

"I like when you say my name," she confessed. "Especially when you're shouting it."

He had the face of a heartbreaker, and Gia knew she was already in danger.

"I like hearing all the things you shout out when I'm inside you." His grin was devastating.

"This whole 'get each other out of our systems' thing doesn't seem to be working too well so far," Gia said, threading her fingers through his hair.

"I guess we'll just have to keep trying," he said before bringing his mouth to hers.

23

*G*ia opened the back door to her little hatchback, and Aurora, having freed herself from the bonds of the car seat, hopped out. "Come on, Mama! Ponies!"

Evan was already out and heading toward the barn, his hands in the pockets of his jeans. His quick pace ruined the casual disinterest he was going for as he hustled over the gravel.

Joey and Carter had invited the kids over for an informal riding lesson while Gia and Summer spent a few hours in the newly finished office talking magazine details.

Joey appeared in the doorway of the barn and lifted a hand in greeting. Gia watched in amusement as Evan ambled up to her and scuffed his sneakers in the dirt while they chatted.

Gia and Aurora caught up just as Carter ambled out of the barn. "Hi!" Aurora said, greeting them as she skipped from one foot to the other. "I get to ride Princess today, right?"

"That's right," Joey said, hands on hips. "But first we're going to get some helmets and go over some basic safety."

"Basic safety," Aurora repeated, fluttering her arms and spinning in a circle.

"You sure about this?" Gia asked Joey.

"Don't worry, I've read all about how to give horseback lessons online. It'll be fine. Now, someone just remind me which end is the front again?" Joey quipped.

"Smarty pants," Gia said.

Carter ranged himself against the barn door. "Looks like we got more company," he said, nodding at the sleek muscle car that rumbled to a stop next to Gia's little red hatchback.

Gia caught Joey's frown as Jax slid out from behind the wheel.

"This is a closed lesson," she snipped at him.

"I'm not here for a lesson. Canon been out yet?"

Joey shrugged a shoulder. "Not yet."

"Good." Jax brushed past her into the stable. The look Joey shot him would have felled a lesser man. But Jax ignored it and stalked inside.

Gia felt herself break into a sweat at the heat pumping off them. If anything were to spontaneously combust, it would be Jax and Joey. Someday.

Carter was grinning until Joey elbowed him in the ribs. His breath whooshed out of him, and Aurora giggled.

"Oh, you think that's funny, pipsqueak?" He grabbed her and tossed the giggling girl over his shoulder.

"Watch out, she's a puker," Evan warned.

Carter carefully sat Aurora back on her feet.

"Again, Car! Please?" she begged.

"When did you last eat?" he asked her.

"Just over an hour ago. You're probably out of the projectile zone," Gia reassured him.

They watched as Jax thundered across the riding ring on a black thoroughbred. Gia held her breath as they approached a four-foot jump. The horse cleared it cleanly without a hitch in his stride and galloped off through the open pasture gate.

"Whoa," Evan whispered.

"Are you sure you don't want me to stay?" Gia offered to Joey.

Joey stared holes in the back of Jax's shirt until he and Canon disappeared over a ridge. She shook her head grimly. "I got this."

Gia reluctantly left her children in Carter's and Joey's hands after Carter promised to text her pictures and wandered back to the farm.

She found Summer on the second floor of the barn. The office was done, finished by Calvin's team with a few Pierce touches. Everything was white and bright. The new windows on either end of the floor let in a flood of natural light. The long wall across from the stairs was done entirely in white shiplap. The wide-plank floor, replete with decades of scars, had been sanded down and stained light.

Summer, in a cozy cowl neck sweater and leggings, sat behind a desk of reclaimed wood angled out from the corner to get a good look out the large window. Bookcases in white wood were built in over the shiplap and a large flat screen TV hung in front of a long, counter-height table of the same wood as Summer's desk. Instead of chairs, six bar stools with graceful metal legs surrounded the table.

"Oh, good! You're here," Summer said by way of a greeting. "What do you think of the layout for the website?"

She clicked a button, and the TV screen on the wall lit up.

Gia moved closer to examine it.

She could hear Summer's pen tapping a frantic beat on her desk.

The design was clean, light. Large stock photos representing features rotated in and out on the home screen.

The navigation menu reminded Gia of the colorful chalk-board menus in coffee shops and juice bars.

She turned, grinned. "It's perfect. The whole thing says healthy and happy in a really clean way. What are you doing about photography?"

Summer drummed a slower beat on her desk. "My friend and brilliant photographer Niko is coming in for the wedding, and I'm hoping to abscond his services for a day or two and convince him to contribute. I've got most of the January features nailed down, and some of those will need freelancer art. The rest we can pay for stock art."

"How can I help?" Gia asked.

"I wanted to talk to you about a thirty-day yoga challenge idea."

"Are you thinking about releasing it in one big chunk, one pose at a time, or amp up the difficulty as the month wears on?"

Summer pointed her pen at Gia. "I knew I was a genius when I hired you! I like the amping up the difficulty as the month goes on. Why don't you take a stab at it, and we'll look at it next week? Then we can have Niko shoot you when he's here. Stills and video, I think."

"Shoot *me*? Wouldn't it be better with a model?"

Summer leveled her gaze at her. "Gia, where are we going to find a model who's as good at yoga as you are? You are the expert. Plus, you're gorgeous."

Gia fanned herself. "Fine, twist my arm with compliments. I'll start with a handful of basic poses, and then as it progresses, I'll add more to it. Modifications, holding the poses longer, adding in more difficult postures. And then at the end we can have a full class that readers can watch online."

Summer nodded. "I love it. I think that's perfect. Moving on!"

She stood up and herded Gia toward another workstation. "This is yours," she said. "Given your boundless energy, Carter designed it to go from normal height to standing."

"You guys made me a desk?" Gia clasped her hands together over her heart.

"I may be a horrible boss, but I wouldn't make you work on the floor," Summer teased. "Now listen, you already have a Thrive email account set up, and I've sent you all the drafts for the features that are done. I need you to give the piece on family-based new year's resolutions an extra good look because these hormones have me sobbing every time in the first paragraph."

"Aye, aye, Captain," Gia said, giving her a mock salute.

"And when you're done with that, I need some ideas for health-ish features for February and March. And help yourself to coffee and water," she said, pointing at the counter and cabinets on the far wall.

Gia settled herself at the wide expanse of varnished wood and went to work.

For two hours, she focused on the article drafts first while making notes on ideas for future pieces. Summer took and made several calls, including one to her friend Niko.

Gia's phone signaled and she opened the pictures Carter sent her. Aurora, in a pink helmet, grinning from the back of a white and gray pony that Joey led around the ring. Then Evan looking so serious while he walked around the ring on a larger bay.

They were growing up so fast. Gia sighed. She remembered the six-year-old little boy who had introduced her to his teddy bear when she met him. And it was hard to reconcile the squalling infant with the little redhead who now feared nothing.

Family. It was the heart and soul of everything. And here in Blue Moon, her family was thriving.

Summer pushed her chair away from her desk and stretched. "Okay, enough sitting." She glanced at the clock on the wall. "Want to walk over to the stables? And then we can find lunch. Lots and lots of lunch."

"Babies hungry?" Gia laughed, packing up her notes and slipping them into her bag.

"Starving. All the time," Summer rolled her eyes.

"Good because I brought massive quantities of eggplant parm with us," Gia told her.

Summer shot her fist into the air. "Yes! And we have about a gallon of vegetable soup left. Let's haul ass to the stables and forcibly drag everyone back to the house for lunch."

Gia reached into her bag and pulled out a granola bar. "How about a snack for the road?"

She snatched it out of her hand. "Bless you. Bless you!"

Summer snacked while they headed around the barn on the beaten dirt path toward the stables. "Oh, hey, listen," Summer said with a mouthful of almond butter and craisins. "The dresses are done and ready for fittings. Can you go with us next weekend?"

"Oh, um. I'd have to see about the kids," she said. Guilt crept in. She already had Carter and Joey watching them today. And her father and Phoebe had taken Aurora last weekend. Not to mention that she depended on Evan to watch Aurora on Tuesday and Thursday evenings. They were her kids, her responsibility.

They started up the slow incline toward the stables.

"It'll be you, me, Joey, Phoebe, and my mom. I'll be trying on my wedding dress, too," Summer chattered excitedly. "I figured we could leave after your morning classes and have lunch, of course."

There was no way Gia could drag Evan and Aurora to a dress appointment. They would wreak havoc on the store. She winced, imagining Aurora exploding a grape juice box on a dozen pristine, white dresses.

She spotted Beckett's SUV outside the barn and felt a rush as her pulse quickened.

"I'm nervous about the fitting. The dress is just incredible, and Sashi's worked out this ingenious way to hide the bump that hopefully won't be huge by Thanksgiving. A week after the wedding, I'm allowed to look gigantic. I've had a talk with the kids, and they promised to stay hidden so it won't look like a shotgun wedding."

"It sounds like a lot of fun. I'm just not sure I can leave the kids. Saturdays are really busy for my dad at the restaurant, and he already took one off this month to help me..." She trailed off as Summer's face fell.

"I understand," Summer told her.

"Understand what?" Beckett strolled out of the stables, looking gorgeous as always in jeans and a zip-up sweater.

Gia forced herself not to lick her lips.

"Summer invited me along on the dress fitting trip next weekend," Gia answered.

"And Gia can't go," Summer interjected.

"Why not?" Beckett asked, sliding his hands into his pockets. His gaze was warm on Gia's face.

"I've got the kids," she said lamely.

"I'll watch them," Beckett said with a shrug of his broad shoulders. "Next Saturday?" he asked Summer.

Summer nodded enthusiastically. "Yep! We'd leave after Gia's yoga class. No wonder you're my favorite soon-to-be brother-in-law."

Beckett winked and pulled out his phone. "Sure. I don't have anything on the calendar that day."

"Hold on. Beckett, I can't ask you to watch Evan and Aurora for me," Gia began.

"Summer, do you mind if I take our friend Gianna here for a walk and talk some sense into her?" Beckett smiled winningly at Summer.

She grinned up at him. "I think I'll just wander in and find my handsome baby daddy and leave you two to hash out the details." She winked at Gia. "See you in a minute."

Gia crossed her arms as Summer scurried into the stables.

"What was that all about?" she demanded.

"That's exactly what I was going to ask you," Beckett said. He slung an arm over her shoulder and guided her along the fence line of the riding ring. "Don't you trust me with Evan and Aurora?"

Gia stumbled. "Of course I do. Don't be ridiculous."

"Don't you want to go?" He was rubbing her upper arm through her thin sweater, his touch distracting her.

"It's not that. I'd love to go with them. It's just, the kids," she said lamely.

"The kids that I'm volunteering to watch that you said you trust me with."

"Beckett, I can't ask you to do that. They're my responsibility." She could feel herself getting upset. Frustration rising up from her belly.

"Red. Stop." He turned her to face him and held her in place by the shoulders. "You don't have to do it all on your own anymore."

"What are you talking about?" She frowned up at his handsome face and tried not to notice the softness in his eyes.

"It's been just you and those kids for a long time. Having someone help out every once in a while doesn't hurt anyone.

Having other people you can lean on doesn't make you weak or dependent."

He'd hit the nail on the head, she realized. She was so used to being the only responsible parent that she didn't know how to let go.

"Most parents share the responsibilities with a partner. And the really lucky ones have extended family they can rely on," Beckett continued. "You now have an extended family of about two thousand people plus me."

Gia glanced over her shoulder to make sure they didn't have an audience. "As my secret lover, I don't expect you to take over childcare duties."

"As your friend, I'd love to watch the kids. They crack me up. If it makes you feel better, I'll bring them over here and let them have the run of the farm for the day."

She knew the kids would love it.

"I just feel like I'm passing them off to everyone these days. Both kids had sleepovers last weekend. They're hanging out with Carter and Joey right now. Evan watches Aurora for me two nights a week because of yoga. And I feel like I'm pawning them off."

"Red, how long have you lived here?"

She shrugged. "Six weeks?"

"And you feel like a sleepover, a riding lesson, and you teaching two evening classes a week is pawning them off?"

She nodded and bit her lip.

"Gianna."

"I know. It sounds stupid to me, too," Gia said, covering her face with her hands.

"Imagine how stupid it would sound if you turned me down and stayed home doing laundry Saturday with the kids instead of being there when Summer tries on her wedding dress."

"I bet juries eat right out of your hand, don't they?"

Beckett grinned. "I go in for the kill with logic, style, and charm. And if that doesn't work, I yell a lot. Don't make me yell, Gianna."

"Are you really, really sure you want to watch them? They can be a handful. Well, Evan can be quiet and pouty. Aurora can be a nuclear disaster."

"I want to. I'll bring them out here, we'll ride horses, play with the pigs, I'll let them do a tasting at the brewery..."

"Okay," Gia sighed.

"Okay?"

"Okay to everything except the beer tasting. I get to sample before they do."

"Good girl. Now, go tell Summer that you'll be happy to join her Saturday."

Gia looked over her shoulder again and, spotting no one, rose up on her tiptoes to kiss Beckett on the cheek. "You're the best secret lover and friend a girl could ask for."

24

$\mathcal{T}$he week hustled by in a blur of kids' school activities, busy yoga classes, and the as-often-as-possible morning or afternoon tryst with Beckett.

Her work with Summer was going well, and she was starting to feel a sense of ownership in the magazine. Between her business, Summer's business, and Beckett's… "business," she fell into bed exhausted and smiling every night.

She had started a load of laundry the other evening, and her heart had taken a hard stumble when she peeked outside to find Beckett throwing a football with Evan in the yard. She and Aurora had joined in until the evening chill had chased them all inside. Beckett worked through an algebra problem with Evan while Gia made her father's famous homemade hot chocolate. They all enjoyed steaming mugs—with Aurora's 'smarsh-smellos'—before she sent the kids up to bed.

She and Beckett had then enjoyed several steaming kisses before she sent him home.

It had been blissfully… normal. And she had more than a fleeting moment of wishing that it could be real life for them all. In the dark of that cool autumn night, lying in bed staring at her little fairy garden, she let herself wonder what it would be like to have Beckett as part of her family.

What it would be like to fall asleep in his arms every night. What it would be like to touch him whenever she wanted, like she wanted to do now as he hefted Aurora up on his hip in Carter's foyer.

Dress fitting day had arrived. Beckett and his brothers had unanimously dubbed it Man Day with a little side of five-year-old girl. Their plans included pizza and wings for lunch, video games, and whatever would tire Aurora out the fastest.

"You're sure you don't mind?" Gia asked, brow furrowed as Beckett tossed Aurora over his shoulder. Her little girl giggled so hard Gia was afraid she'd throw up her breakfast.

"Gianna. Go," Beckett said, jerking his chin toward the door.

"Bye, Mama!" Aurora shrieked with glee as Beckett jostled her.

Beckett met her gaze for one solid, searing second in which she knew exactly what he was thinking. He wanted her, wanted to kiss her goodbye. But they could only share a look as Jax jogged down the hallway.

"Did someone say they wanted to eat lollipops for lunch and play video games all day?" he asked.

Aurora reached for him. "Me! I do! I do!"

Beckett tossed the little girl to his brother and sent Gia a slow wink. "Have a good time today." He turned and sauntered after his brother.

"They have no idea what they're getting into," Gia said to Evan.

"Don't worry, Gia. There's three of them," Evan said, patting her arm. "It'll take her a little while before she wears them all out."

"Just promise me one thing," she said, laying a hand on

her son's shoulder. "Send me pictures if she talks them into a tea party."

Evan patted the pocket with his phone. "I'm on it."

A horn honked outside. "Okay, I'd better go. Good luck." She dropped a kiss on Evan's head. "Call me if anything catastrophic happens."

"Blood that requires stitches or a fire that requires professional intervention," he said, reciting their family definition of the word.

Sandwiched between Joey and Phoebe in the back of Summer's new SUV, Gia let herself fret about Beckett and the kids on the ride. Summer's mother, Annette, rode shotgun. She had a tall, slim build and wore her blonde hair short with a stylish side sweep. Her blue eyes caught Gia's in the rearview mirror.

"Don't worry, Gia. They're three grown men. They can handle her," she said.

"The only thing you should be concerned about is if 'dumbass' becomes part of her vocabulary after spending the day with my sons," Phoebe said, patting her arm.

"I don't know why I'm so worried," Gia sighed. But that was a lie. It wasn't that she didn't think the Pierces could handle her little fiery ball of energy. It was that she was afraid that after spending a day as primary caregiver, Beckett would start to reconsider his feelings for her.

She was a package deal. And she needed Beckett to be okay with that.

~

THE DRESS SHOP was an hour outside the city. Summer had worked with the owner, Sashi, before on a piece on custom gowns and had fallen in love with the woman's breathtaking handiwork.

Summer insisted that Joey and Gia try on the bridesmaids dress first to make sure they approved.

Eggplant in color, the full-length chiffon skirt floated rather than hung. Subtle beading woven throughout the layers caught the light here and there. The fitted bodice dipped just low enough to be interesting without being racy, and the open back took the entire dress to another level.

"Oh my God, Joey. This dress is amazing," Gia said, stroking the fabric with her palm.

She heard Joey's dressing room door open and then the whisper soft rustle of chiffon. "Yeah, I guess it's okay."

Gia opened her door. Joey was turning this way and that in the three-way mirror.

"Holy freaking crap, Joey. You look incredible."

She'd released her rich, coffee-toned hair from its tail, leaving it in soft waves framing her face and shoulders. The top fit her like a second skin, highlighting her subtle curves and slim, strong shoulders.

Joey turned around again and frowned. "It's not bad."

"Joey. Jax is going to have an aneurysm when he sees you in that dress."

The corners of her full lips turned up just a little, and Gia caught a distinct sparkle in her warm, brown eyes.

"Well, let's get out there and show off so we can go to lunch," Joey said with a nod. She turned around and studied Gia.

"You look good," she said with a nod. "Beckett's going to shit bricks."

They hustled out of the dressing area to the front where Summer, Phoebe, and Annette waited. Phoebe and Annette had flutes of champagne.

"Oh!" Summer said, bringing her hands to her cheeks. "You two look amazing! *Please* tell me you like the dress. I know you'll never be able to wear it again. I'm not the delusional bride who promises that. And Gia, we'll have yours hemmed. But it's just so perfect for both of you. Do you like it?"

"Summer, its stunning," Gia said. "You couldn't have picked a more beautiful dress."

"Or more beautiful bridesmaids," Summer reminded them. "What do you think, Joey?"

"It's purple. Very purple," Joey said, studying herself in the mirror. "But I do have a concern."

Summer's face fell by a degree. "What's that?"

"Your dress had better be kick-ass or we're going to outshine the hell out of you."

Luckily, Summer's dress did kick ass. She had chosen the full organza skirt from one dress and combined it with the scalloped lace cup bodice of another. To join the two pieces—and camouflage the baby bump that would be evident in another month—Sashi deftly wrapped a wide piece of organza around and around Summer's waist, tucking it here, tufting it there.

With quick hands, she pinned it into place and took a step back. "What do you think?" she asked, shoving a hand through her thick fringe of bangs.

Summer toyed nervously with one of the delicate spaghetti straps. Her cheeks were flushed.

"I think it's…"

She turned around to face them. Her circle of women, her friends and mother. Gia's fingers flew to her mouth.

"What do you think?" she asked them.

Summer's mother answered first, with silent tears. "Perfect. You're absolutely perfect," she sighed.

"Oh, now there I go, too," Phoebe sniffled, digging through her bag for a tissue.

"You look gorgeous, Summer," Gia told her. "It's exactly right."

Eyes damp, Joey chugged her champagne and nodded briskly. "No one's going to outshine you."

Summer wiped briskly at her own tears. "I'm so happy." She ran the hand wearing her engagement ring over her belly. "So very happy."

"Would you like to see Summer in a veil?" Sashi offered, doling out tissues as if they were cookies.

"Yes!" they all answered.

While Sashi and Summer debated mantillas and head-pieces, Gia's phone signaled a text message from Evan. Drying her eyes, she opened it.

"Oh my God."

≈

Beckett sucked in his cheeks and made a fish face.

"Like here?" Jax said, shoving a fluffy makeup brush in the hollow of his cheek.

"No, dumbass. On the cheekbones." Beckett moved the brush higher.

"What color should I put on his eyes, Roar?" Jax asked.

Aurora looked up from the sparkly clips she was adding to Carter's beard. "Um," she tapped a little finger to her chin. "How about ba-loo?"

"Blue it is," Jax said, smearing blue eye shadow on his finger and reaching for Beckett's face.

"Not like dat, Jazz!" Aurora—her lime green sparkly eye shadow spread across her face like a mask—hopped off Carter's lap and hurried over. She chose a brush that looked like it was meant to apply paint and dragged it through the blue shadow. "Close your eyes, Bucket."

He obliged and felt the feather light pressure of the brush coating his eyes, temples, and part of his forehead.

"Dere! Now you're perfect." She sighed and patted his face happily.

"Thanks, shortcake. How does Jax look?"

She turned to study his brother. "Good." She nodded. "I gotta finish Car's hair and den we can take selfies."

"Selfies?" Jax asked, swallowing hard.

"Yeah, wiv your phone."

"What are you worried about?" Beckett asked. "I gave you a really classic look. You could totally pass for a chick with that cat eye and lip stuff."

"How do you even know what a cat eye is?" Jax demanded, crowding Beckett at the makeup mirror Aurora had found upstairs.

"It's just something you pick up when you date women. And judging by my face, you've only dated blind drag queens."

Jax smirked. "I was going for something a little more abstract."

"Evan!" Carter called from his chair at the table as Aurora tried valiantly to secure his beard with hair ties. "Please tell me your sister takes an afternoon n-a-p."

Evan's head popped up from the couch where he was in a life and death battle as a knight on Carter's big screen. "She will if you gave her enough s-u-g-a-r."

All eyes skimmed to a small pile of empty juice boxes and Twinkie wrappers. "Yeah, that should be good," Evan said, returning his attention to his video game.

"Hey, shortcake. How about we put in your movie so you can watch it while we teach your brother to play poker?"

Evan's head shot up again. "Poker? Seriously? Cool!" He turned off the game and wandered over to the table.

"Not yet, Bucket!" Aurora said, dancing over to him and wrapping her arms around his neck. "Mwah!" She kissed him loudly on the cheek and skipped back to Carter's beard.

"Oh, boy. You're a goner," Carter sighed.

"How could I not be?"

"She's not getting tired yet," Jax pointed out as Aurora danced from one foot to the other humming and twisting Carter's facial hair into a tail.

"I've got a plan."

"You want to lock her in with Dixie and Hamlet?" Carter suggested.

"No! I'm not suggesting we lock her in a paddock with two pigs. What kind of a human being would do that?"

Carter shot Jax a guilty look.

"They were from HCAEDC; they don't count as human children," Jax argued.

Carter shivered. "That one got me by the beard and tried to rip it out."

"Dat's not nice, Car!" Aurora gasped, gently patting his beard. She added a sparkly butterfly clip to it."

"Now do you see why I don't come out here and help on daycare tour day?" Beckett asked.

"Anyway, what's your brilliant idea here? If this goes on much longer, we're the ones who are going to be napping," Carter grumbled.

"We're gonna run the hill," Beckett announced.

Jax groaned. "I haven't done that since we were all in fall sports in middle school."

Carter laughed, remembering. "Dad told us running up to the ridge and back down would make us better athletes."

"Pretty sure he did it just to get us out of the house before Mom could murder us," Beckett recalled.

"That was years ago. Are we even physically capable of this?" Jax asked.

"We'll take turns," Beckett decided.

"It's worth a try," Carter said as Aurora spun in a circle flapping her arms.

"Hey, shortcake, want to run up a big hill outside?" Beckett asked.

"Yeah!" She darted out the side door before any of them were able to get to their feet.

BECKETT WAS bent over trying to catch his breath and not puke when his phone signaled in his pocket.

Beckett spit in the grass and prayed his lunch of pizza and hot wings would stay down.

A text from Gianna.

Gia: Everything going okay?

"I'm winning, Jazz," Aurora squealed, and she hurtled down the hill as fast as her little legs would carry her. Jax gave up running and lay down on the hillside. It was a long, slow grassy rise if you were on horseback or walking. But running? It felt like the last quarter mile of the marathon. And after a heavy, greasy lunch, it was probably the worst thing they could have done.

Aurora had successfully made the climb nine times so far. Thankfully Evan had taken pity on them and entered the rotation.

Carter was laying on his back in the grass, muttering something about "two of them."

Jax rolled the last few feet down the slope stopping at Beckett's shoes. "Your turn," he groaned.

"I gotta answer this..." he waved the phone over Jax's face. "Evan! You're up"

"I really expected more from you guys," the kid said, shaking his head sadly.

"I'll pay you five bucks," Beckett offered.

"Deal." Evan took off with Aurora hot on his heels.

"Oh, shit!"

Beckett swiveled when he heard the panic in Jax's voice.

Clementine, Carter's pet goat and Jax's full-time nemesis, loomed over his prone brother.

"Get away from me, hell spawn," Jax said, his feet scrambling for purchase on the grass.

Clementine bleated and shook her head, brown ears flopping in the fall sunshine.

"Did you see that?" Jax yelled. "She just said 'no.'"

Clementine bleated again and pranced closer. Jax rolled over, trying to crawl away, but the goat was faster. With a four-footed jump, she landed next to Jax and went in for the kill.

Her little goat mouth closed over the flannel of his shirt. "Get her off of me!" Jax yelled, trying to push Clementine away.

"Hang on," Beckett said, opening the camera on his phone. "Okay, just hold it right there... and... perfect."

He looked at Carter who was rolling on the ground laughing.

"Should we help?" Beckett asked.

"Yes, you should fucking help," Jax shouted at the top of his lungs, shoving Clementine's face away. Her mouth took a hunk of fabric with it.

"Hey, there's kids present. You can't use language like that," Carter lectured.

"I'm going to f—"

"Uh-uh. Watch your mouth," Beckett reminded him, switching to video.

"I'm going to freaking kill you guys," Jax growled, rolling onto all fours before regaining his feet. "And I'm going to kill you too and cook up a nice goat stew," he said, reaching for Clementine who danced out of his grip, happily munching flannel.

"She ate my shirt," Jax said in disbelief, staring at the sleeves that bunched at his wrists, the back cleanly ripped open.

Clementine meandered toward the kids.

"Uh, Carter? Is she going to eat us?" Evan asked, ranging himself between the approaching goat and Aurora.

"She's fine. She only hates Jax," Carter called, getting to his feet and going to supervise the impromptu petting zoo.

Beckett followed, just to be sure Clementine didn't suddenly develop a taste for the flesh of children.

As predicted, the goat flicked her ears and tail, charming pats from Aurora and Evan.

"She's so funny, Bucket," Aurora told him, her little hand patting the goat's neck.

"Yeah, she's hilarious," Beckett agreed. "What do you say, shortcake? Are you ready for a snack and a movie?"

Her face lit up and she raised her arms. "Can we watch *Monkeys and Pandas*?"

He picked her up and swung her around onto his back. "Sure, kiddo. Come on, Jax. If you stop whining, I'll buy you a beer out of Carter's fridge."

With Aurora cozied up in front of the TV, the men took

turns washing the makeup off their faces before gathering around the kitchen table for a poker lesson.

Beckett took the opportunity to sit down and respond to Gia's text.

Beckett: Aurora's on her second beer, Evan's playing with firearms, and Jax just got his shirt ripped off by a goat. Totally under control.

She answered quickly.

Gia: Oh good. We passed a fire truck a few miles out, and I was worried the kids burnt down Carter's house already.

Beckett: False alarm. We got to it with extinguishers first.

Gia: My hero.

Beckett: How goes the dress shopping?

Her response had him shifting in his chair as his blood threatened to migrate.

Gia: Summer picked out some really classy pasties with tassels and hot pants with rhinestone crotches for the bridesmaids.

Beckett: Can't wait to see you in it. Gotta go teach Evan how to build explosives.

Gia: Great. BTW, blue is definitely your color. It really brings out the gray in your eyes. You look breathtaking.

"Evan!" Beckett shouted. "Get over here so I can murder you!"

~

"Now remember," Summer whispered as she pushed open the front door. "Not a word to Carter about the dress, got it?"

Gia and Joey nodded earnestly while Annette and Phoebe crossed their hearts.

"Our lips are sealed," Gia promised.

"Thank you ladies so much for coming with me today," Summer said. "It meant the world to me."

"Sweetheart, we wouldn't have missed it," her mother said, grasping her hand. "Your father is going to get a little choked up when he sees you on the big day."

Gia left them to commiserate in the hallway and headed back to the kitchen. It was quiet in the house. Too quiet. There should have been yelling, possibly some crying, or at the very least a few shrieks of laughter.

She found the kitchen empty, but the TV in the great room was lit up with cartoon pandas parading about. That's when she heard the first snore.

Tiptoeing in, she spotted Jax first on the end of the couch, his feet on the coffee table. Evan was sandwiched between him and Carter, his feet on Jax's lap and his head resting on a pillow jammed up against Carter's side.

Beckett was sprawled out on the other couch with Aurora asleep on his chest. She felt something warm and bright open in her heart. She bit her lip.

"Well, if that isn't the sweetest thing..." Phoebe whispered at Gia's side.

Grinning, the two women dug for their cell phones as quietly as they could.

25

---

*B*eckett's lunch on Tuesday magically freed up when the property he visited with his mother turned out to be a bust.

"We're never going to find a place," Phoebe lamented in the car after they left the rundown ranch with mirrored living room walls.

"How many properties have you looked at?" Beckett asked, gripping the handle above his door as his mother accelerated up to a stop sign. She wasn't a bad driver per se, but she was a city driver. Heavy-footed on the gas and the brake, she took some getting used to. She'd often wondered why all three of her boys got carsick when she drove but not when John was behind the wheel.

"Fourteen," his mother sighed. She shook her head and sent her brown bob bouncing. "They're either too big, too small, too expensive, or too ugly. I'm not looking for a fixer upper at this stage in life. We want a comfortable place with room for grandkids."

"You'd better hurry up. You'll have two in no time," Beckett warned, closing his eyes as his mother stomped on the gas.

"Four," Phoebe chirped. "Evan and Aurora are on that list."

Beckett waded through the feeling that statement conjured. Moving in together and sharing grandkids meant that marriage was right around the corner for his mother and Franklin. And while he was doing his best to tolerate Phoebe dating, he worried that marriage would push him over the edge.

He was trying. He would continue to try. It kept the peace not only with his mother but also Gianna.

"That Gia has done an incredible job with those kids," Phoebe said, speeding through a yellow light.

"Yeah, she's great," Beckett agreed. He cracked his window just a little bit.

"Oh, honey, you don't still get carsick, do you?"

"I'm fine, Mom. Just enjoying the fresh air," he said weakly. Beckett made a mental note to call his friend Donovan Cardona and ask the sheriff how many times a week Phoebe Pierce gets pulled over.

"So how's it going with a single mom and two kids living in your backyard?" Phoebe asked.

"It's fine." He shrugged.

"Uh-huh."

"What do you mean, uh-huh?"

"I just mean that I didn't raise idiots," Phoebe continued. "And there's a beautiful, unattached woman living in your backyard."

"Who happens to have kids."

"Who happens to have kids that you adore," his mother countered. "Is that a deal-breaker? You've never dated anyone with kids before."

Was it a deal-breaker? Beckett wondered. He thought back to video game night and pizza night. Evan and Aurora weren't deal-breakers. Somehow they made the deal even more appealing.

"You're smiling," his mother announced triumphantly.

"God, Mom. Don't tell me you've joined the Beautification Committee," Beckett grumbled.

"All I'm saying," she said, slamming on the brakes to turn onto Beckett's street, "Is that with the way you look at her—"

"Just how exactly do I look at her?"

"Like you want to devour her."

"Mom!"

"What?" Phoebe asked innocently. "That's how your father used to look at me. How do you think we ended up with three kids? There would have been more if your father hadn't gotten snip—"

Beckett brought his hands to his face. "Why are you torturing me?"

"She looks at you the same way," Phoebe said, turning into Beckett's driveway.

He had to bite his tongue. "She's not exactly my type, Mom," Beckett said, feeling a twinge of guilt at deliberately misleading his mother.

Phoebe shot him a look that told him she wasn't buying it.

"Beckett, your type bores you. You always were a cautious kid, and now you're a painfully responsible adult. Don't you think it's time to try playing with fire?"

Gia stretched her legs under the linen-draped table in the conference room of the Lunar Inn. She, along with most of the other female entrepreneurs in Blue Moon, were spending their Wednesday lunch hour enjoying a special get-together hosted by the city council and chamber of commerce to honor women in business.

It was a delicious meal with entertaining company, but the timing meant she'd had to give up an hour with Beckett in her bed. These were the tradeoffs of an adult, she supposed.

She'd see him tonight but with their families. With the days to the wedding ticking down, Summer and Carter offered to host dinner in exchange for planning help. In order to get out of any planning, Joey announced she'd give Evan and Aurora another riding lesson.

Gia wondered if she and Beckett would have a chance to sneak off for a quick, hard kiss... or two. Just the thought of it had her fingers flexing in the napkin in her lap. Aurora had already made sure a dozen times that her friend "Bucket" would be at dinner tonight. It seemed even five-year-olds weren't immune to the charm of the Pierce brothers.

As the president of the chamber of commerce was wrapping up her speech, Gia saw her gaze dart just off stage. Beckett waited patiently, his hands clasped in front of him, his eyes searching the audience until they found her.

Gia's lips parted in a secret smile, and she heard the delighted whispers run through the crowd. Apparently women at every age succumbed to that quick grin and those sharp, stormy eyes. No one was safe from Beckett Pierce.

Elvira Eustace wrapped up her comments. "I'd like to now introduce Blue Moon's mayor, Beckett Pierce. Beckett has a few short remarks he'd like to make."

The applause was hearty as Beckett took the podium, shaking Elvira's hand and waving to the crowd.

"Thank you, everyone. I wasn't sure if I'd be able to join you today because I was spending some time with my mother. As you all know her, you're well aware of the fact that Phoebe Pierce is a force to be reckoned with."

The crowd laughed appreciatively. And Gia smiled. It wasn't an exaggeration. She didn't doubt that every woman in the room knew Phoebe.

"I look like my father. My mother tells me I walk like him and argue like him, too. But after spending the morning with her I was reminded of how many things of hers I absorbed. Her impact on me is staggering. And it got me thinking about your impact."

He scanned the audience slowly, making and holding eye contact.

"You are the heartbeat and the backbone of our community, our families. The decisions you make, the boundaries you set, the strength you show all make this world a better, brighter place. Because of you, it never once dared to occur to me that a woman had no business in HVAC or dentistry or town council or the thousand other things you do. Because of you, generations grow up in this town never doubting that a woman can and will do whatever she puts her mind to.

"You've all sacrificed something in order to be here today. Businesses demand your time and your energy, and as women, you are too often faced with unfair standards, sometimes from outside forces and sometimes from within."

His eyes were on her again, and Gia shifted in her seat.

"To do it all and do it all perfectly. But what impresses me the most about each and every one of you is your unwavering dedication to community. You see our community as an extension of family, and you encourage us to come together time and again to support someone when they need it the most... whether they ask for our help or not."

That got another chuckle out of the room, yet Gia strangely felt her throat tighten.

"To be honest, I thought I got my desire to serve this town from my father. But as I step back and look, that's not the whole story. Not even a fraction of it," he said, shaking his head.

"Growing up here, you have all taught me how to be a better person, a better business owner, a better neighbor, and a better leader. And for that, I am eternally grateful.

"On behalf of all of Blue Moon, I would like to thank you for your service to this community and all its generations. You have truly made this town a village."

The applause was thunderous for such an intimate crowd. Gia noted more than a few watery eyes around the room as they all cheered for the man who saw them as they were and loved them for it.

Gia rose, applauding. His gaze, suddenly serious, zeroed in on her face, and she smiled. It was enough to knock the wind out of her, that swift, fierce rush of love.

It took her a moment to realize that heads in the crowd were swiveling from Beckett to her and back again. And that she was the only woman in the room standing. Mrs. Nordeman on one side of the room and Willa on the other took pity on her and stood up, too. Soon the whole room was on their feet, but the attention was still on Gia and Beckett.

When he left the stage, he headed her way, but Gia stopped him with what she hoped was a subtle shake of her head. She dug through her bag until she found her phone and fired off a quick text.

Gia: Don't talk to me. They'll be all over us like sweat on a Pierce in a yoga class.

Beckett pulled his phone out of his jacket pocket. She saw him smirk.

Beckett: Cute. Just like your oh-so-subtle one-woman standing ovation.

Gia shot him a glare.

Gia: Behave yourself. I'll see you tonight. In the company of many.

He gave her a nod and tucked his phone back in his jacket before fading back into the crowd.

Gia took one last look at him before scurrying out the door. She was in love with Beckett Pierce. Now what the hell was she going to do?

GIA DROVE down the lane to the farmhouse as the sun began to set. Evan sat quietly in the front seat while Aurora chattered to herself in the back.

"You're awfully quiet today," Gia said to Evan. "What's going on in that super big brain of yours?"

He shrugged, staring out the window at the pigs in the pasture. "Nothing important. Just some kids and I want to start a debate team at school."

"Wow," Gia said, parking the car next to her father's. "That's kind of awesome."

He shrugged again. "It would be if we could find an advisor. That's what the principal said we have to do."

"And it's up to you?" Gia tucked the keys in her bag. "Doesn't the school usually do that?"

"They're big on independence here." Evan sighed. "I don't know if it's, like, to build up our self-esteem or to dump more of the work off on us kids."

Gia hid her smile. "Hmm. Do you and your friends have any ideas for who you can ask?"

He shook his head. "Not yet. But we have until Thanksgiving break to find someone or we have to 'table the team' until next school year," Evan said, using air quotes.

They climbed out of the car. "Well, good luck with the search, and let me know if there's anything I can do," Gia said.

"Doubtful. Very doubtful." Evan smirked.

"Hey, smarty pants, I deliberately didn't volunteer to be the advisor to avoid your snarky comments on my illogical nature."

"And the team thanks you for that." Evan grinned, slamming the door and heading toward the front porch.

"At least Aurora still thinks I'm cool," Gia called after him, opening her daughter's door.

Her daughter hopped out and started running toward the house. "Whoa, slow down, kid," Gia called after her.

"I want to see Bucket, Mama!"

That made two of them.

Gia had debated all afternoon about whether to tell him that she'd fallen hard for him. They'd never discussed what an actual relationship between them would look like, always assuming that the odds were insurmountable. So why try? But the more intimate they became, Gia couldn't help but wonder, why not try?

She just didn't know how he'd feel about it.

She'd finally decided to give it a little more time before dropping the bomb on him that she had accidentally fallen in love with him. It would give her time to get used to these feelings and give him more exposure to the Decker family to help him decide if he was up for a package deal.

"I don't think he's here, yet," Gia told her, catching her

little fireball on the porch steps. Beckett's SUV wasn't in the driveway yet.

Aurora's lower lip poked out.

"But Grampa's here with Carter and Summer and Jax."

Aurora brightened. "Let's go, Mama!"

Gia debated knocking on the front door but realized that Evan had already walked right in, leaving the door wide open. Aurora made the decision for her and clamored through the open door.

They may not have been raised in a barn, but they sure acted like it sometimes. She followed Aurora's quick footsteps down the hallway into the kitchen where everyone gathered. Evan had already made himself at home on the barstool, an open soda in front of him.

"Jax said it was okay," Evan said defensively when he spotted Gia checking out his beverage.

Gia gave Jax her best disapproving mom look. She pointed two fingers first at her eyes and then at him.

Jax looked guilty. "Oops?"

"Yeah, 'oops' is right, mister."

"Can I just say you're looking particularly ravishing tonight?" he asked hopefully.

Joey and Beckett both happened to enter the room on that statement and glared daggers at Jax.

"Geez, tough crowd," he muttered.

"Hi," Gia said quietly to Beckett. Neither of them had changed from the luncheon. He was still wearing his neat charcoal trousers and tie. Every time she saw him in a tie, she wanted to grab him by it and drag him in for a kiss.

He shoved his hands in his pockets, and she wondered if he shared similar sentiments. "Hi, yourself."

"That was some speech you gave today."

"Way to lead the standing ovation." He winked. Beckett glanced around, making sure no one else was paying attention. "I want to touch you." He said the words so quietly Gia wasn't sure if she heard him correctly. But the hard look of yearning in his eyes told her she hadn't misheard.

"Hail, hail, the gang's all here," Phoebe said reaching for her phone. "Now, everyone be quiet so I can order the pizza for later."

Gia thought it best to get a little distance before one of them did something really stupid. With pink cheeks, she gave Beckett a wide berth and wandered over to her father and Summer, who were studying an array of recipes scattered across the table. She wrapped her arms around her father's neck and gave him a kiss on the cheek.

"There's my girl," he greeted her with a crinkle-eyed smile. "Summer and I were just going over Thanksgiving recipes for the wedding."

"Want to help?" Summer asked, squishing her cheeks between her hands. "We're feeding fifty. Small, casual, family-style."

"Please tell me you're going to have actual turkey and not some tofu-soy-fake bird," Beckett groaned from the refrigerator where he was fishing out a beer.

"Quit your whining," Carter said, smacking him on the shoulder. "When you get married, you can have meat with a side of meat. But for mine, you're eating tofurkey."

Beckett and Jax made gagging sounds that Evan immediately imitated.

"Enough from the gag choir." Summer pointed at them. "There will be turkey *and* tofurkey."

"Do vegetarians eat gravy?" Evan piped up.

Aurora had latched on to Beckett's pant leg and was giggling like a fiend every time he took a step.

"You're not going to get anything done with all of us hovering over you," Gia murmured to Summer. "You'd better assign jobs and get everyone out of here or we'll be eating Ramen noodles at your wedding reception."

"Good idea," Summer nodded. "Everyone, zip it and listen," she said, switching seamlessly into editor-in-chief mode. "Joey and Jax, I need you two to take Evan and Aurora to their riding lesson."

Joey looked at Jax who shot her a devilish grin and then back at Summer. She started to shake her head, but Summer had already moved on.

"Gia, I need the measurements of all of this stuff on the list in the barn so we can figure out what is getting drowned in tulle and flowers and lights. Beckett, I need you to go eyeball the barn's patio and see if we have room for a fire pit—fireplace preferably. A big one, not one of those crappy little ones."

Beckett grinned darkly at Gia. Of course Summer was sending them on the same assignment. Anticipation flashed through her as she wondered if they could steal a few steamy moments.

"Phoebe," Summer continued. "I need your help with the menu. And, Carter, you get to look through all of these vendor quotes and figure out where we're getting the tables, chairs, and linens from."

Everyone stood silently staring at each other.

"Move, people! Meet back here in an hour for food," Summer ordered.

Everyone scattered. Joey rounded up Evan and Aurora and did her best to ignore Jax. Gia snatched up the list Summer had handed her and scurried for the side door, feeling the weight of Beckett's gaze on her every step of the way.

He caught up with her at the bottom of the porch stairs.

"Wait up, Red. It'll be faster if I drive. Besides, I doubt you've got a tape measure in that dress." He eyed her fitted sweater dress appreciatively, and Gia's heart stuttered.

"Behave yourself," she hissed.

"Mama, we're ridin' ponies," Aurora called from up ahead.

Gia shot Beckett a warning look and jogged over to catch up to the riding class crew before they left.

Evan was talking Joey's ear off, and Aurora had wrangled a piggyback ride out of Jax who wielded the flashlight.

"Are you sure you guys don't mind—"

"I'd rather muck stalls than go play with tulle and flowers," Joey said. "If you get done in the barn fast enough, come check us out in the indoor ring." Their little group peeled off toward the stables with Aurora waving cheerfully from Jax's back.

"Alone at last," Beckett said, his voice low and dangerous. Gia told herself the goose bumps that cropped up everywhere were from the chilly evening air.

He dug his car keys out of his pocket. "Come on."

She followed him back to his SUV, careful to stay just out of reach in case any prying eyes from the house were watching. Settling onto the leather of his passenger seat, Gia willed herself to relax. Just because she was in love with Beckett didn't mean things had to change.

As soon as the interior lights went out, Beckett's hand found her thigh. They passed the house and bumped along behind the little barn on the well-worn path. And once they were out of sight, his hand slid higher, finding the top of her thigh high.

The quiet rumble in his chest told her he approved. Gia bit her lip as his fingers dragged the skirt of her dress an inch higher so he could stroke bare skin. The pads of his fingers trailed fire over her flesh.

How could something as benign as the stroke of his thumb consume her? Was this desire laced with love?

Gia shivered and took a shaky breath. In the headlights, the barn loomed in front of them. Dark and isolated.

26

*T*he blood pounded through Beckett's veins as he pulled her inside, carelessly flipping on light switches as they went.

"Wait! I didn't get the tape measure," Gianna frowned, resisting his pull.

But he had other plans.

Beckett, his jaw set, dragged her up the new staircase at the far end of the barn. "What are we doing up here?" Gianna asked. "Aren't we supposed to be—"

Her question was cut off when Beckett yanked her into his arms. Off-balance, she slammed into his chest.

"I can't stand not being able to touch you." His voice was jagged and rough. "It's fucking torture. First at lunch and then at Carter's. I need to touch you."

"Please touch me, Beckett."

He swore. She was begging him, and he wasn't going to be able to stop. They were safer upstairs than they were down, but if someone were to start up the stairs, they'd get an eyeful.

He half dragged, half carried her into the door-less restroom on the other side of the bar. The double vanity had been installed, and Beckett sent up a prayer of thanks that they hadn't gone with floating sinks. He dropped Gianna on the counter between the two sinks.

She came alive under his hands. His palms dove into the top of her wrap dress to free her breasts. That dress had been on his mind since he spotted her in the crowd at the luncheon. Sedate enough to be professional but with a very loud hint at what lay hidden beneath. He pushed away the cups of her bra and spread the material, baring her to his touch.

"God, let me taste you," he breathed, skimming his lips across her delicate collar bone and lower to where his hot breath made her nipples strain.

"Please, Beckett," she whimpered.

He drew one of the taut peaks into his mouth and began to suck. She wrestled with his belt and the zipper on his pants. His long deep pulls at her breast had her fingers fumbling again and again until finally she was able to shove his trousers down just enough.

He groaned against her sensitive skin as her fingers encircled his thick shaft. How could a man want so fiercely? There was nothing that would make him stop.

He released her breast, pressing a wet kiss to the other one and with a deft yank, tore her underwear from her.

"Now, Beckett. Please, now," she chanted, pumping his cock in her hand.

He spread her knees as wide as they would go and hooked the heel of each of her shoes in the sinks to anchor her open.

She leaned back, hands bracing against the wall and counter, and he again marveled at her flexibility.

"Now, baby." Aligning himself with her wet center, he slammed into her, claiming her. Nothing would stand between them here. He wouldn't let it. He belonged inside her, buried in her depths.

He held back just long enough so she could adjust to his size before pulling out and driving back into her. It was going to be fast, but fast was what he needed.

His gaze was drawn to her breasts as they trembled with each thrust.

Her whimpers of need drove him crazy. Every time he touched her, he felt like he was losing another piece of himself. But he didn't care because he was getting a piece of her in return.

Sheathed inside her, he was home. This wasn't something he could hide anymore. He belonged to Gianna, and she belonged to him. He felt the change in her, felt her sliding closer and closer to the edge.

He adjusted the angle just slightly, and it was enough to have her head dropping back against the mirror in silent ecstasy.

"You guys in here?"

They both heard the call from below. Carter.

Gia tensed, but it was too late for them to stop. He could feel the first tremor of her release as she tightened around him. He clamped a hand over her mouth. Leaning over, he brought his forehead to hers. And staring into each other's eyes they came together. A wave breaking, an explosion of pleasure. He stared into Gia's green eyes and gave her another piece of his soul.

"Hello?" Carter called again. The door clicked closed behind him when he exited to search outside.

But neither of them heard him. They were lost in each other.

~

GUILT AND SHAME painted Gia's face as she practically flew off the counter, straightening her dress. "Oh my God! What were we thinking?" She frantically shoved her bra back in place. "Carter almost caught us."

Beckett took his time tucking his shirt back in and righting his pants. He looked at his reflection and frowned. "Can guys have sex hair?"

"Beckett, be serious! I didn't even bring my phone in here. What if something had happened to one of the kids and they couldn't reach me because..."

"Because what?"

"Because I was being selfish and sneaking around having sex when I'm supposed to be helping my friend decorate for her wedding. I'm using my other friend as a baby-sitter while I have a tryst with my... my..."

"Your what?"

"Whatever you are!" She covered her face with her hands. "Beckett, I'm acting like a lovesick teenager. I can't be sneaking around like this. I'm a mother."

"Red, I hate to tell you this, but my mom and dad did a lot of sneaking around when we were living at home. Just because you have kids doesn't mean you have to give up everything else."

"Your parents were your *parents*. They were married, and everyone knew it. We're just... sleeping together."

"We're not *just* sleeping together, Gianna." Beckett kept his tone cool and level even though he felt like yelling some sense into her. How could she regret what they shared? How could she feel guilt from it?

Gianna shoved the skirt of her dress back down and pulled her hair back into a ponytail. She brought her hands to her flushed cheeks.

"What if Carter had come upstairs?" she asked, ignoring his statement.

He grabbed her by the shoulders. "What has you so worked up?"

She stared up at him, eyes wide and full. "You matter to me, Beckett. And this sneaking around feels like... it feels like it diminishes what you make me feel." She shook her head. "I need to think. I'm going to go check on the kids."

Beckett's hands slid from her shoulders to his sides. "You matter to me, too, Gianna." So much more than he ever anticipated. There was no planning for something as unexpected as Gianna Decker.

"I know I do. But I need to think about this, about us. Sneaking around behind everyone's backs, it doesn't make me feel... healthy. Or valuable."

"What are you saying?" Beckett asked, panic gripping his gut.

She brought a hand to his chest. "I'm only saying that I want to get things straight in my head. I want to talk it out with you but not here. Now isn't the time or the place obviously." She smiled weakly.

She held up the crumpled list Summer had given her. "Will you get all these measurements for Summer? Please? I need to go see the kids."

Beckett didn't trust himself to answer and only gave her a curt nod.

She whispered a thanks and hurried through the door and down the staircase, leaving Beckett to stare at his reflection. Her moods changed like wildfire. One second she was an untamed temptress driving him to new heights of pleasure, and the next she was a desolate girl in need of solace.

Predictable she was not, nor logical. His lips quirked

recalling Evan's barely disguised insults about Gianna and her emotional decision making.

And now, she wanted space to think. She wanted a change and rightfully so. But if she were to reason her way out of their relationship... well, he wasn't about to let that happen.

By the time he collected all the measurements on Summer's list and scoped out the newly laid patio for fireplace potential —there was room, and they should have thought of it before— he had worked up a good steam of mad. Rather than calmly talking out her concerns, she went straight to '*I need some time*.'

She kept the fairy garden he gave her on the table next to her bed, which made it the first thing she saw every morning and the last thing she saw at night. This wasn't just some fling, and she knew it.

"I need some time," he mimicked. "You matter to me Beckett. I need some time to decide to dump you. Let me meditate about it or maybe I'll flip a coin. And now let me run out of here without a flashlight so I can fall down in a ditch and hurt myself."

Yeah, he was good and mad. He wasn't about to be ousted from their relationship without a fight.

GIA HURRIED down the dark gravel drive from the brewery to the stables. Relief flooded her when she heard Aurora's giggle and Jax's amused voice inside.

"That's it, Ev," Joey called. "Really nice."

Gia plastered on a happy face before stepping up to the fence. Evan, in a black riding helmet, was posting pretty as you please on the back of a gray horse as it trotted around the ring.

"Awesome," Joey said. "Now bring her down to a walk."

She watched with careful eyes as Evan used the reins to neatly slow the mare's pace. He came to a halt in front of Joey, and his grin was balm to Gia's heart.

He spotted her, standing on the bottom rung of the fence and started to wave but stopped. "What's wrong?" he demanded.

So much for my happy face, Gia thought wryly.

"Nothing," she called brightly. "I'm just really impressed. Are you sure you haven't been skipping school and sneaking over here to ride?"

She could see the pride in his shoulders, but his eyes remained wary.

"You sure everything's okay?"

Damn her intuitive kid. "Everything's good. Really good."

"Mama! Look at me!" Aurora squealed from the opposite end of the massive ring. Jax was leading her around on a white and gray pony that pranced and swished her tail.

"Wow! What am I going to do with two equestrians?" Gia laughed.

"Can I have a pony, Mama?"

"Thanks a lot, Joey," Gia rolled her eyes.

Joey grinned. "You can visit Princess anytime, Roar."

"Yay! Princess, did you hear dat?" Aurora leaned forward a little too zealously to pat Princess's neck, but Jax was there to right her before she slipped.

"Don't you have a slightly shorter steed?" Gia asked weakly.

"Yeah, but she's a goat," Jax said with a grin. "And she's evil."

"Cwementine! She's so funny," Aurora giggled. "She eats shirts. Demon hell spawn!"

They all froze, eyes on Aurora, who was too busy cooing at Princess to notice the attention.

Jax looked guiltily in Gia's direction. "She may have been within earshot of me when Clementine attacked."

"I thought Beckett was kidding about that," Gia said, covering her mouth.

Evan shook his head. "Oh, it happened. And it was pretty awesome. Beckett got video on his phone."

Jax gave Evan a mock glare across the ring. "You watch it, kid, because I'll feed you to her next chance I get."

"What have I exposed my children to?" Gia asked the heavens.

Joey told Evan to take a lap walking with his mount and strolled over to Gia, her long legs eating up the sawdust between them. "He's good," she told her. "Really good. You should think about formal lessons for him if he's into it."

Gia looked at her son's face as he ambled past. Serious, but with that unmistakable sparkle usually reserved for video game victories. She sent him an air high-five that he returned.

"I've got a group class of kids his age twice a week. I could catch him up to them with a few private lessons, and then he could join the group," Joey suggested, watching Evan's form and calling out a correction here and there. She turned her attention back to Gia. "He's, like, really good. I think this could be his thing."

Gia felt the warm glow of pride spread through her. "I'll talk to him and see if he's into it. I'd love to sign him up."

Joey nodded. "Good. Now you don't want to talk or anything about why your face looked like you ran over a litter of kittens when you came in, right?"

Gia shook her head guiltily. More secrets, she supposed. "No. I'm good, thanks."

Joey looked marginally relieved. "Good," she said again. "Because I'm pretty sure the only thing that can put a look like that on a woman's face is a Pierce." She shot a dark look at Jax's back.

GIA SHREDDED the lettuce with a little more force than necessary in Carter's kitchen. She'd returned to the farmhouse with Jax, Joey, and the kids, and Phoebe had put her to work on a salad to go with the soon-to-arrive pizza. Carter had taken a break from his invoices to turn on the lights in the front paddock for the kids to play with Dixie and Hamlet before dinner.

Summer had nailed down the wedding menu with Franklin and only given her an odd look when Gia told her that Beckett was finishing up the measurements in the barn.

"You know what's funny?" Carter said quietly as he leaned against the counter next to Gia. "I went up to the barn to help you guys, and I couldn't find you."

Gia felt her face go fire engine red. "Uh..."

"You look like you could use a beer," he said. "How about I get you one?"

Gia could only nod her head. He *so* knew what she'd been doing.

God. What had she been thinking? She had guilt and just-had-sex written on her forehead. She was an adult, a mother, a business owner. She should know better.

She heard the front door slam and angry footsteps in the hallway. Ignoring the greetings from his family, Beckett burst into the kitchen in a cloud of pissed off. His gaze locked on to Gia's still pink face, and he started toward her with the purpose of a charging bull.

She backed up a pace and was debating about skirting

around the other side of the island when he caught her. His warm hands closed like clamps on her arms.

She shook her head. *She wasn't ready for this. Was he?*

He dragged her to her toes and kissed her fiercely on the mouth. The thoughts flew out of her mind, breath leaving her body. He kissed her, and she tasted anger, possession, and something else. Something dark and sweet.

Before she realized what was happening, he'd pulled away.

"Gianna and I are seeing each other," he announced briskly without taking his eyes off her.

Gia caught a glimpse of the reactions around the kitchen. Jax was frozen with his beer halfway to his mouth. Franklin looked dazed holding the spatula while Phoebe's mouth formed a perfect "o". Carter and Summer were grinning like idiots.

Joey strolled in from the powder room and surveyed the scene. "What did I miss?"

Beckett towed Gia toward the door. "We're telling the kids. Enough with this sneaking around."

It was quiet enough in the kitchen to hear the spoon that Phoebe dropped strike the floor as the door slammed behind them.

"Beckett, what the hell was that?"

He rounded on her. Toe-to-toe in the drive, he was braced for battle. "I'm tired of sneaking around, Gianna. And you should be, too. What we have isn't some fling, some secret affair. It's fucking real."

"I know it's fucking real, Beckett." She saw the beginnings of a smile play across his lips. "But damn it, it's *our* decision to make whether or not we tell people about us. Not yours."

"Don't you want to tell the kids?" Like the flip of a switch, he was back to angry now.

She threw her hands up. "Of course I want to tell them.

I've been dying to tell them. I've started to tell them a hundred times this week alone. They're starting to think I'm even crazier than they already do."

"Then why are you so mad?"

"Because I wanted to be part of this decision. I was working on a speech to convince you. With logic and everything. And you ruined it by going all lone cowboy in there and kissing the crap out of me."

"Red." He cupped a hand to her face. "Sweetheart, you don't have to convince me. I already know."

"What do you know?" she asked stubbornly.

He stepped in on her and brought his forehead to hers. "I know that you care about me." He clapped a hand over her mouth when she started to protest. "And I know that I'm head over heels for you, Gianna. You are never out of my head. I want us to be an official us."

"What about Evan and Aurora?" Gia didn't want to leave anything left unsaid before she let her hopes rocket into the stratosphere.

"You're a package deal and a damn good one. Your kids are one of the best pieces of you."

"You want to be with me... with all of us?" Gia asked breathlessly. Her mind was spinning.

"Yeah. And you want to be with me." He nodded. "I'm tired of playing hide and seek, ducking around corners. I want everyone to know that you're mine and I'm yours."

"I'd still like to have been part of that decision before you devoured my face in front of our parents."

Beckett smiled down at her, his hands stroking her back. "I'm sorry for that. In the future, we'll be partners in decision-making. But I still want to tell Evan and Rora today. Now preferably. Can we?"

She heard the giggles of her kids wafting on the night air.

Her heart swelled, and her eyes stung. Beckett Pierce wanted to be a part of the family she'd built. "I'd like that," she said on a little hiccup.

"Don't do that, Gianna," he said, bringing his hands to her face. "Don't cry or you'll freak them out."

"I'm just really happy," she sniffled.

"Me too, Red. Me too." He brought his lips to hers in a warm, gentle kiss, sealing the deal. They were oblivious to the faces pressed against the glass behind them.

27

She was going on a date. An honest-to-goodness, freaking date. Whatever the hell that meant. Gia held up the short red dress in the mirror and then tossed it on the bed in favor of the soft forest green with elbow-length sleeves. When was the last time she'd been on a date?

Paul, probably a few months before she got pregnant, she thought, tugging the dress over her head. Subtle on top with its crisscross fabric gathered over the bodice, it went sexy with the short, swingy skirt that ended several inches above her knees.

She paired it with her favorite heels in a creamy gray snakeskin pattern.

Gia took a deep breath and looked in the mirror. She'd taken a little extra time with her makeup. Okay, a lot of extra time.

Earlier in the week at Carter and Summer's, she hadn't even gotten the words out before Phoebe and her father were volunteering to take the kids overnight so Gia could go out on her first official date with Beckett. Without the kids to fight for the bathroom, she'd actually had an uninterrupted half hour for a shower and makeup.

This wasn't just a "swipe on some mascara" occasion. This was a date. With the man she loved. This was big.

It called for a sexy sweep of eyeliner and some color to her cheeks. Even some eyebrow grooming. She left her hair down —for now—in its usual long loose curls and pursed her lips in the mirror. Hair up or down?

She grabbed her phone and took a picture in the mirror. Summer would know. With her city style, the woman always knew exactly the right look.

Gia: Hair?

To Gia's relief, Summer responded immediately.

Summer: Definitely down. You look incredible! I'll be surprised if you make it to dinner.

Gia felt her color rise. They'd better make it to dinner. She was starving. But afterward... With the kids designing make-your-own pizzas and watching movies at her dad's, Gia was going to enjoy a sleepover of her own. She glanced over her shoulder at the overnight bag she'd packed. And took a deep shaky breath.

This was a big step, both publicly and personally. In Blue Moon, a public declaration of any kind was huge. And in her world, with two little people watching her every move, officially claiming a boyfriend was a change that would affect them all.

They'd told the kids in the late autumn evening chill while they played with Carter's pigs. Aurora had very seriously asked if Bucket would also date her. Evan had remained quiet, unreadable.

She really hoped Beckett was ready for this.

She checked the clock on her phone. She still had fifteen minutes before he picked her up. Good lord. What was she going to do for fifteen minutes? Wear a hole in her bedroom rug?

Her phone signaled. Startled, she fumbled and dropped it on to the rug. She picked it up and answered, grateful for the distraction.

"Eva!"

Her younger sister's face filled the screen. "Tell me about your date," she ordered with the slightest hint of Carolinas in her voice.

"Okay, now I know you're not a member of the Blue Moon Gossip Group, so how did you know I have a date?"

Evangelina Merrill, her strawberry blonde hair shoved into a knot on top of her head, gave her a coy smile over her librarian-style glasses. "I have my sources. Including Dad, who when I called, had some familiar looking munchkins in the background."

The wave of guilt tumbled over her. "How were they? Did Dad look overwhelmed? Were they having dinner?"

Eva held up her hands. "Chill out, G. You're entitled to a night out, especially if the mystery man is hot and not in a band. What's with the helicopter moming?"

Gia flopped back onto the bed. "I don't know what's wrong with me. I'm tied up in knots about a date with a man I've been sleeping with for two weeks, and I feel guilty anytime I pawn childcare responsibilities off on someone else."

Eva rolled her eyes. "Ugh. I worry every time we talk you're going to start espousing the merits of homeschooling your kids."

"Hey, what's wrong with homeschooling?"

"Nothing. For parents who didn't have your history and math grades. You'd be ensuring that Evan and Aurora never see college if you were in charge of their education."

"Thanks, jerk," Gia pouted.

"Listen, at some point you're going to have to understand that having more people involved in your kids' lives is good for them. Socialization and all that."

"Thank you Ms. Psychology Today." Eva had pursued psychology as a minor in college and wasn't shy about dusting off those textbooks whenever she spotted crazy.

"Deflecting."

"Was there a reason you called, Eva?"

Her sister's mouth spread into a grin. "Besides checking in with my sister to make sure she's not turning into a raw milk-swilling hippie? Pretty much to just get the jump on the date details before Emma."

"You always were the sneaky sister," Gia laughed.

"I've had to hear all about her seeing him first when he showed up on your video chat with a dishwasher. So tell me, is this guy as gorgeous as Emma says?"

Gia closed her eyes. "So gorgeous. Remember how we used to all fight over the shirtless guy in the gum commercial in high school?"

Eva smiled slyly. "Oh, yeah. He was quite the eye candy."

"Beckett makes him look like a pre-pubescent troll."

"Wow."

"You have no idea," Gia sighed. "And not only that, but he's smart and kind and steady and loyal and—"

"Great in bed?" Eva asked.

"Are you taking notes?"

"Maybe. You were saying?"

"Incredible in bed. Like life-threateningly amazing in bed. I'm worried I might die from pleasure."

"I so hate you right now," Eva groaned, pushing her glasses up her nose.

"If I were you, I'd hate me, too," Gia agreed.

She heard the knock and bolted off the bed. "Oh my God. He's here? How do I look?"

"You look a little wild-eyed and crazy, but the rest of you looks smokin'," Eva assured her.

"Okay, I gotta go."

"Yeah, yeah. Go to dinner and get laid. I'll just sit here and find that old gum commercial on YouTube."

Gia disconnected and took one last look in the mirror before hurrying to her front door.

Beckett had pulled out all the stops in the wardrobe department, too, she noted. He wore a navy suit with a gray patterned tie. Glossy shoes in a delicious shade of caramel matched his belt.

His hair, with its slight waves on top, begged for her fingers to explore it. Those smoky eyes, an exact match for the tie, swept her from head-to-toe. She felt his gaze as distinctly as if it were his hands exploring her body.

"Hi," she said, a little breathlessly.

He grinned that devilish grin, and Gia felt her temperature rise by a few degrees.

"Hi," he responded. "You look good enough to eat."

"Oh, no." She shook her head. "You're not getting out of feeding me, Mr. Pierce. This is a *dinner* date."

He took her hand and brushed it with his lips, sending a zing of current through her veins. "Then I can't wait for dessert."

Was it too old-fashioned to swoon? Gia wondered.

Beckett's other hand flashed out from behind his back grasping a clutch of flowers in oranges, reds, and yellows.

"Oh, you're good," Gia said with delight, burying her face in the blooms. "You brought me a bouquet of fall."

"I'm prepared to date the hell out of you, so be prepared to be seduced, Red."

It sounded like a threat.

"Let me put these in water," she said, heading into the kitchen. "Would you like a drink before we go?"

He hummed. "I think it would be best if we left. Otherwise, I'll be tempted to drag you to bed."

Gia laughed, feeling safer with the island between them. She found a gold crackle vase on the top shelf of one of the cabinets and arranged the flowers in it. "Where are you taking me tonight?"

"It's a surprise," Beckett said, eyeing her as she set the vase on the kitchen table. "I think you'll like it."

"Karma Kustard?" she teased.

He reached for her hand and pulled her in. "I thought we'd try some place a little more romantic." His thumb skimmed her palm. "And a little less Blue Moon."

"I'm intrigued," she said, savoring the warmth of him against her.

"You look beautiful, Gianna," Beckett said, cupping her face in his hand.

"Thank you. So do you." Gia flushed. "Handsome, I mean."

They stood touching, gazes locked, for a beat and then two.

"I don't think I'm ever going to get used to looking at you," Beckett said finally. He leaned in and down. Gia's lips parted with jagged anticipation. But instead of brushing her mouth with his, he kissed the tip of her nose and pulled back with a regretful sigh.

"Come on, beautiful. Let's go to dinner."

He helped her into her wool trench, hands lingering on her shoulders and sweeping her fiery curls off her neck. And with another sigh, Beckett led her out the door.

He drove them north, his headlights catching leaves as they tumbled free and floated from their branches. A symphony played quietly through the speakers of his SUV.

"Are you a fan of classical?" Gia asked.

Beckett took her hand and held it. "Mom was very big on music, so growing up we got quite the eclectic education. She always had a radio on. Of course, we always did battle to listen to 'our' music." He smiled at the memory. "Then when Carter came home hurt, we noticed his anxiety was better with music. I guess Mozart and Beethoven got their hooks in me then, too."

Gia squeezed his hand. "It's peaceful. Was it hard seeing Carter like that?"

She tried to imagine the calm, steady man she knew riddled with emotional wounds.

Beckett cleared his throat. "It wasn't easy. He left my brother and came back someone none of us recognized. But he found his way back again."

"And you helped," Gia said.

He shrugged. "Everyone did. Mom smothered him in a way only she could get away with. Jax checked in every day with ridiculous Hollywood stories until he could fly home. We had a lot of help on the farm and in the kitchen. That's one thing we know how to do in Blue Moon, shove our help down your throat."

Gia smiled. She could see it, a never-ending line of casserole-wielding neighbors winding its way through Pierce Acres.

"And what did you do?"

"I punched him in the face. Repeatedly."

Gia blinked. "I beg your pardon?"

"Boxing." Beckett winked at her. "He wasn't just afraid. He was angry. We'd get in the ring and beat the shit out of each other. We both had some anger built up, so we fought it out."

Gia closed her eyes. "I can't imagine you two fighting. It's so... barbaric."

"Says the woman with a heavy bag in her shed."

"A heavy bag doesn't have a face. Why were you angry?"

Beckett weighed his words. "First and foremost, you don't hurt a Pierce without incurring the wrath of the rest of us. And, at the time, I guess I was still pissed that the path he chose, the path that took him away from our dad in his last years, was the thing that almost got him killed."

Gia nodded. "And you felt guilty about being mad at him."

"Of course."

"What did your mother say? About the boxing, I mean."

"We never told her," Beckett said. "We're not stupid."

"Neither is your mother," Gia said dryly. "She had to know. Besides, you can't do anything in Blue Moon without the entire town talking about it."

"Fitness Freak has a ring in the back with its own entrance. Doesn't get a lot of use, but Fran—you know Fran?"

"You mean the coolest woman on earth?"

"Yeah, that's Fran," Beckett laughed. "Anyway, she gave us the key and asked no questions. So we'd sneak in once or twice a week, whenever things got bad for Carter. I held back at first. He had fucking bullet holes in him. But that just pissed him off more." Beckett shook his head.

"Now, *that* I can see."

"He called me a pus—" Beckett shot her a sidelong glance. "Uh, a name, and I just snapped and put him on his ass. It was the first time I'd seen an honest-to-God smile since he'd come home."

Gia stared out her window, a smile playing on her lips. "Men are idiots."

"We're not idiots," Beckett countered. "We're blunt instruments. We walked around with black eyes and cuts on our faces for a few weeks, but since it seemed to be helping, everyone—including Mom—knew better than to ask about them."

She rolled her head on the seat and shot him a smile. "I really like you, Beckett."

She watched the rush of feelings her words conjured sweep across his face.

"You like me because I punched my wounded-in-combat brother in the face?"

Gia nodded. "Yep."

Beckett shook his head. "Women." He turned off the highway and onto a dark country road.

"We are going to a restaurant, aren't we? You aren't just taking me to some rural gas station for candy bars and beef jerky, are you?"

"Gianna, Gianna, Gianna," Beckett sighed. "You should have specified where you wanted to go," he teased.

He made another turn, this time at a wooden placard that said Horseshoe Lake. Gia peered through her window but couldn't see much beyond the soft glow of lampposts and trees that lined the drive.

"How's Evan doing with everything? He seemed pretty quiet when we told him about us," Beckett said, followed the road as it meandered through trees.

"He's very private about how he processes things. The most I could get out of him was that he wasn't surprised."

"He knew your dad was going to tell you he was dating when you came to dinner that first night."

"He did? God, that kid is smart. I didn't see that one coming. A happy surprise, thankfully."

Beckett remained silent, and Gia held her tongue. Sooner or later, he'd either have to get used to his mother dating her father or blow up and spill his guts on why he disapproved.

The tree-lined drive opened up to reveal a sprawling lodge that spread out on the lake's edge. Its cedar shingles and heavy navy shutters gave it a classic New England look. Beckett pulled into the gravel parking lot cordoned off with a split-rail fence next to the building.

"Wow," Gia said, gripping her bag.

"I haven't even taken my pants off, yet."

Gia slapped Beckett on the arm. "Funny guy."

"Let's get you fed so I can take you home and find out what you have on under that dress," Beckett said, his fingers tracing her thigh just under the hem.

"Just consider it dessert," she said, leaning closer and licking her lips. She gave him her best sultry look.

"Evil woman," Beckett said blowing out his breath and getting out of the driver's seat.

They were seated immediately in a cozy corner near a crackling fireplace. Their table offered a view of the moonlight as it sparkled on the lake's dark waters.

"Very, very nice, Beckett," Gia said after the server, a young man with a slight French accent, took their drink order.

Beckett took her hands on the crisp white linen tablecloth. "I'm glad you approve."

"You're very good at dating, aren't you?" Gia said, raising an eyebrow.

"Aren't you?"

"I'm not sure if I've ever been on an actual date. Certainly nothing like this," she said admiring the room. The dining room was a wash of white walls and tall windows. The fireplace that warmed Gia's back was clad in a rustic, local stone. Aged oak floors washed in a light gray carried from the foyer all the way through to the patio doors facing the lake.

Candle flames flickered on every table.

"Then your previous partners were sadly lacking," Beckett told her.

"You may be right," she agreed.

When he looked at her, Gia felt as if he was looking into her. Probing every dark corner for secrets. There was so much behind those smoldering eyes.

"What?" she asked when his face turned serious.

"You deserve better."

"That's why I'm here," she said lightly.

The waiter returned with their wine and recited the night's specials. After an internal debate about which entrée would be most conducive to their after-dinner plans, Gia selected the corn chowder and grilled salmon. Beckett went with red meat.

They sipped and chatted, flirted and teased. Both enjoying the simple traditions of the time-honored date.

28

$\mathcal{J}$t wasn't until Beckett fed her a tender forkful of his steak that Gia noticed the bitter attention of another patron. The woman was tall and sleek. Her dark hair was pulled back in a perfect chignon. And her heavily made-up eyes were shooting poisoned darts at Gia.

She was certain she'd never seen the woman before in her life and did her best to ignore the death darts. But when Beckett reached across their little table to brush a curl back behind her ear, the woman tossed her napkin down on her plate and looked as if she was about to spit flames hot enough to incinerate her dinner date.

The woman obviously had something to say, so Gia decided to give her an opportunity. She excused herself and went to the restroom, making sure to walk past the stranger's table. She was checking her teeth for food when the door opened swiftly enough to create a brisk breeze.

"Hello," Gia greeted her.

The woman stormed in on truly beautiful stilettos that put her a good six inches taller than Gia. She stopped two sinks down and crossed her arms. Everything about her was angry.

"So you're my replacement?" she finally said. Her tone told Gia the woman wasn't impressed with what she saw. "You look like the rest of those idiot hippies in that pathetic town."

Gia decided it best to remain silent and waited.

She withstood the woman's head-to-toe review and derisive sniff. "You're certainly not Beckett's type. How does it feel to be a rebound?"

"A rebound?" Gia pretended to ponder. "Well, to be honest, if that's what I am, it feels really, really good."

The woman uncrossed her arms and clenched her fists at her sides. A diamond tennis bracelet glittered on one wrist. A cloud of Chanel No. 5 tickled Gia's nose.

"He'll come to his senses sooner or later and drop you back in whatever gutter he found you. He needs someone with sophistication and style. Not some frizzy haired child who makes her own goat milk soap."

Whoever this woman was, she had definitely spent some time in Blue Moon, Gia thought.

"I'm assuming you two used to date?"

"Used to date? I'm *Trudy*." She said her own name as if Gia should have it tattooed on her body somewhere. "We were practically engaged. We understood each other," the woman purred, crossing her arms again and drumming her garnet fingernails on her own skin.

Gia decided to give her a win. "Oh, *Trudy,* of course!"

"And we'll be back together just as soon as he gets you and your silly little town out of his system."

Gia debated the threat level and decided it was relatively low. She slid up on the vanity and let her legs dangle. The woman, who had clearly never slouched a day in her life, sneered at Gia's informality.

"It sounds like you two were really serious," Gia prompted.

"We were... are," she corrected herself. "It was just a tiny misunderstanding."

"Misunderstandings happen all the time."

"There was no reason for him to call that bumbling sheriff."

Oh boy.

"He must have just panicked," Gia said sympathetically.

"It was only a small fire. I don't know what the big deal was." The brunette shrugged her courtesy-of-a-personal-trainer shoulders.

"Men have a tendency to overreact, don't they?"

"They certainly do. Take my date for instance," she said, turning her attention to her reflection. "He insisted that I was blowing this out of proportion. But I know that Beckett *knew* I'd be here, and he brought you here just to rub you in my face."

"What's your date like?" Gia asked, changing the subject.

The fingernails tapped faster. "Thomas? He's..." She trailed off searching for words.

"He's very good-looking," Gia supplied, not sure if it was true as she hadn't actually seen his face.

"Yes," Trudy nodded. "And he doesn't come from some bucolic hellhole that smells like patchouli."

"Well that's definitely a point in his favor," Gia decided.

"And he's going to leave his wife in the spring, so there's that," Trudy said, continuing to tally the points. "Tax reasons, of course."

"Of course," Gia nodded.

There was a knock on the bathroom door.

"Come in," Gia called cheerily.

The married, tax-conscious Thomas poked his head in the door. He looked relieved when he didn't spot any blood.

"I'm so sorry. I've been monopolizing Trudy. I'm sure you

two want to get back to your romantic dinner," Gia said apologetically.

"Uh. Yeah." Thomas didn't sound very enthusiastic.

"It was really nice to meet you," Gia said, sliding off the vanity. "Have a great night." She skirted around Trudy, and Thomas held the door for her.

Gia settled back in her seat across from Beckett.

"I was starting to get worried," he said, his hand snaking out to grab hers.

"I think we should go," Gia said firmly.

Beckett glanced down at his plate and half-finished steak and then back up at Gia.

"Check please." With the check paid and the leftovers hastily boxed, Gia led the way out holding Beckett's hand. When they passed Trudy's table, she felt Beckett stumble, and then suddenly he was leading the way, dragging her out of the restaurant.

Gia hid her smile.

"Are you sure you don't mind leaving? We could go back in for dessert," she said sweetly.

Beckett opened her door and all but shoved her into the seat. "No. Let's get you home," he said, slamming the door in her face and jogging to the driver's side. He accelerated out of the parking lot so fast the SUV fish-tailed, and Gia had to bite her lip to keep from laughing.

"Are you okay? You look like you've seen a ghost," she said, putting her hand on his thigh.

Beckett accelerated harder. "Nope. Everything is fine. Just excited to get home and..."

"See what I have on under my dress?" Gia prompted.

"Huh?"

"Do you want to talk about Trudy?"

Beckett's foot slipped off the gas pedal. "Fuck."

Gia did laugh now.

"You wouldn't be laughing if you knew—"

"About the fire?" Gia asked innocently.

"So she followed you into the bathroom. Damnit. I purposely picked this place so we could have a nice, romantic dinner away from the prying eyes of Blue Moon. And instead I march you into the she devil's den."

"Tell me about the fire," Gia laughed.

"Why are you laughing? You were just cornered by a succubus."

"She didn't do anything awful. She just told me I would never be the Mrs. Beckett Pierce that she would because I'm a —and I'm paraphrasing here—gutter-raised, soap-making dirty hippie."

Beckett stepped on the brakes. "I'm going back there and murdering her. I don't think any court would convict me."

Gia laid a hand on his arm. "Beckett, it's fine. The whole thing was funny and a little sad. I got to meet her boyfriend, Thomas. He's married, but as soon as he gets his refund in the spring, he's filing for divorce."

Beckett covered his face with his hands and growled in frustration.

"She had no right to verbally attack you. Mrs. Beckett Pierce, my ass. That woman was gunning for a proposal from day one, and when I called it off, you know what she did?"

"She set something on fire."

"She set my welcome mat on fire, and you know what she did while I was hosing it off?"

"No, but I bet it's something really good."

"She handcuffed herself to the stairs in the foyer and said she wasn't leaving until I gave her another chance."

"Ah. So that's how she became acquainted with Sheriff Cardona."

"You two sure had a lot to say," Beckett grumbled.

"She's a peach. How long did you date?"

"I think it was a grand total of three weeks. She brought a tape measure with her to get drapery measurements."

Gia snickered.

"You shouldn't be laughing. The woman insulted you and tried to make you feel insecure about our relationship. On our first fucking date!"

"Well, I mean the woman is clearly gorgeous and ruthless with impeccable taste. I would have felt deeply insecure if I didn't have such a leg up in the sanity department," Gia placated.

"She say anything else?"

"Only that Blue Moon is a bucolic, patchouli-scented hell-hole and that you *will* give her another chance."

He swore again. "I'd better call Cardona and make sure she doesn't go poking her nose around our place."

Gia felt a warm tickle in her belly. *Our place.*

"Pull over." Her words were quiet, but they carried the weight of urgency.

Beckett immediately veered for the side of the road. "What's wrong? Are you feeling okay?" He found a small pull-off, shrouded in trees, and threw the SUV into park.

"What—"

His question was cut off by Gia's sneak attack. She released her seatbelt and dove across the console, lips finding his mouth.

It took Beckett no time at all to catch up.

"Here?" he whispered the word against her mouth, hands seeking out her curves.

"Here," Gia groaned. She invaded his mouth with her tongue. She could taste the wine he'd had with dinner.

Stroking and sighing, she explored his mouth while his fingers dug into her waist.

"God, I could taste you for days," he murmured.

"Let's start now," she suggested in a breathy whisper.

Beckett's hand snaked under her dress, fingers exploring. She knew the second he found her sexy garter because he growled low and dangerous. She felt powerful, craved.

He hooked an arm around her waist and threw open his door. Dragging her across the console and out the door, Gia didn't have a chance to catch her breath before he was placing her on the hood.

Moonlight filtered through the trees, and the night air was cold, but Gia was warmed by Beckett's body. Her hands slid under his jacket, caressing the warmth of his chest, his broad, strong back.

He ranged himself between her legs, his mouth never leaving hers.

"So fucking beautiful," he told her as his lips cruised over her jaw, down her neck. His hands buried themselves in her hair. "You're in my dreams. Every night. And when I wake up, you're not there."

"Beckett," Gia sighed. "Please don't stop touching me."

His hands abandoned her hair in favor of her legs. He started at her knees and slid his palms higher. Over the lace edge of her thigh-high to the elastic strap of the garter, taking her dress with him, sliding it higher and higher.

"I want you to be there, Gianna."

"I'm here now," she shivered out the words. Her heels found purchase on the bumper, which she used for leverage to grind against him. She could feel the length of him, solid and aching through too many layers of clothing. Her fingers dug into his back, begging him, needing him.

He fumbled with his belt, and Gia felt her breath leave her

LUCY SCORE

as he freed himself. He was magnificent, painfully perfect. The epitome of desire. She felt her lip quiver, need and greed racing through her.

He shoved her dress up another inch, spread her knees farther apart. His eyes, lit from within with desire, sharpened, his jaw tightened when he realized there were no more barriers between them.

Gia would have patted herself on the back for skipping underwear if she wasn't already enthralled by his spell.

"Watch," Beckett ordered her, his voice as rough as the gravel beneath his feet. He guided his crown to her slick center, he stroked down the length of his shaft once, twice, each time parting her folds with the blunt tip of his erection.

Enthralled, Gia watched as he penetrated her slowly, finally. Her sigh of submission threaded its way around his groan of possession. "Watch us, Red," he said again as he began to move in her.

In the moonlight, she couldn't tear her eyes away from the demonstration of his rule over her. Sliding in and out, slick from her desire, he gave and took. She wasn't cold anymore. She was on fire.

She wanted to say it, to tell him that he had her body, her soul, her heart. But there were no words. Only the breath, the beat of the heart, the silent knowing that they were finally complete.

His strokes came faster, harder, layers of control stripping away, and she knew he fought against the sharp teeth of release. Knowing how dark his desire for her was, knowing that she had the power to make him forget his restraint, to let go and leap, Gia felt the truth in her body.

Gripping his tie, she flowed backward, draping over the hood. The waves licked at her, through her, and she gave herself over to the glory of them. Gia heard his half-shout. Her name, always her name. She let him carry them both into the abyss.

~

SATURDAY MORNING HAD Gia waking sore and satisfied in Beckett's bed.

"God, I could get used to this," Beckett said, his voice muffled by pillow.

She stretched luxuriously before snuggling back into him. "Yeah, your bed is way more comfortable than mine."

He pinched her under the covers. "That's not what I meant," he said, his voice heavy with sleep.

His hand skimmed down her naked back, and she winced. "Is that a bumper-sized bruise on my butt?"

Beckett rolled her over to examine her otherwise flawless skin. "That's what we get for having car sex like teenagers," he said, his fingers running over the small bruise.

"I hope we didn't do any permanent damage to your hood," she teased.

"I'm hoping we did. I'd smile every time I looked at the dent."

Gia laughed and yawned. "Mmm, so worth it."

"I'm just glad we didn't get caught." He placed a soft kiss on the bruise and another one on the curve of her hip. "So, listen..."

"Uh-oh," Gia sighed. "This doesn't sound like I'm going to like it."

"Well, I was thinking since we told the families and we had our first official date we should probably go public in Blue Moon." He toyed with a loose curl.

"And how does one do that?"

"I've got that covered. I just need you to look surprised and maybe a little giddy."

"Surprised and giddy?"

Beckett nodded.

"I think I can handle that."

"Great. I'll take care of the rest. By noon everyone in town will know that we're dating."

BY THE TIME her ten o'clock yoga class began, most of Blue Moon already knew. Five minutes before class started, Gia took delivery of a huge bouquet of roses so velvety red they were almost purple. In front of her class of fifteen, she fished the card out of the blooms.

I had a great time last night. Can't wait to see you again.
Yours,
Beckett

After her ten o'clock, Gia checked the Facebook group, and sure enough, there were half a dozen pictures of the flowers from the store to the studio.

The captions ran the gamut from "It's official," to "About freaking time!"

As she scrolled the posts, a new one appeared.

Beckett Pierce installs car seat to accommodate girlfriend's adorable daughter. Looks like this is serious, Mooners!

She switched over to text messages and typed a quick message.

Gia: Does Facebook deceive, or did you seriously just buy a car seat?

He responded a minute later.

Beckett: I'm being practical here. We can't all fit in your tiny little clown car.

To him, it was practical. To her, it was a path straight to her heart. Gia found it oddly easy to look giddy for the rest of the morning.

29

*B*eckett hit send in one window, print in another, and spun his chair around to neatly tuck a stack of papers inside a large envelope. He was an efficiency machine these days. By day, he was filing papers with the courts, structuring trusts, and smoothly sailing the tricky waters of prenups.

And in the evenings, he and Gianna eased into playing house. He'd taken to visiting Evan and Aurora on the nights when Gianna was at class. Last night, after a spirited game of laser tag in the yard, Evan had made him a peanut butter and jelly sandwich for dinner. Beckett reciprocated by sneaking them out for dessert at Karma Kustard.

He and Gianna still did some sneaking of their own. Off to bed whenever either of them had a free hour in the mornings or afternoons. He wished they could spend the night together —nothing beat waking up to Gianna Decker wrapped around him—but they had decided that for the sake of the kids, they'd table the sleepovers for now.

She still stunned him. Not just with her beauty, though

that hadn't ceased to affect him, but with the way she moved through life.

Grace, strength, and compassion were her hallmarks. She could never remember if she locked a door or recall where she put her phone, but Gianna could recite entire family trees of her students and always remembered to ask Evan about his friends and teachers.

Everything she did was garnished with an easy physical affection that baffled Beckett. She used her hands to guide her students deeper into poses and to express an unconditional, abiding care for her kids. And for him.

Beckett found himself getting out of bed with a smile every morning. It stayed fixed in place through Ellery's smug questions about his new tenant. It even held fast—for the most part—when Carter and Jax started speculating how long it would take Franklin to propose to their mother.

Life was good.

He was debating texting Gia to see if she and the kids wanted to come over for grilled chicken that night, when Ellery appeared in his doorway.

"Mr. Pierce?"

With her inky black braids and full-skirted dress, she looked like a 1950s goth Barbie.

"Mr. Pierce?" he repeated.

"Yes, sir. You have a gentleman to see you."

"I do?" He frowned, trying to recall an appointment on his calendar.

"Mr. Evan Decker," Ellery said with a twinkle in her eyes.

"Evan to see me?" Understanding her game now, Beckett grinned. "Please show him in."

Ellery gave a mock curtsy. "Of course. Mr. Decker? Mr. Pierce will see you now."

Evan strolled into the office in what Beckett assumed was the kid's version of meeting casual, chinos and a rumpled button down with a striped tie. His hands were shoved in his pockets.

"Come on in, Evan," Beckett said, gesturing toward his visitor chairs.

"Can I get you something to drink, Mr. Decker?" Ellery offered.

"I'm fine, thanks," he said. "Unless you have Coke?" He darted a glance at Beckett to see if he would argue.

"I think that can be arranged," Ellery winked. "Anything for you, Mr. Pierce?"

Beckett hid his grin. "I'll take a Coke, too."

He waited until Ellery had shut the door behind her.

"So what brings you to the office, Evan?"

The boy leaned forward in his chair. "I've got a proposition for you."

Beckett's interest was piqued. "What kind of a proposition?"

Evan interlaced his fingers on the desk in front of him. "As you know, I go to Blue Moon Middle School. What you may not be aware of is that the school doesn't have a debate team."

Beckett pursed his lips. "I was not aware of that."

"The high school has one, but that's a few years away. Some fellow students and I thought it would be a good opportunity to start a middle school team so, by the time we get to high school, we already know the basics and can focus more on competition and fine tuning our tactics."

Ellery returned with heavy tumblers of ice and soda.

"Thank you, Ellery," Evan said politely.

She grinned, a dark burgundy lipstick smile. "You're quite welcome." She left them again and closed the doors, wiggling her eyebrows at Beckett.

"So, you want to start a middle school debate team," Beckett recapped.

Evan nodded. "Yeah."

"And there's something standing in your way?"

"Just one small obstacle. We need an advisor."

"And your teachers..."

"Already have their activities. And if we don't find an outside advisor now, we'll have to wait until the next school year."

"I see."

"So, I thought, given your background on the high school debate team and your current prof—"

"How do you know I was on the debate team?" Beckett asked.

"Carter let me look through his old year books. You were president of the Debate Club."

He'd also been team captain of the cross-country team, but of course Carter wouldn't have pointed that out to the kid.

"So you're looking for an advisor."

"It would only be an hour of your time a week, after school." Evan leaned in. "You could give us pointers and help us get ready for some events in the spring."

"And you want me because everyone else said no?"

Evan shook his head earnestly. "You're the only one we've asked. We want the best."

How the hell was he supposed to say no to that? Beckett wondered.

He pinched the bridge of his nose. "An hour a week?"

Evan nodded. "On Wednesdays. I checked with the library, and they have meeting space we can use."

"How many of you are there?"

"Seven. Eight if you count Oceana, but she's at some wool-spinning workshop for two weeks after Thanksgiving."

He slid a piece of paper across the desk. "These are the competitions we want to enter in the spring, so we need to be good by then."

Beckett picked it up and studied the list. "Okay."

"Okay you'll do it, or okay you'll think about it?"

"Okay, I'll do it," Beckett clarified.

"Cool." Evan nodded as if he'd expected the yes. "Meetings start the week after Thanksgiving at the library." He stood up and extended his hand to Beckett.

Beckett rose and shook the boy's hand.

"You won't regret it," Evan said confidently.

"We'll see about that."

"Thanks, Beckett. See ya around," Evan said, draining his glass before he left.

Beckett sat in his chair feeling slightly manipulated and not the least bit upset about it. He saw Evan close the sunroom door behind him on the porch and break into a victory dance.

Nope, Beckett wasn't the least bit upset about it.

He called Ellery's desk. "Can you set a reminder for me to call the middle school principal about this debate team thing?"

"Already on your calendar."

BECKETT ANSWERED the evening knock on his front door with a beer in one hand and his phone in the other. Gianna had regretfully turned him down for dinner tonight in favor of getting some magazine work done for Summer. So he'd settled for a sexy text exchange while he caught part of the basketball game on TV.

His brothers ranged themselves in the doorway.

"Haven't seen you in a while," Carter said, pushing past him into the house.

Jax followed suit, slugging Beckett in the shoulder on his way through the door.

"Got any more of those?" Carter asked over his shoulder, pointing at the beer.

"Fridge." He followed his brothers down the hall to the kitchen. It had been a while since he'd seen them.

"Don't get your beard hair on any of my food," he warned Carter as his brother started to dig through his fridge.

Carter pulled out two beers and handed one to Jax. He stroked a hand through his thick beard. "Sounds like jealousy to me, Jax."

Familiar with the game, Jax grinned. "Sounds like it. I bet Beckett couldn't grow more than a sad, scraggly patch or two in a week."

"What brings you esteemed gentlemen to my kitchen, besides insulting my face?" Beckett asked, letting his gaze skim between them and through the back window. Lights were on all over Gianna's house.

"He's got it bad," Jax sighed, sliding to the left to block Beckett's view of the window.

"Who's got what bad?" Beckett asked, playing it cool.

Carter pulled out his phone, skimmed a thumb over the screen.

"Beckett Pierce sends flowers, buys car seat, seen smiling in grocery produce aisle," he read.

"I like grapefruit. They were on special."

Jax snorted.

"You two didn't come all the way over here to talk about me and Gianna, did you?"

Carter and Jax shared a look.

"What?"

"Summer kicked us out," Jax said, rubbing the back of his head. "Something about not being able to concentrate with so much testosterone in the house."

"What exactly were you doing that earned you an exile?"

Carter shrugged. "We may have been just fooling around wrestling."

"She got pretty pissed when we kicked over that lamp," Jax said, taking a sip of beer.

"Was it the lamp or the table she was mad about?" Carter frowned.

Jax shrugged. "All I know is one second we're just goofing off and the next she's throwing car keys at us and telling us to get out."

"Is this pregnancy hormones or bridezilla issues?" Beckett said, pretending that Summer wasn't perfectly within her rights to evict two overgrown teenagers.

"Man, I think the hormones are double with twins," Carter sighed.

"Or it could be the fact that you're smothering the shit out of her," Jax said affably. "'Can I get you a pillow, sweetheart? How about you sit down and take a break? Why don't you let me chew your food for you?'" Jax said in a spot-on, lovesick Carter imitation.

Carter cuffed his brother upside the head, which resulted in another scuffle.

Beckett pulled them both apart by the backs of their shirts. "If you break anything in here, I'll do worse than kick you out," he said mildly.

Carter straightened his shirt and grinned. "We figured we'd give her some time to cool off, swing by and make fun of you, and maybe hit up Shorty's for a round and some wings."

"And if we bring Summer cheese sticks, she'll forget she was pissed," Jax added.

"Good call," Beckett nodded. "I'm in. Let me get my wallet."

"Just so you two know, this doesn't count as a bachelor party," Carter warned.

∼

BECKETT RAPPED on Gianna's front door, a greasy paper bag wafting the aroma of deep-fried onions into the night air. A low-key evening with his brothers and getting to drive Jax's souped-up Chevy Nova back from the bar had put him in an even better mood.

Imagining Gianna's thank you for the snack could potentially make the grin on his face permanent.

Expecting to see her beautiful face or one of the kids grinning up at him, he was surprised when a thin man wearing boot cut jeans and a tight, black button-down answered the door.

"Can I help you?"

"Gianna here?" Beckett asked, his eyes narrowing.

"Sure." He leaned back. "G, babe. Someone here to see you."

Gianna, her cheeks flushed hurried down the stairs. "Beckett."

She stopped just inside the door. "Beckett, this is Paul, the kids' dad. Paul this is Beckett, my..."

"Landlord," Beckett finished for her. He took the hand that Paul offered.

"Cool," Paul said.

Beckett's eyes tracked to the bags and suitcases just inside the door and felt the blood in his veins go icy.

"You just get into town?" he asked.

Paul nodded. "Yeah, I was missing the fam," he said and

tossed an arm around Gianna's shoulder and pressed a kiss to her temple. "This is a great place you got here. I hope you don't mind one more in it."

Gianna's wide eyes never left his face.

"Daddy!" Aurora's little voice piped up from the stairs. "Come color with me!" She spotted Beckett and hurled herself down the stairs and jumped into Beckett's arms. "Bucket! Wanna color with me and Daddy?"

Beckett held on a minute longer than necessary before setting the little girl back on her feet. "Sorry, shortcake. I've got to go do big people stuff."

Aurora threw her arms around his legs. "Okay. We'll play later. C'mon, Daddy!"

Paul left them in the doorway and chased Aurora up the stairs with the five-year-old shrieking the whole way.

"Beckett," Gia began.

"I need to go." Blindly he stepped off her porch and started toward his house.

"Beckett!" Gia dashed after him, pulling on a sweatshirt. "Wait!" She caught up to him and grabbed his arm. "Where are you going?"

"I'm going home." He yanked his arm out of her grip and kept moving.

He was waylaid again when she jumped on his back and wrapped her arms around his neck. "Gianna!" He grabbed her by the wrists and slung her off his back. He was so angry he was shaking. "Is this why you couldn't come over to dinner? Because your *husband* is back?"

"Beckett, please talk to me," she begged. "There's nothing to be upset about. Tell me why you're so angry."

"Why am I so angry?" He turned on her. "Your husband just answered the door. Your husband who misses his family."

"My ex-husband," she corrected. "And of course he misses his family. Who wouldn't miss those kids?"

"Then why are you trying to take them away from him?"

The words pushed her back a step. "What are you talking about?"

"You heard me. You broke up your own family. Paul doesn't look like he's done being a father. It's obvious he still cares for you."

"I don't understand what you're saying. Of course Paul isn't done being a dad, and of course he still cares for me. I still care for him. But what does that have to do with you?"

"You've got me filling shoes that aren't even empty," he snapped.

"Excuse me?" Gianna's tone was ice cold. She wrapped her arms around herself.

"There's a man in there who doesn't look disconnected and disinterested to me. And you've already got me lined up, falling for you, falling for your kids. Well, I've got news for you. I'm not poaching someone else's family."

"You need to stop now before you say something that can't be taken back." Gia was getting fiery. Matching anger with anger.

There was no stopping the tirade now. The words tumbled out of his mouth.

"Maybe it's a family trait. You and your father just shuffling people in and out of relationships, rearranging families."

"Beckett, I'm going to give you a chance to calm down, and then you're going to give me a chance to explain why Paul is here." Her jaw was clenched.

"No." The word cracked across the backyard with the force of a whip. "I don't need you to explain to me what he's doing here. He came to ask for a second chance, and you're not going to use me as an excuse not to give him one. I'm not stepping in to play daddy when he's here, ready and willing."

She shivered from the ice in his voice. He too felt the cold from the inside out.

"You can't take a man's family from him, Gianna."

"I'm not taking anyone's family away from anyone."

"You just decided you were done. He's clearly not done with you or the kids. Not all families are lucky enough to get the choice to stay together. Sometimes we lose people and we can't get them back." His throat clogged with emotions. Anger, frustration, and that bitter sadness that had never dulled, never faded.

"I did what was right for my family," Gianna snapped. "I would have thought you of all people would understand that."

"No, you did what you thought was right for you. You've got a chance to make it right for everyone, and you're selfish if you don't."

"So that's it then? You don't even want to hear what I have to say?" Gianna's words were clipped. "Once again you make a sweeping decision that affects me *and* my kids, and we don't even get to talk about it?"

The ice lodged in his gut. Somewhere along the line, he'd started to think of all of them as his. But they weren't. They belonged to a man named Paul who was waiting for his wife to come back.

"Go home, Gia."

30

*G*ia had never been so grateful for Paul than when she went back in the house. He took one look at her face and volunteered to watch the kids. Her expression must have said it all. She was so angry, so hurt. A rage headache pounded behind her eyes. Even the heavy bag wouldn't be enough to work off this mad. Nothing short of pounding in Beckett's face would make it stop.

She climbed in her car and briefly entertained a fantasy of taking out Beckett's mailbox as she backed down the drive. She'd found early on in her marriage that entertaining violent fantasies usually prevented her from physically following through on them. She thought of Trudy and suddenly felt a kinship to the crazy woman.

How dare Beckett place judgment on her like that? How dare he filter her life through his own issues? He missed his father? That was no excuse for trying to make her feel guilty for doing what was best for her kids.

It was best, wasn't it? Dragging Evan out of the school he'd just started to get used to because Paul had a "new gig" with a "guaranteed record deal." The permanent ambivalence with which he'd viewed his parenting responsibilities. He wasn't a "bed and bath time" kind of dad. He was a "spend the night at the recording studio" or "call from the road" dad. He'd missed birthdays, anniversaries, story time, groundings, and bad dreams.

She brought up the last straw in her mind's eye. She'd come home from a yoga class. She'd just started teaching a few months earlier as a way to earn some extra money. When Paul had lost his job again, she picked up a few extra classes at one of the studios where she worked.

It was after nine, she hadn't eaten, she still had to pack Evan's lunch for the next day, and the school bake sale she'd promised brownies to had snuck up on her.

She stopped at the grocery store for brownie ingredients and crossed her fingers that her debit card wouldn't be declined. Money was tight, and Paul once again was making noise about following his music career rather than buckling down and making ends meet.

"It's my dream, G. Can't you understand? If I lived like every other stiff in a suit out there, I'd wither up and die," he'd told her over and over again.

But things were different when there were little mouths to feed and feet to cover and back rent to pay. Dreams had to be shuffled into the luxury folder, at least until basic necessities were met. She'd had dreams too and had nearly given up on every single one of them while she became the sole breadwinner, the primary caregiver.

Carrying her measly bag of eggs and brownie mix, she'd come home to chaos. A couple of Paul's friends had stopped by. The sink was filled with empty beer cans and stale cigarette smoke, and raucous laughter wafted into the house through the open patio door. She could hear them out there, someone fiddling with an acoustic guitar while another one told a loud story about a prostitute who played a mean keyboard in Des Moines.

There was an ashtray with a joint in it on the third-hand coffee table.

And Evan was in his pajamas on the couch trying to comfort a crying Aurora.

Gia had been mad then, too. But then it had been more resignation than rage. Because she'd expected it, she realized. Paul was up front about who he was and what he wanted out of life. She'd been the one to think she could deal with it or, worse, change it.

But watching her ten-year-old play parent to her daughter while their father chased his dreams in the backyard made her realize she couldn't do either anymore.

She'd shut the patio door, tucked the kids into bed, and made three dozen brownies. And when Paul came inside to try to charm a plate of brownies out of her, she'd quietly told him she was filing for divorce in the morning.

There had been no fight, no discussion. No requests for custody or even visitation. And that's what broke her heart for her kids. He should have wanted them. He should have wanted her. But he didn't. Not then.

And not now, either. Beckett was wrong.

She parked on the street and stared at the cozy townhouse. She could see the TV flickering in the front room through the window.

On autopilot, she got out of her car and climbed the steps to the front door. She rang the bell, and when the door opened, she fell into the arms of the only man who had never let her down.

"Hi, Daddy," she sniffled in his warm, safe embrace.

Franklin had seen enough female tears in his time to know that now wasn't the time for words. It was time for the silent comfort that only a father could give. She let him guide her into the living room and was beyond mortified when she realized Phoebe was curled up on the couch, a Cary Grant movie paused on the TV.

"Oh! I'm so sorry, Phoebe. I wasn't thinking." Gia wished the cream-colored carpet would swallow her up and put her out of her misery.

Phoebe gave her a warm smile as she rose from the couch. She was wearing cotton pajama pants and a tunic length sweater. A bowl of popcorn sat on the coffee table.

"Don't be silly." Phoebe patted her hand. "I'm going to go make us some tea." She laid a gentle hand on Franklin's shoulder as she made her way back to the kitchen.

The gesture wasn't lost on her, even in her current state of rage-induced hysteria.

"You two really love each other, don't you, Daddy?"

Franklin gestured toward the couch, and Gia flopped down, hugging a corduroy pillow to her chest. He sat down next to her, a smile breaking through the worry on his face when she nudged him with her foot. "Don't you?" she said again.

He nodded. "I never expected to find this at my age." He sighed.

"At your age?" Gia rolled her eyes. "You make it sound like you're a million years old."

Broad-shouldered with his kind, crinkle-eyed smile, he'd always been handsome. In high school, all the friends who'd crossed their threshold did so carrying a torch for Franklin Merrill. Even when his hair had gone from dark to silver, it only made him more distinguished.

"I'm a lucky man," he sighed with contentment.

"Phoebe's a pretty lucky lady," Gia said, nudging him again with her toes. "I hope I'm that lucky someday."

"Your luck seems to have been improving," Franklin said, patting her knee. "Beckett is about as far from Paul as you can get. He clearly cares about you and the kids."

"And yet he just broke up with me."

Her father frowned. "Has he suffered a recent head injury?"

Gia laughed in spite of herself. She shook her head. "No, but he may end up with one if I have anything to say about it."

"Uh-oh," Phoebe said, carrying a tray laden with steaming mugs, slices of lemon, and a box of tissues. "Beckett?"

"I don't want to speak ill of the soon-to-be-dead in front of his mother."

"Sweetie, you can't say anything that I haven't already thought about all of my boys. I love them to pieces, but every single one of them can be an idiot."

"Do they ever snap out of it?" Gia helped herself to a tissue and blew her nose.

"Eventually." Phoebe sank down in the armchair across from them. "How big of an idiot was he?"

Gia relayed the gist of the fight.

"He wouldn't even let me explain what Paul was doing here in the first place though, being my attorney, he should have figured it out." Gia took a sip of her tea, and her eyes widened.

"I hope you don't mind a little whiskey in your tea." Phoebe smiled. "It seemed appropriate."

"Bless you," Gia sighed and took another sip.

"What is Paul doing here?" Franklin asked.

"He starts a new gig in the city next week and swung through to sign the guardianship papers for Evan. I thought he could spend some time with the kids, you know, present a united front to Evan when we explain what the paperwork means. I don't want him thinking his father just abandoned him."

"Did you give Beckett a head's up that Paul was coming?"

Gia shook her head. "That would have required Paul telling me he was coming and not just showing up fifteen minutes before Beckett knocked on the door. I'd left Paul a voicemail yesterday asking if he'd be up for a visit soon."

Phoebe closed her eyes and shook her head, her stubby ponytail twitching. "And Beckett decided that Paul was here because he wants a second chance."

"And he feels very strongly that I should give him one." That stung as much as anything. Not only had Beckett accused her of selfishly splitting up her family, but he walked away from her without a look back. Just like Paul.

"Dad, did I give up too quickly with Paul?" She shoved the words out before she could bury them again. "Would the kids be better off if I had stayed?"

Her father took her hand, squeezed it reassuringly. "I know you kept quiet about many of the details about why you and Paul ended things, but your sisters have big mouths. What does your gut tell you? Do you think you should have stayed?"

Gia closed her eyes, went back to that night again in her mind. She was already shaking her head. "No. If anything I should have done it sooner." She opened her eyes, blew her nose again. "So what do I do? Evan and Aurora love Beckett. But he just walked away. He didn't even try."

Phoebe picked up her mug, and Gia could have sworn she heard her mutter "asshole."

Franklin squeezed her hand again. "It sounds to me like he's hurting. The Beckett Pierce that I know is a rational, loyal, kind man. Usually the only thing that can turn men like that into raving lunatics is love. You must really matter to him to have him act like such an idiot."

Gia gave her father half a smile. "Thanks, Dad."

"He's a good man, honey. Give him a little time to realize how stupid he was, and I promise everything will work out."

She heaved a mighty sigh. "Thanks for letting me barge into your quiet evening like this. Both of you," she said.

"I'm glad that we're close enough for barging in. I've missed you and your sisters. Missed being needed."

Gia crawled over and wrapped her arms around his neck. "You'll never not be needed, Daddy."

Franklin and Phoebe waved a stronger, steadier Gia off from the porch. Phoebe was already dialing her phone as Gia eased away from the curb.

"Now, who are you calling at this hour?" Franklin asked, sliding an arm around her waist.

"I'm calling in the reserves," Phoebe said. "My sons have a diabolical stubborn streak that doesn't usually right itself. Beckett's going to need a pretty good push."

31

_B_eckett refused to look at his phone when he got out of bed the next morning. He had no desire to see any apology texts or voicemails from Gianna. And then— when he finally broke down at lunch and checked—he was even more pissed to find there were none.

It was only a matter of time before the whole town knew they were through. Ellery had certainly gotten the message loud and clear that morning when he'd told her not to worry about finishing Evan's guardianship papers before slamming his office door.

She'd communicated with him via email for the rest of the morning.

He felt bad about being a dick to the one woman he could always count on and offered to buy her lunch. He gave her extra cash and ordered a smoothie from OJ's just to keep her out of the office a little longer so he could fester in peace.

He couldn't believe Gianna would do this to him. Just as he'd been thinking about the future...

Thinking about their future got him knocked on the ass by her past. Her present, he corrected himself. Paul was back.

And no matter what Gianna's argument was, Beckett wasn't going to step between a man and his family. Not one that had the opportunity to be reunited.

He closed his eyes and brought his father's face to mind. The sharp gray eyes, the lines carved by time and sun. A mouth that always looked as if it was smiling at some inside joke. Beckett could almost hear the sound of his laugh, a raspy chuckle. He would have laughed last night at his boys cruising the town square, razzing each other and reminiscing. John Pierce would have been there with them, riding shotgun in his worn flannel.

He would have been there if he could. But Beckett's family wasn't one that could be put back together.

However, Gianna's could.

By mid-afternoon, Beckett's curiosity got the best of him. He put aside deposition transcripts that he'd been staring at without seeing for an hour and logged into Facebook. The news had surely gotten out by now. Maybe someone had posted a picture of how Gianna was coping.

Not that he cared.

He frowned at his screen. The link was always there on the left, but it was missing now. He tried the mobile app with the same results. Dismissing it as a glitch, Beckett retreated back to his dark mood and work.

It was another thirty minutes before he gave up entirely.

He wasn't accomplishing anything moping in his office.

Like a coward, he emailed Ellery from behind closed doors and told her he was calling it a day. He headed upstairs and changed into running clothes and headed out at a hard run toward the trail that snaked through woods and fields.

By mile three, his pace had him gasping for breath. He slowed just enough to not have a heart attack. He heard footsteps on the trail behind him, light and quick. He knew the tread.

"Hey, Beckett," Taneisha breathed as she loped alongside him, her long legs eating up the gravel with ease.

"Hey." His greeting sounded like someone was strangling the breath right out of him.

"Sorry to hear about you and Gia," she said conversationally.

Beckett stumbled but recovered quickly. "You heard, huh?"

She shot him an "are you stupid" look. "Yeah, I heard. It's too bad, but that Paul's a hell of a guy."

Beckett swiveled his head on his neck so fast he heard a snap. "Paul? You met him?"

"Yeah, he was in the lunch yoga class today. He's incredibly limber."

Beckett grunted. Of course he was. Dick.

"You can tell there's a long history there," Taneisha continued, oblivious to Beckett's internal conflict. "Anyway, I better pick up the pace." She winked and shoved her earbuds back in her ears.

"Break a leg," Beckett muttered.

"What was that?" Taneisha slowed down and pulled out an earbud.

"Uh, I said good luck."

She waved and took off, her antelope strides leaving him behind to stew in his funk.

IT HAPPENED EVERYWHERE. Everyone wanted to talk about Paul. And no one seemed interested in the fact that Beckett was devastated and furious over the breakup. No, Fran at the gym wanted to tell him all about Paul's superior squat clean and how he knew one of her drummer friends.

When he ran into Ernest Washington at the gas station, he made sure to tell Beckett about Paul's interest and extensive background in the VW culture. And Bruce Oakleigh called him just to tell him that Paul had a "really terrific suggestion" about a town battle of the bands festival for the summer.

Beckett's own mother didn't even ask how he was feeling before launching into singing the praises of Paul who had apparently joined Gianna and the kids at Franklin's house for a nice family dinner. "I just think it's so amazing that he's instilled a love of music in his kids. Did you know that Aurora can name all the members of the Beatles?"

No, Mother. He didn't know that. And quite frankly he didn't really care. Not that he said that to Phoebe. But he sure thought it.

"You realize this means that Gianna and I broke up, right?"

Phoebe chuckled. "Darling, if you were serious about her, you wouldn't have let a little competition get in your way. You're probably relieved. I'm sure it was tricky for you dating a woman with kids. Now you can go back to your Trudys."

Beckett felt sick at the thought.

The last time he answered his phone, it was Anthony Berkowicz calling to get a quote from Beckett on Paul Decker's musician chic wardrobe. "We're trying to expand the readership of *The Monthly Moon* with a fashion section," he'd explained.

Beckett had hung up on him and narrowly avoided throwing his cell phone through the leaded glass window.

By Day Three of the breakup that nobody else cared about, he'd not only given up answering his phone, but also shaving, protein shakes, and client meetings. Whoever was calling or on the schedule was just going to tell him Paul Decker got nominated for a Nobel Peace Prize or saved Mrs. Nordeman from a choking death with the Heimlich maneuver. And Beckett could live without that knowledge.

But he couldn't live without food. The only food left in the house was cereal and sour cream, a combination he'd been desperate enough to sample at lunch. A choice he regretted immediately. Beckett pulled the hooded sweatshirt over his head, hoping to go unrecognized in downtown Blue Moon. It was a risky move while it was still light outside, but he had no other choice.

He called in a to-go order from Peace of Pizza to be ready in half an hour and took a deep breath as he stepped out on to his front porch. He could do this. He'd swing by the library to check out the space for Evan's Debate Club—if Evan still wanted him to be the advisor. And then he'd sneak into downtown to pick up dinner.

In, out, no need for anyone to talk to him about how great Paul Fucking Decker was.

Luck was on his side, and he was able to avoid all human contact besides friendly waves and "hey theres" on the way to the library.

It was one of the oldest buildings in Blue Moon. Originally a school, the brick three-story building now housed the town's eclectic collection of literature. There was an entire section dedicated to tie-dye crafts.

A man on a mission, Beckett quickly walked past the front desk. Usually the combination of scents of old books and the new carpet the board had installed last year made him feel nostalgic, but today he had no room for nostalgia. Taking the stairs in the atrium at the center of the building, he jogged up to the second floor.

There were more books here, including a special wing dedicated to Woodstock and the rest of the sixties. The back half of the floor was still cordoned off into the original class-rooms that were now used as meeting spaces.

He picked a door at random and opened it. And stepped into a fresh hell.

Willa, Rainbow and Gordon Berkowicz, Bruce Oakleigh, Bobby from Peace of Pizza, and Wilson Abramovich, the town jeweler, sat around a conference table listening intently as Ellery walked them through a three-point plan for something.

The TV screen on the wall had two pictures on it. Gia's and Paul's. There was a hand-written timeline on a white board behind her with the last event listed as Happily Ever After.

There were iced heart-shaped cookies on a platter in the center of the table. Everyone had a ruby red notebook in front of them with the initials B.C. embossed in a heart on the covers.

"Oh my God."

All eyes flew guiltily to him. Gordon was the first to react. He jumped up and tried to cover the TV screen with his slight build.

"Oh, hey there, Beckett," he said, lacing his fingers behind his head and spreading his elbows wide.

"Ellery?" Beckett's betrayal was complete. He sagged against the doorframe. "You, too?"

She looked like a little kid caught stealing cookies. "I'm sorry, Beckett. I thought this is what you wanted. You broke up with Gia so she could get back with Paul, and he's such a great guy."

The table murmured their agreement.

"You know Paul?" Beckett asked.

"Sure, he came into the office today." Guilt turned to excitement. "Oh my God, did you know he opened for the Flying Spiders?"

She must have taken Beckett's blank look as permission to keep going.

"The Flying Spiders are the hottest goth grunge band this side of the Mississippi. Paul was opening for them and ended up playing a set with them when their drummer was too strung out—"

He cut her off. "You all should be ashamed of yourselves, meddling in people's lives. What if they don't want your help? What if there's someone else out there, better for... someone?" He wasn't making any sense now.

"But Beckett, we were just following your lead. Getting Paul and Gia back together. It's what you wanted," Ellery said, her dark eyes wide and sad. She looked like a kicked puppy, and Beckett felt like the victim of an elephant stampede.

He glanced at the whiteboard again. Within the bounds of a red heart the numbers 27-0 were written. The Beautification Committee's record of wins in love. They had never failed in a match. Why did he want them to fail this time? This was the right thing, wasn't it?

He backed out into the hallway, shutting the door with a click, and missed the satisfied grins around the table.

BECKETT LEFT the library under a cloud of doom. With the involvement of the B.C., it was only a matter of time before Gia and Paul were remarried and working on baby number three. Most likely in his backyard.

He wanted to throw up.

But it was what he wanted or at least what was right—

wasn't it? Then why did he feel like shit? And how had he not known that Ellery was a member of the B.C.?

Maizie at Peace of Pizza told him it would be another couple of minutes, and rather than wait inside with people, he chose to head across the street to the solitude of the park. If he stayed on this end of it, he wouldn't get too close to the yoga studio, wouldn't witness Paul doing some flying swan hand-stand pose or something equally awesome.

He was just stepping up onto the curb when a little flash of red flew at him. "Bucket!"

Aurora, bundled up in a purple coat, launched herself at him. Without thinking, he swooped her up and held her high until she giggled.

"I missed you, Bucket!" she said when he settled her on his hip. "Mama says you're busy."

He felt a pang of guilt. "I'm sorry, shortcake. I miss you, too."

She had little pink mittens on her hands, and her ponytail was askew. "I'm hungry, Bucket. Can I have a snack?"

Beckett wished with all his might that he had a snack squirreled away in a pocket to give her. "Sorry, kiddo. I don't have anything with me."

Her face fell, hungry devastation.

"Where's your mom?" he asked, realizing that a panicked Gianna should have come running by now.

"She's at da school wiv Evan for somethin'."

"Did you run away from the school?" Beckett was already digging for his phone before realizing it was still at home.

"No! Silly!" she giggled. "I'm wiv Daddy."

"Okay, then where's Daddy?" Beckett asked. Darkness was starting to fall, and the park, even in Blue Moon, was no place for a five-year-old by herself.

"I dunno. His phone rang, and he says 'Rora, you hang out

here!'" she said in a deep voice. "So I hopped, hopped, hopped on one foot, but I think I hopped too far. Can I go home wiv you?"

Beckett wanted that more than anything. "How about we find your dad first, and then we'll figure it out, okay?"

Aurora sighed. "Okay. Thanks for finding me, Bucket." She patted his shoulder and stared at him cocking her head from one side to the other. "I like your face blanket," she said, bringing her mittens to his cheeks. "Scratchy!"

Face blanket? God love this kid. He hugged her a little tighter to him.

Five long minutes later, during which Beckett began to wonder if Aurora had been abandoned, they spotted Paul pacing in front of a park bench having an animated phone conversation.

He paused when he spotted them and raised a hand that held a cigarette in greeting. "Yeah, yeah. Listen, just do what you have to do, and we'll figure it out in a couple of days, okay? No, man, I'm still in. We'll figure it out. Cool, cool. Okay, listen, I gotta go. There's a gorgeous redhead making eyes at me. Ha. Yeah. Later."

Paul hung up and took one last drag of his cigarette before stubbing it out on the trashcan.

"There's my Rora Borealis," he said, holding out his hands to her.

Beckett paused for just a second before handing his daughter over.

"Thanks for entertaining her. Business call went a little longer than expected."

"No big deal, I just found her across the street in an alley," Beckett said, stone faced.

"Oh hey! You're Beckett, Gia's—"

"Landlord," Beckett supplied.

"Cool."

The guy was way more excited than he should have been.

"I've been hearing a ton about you from the kids. Haven't I, Rora?" he tickled her until she giggled.

"Daddy, I'm hungry," she said between fits of giggles.

"Okay. We can fix that. Is there any food at home?"

"Daddy! I don't know. Can you make pancakes wiv chocolate and bananas?"

Paul frowned. "I don't know how to make that. Sorry, kid. What's next on the list?"

Aurora was starting to look concerned. "Can I have Fruity O's and soda?"

Paul looked at Beckett. Beckett shook his head, imagining the fit Gianna would have if Paul were to pump her daughter full of eight thousand grams of sugar before bed.

"Uh, sorry princess. No on the Fruity O's. Oh, shit. Don't do that."

Aurora's lip was out, and her eyes were tearing up. "Daddy said 'shiiiiiiiit,'" she said on a tearful wail. "I'm so hungry."

Paul jiggled her up and down, looking left and right like he was looking for a place to stash her. Beckett swooped in and pulled her out of his arms. "Hey, shortcake, do you and your daddy want to come have pizza with me?"

"Yes!" Her eyes cleared, her lip stopped trembling and now she was bouncing up and down on Beckett's hip. "Yes! Yes!"

"Dude, you're like the Kid Whisperer," Paul said with admiration.

Beckett almost cracked a smile. Almost.

Paul's phone rang again, of course it was a Led Zeppelin guitar riff.

He looked at it. "Oh, I gotta take this. Would you mind?" He tilted his head at Aurora.

Beckett looked at the bouncing Aurora. "Uh, sure. Just

head over across the park to Peace of Pizza when you're done. I'll get a table."

∾

BECKETT HAD a splitting headache after dinner with Paul and Aurora. The guy was charming, interesting even. Beckett would give him that. But holy mother of God, he should not be allowed to play a role in raising children. Not even his own. Especially not his own.

Not only had he let Aurora wander off into the night in a park by herself, he'd tried to put hot pepper flakes on her cheese pizza, let her order a soda and a chocolate milk, and then expected her to find the restroom by herself.

Instead of coloring on the placemat with her like she'd asked, he'd taken two more phone calls.

Band business, he'd mouthed to Beckett.

With Aurora leaning against his arm on their side of the booth, Beckett picked up a red crayon and tried not to kill Paul with it.

Beckett ended up walking home a block behind them, just to make sure Paul took Aurora home for bed and not to a strip club or bakery.

That night, he hadn't even tried going to bed. Sleep was for happy people in committed relationships. He was alone, and he'd done it to himself.

Beckett had sat on the couch letting the tick of the grand-father clock mark the passing of the night into dawn. How had he so royally fucked it all up? His harsh words to Gianna kept coming back to him, chipping away pieces of his heart. She wasn't the one who owed the apology. It was him. And he was pretty sure there weren't enough 'I'm sorries' in the world to make up for the things he'd said.

He had literally shoved Gianna into the arms of another man. A man who—despite the town's stellar opinion of him—had no business raising children or being married to Gianna.

He, Beckett James Pierce, was the biggest fucking idiot on the planet.

Ellery had taken one look at him that morning when he stumbled into the office in a fog and rescheduled all his appointments for the week. He'd putzed around doing absolutely nothing except for avoiding calls from his family until five.

And now he was having scotch for dinner.

He was sitting on the couch in sweatpants staring at the TV he'd neglected to turn on and debating a third scotch when Carter and Jax walked in.

"Shit." Carter muttered. "He's growing a damn beard."

"Put down the booze and go find some shoes," Jax ordered.

"You put the booze down and go find shoes," Beckett snarled.

Carter threw something shiny at him. "Let's go, asshole."

Beckett stared down at his lap and picked up the key ring. He recognized it without having seen it for a few years. "You want me to kick your ass again?" he sneered. If there was anyone he wanted to punch in the face until he heard the satisfying crunch of cartilage, it was himself... and maybe Paul.

Carter remained silent while Jax stomped upstairs.

"Hey! Don't touch my stuff," Beckett yelled after him.

Jax returned and threw sneakers at him.

"Put 'em on or we make you put 'em on," Carter said, arms crossed.

32

*T*he glove plowed into his face, and this time Beckett tasted blood.

"It's no fun if he doesn't fight back," Jax complained to Carter.

Carter hung over the ropes in the corner. "Beckett, put up your gloves and punch your brother in the fucking face."

"Maybe I want to punch *your* fucking face," Beckett said, his tone surly.

"I'm getting married in six days. Summer said if I came home with a broken nose in time for wedding pictures, she'd shave my beard."

"All the more reason for you to get in the ring."

"Ah, there's a sad little joke out of the sad little clown," Jax said, jabbing him in the ribs. His younger brother, stripped to the waist, ducked and weaved, trying to draw an attack.

"You look like you're on a damn pogo stick," Beckett carped.

"A damn pogo stick that you can't hit," Jax retorted.

"If I make him bleed, can I go home?" Beckett asked Carter.

"We'll see."

Beckett growled in frustration. "I don't have fucking issues to work out by pounding on my brother."

Jax shuffled around the ring throwing shadow punches. "This is boring!" he whined. "Carter, this was a stupid idea. He probably doesn't even miss Gia. He's probably happy she's back with Pau—"

Beckett's right cross caught him off guard enough to knock him back a few steps.

"Oh, so that's the trigger," Jax said, his grin cocky now. "Don't you think it's weird how the whole town just loves this guy?"

He blocked Beckett's next shot and gave him a one-two combination to the ribs.

"I mean, Mom even said he's like this musical genius." Jax wasn't lucky enough to block Beckett's jab. But he countered with a solid shot to the low gut.

"If you punch me in the balls, I swear to God I'll—" Beckett's threat vanished in the heat of the exchange. Punches were thrown fast and hard until sweat and blood began to cloud his vision.

Distantly he heard the ringing of the bell and then realized it was Carter in the corner. "Hey, take a break before someone gets brain damage." He tossed Beckett a towel and Jax a water.

"Can we be done now?" Beckett grumbled, testing out the swelling flesh under his left eye.

"That depends," Carter said conversationally. "Do you feel better?"

"No, I don't fucking feel better. This was your thing, not mine. I'm not fighting some inner demons. Taking swings at someone isn't going to make me feel better."

"I was hoping you'd say that," Carter said, slipping on gloves. "I'm tapping in, Jax."

"Summer's gonna kiiiiill you," Jax sang as he hobbled out of the ring.

"Break my nose, and my wife-to-be will murder you. Got it?" Carter said to Beckett.

Beckett answered with a jab to the chin.

"You fucker."

It was like the old days. Only Carter wasn't handicapped by bullet wounds anymore, and Beckett hadn't slept in three days.

"You're such an idiot," Carter said conversationally as they sparred back and forth. "You're in love with this girl, and you put her on a goddamn platter for someone else."

"I thought it was for the best," Beckett grunted, driving his fist into Carter's face.

Carter shook off the blow. "Like I said. An idiot."

They sweated out another fast exchange of fists with Carter finally dancing out of his reach.

"It's my business," Beckett wheezed. It was his business that he'd colossally fucked up, and now it was up to him to fix it.

"So what are you going to do?" Carter's fist flew into his line of vision, glancing off his jaw.

Beckett stumbled back a step. "I'm gonna fight."

He didn't go down in a blaze of glory. It was more like a soupy splatter on the mat. But damned if he didn't go down swinging. And smiling.

Jax crawled back in with water and more towels, and the three men lay on their backs staring up at the fluorescent lights.

"Feel better?" Carter asked, his breath coming fast and shallow.

Beckett swiped blood off his forehead with the towel. He did. He really did.

A good fight was exactly the primer he needed for an even bigger fight. Gianna didn't belong with Paul. She belonged with him. She deserved more than what that skinny "hey man" musician could give, and he was going to see that she got it.

"Ever think about patenting this as some kind of therapy?" he asked.

IF ONE MORE STUPID person mentioned Beckett Pierce's name to her without attaching the words "is an asshole," she was going to give up on her heavy bag and just start decking people in town, Gia decided.

Blue Moon was obviously Team Beckett.

Ever since the breakup, she'd heard nothing but "I'm so sorry to hear about you and Beckett. He's such an amazing blah blah blah."

After some kind of login glitch with the gossip group, she was granted access again only to read the brief, terse post on Facebook about their breakup. It was the only mention of them before the group had started singing Beckett's praises.

She thought this town had been rooting for them. But she'd been wrong.

For Throwback Thursday, someone had posted a picture of Beckett rescuing a kitten from a porch roof. Another Mooner had posted video of Beckett's speech at the women in enterprise luncheon.

Oh, and she didn't want to forget to talk about how "great" it was to see Beckett treating Paul and Aurora to dinner at Peace of Pizza. Gia didn't even want to know how that came about. Beckett was probably offering to officiate their second wedding.

She knew he was Blue Moon's fearless leader and all, but didn't anyone care that the man had just given up and walked away from their relationship on a stupid misunderstanding?

Team Gia was feeling very lonely. And excessively angry. Between the "yay Beckett" from the entire town and the fact that Paul was driving her insane at home, she was afraid she was going to develop a rage problem. Especially since she wasn't about to give Beckett the satisfaction of seeing her head to the shed to beat out some problems.

Not that he was looking in the backyard. He'd made it clear he was done. Done with her and done with them. Just making way for Paul.

The thought that she would take Paul back was laughable. To both her and Paul. The entire reason for his visit was to sign the guardianship papers, which they had done with Ellery in Gia's kitchen two days ago. Beckett clearly had no interest in helping with the process anymore. And now Paul was just killing time before his new gig started in Brooklyn.

Every time his phone rang, Gia prayed it was the band telling him the timeline moved up. She didn't want to cheat the kids out of time with their father, but she also didn't want to murder him in front of them. She was spending every spare moment of the day with Summer on the magazine just to avoid being around Paul or in Beckett's backyard.

As Thrive took shape online, Gia felt like everything else was spinning out of control. Her only safe place was the desk in Summer's office.

Things with Paul were exactly the same as when they split up. Gia cooked, cleaned, and worked. He brokered deals and played video games and told everyone exciting stories about life on the road.

Between her rage at Beckett and Paul's all-night first-person shooter video game marathons on the couch outside her bedroom, she wasn't sleeping well. And an unrested Gia was an even more distracted one.

Evan went to school with no socks today because she hadn't switched the laundry over to the dryer. The glue sticks she'd promised Aurora's art teacher were still at the store because she forgot to buy them. Again.

And at this exact moment, she was standing outside her studio staring at the locked front door.

Gia knew what she had to do. But she didn't want to. She didn't want to hear that voice or ask him for anything. Unfortunately, she had a class starting in fifteen minutes, and it was going to happen on the cold November sidewalk if she didn't get into the studio.

She took a deep breath and dialed. Gia closed her eyes. "Please be Ellery. Please be Ellery," she chanted.

"Pierce Law," Ellery's chipper voice rang out.

"Oh, thank God," Gia said in a rush. "Ellery, it's Gia."

"Hey, Gia! It's so good to hear from you! How's it going?" Ellery's voice was unusually loud in her ear.

"Uh, it's fine. I'm locked out of my studio, and I can't find my keys. I think Beckett said he hid a spare somewhere. Can you—"

"Gia?"

She inhaled sharply at the sound of his voice. Deep, smooth, with a warm liquid pull like bourbon.

She closed her eyes. "Hi," she said, going for brisk.

"Ellery said you had an emergency."

Gia added Ellery to her growing list of people to kill.

"Is everything okay?" Beckett asked. "The kids?"

"Everyone's fine. I just need you—I mean..." She was getting flustered.

"You were saying you need me?"

Was that hope she heard in his voice?

She shook her head. It didn't matter. "I need you to tell me where the spare key for the studio is. Please," she added hastily.

He was silent for a beat. "Sure. It's around back. Just stay on the phone so I know you found it."

"Uh..." She didn't care for that idea.

"Are you walking around the building?"

Gia sprang into action and jogged around the side of the building toward the alley. "Yes, I'm almost to the alley."

"So how are the kids?"

"You should know since you just had dinner with Aurora," Gia grumbled.

"She said you were at the school with Evan?"

Gia hurried into the alley. "Uh, yeah. It was an art exhibit night for the middle school. They'd done some pottery stuff, and I was afraid Aurora would go Tasmanian devil on the displays. I'm in the alley now."

She thought she heard him bite back a sigh. "There's a loose brick just above ground level under the first window by the door. Do you see it?"

She spotted it, wiggled it with her foot. "I got it."

"It's tucked in behind it—"

"Thank you. I've got to run," Gia said, interrupting him.

"Gianna, wait. I wanted to apolo—"

"I've got to go. Thank you," she said flatly before disconnecting the call and wondering how hard it would be to break a lease.

33

With less than a week to the wedding, Beckett opened his house to Carter's bachelor party. Poker, hot sausage subs—a lame veggie sub for the groom— beer, cigars, and scotch. It was man heaven.

It was also step one of his plan to win Gia back. Beckett hoped Carter didn't mind his party working a little double duty.

"This is quite the setup," Carter said, snagging a chip out of the bowl on Beckett's dining room table.

"Food's in here. Poker's in the parlor," Beckett said, dumping a stack of paper plates on the table. "I hope you don't mind, but I invited Paul."

Carter stopped mid-chew. "You invited Paul?" He swallowed hard.

"Yeah, and Evan."

"Evan's cool," Carter said, still eyeing him.

"What, don't you love Paul like the entire rest of the universe?" Beckett asked.

"I think he's great," Carter said blandly. "I'm just surprised you don't mind him. Seeing as how he's your woman's ex-husband and all."

"My ex-woman's ex-husband," Beckett clarified.

"So you're starting to come around to him?" Beckett could see his brother trying to work it out.

"Let's just say keep your friends close—"

"And your enemies closer," Carter finished. "Just what are you up to?"

"Just being neighborly." Beckett shrugged. Step one was to figure out where everyone stood. Was Paul serious about getting back together with Gia? Was Gia now seriously considering it since Beckett opened his big, fat trap? And what did Evan think about the situation? It was time for some reconnaissance.

The front door opened, saving him from further interrogation.

Jax and Franklin strolled in.

The greetings were fast and easy. Beckett played host and doled out the first round of beverages. Franklin was another good source to tap, he decided, watching the man unload a tray of seafood bruschetta.

"Listen, Franklin, I was wondering if you had a minute," Beckett began awkwardly. He'd been nothing short of rude to the man for six months, and now that he needed something he was all buddy buddy. It was despicable, and he wouldn't blame Franklin for not wanting to hear him out.

"I was actually hoping to talk to you and your brothers tonight about something, too" he said, sliding a hand in the pocket of his khakis. He was wearing another loud Hawaiian shirt tonight. This one had pink and blue surfboards on it.

"Well, you first," Beckett said.

Franklin pulled his hand out of his pocket clutching a black velvet jewelers box. Beckett's mouth fell open.

"Holy shit." Jax and Carter were frozen in the doorway between the dining room and parlor. The bowl of chips Jax held tumbled to the floor.

"Anybody home?" Gianna with Evan and Aurora in tow poked her head into the parlor from the foyer.

She took in the scene in about two seconds flat and recovered even faster. "Can I see you three in the kitchen?" she asked through gritted teeth, pointing at Beckett and his brothers.

When no one moved she gave them all an icy glare. "Now!"

"I'll just stay out here with Evan and Aurora?" Franklin looked at Beckett with a mix of pity and relief. "Good luck," he whispered.

They filed past Gianna into Beckett's kitchen.

"This has gone on long enough," Gianna snapped. She stationed herself in front of the door, legs braced and hands on hips. "Talk."

"Talk about what?" Beckett growled.

"About why *you* don't want your mother and my father together." She was still mad. Beckett considered that a good sign. She still had strong feelings for him, even if they all were rage-related.

"Gia's right. They seem happy," Carter started. "Why don't you want her with him?"

Beckett remained sullenly silent, and Gia actually stomped her foot.

"You took your issues here out on me, but I swear to God if you try to do that to my father—the man who loves your mother, the man who defended you to me after you were a complete and utter asshole—" Her finger drilled into his chest. "I will destroy you. No one hurts my family and walks away from it."

Beckett shoved her hand out of the way and fought the

overwhelming urge to shove her back against the door. He wasn't sure if he wanted to shake her or kiss her. Probably both. She'd always had that ability to stir him up, to shake his control.

"Exactly what issues are you accusing me of taking out on you?" he asked.

She didn't even flinch at the tone that had been known to terrify others. The finger was back in his chest, sharper than ever. "That you were the only one here to pick up the pieces after your father died. And that's why—"

"Whoa, whoa. Hold on there—" Carter started.

"Shut up, Carter," Gia ordered without taking her eyes off Beckett. "Tell them. Tell them why you'd stand in the way of a good man who loves your mother."

"You weren't here." Beckett's tone was cold, sharp. But he was talking to his brothers now. "You didn't see her after Dad died. After everyone else went back to their lives, and she was left here. Alone."

"She wasn't alone," Jax argued.

"Aunt Rose and Uncle Melvin left a few days after you two did. I went back to school. The man that she had spent every day with for twenty-six years was gone. She was alone, grieving and facing the loss of the only thing she had left."

"What the hell are you talking about?" Carter demanded.

"We almost lost the farm. Dad had been sick for so long, we were falling behind on everything. If it wasn't for Rainbow at the bank, you both would have come home to nothing," he snapped. "She gave me a loan when there was no way in hell that I could have qualified for one. I was over my head in law school loans. But she gave me just enough to get us by."

"If you needed money, why didn't—" Carter began.

"Mom wanted to do this by herself. She was so pissed when she found out about the loan." Beckett crossed his arms and leaned against the counter. His lips turned up a little. "It had been so long since I saw anything but sad on her face. We had ourselves a good, long screaming battle in the kitchen."

"The transom," Jax said suddenly.

Beckett nodded, a sad smile played on his lips. "She threw a cast iron skillet through the window above the kitchen door."

"You two were so vague about how it broke," Carter remembered.

"Made me swear never to tell anyone. It was the first night that she didn't cry herself to sleep."

Carter stared at the floor.

"So don't fucking tell me you know what it was like. You had the Army, and you had your big-time career," he said pointing to his brothers. "Mom and I had the land and each other. Even with the help from town, she worked herself to exhaustion every single day until you came home, Carter."

"Why didn't she tell us to come home?" Jax kicked at the leg of a barstool.

Beckett shrugged. "I don't know. She wanted you to live your own lives, make your own choices."

"Why didn't she just let the farm go?" Carter swiped a hand through his hair, guilt radiating off him. "Start over?"

"Because it was the only thing we had left of him," Beckett said, his voice breaking. "She didn't want all of us to lose the last thing we had."

Gianna laid a hand on his back but said nothing.

The fight had gone out of him.

"I guess that's why I can't wrap my head around Franklin. He's not Dad. He can't be Dad. But she loves him. And that's fine." He ducked his head when Gianna shot a searching glance his way.

"It really is," he told her. "But it means she could get hurt again. And I'd do anything to make sure she never goes through that again."

Carter and Jax absorbed it all. The hurt was palpable.

"It almost broke her, and that almost broke me," Beckett said quietly. Silence descended on the kitchen.

"Good," Gia said, breaking the silence.

"Good?" Beckett's hands clenched to fists at his side.

"You finally said what you needed to say instead of keeping it all locked up." Gia nodded. "Let me ask you this. Do you resent your brothers for not being here when you needed them?"

Beckett looked from Carter to Jackson. There had been a time when he had. When he was so tired of carrying the burden alone. But his brothers, he learned, had burdens of their own.

He shook his head. "Not anymore."

"Good," Gianna said again. "The way it looks is that each of you had your own path to follow, and they all brought you back here. So now it's up to you to decide what to do with that."

"Where are you going?" Beckett demanded when she started for the kitchen door.

"I'm taking my daughter to a bachelorette party." She bustled out the door and down the hallway, returning a moment later with Aurora.

Beckett followed her out the door and onto the back porch. "Don't you want to know what happens?"

"I already know," Gianna said, pausing as Aurora skipped down the steps and scampered toward home.

He snagged her wrist and pulled her back to him. "Tell me."

"You'll make the right call," she said quietly, staring into the middle of his chest refusing to meet his gaze. "Because you're Beckett Pierce, and you have the biggest, kindest heart. And as much as you want to protect your mom from pain, you'd rather see her happy. Now, go make your dad proud."

This time, she raised her gaze to his. He could see tears swimming in her eyes but didn't know why.

"Gianna." He didn't know what else to say. It was only her name on his lips.

"You're a good man, Beckett. You'll do the right thing. Or I will make Trudy look like a walk in the park."

IT HAD the makings of the lowest key bachelorette party in history. Gia opened up the studio to Summer, Joey, Phoebe, Annette, and a few of the ladies from town for a yoga class, snacks, and bridal shower.

She couldn't have been worse company.

While Aurora helped Summer attack her giant pile of wedding and baby gifts, Gia stood in the corner and sulked into her wine glass.

"What the hell is your problem?" Joey sidled up next to her with a plate of crudités. "Also, why is there no meat here?"

"Men are idiots, Joey. Complete and total idiots with no regard for anyone else's feelings," Gia ranted.

"Are men behind the no-meat thing?"

They applauded politely when Summer unwrapped a jumble of macramé.

"Oh! Is this a plant hanger?" she asked, trying to hide her confusion.

"No, dear," Elvira Eustace giggled. "It's a baby swing."

Summer held up her treasure and smiled widely for the camera. "It's wonderful. Thank you so much."

"Ten bucks says she puts the kid in that and they're flat on the floor in less than thirty seconds."

"I'm not taking those odds," Gia agreed.

"So you were saying something about men being idiots?"

Gia looked over to where Phoebe and Annette had their heads together over a set of lumpy, handmade mixing bowls. "I can't say much here."

"How much can you say at Shorty's in half an hour?"

"I can't take my daughter to a sports bar." Gia rolled her eyes and felt the slightest bit guilty that she had considered it for a second.

"You're not," Joey said. "Phoebe's taking Rora back to your house after this shindig wraps up. When Paul comes home from Beckett's, she'll head out. She gave me fifty bucks and told me to buy ourselves a bottle of something strong and Summer every fried menu item."

"God, I love that woman," Gia sighed.

Shorty's was Blue Moon-famous for wings and pool tournaments. And Gia could think of no better place to unwind.

"I'm a built-in designated driver," Summer screeched over the twangy country someone played on the jukebox. "So you all have at it."

Julia from OJ's cracked open a drink menu. "No breast-feeding tonight!" she announced cheerily. "Ed, my friend," she said to the bartender. "A dirty, dirty martini for me and whatever these lovely ladies want." Her pink-tipped silver blonde hair shimmered under the bar lights.

"Cranberry juice for me," Summer sighed. "And a cheese quesadilla. Oh, and the fried pickle chips. To start." She smiled prettily at him.

Ed grinned back. "How about for you two troublemakers?"

he winked at Gia and Joey.

Joey looked at Gia. "Well, Ed, my friend and I are in the market for something strong and mean."

Ed ranged his long frame over the bar and winked. "I got just the thing."

A minute later, he passed a sexy looking martini to Julia and slid two rocks glasses full of something dangerous looking in front of Gia and Joey.

Gia picked hers up and sniffed it. The fumes were startlingly strong.

"I wouldn't do that if I were you," Ed warned her. "These are Ed's Erasers. Won me back-to-back awards at the Bartenders Beat Down in 2012 and 2013."

"To Summer," Gia announced, holding up her glass.

"To me." Summer held up a greasy slice of cheese quesadilla.

They toasted their friend with spirit. The Eraser burned on the way down, and Gia liked it.

"Another one," she gasped when she set the glass down.

"You got it, Red." Gia flinched on the inside when Ed used Beckett's nickname for her.

Summer squealed from two barstools down. She held up her phone. "It's Niko! He'll be here on Wednesday. Which means, Gia, he'll want to shoot your yoga piece on Friday. I can art direct—"

Gia, bit her lip. "Summer, do you really want to art direct an all-day photo shoot the day after you get married?"

Summer's face softened. She grinned dreamily. "You guys, I'm getting married!"

"You are getting married and having babies," Gia corrected her.

"I really hit the jackpot, didn't I?" she asked, stroking her belly.

The goofy grin on her friend's face teased a smile out of Gia. "To Mrs. Pierce," Gia said, holding up her fresh Eraser.

"To Mrs. Pierce," they echoed.

After two Erasers, Gia decided to play it safe and switch to beer. She already felt kind of floaty.

"So spill," Joey ordered. "What's got you spitting fire all night?"

"Beckett Pierce." Gia spat his name out like it was poison. She missed the look Joey shot Summer. "Not only did he break up with me and tell me to go back to my irresponsible ex-husband, but I walk in there tonight to drop Evan off, and my dad—"

She stopped and looked around. "Look, I know that gossip is the lifeblood of this town, but is there any way we can never discuss what I'm about to tell you in case Beckett didn't ruin it already and it actually happens?"

Julia frowned. "I think the Current Silence to Protect Future Events Code works here."

"Perfect!" Gia said, slicing her finger wildly through the air. "So per the Current Silence uh... that code that Julia said, no one can say anything in case Beckett wasn't an asshole and didn't tell my dad he couldn't propose to Phoebe."

"Franklin's going to propose?" Summer gasped.

"I don't know! He had a ring, and he was talking to Beckett, and Beckett looked like he was staring into the abyss or something." She mimicked his expression.

"We are so doing this again after the twins," Summer announced, sipping her cranberry juice.

"So why was Franklin showing Beckett the ring?" Joey asked.

"My dad's old-fashioned. He was probably asking them for their permission, which who knows if Beckett will give since he's an ass!"

She punctuated the word by setting her beer bottle down hard.

"Oh boy," Joey said.

"Oh boy is right," Gia said, poking her friend in the shoulder. "What's wrong with that guy, anyway?"

"Beckett's a great guy," Summer started.

"No! Don't you do that, too," Gia pouted. "All week everyone in town is 'Oh, Beckett is the best ever and everything, and we love him.' No one cares that he sucks. He dumped me, he dumped my kids, and told me to get back with Paul 'I sleep around and don't remember my kids' birthdays' Decker."

"Can we get a water over here, Ed?" Joey asked.

"Yeah, a water so I can throw it in Beckett's dumb face," Gia agreed. "Why's his face all bruised, anyway?" she asked no one in particular. She'd noticed all three of the brothers had been sporting bruises and cuts tonight.

"We aren't talking about that," Summer said with uncustomary ire. "Those idiots are going to be wearing layers of makeup for the wedding pictures."

"What if—and I'm just spit-balling here—" Julia said, trying to get the conversation back on track. "What if he realized he was an idiot and was really sorry?"

Gia frowned. "That would be moderately better."

"And what if he gave you a really great apology?" Summer suggested.

Gia shook her head. "Oh no. I've heard too many apologies in my time. 'I'm sorry' means shit—sorry, crap—to me. It's not the words that are important, it's the actions. Beckett can say he's sorry until he's blue in his sexy, stupid face, but until he starts acting like a human being toward my dad, I don't have time to listen to any 'I'm sorries.'"

Summer, Julia, and Joey shared a long look.

34

---

*W*ith no appointments for the rest of the afternoon, Beckett had a late lunch and cut out of the office. Carter's text had lightened the dark mood that hung like a pall over him for the past ten days.

Carter: Batch is done. Sampling day. Get your ass over here.

The first official sampling of the first official John Pierce Brewery product. This meant more than just a drink with his brothers. It was a toast to their future. A future that was looking brighter for some than others. Carter's wedding was in four days. And Beckett would spend the entire day watching Gianna from afar.

Except for when he walked her down the aisle.

His plan to figure out where everyone stood had gotten off to a slow start. Evan was unreadable. Paul seemed to be more inclined to talk road stories rather than family. And Franklin's surprise announcement had left him reeling enough to not even bring up the subject of his ex-son-in-law.

He needed a new plan.

Beckett pulled up to the barn and admired the progress. The exterior lighting was up, and a split rail fence now defined the parking area. They'd gone with gravel for the parking lot and the drive for now. It would keep traffic slow and give them the option of changing the flow in the future if need be.

He entered through the new commercial glass doors and was pleased with what he saw. Calvin's crew had hauled ass on the main floor to get it ready for the wedding. The floors had been sanded and sealed, hundred-year-old flaws preserved in the wide planks beneath their feet. The massive chandelier they'd let their mother choose hung from the rafters. The wrought iron of its curvy arms kept the piece from being too delicate in a space that echoed rustic masculinity. Though he imagined the girls would have it draped in some poufy material for the wedding.

His brothers waited for him at the still stool-less bar.

Carter, in his daily uniform of worn jeans and a ripped Henley, stood behind the bar with three empty glasses in front of him. Jax leaned across from him, the family resemblance unmistakable in the way he held his shoulders and the quiet assessment in his gray eyes.

Beckett knew his brothers better than he knew himself. And it was clear they were up to something.

"Nice of you to join us, Mr. Mayor," Carter grinned, grabbing a glass and turning to the tap.

"How'd he get to be bartender?"

"Pulled the 'I'm the oldest' card," Jax said with a shrug.

They watched with satisfaction as beer flowed from tap to glass. Carter filled the other glasses and doled them out. Beckett tilted the glass and inhaled. "There's the lemongrass," he sighed.

Jax and Carter sniffed cautiously too. "Good call there," Carter agreed. "Kind of citrusy and grassy at the same time."

"Ready?" Jax asked, raising his glass.

"To John Pierce Brews," Beckett said. The clink of glasses rang through the empty barn.

"To John Pierce Brews," his brothers echoed.

Beckett sipped, frowned, and sipped again. "Damn."

"That's pretty decent." Jax nodded his approval.

"Decent? This is a damn good beer," Carter argued, taking a deeper drink. "This is a fish-on-the-grill-hammock-on-the-beach kind of beer."

"What are we going to call it?" Jax asked, polishing off the rest of the beer in his glass.

Beckett grinned. "I think I have an idea."

"What? *Habeas corpus*?" Carter snorted.

"Now you're going to feel like an asshole when you hear it. Summer's Wheat."

His brother frowned, thoughtful. "Seriously?"

"We're serving it at your wedding, aren't we?"

Jax grinned and nodded slowly. "I can already see the labels."

Beckett watched a flood of emotions sweep across Carter's face. "Are you sure? This is a big deal. It's *our* first beer, not just mine."

"Summer's Wheat," Beckett repeated.

"Damn." Carter ran a hand through his hair. "It should have been my idea," He grinned.

"Yeah, it should have," Jax agreed. "Obviously Beckett here is more thoughtful and sensitive than you, Farm Boy."

Carter surprised them both by yanking them in for a half-headlock half-hug over the bar. "I'm not gonna get mushy here. But I will say I wouldn't be who I am today without you assholes."

"Yeah, yeah." Beckett slapped Carter on the back. "You're just hoping I don't tell Summer it was my idea."

"What'll it cost me?"

"Naming rights for one of your kids."

"Done."

A second round of Summer's Wheat and some more back slapping and razzing removed any leftover clogged emotions. Beckett was just considering slipping downstairs to check out the equipment and maybe start thinking about the next batch of beer when Jax cleared his throat. And Beckett braced for the unknown.

"How much was the loan?" His younger brother didn't do serious often, but when he did, it was enough to stop and take notice.

"What loan?" Beckett asked innocently.

"The one you took out to save the farm." Carter's tone was serious.

"Are we back on that again? What does it matter?"

"We're paying our thirds," Jax announced, whipping a checkbook from his back pocket.

"I don't want your fucking money," Beckett bit the words off, the good mood from moments ago dissolved.

"We don't fucking care," Carter said good-naturedly. "And you're an asshole for thinking we'd let you carry the financial burden alone like that."

"I'm not an asshole."

"Then prove it. Let us pay you back," Jax said. "How would you feel if one of us had done what you did?"

Beckett blew out a breath. "That's beside the point."

"That *is* the point. Dick," Carter countered.

"It was years ago. I don't need your money."

"It's not about needing the money," Jax argued. "It's about doing the right thing. Prick."

"I might have a better idea. You know how Mom and Franklin haven't been able to find a place to live?"

His brothers nodded, and Beckett filled them in on his plan.

Jax whistled. "You are on a roll today."

35

*B*eckett sat by himself at the bar and watched the festivities. Summer glowed in her gown and Carter, buoyed by happiness, practically floated off the floor during their first dance as husband and wife.

Nikolai Vulkov, Summer's best friend from the city, captured the moment through his camera.

Beckett noticed that Niko's gaze had more than once found its way to Gia. But who could blame him? Her dress, a dusky purple, nipped in at the waist and dipped low in the back, leaving that long line of flawless ivory skin bare. It was sophisticated and stylish, just like Summer. But on Gianna, it was even more. Sensual. Stunning.

When she twirled, as she was now holding Aurora, the skirt floated away from her legs and the lights caught subtle beading woven throughout the material.

He'd walked her down the aisle and wanted to do it again.

He rubbed a hand over his jaw, minding the fading bruises from Jax and Carter.

Jax, his black eye now more green and yellow, strolled up to him. Summer had threatened to plaster makeup on them for pictures until Niko gave his word he'd edit out the cuts and bruises.

"Think we'll ever be that happy?" Jax asked, tipping the neck of the bottle toward Carter.

"It's not humanly possible to be that happy." Beckett shook his head.

"Maybe they put something in the beer because Mom and Franklin are looking pretty cheerful, too."

Jax wandered off while Beckett's gaze found his mother standing on the edge of the dance floor with Summer's parents. She was watching Carter and Summer as they danced, her hands clasped to her heart. Franklin's arms were wrapped around her, holding her close. Together they swayed silently to the music.

He wanted to be that happy.

With Gianna.

"So you gonna marry her or what?"

Beckett choked on his beer.

Evan climbed up on the stool next to him.

"Barkeep, a soda for my friend," Beckett said. Skye, the busty bartender from the caterer, gave Evan a slow-eyed wink and poured a Coke into a tall glass.

Evan swiveled on his stool to face the dance floor. "So, are you?"

"Pardon my bluntness, but shouldn't you have some deep-seated need to keep your parents together?" Beckett asked.

Evan smirked. "You met my dad. And he's great and all, but Gia deserves better. So do Rora and me."

Beckett's gut paused mid-churn. "And you think I'm better?"

"Even when Gia and my dad were together, she still did everything for us. Made our lunches, came to all my games, took care of us when we were sick. With you, it wouldn't just be her. I try to help out when I can, but I'm still a kid. You'd want to be a team. You wouldn't make her do everything alone. My dad left, you know."

"Left, like for good?"

"He was just visiting between gigs," Evan said. "He wasn't going to stay with us."

Beckett's heart hurt for the kid who should be wanted. "Does that bother you?"

"I live with Gia. We talk about feelings and stuff a lot. It's mostly annoying, but I get it. Dad isn't focused on being a dad. He just doesn't have that gene. And me getting mad at him for not being who I want him to be is a waste. He's not a bad guy. He just doesn't know how to be a dad."

The kid yanked at his tie. "Plus, you're sitting here looking at her like you wanna cry. My dad never looked at her like that. So I'm thinking this could be a win-win."

"I am *not* looking at her like I want to cry." Beckett was insulted.

Evan snorted. "Please. You're all like misty-eyed over here watching her dance. Just go talk to her."

"I messed things up pretty bad," Beckett confessed.

"No shit." Evan shot a look at Gia to make sure she hadn't heard him swear. "But doesn't she deserve someone who's willing to fight for her? Even if he messes stuff up sometimes. You just have to fix it bigger than you messed it up."

The kid was right.

"So you're saying you'd be cool with me being with your mom?"

"I'm saying she does everything for us. I think she could use some happiness of her own and someone to help her out. I figure if she's all happy in love with you, maybe she'll lighten up on me. You know, let me stay up later, eat more junk food."

"And maybe you'll end up with the bedroom with the secret passage?"

Evan nodded. "And a debate team advisor."

"You know, for a punk kid, you know a lot about life."

Evan leaned back against the bar. "Yeah. I know. So, you gonna sit here moping, or are you gonna ask her to dance?"

"I'm gonna go ask her to dance," Beckett said, ruffling Evan's hair. "Thanks for the pep talk, kid."

He didn't so much to ask as pull her into his arms on the edge of the dance floor. Those wide green eyes burned into him.

"Gianna, I don't know how to start to say how sorry I am."

She started to wriggle out of his grasp, but he tightened his hold and pulled her back in.

"I don't really want to hear your apologies," she said frostily.

"Too bad. You deserve them, and you're going to get them. I'm sorry. I was the biggest ass imaginable. I jumped to conclusions and then used that as an excuse to reinforce my own family issues," Beckett said, his eyes never wavering from hers.

"You questioned my very personal, very difficult decision and made it sound like I ended my marriage on a whim. Do you think it was easy for me to leave Paul? The kids adored him. Why do you think Evan doesn't call me Mom anymore? You accused me of walking away because I felt like it. But you don't know." Her voice was shaking.

Beckett stroked her back, reveling in the feel of her bare skin beneath his hand.

"Beckett, you don't know how many nights I cried myself to sleep on the couch. You don't know how many extra jobs I took on to pay the rent because following Paul's dream meant no steady paycheck. You don't know how many times he let the kids down, disappointing them over and over again. You have no idea what he carelessly exposed them to in their own home."

The sick, familiar guilt slid through him.

"The worst part is, you made me doubt myself. You made me wonder if I'd made the decision selfishly."

Beckett felt it like a knife in the gut. Lashing out at her had made her doubt a very difficult, very personal decision. That was unforgiveable.

"I didn't walk away on a whim. You're the one who did." She tried to step out of his grasp, but again, he wasn't giving up.

It was true. Everything she'd said was true. But that wasn't how it was going to end with them. Not with him being an ass, and her confidence shaken.

"I'm not letting you go this time, Gianna."

"I'm not asking you to hold on, Beckett. You hurt me."

"I'm sorry, Red. I'm so sorry." He pulled her in closer, stroking her back. "But I know it's not going to be the last time. When you love this much, people get hurt."

He felt her intake of breath on the word love and continued.

"They get glued back together, and they jump back into it. Between the highs and the lows, what keeps you going, what keeps you coming back together, is knowing that your heart beats for that one person. My heart beats for you, Gianna. It has since the first moment I saw you."

"In the bathroom? You fell for me in a bathroom?"

Beckett shook his head. "That's not the first time I saw you. The night before, you were painting your studio." He brushed a curl back from her face, slid his fingers down the silk of her spine. "You were taking a break, working on some crazy upside-down pose. You fell, and you laughed. And then I fell for you."

Gia stared at him, her sea green eyes mesmerized.

"In that moment, my heart started beating because it knew you. I didn't understand it at the time, but what my heart was saying was 'There you are. Finally.'"

"Beckett."

He shook his head. "Here you are, my Gianna. And I'm not letting go."

"I need some time to think. Pretty words don't just make the hurt go away."

"And they shouldn't. I will make this up to you. And though I can't promise I won't hurt you again—because we will fight, a lot—I can swear to you that I will never make you doubt yourself again. You are the strongest, most fearless woman I know. And I believe in you."

"I don't know how to start over."

"Red, we're not starting over. We're moving forward. I want you, and I want those kids. I want to be there to find your keys and phone for you every day. I want to take Evan to the stables so he can gawk at Joey. I want to scare away Aurora's first boyfriend." He turned them around and pointed at Carter and Summer, swaying to their own music oblivious to the barn full of people. "I want that."

"I want that, too," Gianna whispered, her eyes damp.

"Then give me another chance, and I will give you everything."

The song ended, but still he held her. "I love you, Gianna, and I love those kids. I want us to be a family. A big, sloppy, loud, temperamental family."

She laid her hands on his chest and took a deep, shaky breath. "I need to think about this, Beckett."

He brought his forehead to hers. "Take some time. But understand that I'm not backing off, I'm not letting you go. I'll be there nudging you along."

"Bucket! Can I dance wiv you?" Aurora appeared next to them, her face smeared with cake.

"Of course you can, shortcake." He hoisted her up on his hip, but instead of letting Gianna go, he pulled her back in. "Now we can all dance."

"Rora, don't get cake all over Beckett," Gianna warned.

"K, Mama," Aurora grinned and put her head down on Beckett's shoulder.

Over Gia's head, Beckett spotted Evan on the dance floor with Joey. The kid gave him the nod, and Beckett returned it.

Yeah. This time he wasn't letting go.

As the sun began its slow descent in the November sky, the party was wrapping up. Most of the non-family guests had left carrying thoughtful boxes of their Thanksgiving favorites.

Aurora was yawning mightily, having exhausted herself dancing all afternoon. Gia was feeling a little worn out herself. The man of her dreams told her he loved her. But just like an apology, they were only words. It was the actions that mattered, and so far, his had left much to be desired.

She slipped her shoes off under the table and reveled in the freedom for her toes.

Summer was dancing with Niko and laughing. He was handsome. There was no doubt about it. All that thick, dark hair and olive complexion. Even without the name Vulkov, there was something exotic about him.

He'd casually flirted with her before the ceremony, and Gia understood that it was just his way. He wasn't a womanizer per se. He was an adorer of all things female. She was looking forward to their shoot tomorrow. His work would help put Thrive at the top of the game.

Across the floor near the patio doors, Evan was in conference with Franklin and the Pierce men. Even with the fading bruises—that Niko had promised Summer he could edit out —they still made quite a picture.

She hadn't asked what the outcome of the bachelor party had been, but given the mile-wide grin on her father's face, she imagined it had gone well. After all, Beckett was standing next to him, relaxed and smiling. Finally.

At least he'd gotten it out of his system, and now her father could be a welcomed part of that family.

Gia picked up her glass and sipped. *Summer's Wheat*, she thought with a smile. The thoughtful sentiment had Carter written all over it. She made a mental note to ask him sometime how he talked the other two into naming their inaugural beer after his bride.

The men dispersed, each looking as if they were on a mission. Evan and Jax headed outside to bank the flames in the patio fireplace. Her father wandered over to Phoebe while Carter snuck behind the bar and pulled out a skinny rolled up paper. He nodded at Summer, who winked and tugged on Niko's sleeve.

Niko abandoned her to grab his camera while Summer floated to Carter's side.

They were a perfect team. Gia only had to look at them to know theirs was a love that would last forever. For just a second, when Beckett had guided her back down the aisle, she let herself pretend it was their time, their love.

But pretending was foolish. He'd hurt her, and now she had to decide whether she could forgive. He'd given her the words she'd longed to hear, but without the action to back it up, there were no guarantees.

She'd been hurt before, had forgiven again and again. But

the outcome never changed. She and Paul weren't destined to be together, weren't part of the same team.

Her gaze found Beckett as it had all day. She watched him tickle Aurora and give Evan a high five through the glass.

Gia just needed some time to think. Maybe after she had wrapped up the rest of January's content for the magazine, she could just take a day and really figure everything out. Pros and cons. Try to logic it out since her feelings were so conflicted.

"If you guys have time for one more toast, let's head out onto the patio before my wife and I call it a night," Carter announced, putting his arm around Summer's shoulders.

Summer beamed at him. "I can't believe I have a husband," she sighed happily.

Beckett appeared at Gia's side and waited until she put her shoes back on. When she stood, he draped his jacket over her shoulders. "It's a little chilly out there," he said.

"I'm coming, too!" Aurora announced. Beckett lifted her daughter up, and she snuggled into him. "I love you, Bucket."

Gia saw the slight hitch in his stride and knew that Aurora's words hit their target.

"I love you too, shortcake." His voice was gruff and thick with emotion. And Gia knew he meant the words.

"Mama, do you love Bucket?"

Gia pretended she didn't hear the question and held the door open for them.

The evening air was brisk, but the heat from the fireplace took the chill out of it. Joey and Phoebe came out followed by Franklin who was toting a bottle of champagne. Jax doled out empty flutes from a tray, and Evan's eyes bugged as he got one.

Franklin, looking dapper in his dark suit, made a lap around their little circle pouring a little for everyone, including a sip for Summer and one for Evan as well. Her son was thrilled at being included with the adults.

Niko joined them, snapping away with his camera, trying to make the most of the day's dying light.

Gia pulled Beckett's jacket tighter around her and let his scent envelop her. God, she missed him. She missed his touch, his laugh, those sterling eyes on her, always watching. She could and would forgive. But she couldn't just forget the hurt, the rejection.

She looked around their cozy circle, at Summer and Carter glowing with love for one another, excited about the start of their family. She wanted that and wouldn't settle for less. Not this time.

Her father set the bottle down and joined Phoebe where she leaned against the warm brick of the fireplace. Her deep violet gown a compliment to the bridesmaid's dresses.

"I'd like to propose a toast," Franklin announced.

Gia could feel the shift in mood immediately. She glanced at Summer and saw her friend's mile-wide grin. Everyone seemed to be holding their breath. Could this be it? Could her father be ready to reach for his own happy ending?

"To family," Franklin continued. "To the blood that binds us and the love that forges us. As Summer and Carter begin their own family, they blend two others. It's this blending that builds community. This blending that allows for an old restaurateur to fall for a beautiful farmer and decide that he finally wanted to live happily ever after."

He pivoted toward Beckett, who tossed him a velvet jewelers box. Phoebe's jaw fell open as Franklin neatly sank to one knee. There was a significance in having Beckett keep the ring for him, Gia realized. A message to his mother that he was on board. Recognizing this, Phoebe's eyes welled up.

"Phoebe Pierce, would you do me the honor of being my wife, of blending our two loud, crazy, wonderful families, of being my partner—"

Franklin didn't get to finish what was sure to be a sweet sentiment because Phoebe was kissing him.

Gia looked up at Beckett. His eyes looked the tiniest bit damp as he watched his mother look into the face of the man she loved as he slid the ring on her finger.

"Oh!" Phoebe said, admiring the ring on her finger. "I just don't think I can possibly take any more happiness this year."

"Well, then you're not going to want to hear what we have to say," Carter began.

"If you say the word triplets, I will have a heart attack on the spot," Phoebe threatened.

Carter pulled the roll of paper out from behind his back and opened it on the small patio table.

Phoebe and Franklin peered at it and everyone else crowded around.

"This is the farm," Phoebe said, frowning at the map.

"And this," Carter said, pointing to a swath of land, "is where you and Franklin can build your new home."

Phoebe's fingers flew to her mouth.

"It was Beckett's idea," Carter told her. Gia's eyes darted back to Beckett who was bouncing Aurora on his hip.

"We talked to Franklin about it when he asked us for our permission," Jax chimed in. "He gave us your list of must-haves in a house, and we talked to Calvin."

Carter peeled back the top paper to reveal a house plan and elevation sketches. "And this is what he came up with. It's rough, and you can change anything you want, but we wanted you to get an idea of what you could build."

"What's that upstairs?" Phoebe tapped the second-floor plan.

"That's the bunk room. For all your grandkids," Beckett told her.

Gia bit her lip as Phoebe's mouth opened and no words

came out. She kissed Franklin again and then pulled each of her boys in for a hard hug, strangling the breath out of each one.

Beckett closed his eyes tight as his mother embraced him. Aurora patted Phoebe on the head. "Hi, Miss Phoebe!"

"Hi, sweetheart," she sniffled. "I guess I was wrong. I have a little bit more room for happiness."

Beckett raised his glass with his free hand, his gaze locked on to her face. "A toast. To family."

36

*B*eckett was just early enough for the first Debate Club meeting to handle a little personal business first. He burst into the second conference room on the left without knocking. A half-dozen faces looked up from the large conference table and smiled expectantly.

"I need your help," he announced.

"It's about damn time," Willa said with a satisfied smile.

Ellery grinned at him from the front of the room.

He glanced at the board and noted a large X had been drawn over Paul's picture. "Phase One" was written underneath. His own picture, one taken at a recent chamber event, had been added next to Gia's above the words "Phase Two."

"What's all this?"

Ellery joined him at the front of the room. "You're a stubborn man, Beckett. You didn't know how much you wanted Gia until you couldn't have her."

He turned to his paralegal. She was dressed in platform suede boots and a dress with spider web sleeves. "You're diabolical."

"Thank you," Ellery said with a mock bow. "And now that you know what you want, we're here to help you get it."

"Want a cookie?" Gordon Berkowicz offered up a tray of heart-shaped cookies with icing.

"I do. I really do."

～

GIA HUSTLED out of her studio and cut across One Love Park for the movie theater. The Facebook group alert had said it was a mandatory emergency town meeting tonight. She was curious about the reason for the meeting. Maybe Bruce was finally getting to the conclusion of his powdered wig argument? A smile tugged at her lips and felt foreign on her face. It had been a week since she and Beckett last spoke. But he'd made his presence known.

He'd sent lunch to the studio for her and Niko during the photo shoot for Summer's magazine. She found a rose and a note on her car in his sharp, sloppy script reminding her to schedule an inspection. During her Tuesday night yoga class, he'd taken Thanksgiving leftovers to Evan and Aurora. When she came home, she found a basket full of clean, folded laundry. And last night, he'd advised Evan's first Debate Club meeting which, from Evan's description, had been a huge success.

He hadn't been kidding about not leaving her alone. It was more than apologies. Now he was showing her what kind of partner he wanted to be for her. But she was still hurt, still scared.

Glancing around the town square, Gia wondered where everyone was. The last town meeting had made downtown look like a parade. But tonight, she was the only soul hurrying

342

through the milky pools from the streetlights to the movie theater.

How late was she? The alert had said 7:15. Unless she read it wrong, which was a strong possibility. She hadn't exactly been on top of her game lately.

Not wishing to cause a commotion, Gia quietly opened one of the theater's doors, intending to slip into the back row unnoticed.

"There she is!" Mrs. Nordeman fluttered out of a group of townspeople milling about in front of the snack stand. "Now you just come along with me." The older woman grabbed Gia's wrist and started dragging her through the crowd.

Everyone was staring, and Gia felt her cheeks warm. "Uh, Mrs. Nordeman, I was just going to sit in the back..."

"Nonsense. We saved you a seat right up front."

"Up front?" Gia squeaked.

"We've got her," Mrs. Nordeman announced to the crowd. "Now we can get started."

Beckett and the rest of the council were already on stage, and Gia wanted to curl up into a ball and die of embarrassment.

She was shoved into an empty seat, front and center in the first row. Summer and Joey sat on either side of her, grinning like hyenas. Jax and Carter sat on either side of them. Gia noted Jax's frame sprawling out of his seat and crowding her friend.

"What is going on?" Gia hissed.

"Don't look at me," Summer shrugged innocently. "I'm new here."

Gia shot Joey a look.

"I've lived here all my life, and I've never seen this before," Joey said with a wicked grin. "I can't wait."

Gia made the mistake of looking up at the stage. Beckett's

gray gaze was fixed on her. He subtly flashed his phone at her. She frowned and dug through her tote bag until she found hers.

She had a text from him.

Beckett: Fair warning. I'm fighting for you and I brought an army with me.

Gia shot him a look before responding.

Gia: Why do I feel like my request for space is about to be completely ignored?

She saw the corner of his mouth lift as his thumbs flew across the screen.

Beckett: Because you're not an idiot. Now sit there and prepare to enjoy Blue Moon at its finest.

She shot him another dark look. He knew she didn't like being manipulated, yet here she was, front and center with an entire town scheming against her.

Summer reached across Gia to help herself to some of Joey's popcorn, her new wedding band glinting under the theater lights.

"How are you feeling so far?" Gia asked Summer, tucking her phone away to ignore any more messages from Beckett.

"Like I've run a marathon every day before two. By the time three o'clock rolls, around I have to nap, or I'm in bed by seven," Summer lamented. "Please tell me this phase passes quickly."

"You'll breeze right through your next trimester. And then you'll wish that you could sleep twenty-three hours a day."

Summer sighed and took another handful of popcorn. "And then there's the no sleeping because they're newborns. And the no sleeping because they're toddlers and climbing out of their beds and trying to set house fires. Oh, and don't forget the no sleeping because they're teenagers and who knows what they're up to."

"That about sums it up," Gia said, her eyes scanning the theater for an escape route.

"Don't even think about it," Joey said mildly. "Jax and Carter will just haul you back in here and embarrass the hell out of you."

"Too late for that," Gia muttered.

She avoided making eye contact with Beckett until Bruce Oakleigh took the stage. Gavel in hand, he crossed to the podium.

"If I can have everyone's attention," he said, leaning into the microphone. The noise level lowered to a dull roar. He banged the gavel twice, and the last of the conversations in the crowd died away.

"We all know why we're here tonight—well, except for you, Gia." He smiled brightly at her through his silvery beard. "We're here to host an open forum that will decide whether or not Gianna Decker should give Beckett Pierce a second chance."

The theater erupted in chatter, and Gia tried to bolt out of her seat, but Joey shoved her back down.

"Just try and remember that they're doing this because they think they're helping," she whispered. "And if that doesn't work, know that Evan and Beckett came up with the idea together. So running out of here won't just disappoint the whole town, you'll have to deal with the kid's sad face."

"Evan did this?" Gia stopped fighting the grip on her shoulders.

"He and Beckett put all of this together," Joey told her. "I wouldn't be surprised if he ends up as mayor after Beckett."

Gia took a deep cleansing breath. And then another.

"Is she going to hyperventilate?" Joey hissed at Summer.

Summer shook her head. "I think she's just trying to relax."

The gavel banged again, bringing order to the crowd. "Let's quiet down here. We've only got fifty-three minutes to come to a decision."

"Oh. My. God," Gia whispered. The town was planning to debate her relationship status for fifty-three minutes. She fervently hoped that the floor beneath her feet would open up and swallow her.

"Let's get started with Beckett Pierce, the 'forgivee' in question," Bruce announced, waving Beckett to the podium.

"Shit. They're not expecting me to talk, are they?" she gasped.

Joey shook her head. "They got you a proxy."

Gia put her face in her hands. "I am going home to pack. This town is insane."

She could tell Beckett had taken the podium because the theater had become quite quiet again.

"Gianna Decker placed her faith and trust in me as a potential partner, and I let her down," Beckett began. "I refused to listen, I made snap judgments, and on more than one occasion, I let my agendas and personal issues be excuses for lashing out at her."

A grumble went through the crowd. Joey booed.

"Joey!" Gia hissed at her.

"Team Gia," Joey whispered.

Beckett zeroed in on Gia's face. "I was an idiot. I refused to be a team player. In a few bull-headed moments, I forgot what being a partner meant and tried to make decisions for us both.

I hurt the woman I care very deeply for and made her doubt herself. I'm so very sorry, Gianna. Hurting you has been the worst mistake of my life. And that's saying something since you've already met Trudy."

A chuckle rose up from the crowd.

Apparently there were no secrets in Blue Moon. At least none that involved fire and handcuffs.

"Gianna, I know I don't deserve this. But please give me another chance to show you the kind of partner I can be. I want to be with you and Evan and Aurora."

A generous round of applause rolled through the audience.

"Ugh, Mooners are too easy," Joey grumbled.

Beckett was so busy staring at Gia that Bruce had to physically push him away from the podium.

"We've got a really wonderful proxy stepping in to speak on Gia's behalf. Please welcome, Evan Decker," Bruce said, stepping back from the podium and clapping.

Gia was halfway out of her seat when she spotted Evan strutting down the aisle toward the stage. He was wearing a suit and tie and his hair was neatly combed. He waved with both hands as he walked like the perfect Mini Mayor.

By the time he reached the podium, the audience was standing and applauding. *The kid definitely had a future in politics.* Gia sighed, clapping along with the rest of the crowd.

Evan couldn't be seen over the podium until Beckett pulled a crate out from under his seat and arranged it behind the podium.

He gave Beckett a polite nod and shook his hand before turning to face the crowd. He shot a grin at Gia and waved.

Weakly, she waved back.

"Ladies and gentlemen, I would first like to thank you for

joining us tonight. When two people as stubborn as Gia and Beckett fight, it takes a village to bring them back together."

The crowd laughed appreciatively.

"Best town meeting ever," Joey muttered, her popcorn forgotten in her lap.

"We've heard my esteemed colleague say his piece," Evan continued. "And now I'd like to educate you on the opposing position."

Evan took a moment to organize his notecards before looking out over the audience. "Gianna Decker isn't my mother."

Gia slumped lower in her seat and closed her eyes. "For the love of—"

"At least not biologically. But in every way that counts, she is."

Gia chanced a peek out of one eye.

"She married my dad when she could have done better because she loved me. After letting my dad pursue his goals, she realized that we needed more stability. We needed family. She divorced my dad and moved us here to be closer to Grampa. But we found a lot more family than just him. We found the Pierces."

He looked over his shoulder at Beckett. "Beckett made dumb mistakes. Really dumb ones. Like incredibly stupid ones."

"Move it along, kid," Beckett grumbled.

Evan grinned. "But he made them with what he thought was our best interests at heart. When my dad makes decisions, he makes them because it's what he wants, not because it's for the best for everyone. So even though Beckett was wrong, his heart was in the right place."

Evan shuffled his cards again. "Okay, now we get to the part where Gia was wrong."

Gia straightened in her chair.

"See, Gia got really used to being in charge. Even when she was married to my dad, she did everything for us, and he didn't want a say in it. Beckett wanted a say, and Gia didn't know how to handle that. For instance, she's probably really mad right now and feeling like we're trying to tell her what to do. But that's not true," Evan said.

He looked directly at her. "We're just trying to help you make a decision that works for all of us. Please don't ground me. Thank you for your time."

The applause was thunderous, and Evan waved again while he took a seat next to Beckett. They solemnly high-fived, and Gia knew she was screwed.

Bruce was back at the podium again. "At this time, we'd like to open up the floor to comments."

"Oh my God," Gia whispered.

Willa from Blue Moon Boots was the first to stand. "I'd just like to say that I've seen the way these two look at each other, and they're a strong, solid match. Family and community are so important to them both that if they can work things out, we'll all benefit." She curtsied to the warm applause and took her seat.

Donovan Cardona stood up next, his uniform shirt stretched tight across his broad chest. "I'd like to throw my two cents in as a fellow town leader. I haven't yet been called to Beckett's house to settle any kind of dispute between him and Gia, so, in my book, that's a huge improvement."

People around him nodded in agreement.

It went on like that with townspeople debating their relationship for another fifteen minutes until Mrs. McCafferty of McCafferty Farm Supply stood up. "What I want to know is what kind of guarantee is this girl going to have that Beckett isn't going to pull the rug out from under her again?"

Joey applauded with the rest of Team Gia.

Carter stood up. "Miz McCafferty, I give you my word that if my brother tries to do something else stupid like that again, I'll beat some sense into him."

Gia was suddenly suspicious that that's how the brothers had gotten their bruises in the first place. Mrs. McCafferty frowned thoughtfully. "I think that's a fair solution." She nodded and took her seat again.

Julia, her pink-tipped hair pulled back in a perky ponytail, stood up. She had a chubby infant on her hip. "How do we know that Beckett really cares about not just Gia but you and your sister?"

Evan climbed back onto the crate at the microphone. "I'm glad you asked. I'd like to submit as evidence a few pictures that prove that Beckett likes us a lot."

He pointed back at the control booth, and the house lights dimmed a little as the heavy velvet curtains parted to reveal the screen.

The first picture showed Beckett, Evan, and Aurora mugging for a selfie in Beckett's kitchen. The next was Aurora carefully swiping bronzer over Beckett's made up face as he sucked in his cheeks. The crowd laughed loud and long for that one.

Next up was a grinning Evan raking in the poker chips during a card game while Beckett sat back next to him looking proud. Jax was pointing a threatening finger in Evan's face while Franklin laughed.

"I want my money back," Jax yelled at the stage.

Summer's friend Niko had taken the last picture. Gia and Aurora were in Beckett's arms on the dance floor at the wedding. Niko had captured a very raw, intimate moment, and the feelings translated clearly through the lens. A chorus of "awws" rose up.

"I respectfully withdraw my question," Julia said, winking at Evan.

Bruce returned to the podium. "I think we've got just enough time for one more statement before we put it to a vote. Who's it going to be?"

"Do you love her?"

The question came from the back of the theater. Gia craned her neck along with the rest of the crowd to see who it was.

Ellery grinned from the front row of the balcony.

"That's a valid question," Bruce announced. "Mr. Mayor?"

Beckett returned to the microphone and looked directly at Gia. "More than anything in this world. My heart is yours. I love you so very much, Gianna. Please forgive me."

The women in the crowd sighed as one.

Bruce elbowed his way back to the microphone. Beckett sat back down, and Gia watched as Evan gave him a hearty thump on the shoulder. And her decision was made.

"Okay folks, let's put this issue to a vote. Those in favor of Gianna Decker giving Beckett Pierce a second chance, raise your hands and hold them up so we can tally them."

She could hear the arms going up like a flock of birds taking flight. Evan and Beckett raised their hands on stage.

Bruce and the rest of the council members appeared to be attempting to actually count the votes.

"Well, it would appear that the vote is almost completely unanimous," he said, looking pointedly at Gia.

"Oh, what the hell?" Gia muttered and raised her hand.

37

He came home with her after a second unanimous vote to have council members wear powdered wigs. Beckett helped Evan with his homework and told Aurora a bedtime story about dragons and kittens. Gia watched as he gently kissed the forehead of her sleeping little girl and felt the tightness in her chest that had been there for perhaps years finally loosen.

They tiptoed back downstairs. Evan took one look at them and announced he was going to go watch a movie in his room.

"You're sure I'm not grounded?" he asked Gia from the steps.

"I'm sure. But let's not make this a habit," she warned him.

Evan looked to Beckett. "Will you be here in the morning?"

Beckett looked at Gia. "Yeah, he'll be here," she told her son.

"Cool," Evan nodded. "See you in the morning."

"Night, Evan."

Unsure of what to do now that they were alone, Gia wandered over to the couch. Beckett busied himself locking the front door and pouring two glasses of wine. He carried them over and settled himself on the couch next to her.

"Where would you like me to start explaining?" he asked.

She threw her head back and laughed. "Let's start with how you got those bruises?" She trailed a finger over his jaw, still sharp with stubble.

"Carter and Jax and I beat the shit out of each other in the ring to cheer me up."

"Did it work?" Gia asked.

Beckett nodded. "I had some sense knocked into me."

"I can't believe Summer let you three do that."

"She was not very happy." He grinned.

"Okay, so that explains the bruises. Now how did you get the entire town in on this?"

Beckett chuckled. "I was late to the game. They were already in on it by the time I wised up." He quickly recounted what Ellery had told him.

"So the reason I couldn't get into the Facebook group that day—not that I tried to see if there were any posts about you suffering horribly from our breakup," she added, "was because the Beautification Committee kicked us out to post a town-wide message about how to handle the situation?"

"Yep. They decided they were going to make sure I was convinced that Paul was the coolest thing since Bob Dylan so I'd feel jealous and insecure."

"And they wanted to remind me of how great you were—are," she corrected herself when Beckett pinched her.

"Once everyone had seen the message, they deleted it and let us back into the group. Business as usual."

"But how about the town meeting?"

"I had accidentally stumbled upon the BC's last meeting, and when I walked in, it looked like they were trying to match you and Paul up. Total dumb luck on their part that I came in when I did. A minute later, and I would have seen their whole plan on the slideshow. But when I barged in, Ellery's pointing at the screen, and there's you, and there's Paul, taunting me with his cool guy smile."

"Ugh," Gia groaned.

"My sentiments were a bit more gut-wrenching. I realized then that I didn't want you to be with anyone else, not even Bob Dylan 2.0. And after dinner with him and Aurora, I realized I'd made an even bigger mistake by insinuating that you did the kids a disservice by divorcing him."

"How exactly did you end up having dinner with him?"

"Aurora wandered off in the park while Paul was watching her, and I found her."

Gia smacked a hand to her forehead. "I knew he couldn't be trusted with kids!"

"He also let her order a soda and chocolate milk for supper."

"Ugh, he's the worst!"

"No argument here. When he visits again, one of us needs to stay with him and the kids at all times to make sure he doesn't talk them into quitting school and joining a band."

Gia sipped and laughed.

Beckett continued. "So, after the beating and dinner, I decided I was going to win you back. But my slow, methodical approach to analyzing the situation and getting feedback from all the important players—you, your dad, Evan—was taking way too long. So after the wedding, I called in the big guns."

"The Beautification Committee?"

Beckett nodded. "Evan was the one who came up with the general idea. He doesn't put a lot of stock in your ability to reason out logical arguments. He was worried that you'd overthink us to death."

"Uh-huh. So you both manipulated me with a scripted argument."

Beckett pushed her hair back so he could lean in and nibble her neck. "A debate, Red. Totally different than an argument."

"But you still manipulated me."

She felt him smile against her neck. "I don't know, Beckett. Yoga is really hard. I don't think you can handle it because you're not manly enough," he said in a high-pitched voice.

She giggled and tried to push him away. "I do *not* sound like that."

"You're a conniving temptress," Beckett said, taking her glass from her and gently pushing her back on the couch.

"Is that supposed to be a compliment?" she whispered, her voice breathy and low.

"Of the highest kind," Beckett whispered back, his lips moving gently over hers.

He ranged himself over her, and she threaded her fingers through his hair, tugging him down. She'd missed this, the weight of him on her, his scent on her, all of her senses on fire because of him.

Beckett teased the strap of her tank down, his fingers branding her as they went.

"I don't know how to do this with kids in the house," he whispered against the upper curve of her breast.

She sighed, her breath tickling his hair. "I'm not sure either. But let's start by moving to the bedroom."

Beckett unfolded himself from the couch, and keeping his hands on her hips, he followed her into her room. She shut the doors firmly and led him to the bed. While he stepped out of his shoes, Gia worked her magic on his tie and the buttons of his shirt. She moved her attention to his pants next.

The belt hit the floor next to his shoes. She took her time, trailing her fingers down his chest, over his rippled stomach. Her smile was feline when the tickle of her fingertips had him drawing in a sharp breath.

Deftly, she opened his pants, shoved them down. And when he stepped out of them, she skimmed her hands back up his legs to his briefs.

Her purr of pleasure had him gritting his teeth. "Gianna," he whispered.

"I'm here," she answered. She slid her hands into his underwear, cupping his ass and then sliding the fabric down, freeing him.

"God, you're gorgeous," she whispered. Her breath next to his erection made him tremble.

She skimmed a hand up his leg and over his thigh. But just before her fingers closed around her target, Beckett was pulling her to her feet.

"My turn," he whispered against her mouth. He drew her tank top over her head and made quick work of her leggings. She had on tiny black briefs and a strappy sports bra with a zipper front. "Oh, I'm going to like this," he murmured against her neck.

Beckett backed her against the bed and slowly lowered her to the mattress. Gia's breath was a gasp when he settled himself between her legs. They were separated by just that thin layer of fabric, and yet it felt like miles.

"Beckett, please," she pleaded.

He tugged at the zipper of her sports bra. Inch by inch, it lowered until the fabric parted, and her breasts were freed.

"I'm never going to have enough of you, Gianna," he whispered, nuzzling a taut peak.

He tasted and tantalized, using his tongue to drive her wild. First one breast, then the other until Gia found herself writing under him. The sweet relentless torture had her biting her lip to keep from sobbing.

He moved back up her body, and when he gripped his shaft, she thought that the torture had come to an end. "Let's make sure you can be quiet," he said, a quiet rumble in her ear. He pressed himself against the damp fabric of her underwear and Gia moaned.

"That's why we're practicing," Beckett said, clamping a hand over her mouth. He ground his hips into her, and this time her moan was muffled by his palm.

"Good girl," he whispered.

He lowered his head to recapture the tip of her breast and continued his short thrusts against her. It wasn't enough for her. She wanted more from him. She wanted to feel every inch of his thick shaft buried in her, stretching her until she could take no more.

But his attack was relentless.

With every stroke, he swept the head of his penis over her swollen mound, and Gia saw stars. She'd never come like this before but knew that she would tonight.

With a deft tug, he pulled her underwear to the side and grunted as her slick folds welcomed his swollen crown.

The skin-to-skin contact destroyed her.

Beckett stroked himself against her, and Gia came, arching up violently. Her lips moving against his palm in a silent scream.

"God, I love how you come for me." Beckett's voice was strained, breathless. He pulled his hand away from her mouth and kissed her, so gently. "I love you, Gianna. Tell me you're mine."

Gia lifted her hips for him as he yanked her underwear from her. "Tell me, baby. Say you're mine."

Beckett held himself positioned just outside of her entrance. Trembling, he waited.

Gia grasped one of his hands and pulled it to her breast where her heart thundered for him.

"I'm yours, Beckett. I belong to you."

Finally, finally. He thrust into her, staking his claim.

Gia buried her face in his shoulder and sobbed. She was his. He fought for her and won.

"You're mine, my beautiful Gianna." He whispered the words over and over again as he began to move in her like music, a dance as old as time. She welcomed him into her.

His mouth met hers, and she feasted on his lips, his tongue. The heat of their love warmed every dark corner of her heart, freed her. She felt the light as it spread through her body, gilded and glowing.

His gaze locked with hers as he drove into her again and again. "I love you, my Gianna."

She felt the words in her soul, in her body. The vibrations set off a chain reaction. As her body gave itself to him, the last shield fell away from her heart. "I love you, Beckett." She whispered the words as they came together. Beckett, fully sheathed in her, shuddered his release into her as she fell apart around him.

This was love. This was life. They belonged to each other with an unbreakable bond forged of heartbeats and breath, of forgiveness and faith.

They whispered the words over and over again long after the last waves had receded.

GIA'S EYES fluttered open to the sunny morning light. She smelled... breakfast? The giggles of Evan and Aurora floated into her room, and she started to wiggle out from under the quilt when a distinct sparkle caught her eye.

Her fairy garden, the first thing she saw every morning, was different. A third polished rock rested front and center, the word *love* etched into its smooth surface.

And on it rested a fairytale diamond ring.

Gia shot out of bed, her shaking hands nearly upending the globe as she reached inside.

It was real. Cool to the touch, the emerald cut center stone picked up the morning sun in rainbows of sparkle.

Was this really happening?

Clutching the ring in her hand, she hastily pulled on shorts and last night's tank top and opened her bedroom doors. She paused in the doorway to take it all in.

Beckett in pajama pants and a t-shirt had a dishtowel draped over his shoulder and was expertly flipping pancakes to Evan and Aurora's delight.

He scooped one up with a spatula and tossed it onto Evan's plate. Her son was ready and waiting with the syrup.

The next one landed on Aurora's plate. "Wow!" she gasped.

"Wait 'til Mom sees these," Evan said. "Heart-shaped pancakes. That'll kill her."

Gia brought her fingers to her mouth. It was so blissfully normal. Sunday morning family breakfast. And Evan called her "mom."

She felt the tears prick her eyes.

Beckett spotted her first, and the rush of love she felt in her chest was echoed in his face. He lit up just looking at her. She mattered to him. They all did.

"Told you she'd cry," Evan muttered to Beckett.

Beckett smacked him lightly with the spatula. "Don't you have homework to do or robots to build?" he teased Evan.

Her son snorted. "I'm not missing this show for anything." Evan made himself comfortable on the stool.

"Hi, Mama!" Aurora chirped. "Bucket made pancakes!"

"I see that, sweetie."

Aurora clapped as Evan dumped a river of syrup on her plate.

Beckett skirted the island and met her in the living room. He took her hands in his, finding the ring in her grasp. "I see you found it." He smiled down at her with such tenderness that Gia couldn't stop the tears from spilling over.

She nodded.

Beckett brushed his thumbs across her cheeks, swiping away hot tears.

In the tiny space that separated them, Gia could feel the warmth, the strength of him. His steadfast loyalty, his love.

"I love you, Gianna."

"I love you, too, Beckett." She sniffled.

"I know I screwed up. Big time," he said, holding her hand in his, his face close to hers. "And I'm pretty sure I will again, but I can promise you that I will stick, and I will fight, and I will be there, every day. For you and for Evan and Aurora."

Gia was getting perilously close to humiliating herself with a tearful wail.

"I've asked your father, I've asked your kids, I've asked this whole damn town, and now I'm asking you. Gianna Decker, will you be my partner, my wife, my other, better half?"

Gia closed her eyes and let her heart tell her what to do. "Yes." She had barely whispered the word when she was swept up in a crushing hug. Beckett spun her around, kissing her until she was too dizzy to stand on her own.

Evan and Aurora jumped around them cheering and laughing. Evan jumped on Beckett's back, and it was just enough for everyone to lose their balance. They landed in a heap on the living room floor, laughing like idiots.

"Mama! Bucket said 'damn.'"

"Dibs on the secret passage room!" Evan hooted.

Beckett found Gia's hand in the pile of chaos and slid the ring onto her finger.

"*Y*ou look pretty nice, Mom."

Gia wasn't sure if it was the hard-won compliment, the "Mom," or the fact that she was wearing her dream wedding dress about to marry Beckett Pierce that did it.

Whatever it was, she was blinking back tears and pursing trembling lips together.

"Thanks, Ev," she said, grabbing her stepson for a fierce hug.

"Geez. Don't mess yourself up," he said. But his arms tightened around her.

"I won't," she promised, resting her head on top of his. Her boy was getting so big. In his tuxedo, he looked older than his twelve years. And in another minute or two, he'd be standing up with Beckett and his brothers on the stage at the Take Two Movie Theater while she said vows to a man who had welcomed them all into his life as if he'd been waiting for them.

"Mama! Do you think Bucket will like my dress?" Aurora twirled in a fussy white princess dress. The sparkle on the tulle skirt caught the yoga studio lights with a hundred glimmers.

"Bucket is going to love your dress, Roar," Gia promised. The man loved every damn thing the little girl did.

"Last glass of single champagne," Gia's sister Eva announced, holding the bottle aloft. "Gather 'round ladies."

The women in Gia's life encircled her, and she felt the energy of their love, their happiness. Phoebe, her soon-to-be mother-in-law and maybe stepmother, beamed at her. Gia's own mother wasn't in her life. And Phoebe made her notice that hole less.

Summer, blonde and fashion-forward, was dazzlingly beautiful at six-months pregnant. Joey, the antisocial tomboy, looked like she would be breaking a few hearts. Eva, her younger sister, in a slim rose gold column with a delicate comb in her wild red hair, poured champagne while Emma, the oldest, gave everyone the once over. She tamped down stray flyaways, adjusted straps, hid tags, and consulted her watch every minute or so.

"Are all the men here as good-looking as your sons?" Eva teased Phoebe.

Joey snorted. She'd grown up with the Pierces and had her heart broken by Jax, the youngest, so she wasn't as generous with the compliments.

"We're a very good-looking town," Phoebe said with a wink.

"How about that sheriff?" Eva said, fanning herself with her bouquet.

"He'll be there tonight. Maybe you'll get a dance out of him," Gia said.

"He's not my type," she sighed. "Too put together. I need my men a little messier. But he sure is pretty to look at."

Emma smirked. "Organized men are sexy."

Gia laughed at her sisters. "Eva needs a steady, organized man, and you, Emma dear, need someone wildly unpredictable."

"I don't find wild unpredictability remotely attractive," Emma insisted.

Summer and Gia exchanged knowing looks.

Evan cleared his throat. "I'd like to make a toast," he said.

"If you make me cry, Evan, I swear I will change your name to Goat Sniffer Decker," she warned.

"So... I know things haven't always been easy," he began, rocking back on his heels. "But I think this is where you were always meant to end up. And Roar and I are really happy here. So maybe we were meant to be here too."

"Oh, no," Summer whispered. The poor hormonally charged woman had tears streaming down her face. Phoebe handed her a tissue, then another one.

"Oh, hell," Joey grumbled, tilting her head toward the ceiling trying not to look at anyone.

"Anyway, you deserve to be this happy and loved this much. And Roar and I," he glanced down at his little sister who was adjusting disco ball sunglasses and dumping grape juice on the floor. "We really like Beckett. Because he's good enough for you. And you deserve someone who's going to be there for you always."

"Oh, shit," Gia whispered.

"Mama said 'shit!'" Aurora announced.

"I mean, Roar and I won't always be around to find your keys or remind you to put on shoes before you leave the house."

"Okay, okay," Gia said, sniffling. She pressed a hand over Evan's mouth and gave him a loud kiss on the forehead. "Let's call it quits there."

"To my mom," Evan said through Gia's hand. He raised his glass of grape juice.

"To Gia," the rest of the women echoed.

"Ladies, it's time." Franklin, Gia's father, looking dapper in a new haircut and a long coat, poked his head into the studio.

It was giggling, glamorous chaos as they chugged the champagne and helped each other into coats and shoes.

The evening air was cold and crisp. It was New Year's Eve, and the town was still decked out for Christmas. Lights sparkled, tie-dye bows on wreathes danced on the winter wind. Across the street in One Love Park, Eva saw the huge, white tent where the celebration would take place. Patio heaters were on full blast, though once the dancing started no one would have trouble staying warm.

Gia took her dad's arm. "It's really happening."

"This is your happily ever after, honey."

"It really is."

"It takes a good man to open his heart and home to not just a wife but an entire family."

And that was Beckett to a tee. A good man with a limitless heart.

"We're going to have to get a dog," Gia whispered half to herself.

"Did you say a dog, Mama?" Aurora paused mid-twirl.

"Shit."

Franklin chuckled beside her.

She peeked. She couldn't help it. She needed that picture in her head to soothe the nerves. All of Blue Moon had turned out for it, packing the seats of the art-deco movie theater. And there at the front were the brightest lights in her world. The foundation of their life together.

The women shimmered in rose gold, a color that spoke of love and affection.

Beckett and his brothers and Evan lined up looking handsome in classic tuxedos.

Beckett. The love of her life. The man of her dreams. The irresistible charmer was waiting for her, and she couldn't wait to get to him.

Phoebe cupped Gia's face in her hands. "Thank you for making my son so happy, Gia."

"Thank you for making my dad so happy," Gia whispered back.

They embraced, and Gia felt nothing but a mother's love.

"Good luck out there and remember to breathe," Phoebe said. She turned her attention to Franklin and straightened his bowtie. "I'll save you a seat."

"And a dance," he insisted, pressing a kiss to her mouth.

"Not in front of the kid," Gia teased.

Phoebe hurried down the aisle and took her seat in the front row. And then the music started. They took their first steps into the theater, and Gia felt the overwhelming love.

It wasn't just Beckett. It wasn't just the Pierces, Joey, Summer. All of Blue Moon was part of Gia's family now. She'd vow to honor and protect them all. To support them and love them for all the days of her life.

But first... first, she'd marry that fine-looking mayor in the tuxedo down front.

∾

Beckett

"I CAN'T BELIEVE this is happening," Beckett said for the third time in a row. His wife—because he could call Gianna that now—laughed again and threw her arms around his neck. The ceremony was over. The dinner devoured. And now they had nothing better to do but dance until midnight and ring in the New Year with a married kiss.

"This is the best day of my life," Gianna said, peppering his face with kisses. Her lipstick had been worn away hours ago between sweet kisses and glasses of champagne.

"I'm either drunk or delirious," he announced, picking her up and holding his fairy princess bride off the dancefloor. Her dress was breathtaking and oh-so-Gianna. The bodice was cut straight across the chest, but the back was a sexy swatch of lace and skin. He wanted nothing more than to peel it off her slowly until she was completely naked.

"Why not both?"

"What were we talking about?"

She threw her head back and laughed. Those divine red curls exploded like the secret fireworks Beckett had planned for midnight.

"You're beautiful, Red," he told her, letting her petite body slide down his in a not-appropriate-for-public caress.

"And you're everything, Beckett. I feel like the luckiest girl in the world tonight."

"I promise to stick, Gianna. Through thick and thin. You're the girl I've been waiting my whole life for."

"You don't mind my baggage?" she teased, nodding in the direction of the cake table. Two pairs of legs stuck out from underneath.

"That's not baggage, Red. That's our family."

The tears flowed fast and hot from her beautiful gray-green eyes. "You make me feel cherished, Beckett. Loving the things I love. Making room for what's most important to me." Her gaze shifted to where her father and his mother were dancing in the center of the dance floor.

He saw love there too.

He saw love everywhere he looked. And maybe it was the

champagne. Or maybe it was the special rose quartz crystals Willa had tucked into each napkin. Or the smudging Gordon and Rainbow Berkowicz performed before the ceremony.

Or maybe, just maybe, it was John Pierce smiling down on his town. His family. His son. Beckett felt it then. A squeeze on the shoulder from an invisible hand and knew his father was here.

Just like he'd be there for Evan and Aurora and anyone else who came along.

"What do you say we get some cake, Red?" Beckett offered.

"It's almost midnight," Gianna reminded him.

"There's no place else I'd rather be."

And so they rang in the New Year and their wedding night under the cake table with Evan and Aurora. And when the clock struck midnight, when Beckett's mouth found Gianna's, he knew his life would never be the same and would always be better.

AUTHOR'S NOTE TO THE READER

Dear Reader,

I'll let you in on a little secret: Beckett Pierce is always going to be one of my all-time favorite heroes. I think it's because he reminds me the most of Mr. Lucy. Beckett's desire to do the right thing by his family, his town, and the woman he loves is what made me fall face over butt for him.

This story was so much fun to write because, not only did I get to follow up with Carter and Summer, but I also got to delve deeper into Blue Moon Bend. And man, is that place fun! They take the "it takes a village" sentiment seriously, especially when it comes to love.

One of my favorite things about Beckett and Gia's story is that I got to explore the idea of family being much more than just blood. Gia's raising her stepson as well as her daughter on her own and watching Beckett bring them all into the fold as his own was a heart-melter.

Favorite scene: Babysitting Aurora makeovers.

Jax and Joey are up next in *The Last Second Chance,* and they have a *lot* of history to overcome.

Thank you again for reading! If you loved *Fall Into Temptation,* please feel free to leave a review. And if you're totally feeling the love, sign up for my newsletter and follow me on Facebook and Instagram. I'm super nice. I promise!

Xoxo,
    Lucy

ABOUT THE AUTHOR

Lucy Score is a *Wall Street Journal* and #1 Amazon bestselling author. She grew up in a literary family who insisted that the dinner table was for reading and earned a degree in journalism. She writes full-time from the Pennsylvania home she and Mr. Lucy share with their obnoxious cat, Cleo. When not spending hours crafting heartbreaker heroes and kick-ass heroines, Lucy can be found on the couch, in the kitchen, or at the gym. She hopes to someday write from a sailboat, or oceanfront condo, or tropical island with reliable Wi-Fi.

Sign up for her newsletter and stay up on all the latest Lucy book news.
And follow her on:
Website: Lucyscore.com
Facebook at: lucyscorewrites
Instagram at: scorelucy
Readers Group at: Lucy Score's Binge Readers Anonymous

LUCY'S TITLES

Standalone Titles

Undercover Love

Pretend You're Mine

Finally Mine

Protecting What's Mine

Mr. Fixer Upper

The Christmas Fix

Heart of Hope

The Worst Best Man

Rock Bottom Girl

The Price of Scandal

By a Thread

Forever Never

Riley Thorn

Riley Thorn and the Dead Guy Next Door

Riley Thorn and the Corpse in the Closet

The Blue Moon Small Town Romance Series

No More Secrets

Fall into Temptation

The Last Second Chance

Not Part of the Plan

Holding on to Chaos

The Fine Art of Faking It

Made in United States
North Haven, CT
30 June 2022

20812576R00228

"Your kids are great," he said, changing the subject.
"Don't be sweet. I can't resist sweet," Gianna warned him.
"Your kids are monsters, and I hate your face."

Beckett Pierce is the most eligible bachelor in the nosiest small town in upstate New York. But after his last girlfriend handcuffed herself to his porch and set his welcome mat on fire, he's not looking for any more roman

Especially if it lands right in his own backyard. And has miles of red hair.

Gianna Decker has her hands full—no, overflowing—with problems. With two kids, a useless ex, and a bra new yoga studio, the last thing on her mind is finding a man who'll demand more of her time.

Fantasizing about her hot, broody landlord? Mistake. Lusting after the sexy mayor of her new town? Terrible Getting naked with the "favorite" son of her father's new lady friend? N-O. Getting involved with Beckett ha disaster written all over it.

Those stolen kisses were accidental. A few moments of strings-free, sizzling passion couldn't possibly cause ar trouble. At least, not until tempers flare when their families complicate things and the interfering citizens of I Moon step in with their special brand of chaos.

Fall into Temptation

LUCY SCORE

WWW.LUCYSCORE.NET

ISBN 9781945631405